DEADLY CONSEQUENCES AND CONVENIENT HEROES

DEADLY CONSEQUENCES AND CONVENIENT HEROES

K. Patrick Bonovich

authorHOUSE®

AuthorHouse™
1663 Liberty Drive
Bloomington, IN 47403
www.authorhouse.com
Phone: 1-800-839-8640

First published by AuthorHouse   09/17/2011

ISBN: 978-1-4567-9601-3 (sc)
ISBN: 978-1-4567-9600-6 (ebk)

Library of Congress Control Number: 2011915300

Printed in the United States of America

CHAPTER 1

A COMMENDATION

The window frame crunches and shatters, glass explodes inward, and a disgusting brown-gray smoke momentarily fills the void before bleeding out in a wide, thin ribbon spiraling upward. Tim Bridges pauses, framed by the gush of smoke swirling around him, and steadies himself on the small awning just beneath the window ledge. He bends, sliding one leg into the opening he's just created, and his entire body disappears into blackness.

For a few seconds Bridges can identify the room he has entered—a bathroom, tiny, cramped, and rapidly filling with smoke. He drops to his stomach on the floor amidst chunks of wood and shards of glass; breaking and entering, Neanderthal style and crawls toward the doorway. The heat escalates exponentially, courtesy of the blast furnace of fire pushing up the stairway across the tiny hallway from the bathroom.

Bridges (known as Darth Vader to the rest of his team), breathes behind his mask and crawls on his stomach into the hall. If this scene were played out on television there'd be plenty of room to stand and look around, knowing his precise location. So much for cheap imitations. Tim is lying on the floor of a filthy bathroom, unable to see more than two feet in any direction and weighed down with nearly seventy pounds of equipment. Behind him the hole that had once been a window, acts as a flue for smoke and heat drawing from the fire

1

roaring through the first floor and bringing the flames up, over, and around the fireman crawling just outside the bathroom.

Damn!! He has to push himself back into the small room; the heat beating on him is too great . . . and is intensifying. Tim casts a glance upward. Heavy black flakes of charred paper and ash layer him. The smoke is lower and banking lower. *Well this sure doesn't look good,* the thought rushes through his mind. His limited vision of just seconds ago is gone. Stuffing your head in a black sack and laying on top of the broiler will give you a good idea of the feeling.

Moments before Bridges and Mark Hagan stumbled through the rubbish strewn alley behind the rowhouse, carrying the ladder that had enabled Tim to enter the second floor bathroom. Somewhere outside, beyond the smoke and heat, Mark Hagan is working to enlarge the hole in the wall so he can follow Bridges. Two small children are supposedly trapped in this dilapidated house according to the hysterical shouts and screams of what seems like half a hundred people down on the street.

Bridges has to retreat further into the bathroom, feeling around in the blackness. His heart races and he forces himself to breathe in a steady, easy pace. He can hear the fire in front of him—a constant, muffled baritone rumbling. Glass shatters somewhere, but the smoke seems to absorb the noise, distorting it, confusing it's direction, and isolating anyone caught in it. The Garrity light strapped to the side of his helmet is of no use to Bridges; neither is the 'Big Ed' light hanging from its clip at the front of his coat. The soupy smoke, bunching tighter around the man, swallows the illumination. The line of fire engines and collection of men in the street is reduced to the lonely struggles of anyone inside the burning dwelling.

Bridges *isn't* trapped. His progress *is* effectively blocked and the whereabouts of the two children become moot as long as he remains stationary. From the stairway a few feet away heat continues to build; the occasional stream of orange flame twirling up through the brown and gray smoke giving a worthy impression of Dante's Inferno.

Tim knows water is being brought to bear on the fire from somewhere below; enough time has elapsed that even the slowest company could accomplish that feat. But for Bridges to escape the heated, blinding confines of that small second floor room, time is dwindling. Tim entered the second floor first to search the rear of the building, while

Mark Hagan, still outside on the awning, will search the front. For a split second Bridges considers backing out the shattered window, but that consideration is immediately terminated when a deep throaty roar of water rushes over his right shoulder.

"We got it, Tim," voices muffled by the masks rise over the cascading water and sharp defined shafts of light bob around inside the bathroom. From the awning outside two men direct the nozzle of a hose, hitting the stairway in the hall. The change in the atmosphere is dramatic. Smoke falls around Bridges and the intense heat vaporizes the water from the hose and super charged steam fills the room with suffocating humidity.

In an instant the fire pushing up the stairs darkens, and in that instant Tim scoots from the narrow doorway and scuttles left, arms outstretched feeling his way like a blind man. From behind him comes the sound of ripped, splintering wood, and the loud thuds, even though muffled, tell him other men have gained entry to that tiny dirty bathroom. Hagan has to be one of them. He and Bridges will operate separately, searching both ends of the second floor. In a crouch—or when needed sliding on their bellies—both men feel their way along, around and through rooms cluttered with piles of charred clothing and furniture, stumbling over children's toys.

Along the ceiling fire flows like liquid following the surface contours, flicking and lapping the combustible material. Smoke hangs in the air a few inches above the floor and both men. Bridges in a back room, and Mark crashing and reeling somewhere in the front, keep themselves low, calling loudly and hoping for a response . . . any kind of response. Between them three other firemen are advancing a line, hunched over and leaning forward against the backpressure of the nozzle. The water crashes into the ceiling, gouging chunks of plaster and wood, sending them careening in different directions and inundating the floor with the debris.

Satisfied there are no children in a rear bedroom, Tim crawls forward to rendezvous with Hagan. He rises to a crouching position and when he steps forward his boot sinks though the thin carpet, breaking through the wooden floor. In an instant Bridges' leg has fallen through the floor, his remaining limbs forming a crooked tripod for support.

"Damn!" He yells through his mask. Beneath him, the first floor remains a mass of orange and red flame, undulating and snaking about the room below. Tim can feel the heat on his leg, momentarily grateful for the bulky bunker pants he is wearing, heavy pants saturated with flame retardant and insulated against the heat.

Leaning to one side he braces himself and pulls the entrapped leg back toward his body. The men hunched around the hose line are out of sight, lost in dense clouds of smoke and steam, although the drumming of the water tells Bridges they are nearby. His leg is freed from the hole, and with a quick glance down Tim sees the rolling swirling flames that seem to have consumed everything on the first floor. His breathing more labored, the fireman moves out of the bedroom, colliding with Hagan who has returned to the hallway looking for Tim.

"I got nothing," Hagan yells and jerks his head back from where he'd come, his eyes are wide behind the clear plastic face piece. "Are you sure they said there was two kids up here?"

Tim puts a hand atop his helmet, holding it in place and nods affirmatively. "They said there was two . . ." He holds up two gloved fingers. "I got nothing in the back either."

"Then let's switch," Hagan replies loudly. "You go front and I'll take the back. Maybe we'll see something the others missed." Bridges nods and the men clumsily move past each other, air tanks clanging as they brush together.

It is easier for Tim to get forward. On his right is the charged hose line operated by the three men who'd followed him inside. Gripping the rock hard hose loosely, he shuffles forward, feeling the line move back and forth like a sluggish snake, almost two hundred gallons of water per minute rushing along its interior. Around him lays the clutter and debris of a room destroyed by fire and the men fighting it. "The only job in the world that pays you for breaking glass and ruining everything," he once told his parents.

The smoke is still heavy and remains bunched along the floor. Somewhere in front of him, Bridges hears that steady, full rush of water and the sound of things falling to the floor. Out of the smoke looms the bulky figures of men with a hose line and Tim rises to kneel behind the closest figure. The weight of his body against the other man makes him turn. It is Dan Kemp, the captain of Engine 50 and the eyes behind the air mask's face piece narrow in recognition. Bridges gives a weary nod and Kemp moves slightly to give Tim room to move.

"Ain't nobody in this blasted room." Kemp calls loudly. "Right after Mark came out of it the whole place lit off. Nothin' but toast in here now."

Bridges leans forward, peering over the broad, hunched backs of the two men at the hose, Burger and Miller. Neither of the men look at Tim and he slaps Burger on the back and slides back in the direction he has just crawled.

The smoke begins to lift and thin dramatically, the result of ventilation holes cut in the roof above the windows broken out in both front and rear bedrooms. Hagan has returned to the tiny hall by the stairs, squatting and looking into the charred dark interior of the back room. At Bridges' arrival he raises a gloved hand and indicates a window in the room.

"There's a ladder at the window," he says loudly. "We looked everywhere for them kids and didn't find anything. Let's get out the window and maybe try the back of the first floor." Bridges agrees and the two crawl on all fours toward the opening indicated by Mark. They reach the ground and the two other firemen momentarily kneel at the foot of the ladder, helmets off, pulling their own air masks over their heads. Standing, they mount the ladder with a second hose line.

Hagan has already retrieved the tools they'd carried with them in the narrow concrete backyard. They crouch at the back door, an open, dark rectangle with smoke pouring from its frame. Both men enter in a crab-like scuttle, separating and moving along opposite sides of the room. The interior heat is incredible. Indistinguishable blackened rubble fills the room; the walls still steaming and small tongues of flame dart across a hundred little holes burned through the plaster and wallboard. Black water sloshes loudly over their boots as they pull and throw charred furniture out of their way. In the corner of the room a sink hangs from the wall, its fixtures melted in the ferocious heat, turning into a molten metal sauce. A kitchen drawer hangs open, it is the consistency of charcoal, and its contents—formerly flatware—have congealed into a shapeless mass.

"*Oh hell!!*" The shout comes from Hagan. Bridges turns and sees his partner frantically scooping handfuls of burned, soggy material and tossing them aside. "I found a kid!" Bridges stumbles in Mark's direction, pushing aside anything remaining in the room bulky enough to form an obstruction. He is at Hagan's side in moments and helps pull misshapen objects, wood, plastic, and metal away from what looks like the arm of a doll jutting from beneath a large basin.

"Oh my God . . ." Their sense of defeat is bitter. Two small children, blackened, lie on top of each other, only small pieces of reddish pink material give some clue they had once been human beings. The firemen had been told the children were on the *second* floor. There'd been no mention of any child or adult, male or female, on the first floor.

Hagan scoops the first infant in his arms and steps out the back door, Bridges following. Not only had the two children been on the first floor, they'd been right by the doorway. A few moments with the correct information and the two charred corpses would be alive. Instead of fighting to get through the smoke and fire on the second floor someone would have crashed in the backdoor and grabbed both kids. Now Bridges and Hagan stand in the backyard as more firemen gather around them forming a loose circle, masks off and dangling at their sides, dirty faces gazing at the small bundles in their arms.

"Somebody get some sheets or something," Hagan yells. He places the small bodies on the ground, out of the way of the firemen making their way into the rear of the dwelling. The air outside is cold, a strong February wind whips through the alley and the heat of the fire is forgotten as icy air chills the sweat on the men. Hagan's helmet is off, his hair wetly plastered over his forehead, twisted in clumps and sticking out along the collar of his turnout coat.

Bridges walks numbly toward the alley, his mind reeling. The front of his coat is open and the chill bites deeply through his clothing. Each time he exhales an immense cloud of vapor forms around his head. From the darkness comes a paramedic, two large sheets in his hand. Tim waves in the general direction of the two children and turns back quickly, not wanting to be reminded of the bodies.

The street in front of the house is ablaze with man-made light. Hoses are sprawled and twisted across the sidewalk, water spraying from couplings and running into the gutter where it forms a fast moving stream that gradually turns into an expanding delta of solid ice at the street corner. Ladders are raised against the roof above the second floor windows, hoses snaking up the rungs disappear into the sooty blackened openings. Debris and rubble from the interior of the rowhouse is forming an impressive pile on the sidewalk. Soggy and steamy, the object of the stream of water intermittently played over it, gradually soaking the rubbish and preventing it from rekindling.

With the narrow street choked with fire department vehicles, a mass of spectators has gathered just beyond the apparatus, most bundled in garishly colored clothing to warm themselves against the icy air. It is a mob of ignorance; no one understands what is going on inside the gutted house. They have gathered to participate in one of the oldest forms of entertainment, witnessing someone else's tragedy. There are high pitched yells and laughter, an easy banter tossed back and forth in the incomprehensible street jive that serves as a language, a rapid fire staccato beat whose words keep repeating themselves in all it's grammatical forms. It is almost like a chant.

Red and white emergency lights flutter, sending shafts of colored light circling off the face of crumbling bricks, dirty windows, and cheap doors, all covered with accumulated layers of neglect and grime. The radios of the department vehicles blend, forming a continuous, echoing chorus of metallic voices with every transmission; some from the Communications Bureau and others from fire ground radios at the scene.

Thomas Loughlin, the battalion chief supervising this operation, stands at the front of his red Chevy Blazer, his face scanning the blackened windows of the second floor as he intermittently brings his radio to his lips transmitting instructions to men inside the house. Loughlin—slender, with hair as white as the helmet he wears—sees Hagan and Bridges slowly making their way around the corner of the row of houses that stretch down the block.

With effort Mark shrugs off the harness and straps holding the air tank on his back, setting the breathing device on the street. He remains bent over, helmet off, hands on knees, breathing deeply. Beside him, Tim Bridges sets his breathing equipment upright and leans against the side of one of the engines. The motors of the big vehicles pulse with a deep gut-rumble, a steady throbbing of pumps pushing water through any of a half dozen hose lines. A thin crust of ice already layers the street and Loughlin will be calling the city's maintenance crews to provide salt to melt the rapidly accumulating ice.

"You guys did good," Loughlin confronts the two weary firemen. Neither man responds immediately to the chief. Their eyes are reddened and puffy as they glance at the street, the cluttered sidewalk, and up at the second floor windows. Think of Ward Cleaver wearing a white helmet, hair brushed straight back, somewhat large nose and intense eyes and you have Loughlin. But this speech is not to Wally and the Beaver.

"It was screwed up Chief," Bridges shakes his head and finally gives Loughlin a quick glance. "We figured the two kids were up on the second floor. Nobody said anything about them being downstairs." He takes a cigarette that Hagan has shaken from a pack tucked in his coat and waits for the other man to light it.

"You didn't know that," Loughlin points out. "You two did a helluva job getting in there and doing a search, okay?" His words are sincere, not the sympathetic feel-good encouragement handed to losers. Loughlin continues, "Kemp said there was a hurricane of fire comin' at you upstairs," referring to the captain of Engine 50. You did everything just like you're supposed to."

"Yeah, well . . ." Bridges' voice trails off.

"It's cold out here," Hagen interjects, changing the subject. He hikes his heavy coat higher on his shoulders and takes another hit on his own cigarette, staring at the swiftly crystallizing water around them.

"I'm gonna put you two in for a commendation," Loughlin announces. You couldn't get those two kids but you put your own lives at risk."

"What happened to the parents?" Hagan juts his chin towards the smoking row house. "Where did they go?"

The mother dove out that upstairs front window," the battalion chief points to the upper left window. "She did a header on the sidewalk just as I was pulling up. A couple of paramedics got her in an ambo, but her head and face looked like spaghetti sauce." The description is accompanied by a shrug. "The father . . ." Loughlin pauses and rolls his eyes, "at least I guess he was the father, is a goner too. Two guys from 64 Engine found him just inside the front door." He returns his gaze to the two men in front of him.

"You two take a little break, change air bottles on your gear and then go back in and start overhauling. I just wanted to let you know first-hand I was gonna write you up for a commendation." His speech done, the chief begins to move away.

"Hey chief," Hagan calls after the other man.

Loughlin turns back and gives Hagan a smirk.

"You think you could change that commendation to maybe a couple cases of beer?"

CHAPTER 2

THE FORT

Two jagged lightening bolts bracket a grinning Death's Head adorned with a fire helmet; beneath the skull a miniature fire hydrant criss-crosses a small ceiling hook. Bold black letters curving over the top of the image spell: 'East Side'—under the image in identical font is: 'Lightening'. It is the official icon, the customized logo, of the two companies operating from the big granite firehouse on Fort Avenue. As a patch, it is sewn over the left breast of the dark blue sweatshirts, golf shirts come with adhesive. Emblazoned on the backs of helmets and affixed to their personal vehicles in the corners of windows or bumpers, in short, any space available is used to identify the bearer as a member of The Big House, 'The Fort'; the aggregation of 'hot shots' working the city's legendary east side.

Here's the job. You work a trick—a combination of days and nights comparable to shifts—of ten-hour days followed by two fourteen-hour nights before getting four days off and starting the routine over again. Working days means you're out of bed by four so you arrive at the firehouse by five-thirty-six o'clock tops. You don't officially start work until seven, but the guy you're relieving wants to get home and you know your own relief will arrive early at the end of your shift so you can leave fast. Your tour ends at five, but because your relief arrives early-like you did—every thing evens out, each shift complementing the other. And when you work nights your shift begins at five, runs until seven the next morning and you make sure you are in the firehouse by four o'clock.

You prefer working nights, the atmosphere in the firehouse and throughout the department in general is more relaxed, less formal. There are fewer supervisors in white hats running around during the night shifts-self-absorbed white hats whose joy involves seeing how much busy-work they can create. Busy-work interrupting your own paper work, scut-work, anything unrelated to what means most to you, fight fires. Regardless how insulated you believe you are from those white hats, you know they can make the smallest anthill seem Himalayan simply to justify their existence. More importantly, it seems like there's more fires at night on the east side or most places throughout the city for that matter. Whether fires suddenly become more numerous by a quirk of physics or by the emergence of the darker side of humanity-the firestarter side—when the sun goes down, you can't be dogmatic. You just know things burn more frequently at night.

Firehouse meals are bigger at night, no bag lunches or quick stops at fast food places like daytime. No, at night the firehouse meals become monstrous affairs—four and five courses with everyone gathered around the long kitchen tables, plates heaped with steaks and lasagna and spaghetti. Everyone stuffing food down until they can't move or until dinner is interrupted by a run.

Working nights means the light blue uniform shirts can come off at seven o'clock and dress becomes casual. You end up wearing the dark blue tees with 'City Fire Department' printed in large white letters across the back and the Maltese Cross on the chest, informal and relaxed. When the weather turns colder the dark blue 'job shirts'—heavy sweats with corduroy collar and elbow patches—and that "Eastside Lightening' patch—are perfect. Besides, after nine p.m. you can head upstairs and rack out on your bunk, if nothing's burning in the district.

That's the kicker to the job, when the fires begin. Timing is everything and you can bet that at the precise moment you've started the perfect dream, the bells will start to clang. From crypt-like silence everything gets shattered by that damned triple *clang* from the gong on the wall and every light in the firehouse flashes on. And if you really need further annoyance, the alarm bell is followed by that crazy, irritating warbling tone, that rising and falling slightly off-key sound you hear on those European police sirens in the foreign movies you hate. Everybody around you is yelling and cursing and you join in because with this group you have maybe thirty seconds to go from the arms of Morpheus into overdrive. And people wonder why firemen always have some kind of heart trouble.

You hit the brass pole closest to your bunk and slide down to the apparatus floor where you start pulling on your turnout pants, those heavy, outsized pants that resemble black canvas ski bibs and boots, grab your turnout coat which weighs ten pounds and you climb up into your assigned seat on the apparatus. Around your neck you wear a flame-retardant, heat-resistant hood-like a race car driver and on the way to the fire, when you know it's going to be a crapper, you pull that hood over your head so you look like one of King Arthur's knights in chain mail and slap a three-and-a-half pound helmet on top of that. A helmet with the most famous and recognizable silhouette in the world. By the time you arrive at the scene your spinal column has been rearranged from hitting so many potholes you think you drove through a prairie dog village and you're so bulky with protective equipment, you feel like if someone knocked you over you couldn't get up.

Too bad, deal with it. It isn't any consolation, but there's five or six other companies that have joined you on this night-time call and every one in those companies has just gone through the same routine. You think they're concerned with your little discomforts?

There's always somebody awake and on the streets at whatever hour you caught this run. Some nights it's a carnival outside—even at two in the morning. But this is the 'hood', the famous 'cement jungle' and just like it's vegetative counterpart, this jungle has it's predators too. You spot them in a second, the home boys and bloods looking at you from across the street. They're not there to cheer. There's always a couple of groups, threes and fours, weight shifting back and forth with hands deep in the pockets of baggy pants or down the front of equally baggy sweatpants, usually holding the handle of a knife or gun. And the crowd grows if it is a real fire until you wonder if this isn't some kind of parade route. They watch you without a clue, somebody always counting the number of engines that show up, thinking that the number of vehicles equals the number of alarms. All it means to them is that another crumbling, rancid rat hole in this neighborhood is burning and since it isn't their rat hole all the excitement is late night entertainment, ghetto style.

The moment you pull up to the address-and there's no guarantee how correct it is—you're strapping your air tank and adjusting your breathing mask. If you need tools you grab them as you get down out of the cab, so before you have even set foot in the burning building, you are already carrying about sixty to seventy extra pounds and you have to strain the next few hours just carrying all around with you. God help you buddy if there is some derelict citizen needing to be rescued. Not only do you have to deal with almost an extra hundred pounds of your own equipment, but you are going to have to drag, carry, and support the weight of whoever needs your help.

You didn't take this job because you love the neighborhood, did you? If you are not putting out fires, you can't wait to go home, otherwise you get caught up in what they call 'community service'. If you were so concerned about the community, you'd be a member of some volunteer department instead of working in this hole. One of the reasons you drive a little faster to get home after every shift is because this neighborhood looks more like a poverty-stricken, Third World Enclave, the kind of place National Geographic does exploratory videos.

And you don't do this job for the pay either. You're in one of the top ten Most Dangerous Jobs in the civilized world and the city pays you as well as it does the trash collectors, sometimes less depending how the collective bargaining went during the last contract negotiations. Besides, how do you quantify crawling around on your stomach doing a modified breast-stroke in one of these filthy, housing projects with smoke so heavy it's like black paint flowing around you? You can feel the rapid, petrified scampering of mice and rats running over your back trying to escape from the toxic fumes into which you are determined to go.

Take it to the bank, whatever you think it's worth the city doesn't care. You don't do this job for love of city and community, but because it is something that needs to be done and your conscience allows you to sleep better for doing it. Those same people who pat you on the back for saving grandma or mother would just as soon meet you later on a dark street and do you bodily harm for whatever is in your pocket

A couple of generations ago you wouldn't get through a day without somebody in the neighborhood stopping at the firehouse to deliver something to eat or to express their gratitude for your efforts. Now anything not nailed down in the firehouse with the doors not bolted shut is stolen. You do a great job and 'The Big House' is a community institution, but you get paid for doing it; you don't need a show of appreciation.

You do this job for one consuming reason: you love it!

You love the guys you work with, that bond between people who've been through serious times together. The ones who have been injured with you, broken bones, cuts, gashes, burns or vomiting because you've inhaled too much smoke. In every circumstance, whether it's a super heated room or moving over the roof of some rowhouse that's blowing smoke out of every window, it doesn't matter, you know they are watching out for you just like you are watching for them; no words exchanged.

At the firehouse everybody makes bodily noises, flicks rolled-up objects at each other and can't usually get a sentence out without using profanity without a second thought. Those conversations are special too because with each other you can be real. Conversation can be trilingual, that art form that is reserved for the firehouse. Not the language you use at home with the spouse and kids neighbors. Sometimes the challenge is knowing when to slip into and out of the variety of dialects not understood completely by outsiders. Part of the rich tapestry of language utilized by the firefighter is the flexibility of words used to describe many different circumstances.

To be faced with a one room fire that is extinguished within a few minutes after arrival is commonplace to the firemen. However, if that same fire is given time to grow, extend and involve another room to the point where both rooms are burning fiercely and freely, the result is a 'crapper'. Any fire that becomes labor intensive, requiring all personnel involved, up to and including additional alarms can be considered a 'crapper.' Even the more dramatic multi-alarm fire where the basic tactic is one of 'surround and drown' can legitimately be categorized a 'crapper' if the work entailed in controlling the blaze becomes time consuming and exhaustive.

"You don't knock down a crapper in five minutes," Bill Burger explains. "You end up filthy and sweating and wanting to take a break."

"Most good, busy companies look forward to a good crapper," Donald Holland has pointed out, "It's those one alarm jobs that tax your limits, that kind of teeter between a working fire and a second alarm . . . those are really bad."

That same word, however, still used in adjectival form, is used to convey frustration and futility when department resources are squandered—the basic 'crapper run.' It is the one-eighty of a crapper; a call of little or no consequences other than taking time and energy. Viewed in that light, the ubiquitous 'pot of food' left too long on the stove, filling a dwelling with noxious smoke, is a 'crapper run;' multiple companies converging on the same location, each with uncertain expectations about the dispatch that said, "odor of smoke . . ." The first company arriving at the scene handles an 'emergency' that could have been averted simply by taking the blackened, smoky pot from the burner and putting it in the sink. Department sources are wasted, interrupted with no more consequence than one more 'run' credit to the responding companies—a 'crapper run.'

More flexible and in far more widespread usage is the 'queen mother' of four letter words—'the F word.' In the firehouse, on a fireground, during conversation, on the hoboes with another firefighter, the word is used in every conceivable linguistic form—noun, pronoun, verb, adverb, *ad nauseum*. The word's incredible flexibility is exceeded only by the frequency it finds in a single sentence.

During one exchange in Gulfee's office, the Truck Company Office on the second floor, Mark Hagan complains about the City Hall Metrostrat 'suits'—that word was used in seven references in one short commentary. In his first week working at the firehouse, Tim Bridges sat in the lounge listening to a general conversation between March, Burger, Holland and Killen counting the word in one form or another thirty-two times in the space of a short discourse. The practical complication of such ease of use comes when the same firefighters are outside the firehouse in social conversation, with people whose daily language is as alien in form and content as that used by firemen.

"I just get finished talking with Jerry on the phone," Sam Killen confesses in the midst of his 'jungle blush,' "and turn around and there's an audience of kids with their mouths hanging open because of how I talked."

Once the city accepted you for this job you spent four months at the Fire Academy, six days a week, ten hours a day, learning the basics. The instructors taught everything in a strictly controlled environment with precise, anticipated outcomes. You learned how to raise the ladders and carry hoses and the physics of combustion. At least twice each week you went through the 'Maze,' that twisting, turning jumble designed to confuse your mind and make you think independently. And to make it all more interesting the instructors made sure your struggle inside the 'maze' occurred in total darkness. You can't see your own hand one inch from your face. You get taken into the 'burn building,' nothing more than four walls, a roof and cement floor, filled with smoke, and once you acclimate yourself, some instructor tells you to take off your mask and inhale deeply. That was always memorable, your stomach twisting and turning and shaking like a washing machine until you've vomited everything inside you.

You learn some things by rote, others by calculation and logic. If you've been blessed with more than half dozen brain cells, you realize you are gradually accumulating knowledge, enough to promote self confidence, but not nearly enough to turn you loose just yet.

About two weeks before the end of your academy training Roscoe Harrington, the captain at the Fire Department Headquarters responsible for personnel assignments, pulls out his file of CGA35's—the Company Graduate Assignment forms—and begins matching the names of your classmates with vacancies among the various companies scattered across the city. Most New Guy's end up being assigned out in the boonies, firehouses on the fringes of city/county lines where a 'busy' company might actually get a thousand calls a year. That's where the majority of the academy graduates begin their careers and many remain there, never making the next step into the busier districts.

But if you are lucky, if the astrophysics of galactic rotation are just right—and if you have the slightest amount of influence—Roscoe has been known to drop a graduate into a busy company. Rumor has it, he has a distinct fancy for a certain Tennessee Bourbon and some guys make sure his bar is heavily stocked. Miracles take place, however,—'69 Mets for example—and in those humbling moments when the veritable Hand of God is on your career, you open your sealed orders and discover you've been assigned to one of the legendary companies of mythic proportion. They'll be companies with waiting lists of firemen wanting to transfer in, companies that only the department 'insiders' really know about.

Some units in the city are busy by 'the numbers', they get a lot of calls, but many are of little consequence; nuisance runs, medic assists, bad electrical wiring, anything that would prompt a tax paying citizen to dial 911 and ask for emergency services. There are other companies, however, units sitting in old crumbling firehouses topping the list for media photo-ops, busy by 'quality.' They call it 'First-in-Fire;' balls of flame and smoke, people trapped inside and needing rescue—companies who always seem to be at that cutting edge of action becoming fire department legends. Don't misunderstand, however, the crap runs still exist. They are the miserable parentheses of time idling in the street, assisting an ambulance or checking to determine if the pilot light went out on the water heater at two in the morning. Those idyllic moments are made the more maddening when in your companies absence, a real fire alarm comes in. Yet, the minute this fire department concluded the Emergency Medical Service would be included under its aegis, the firemen become jealous of doing what they signed up to be—firefighters. Baby sitting ambulance work is a necessary evil.

Half the ten busiest companies in the city fire department are still in the east, but the growing trend shows the west will be the place to be for the future—save for one stretch of city property that stands like a forbidding western rabble-hole—a last reminder to the wary traveler that what looms ahead doesn't get any better.

This modern Rubicon stretches east-west through what the city police department cautiously acknowledges as 'potentially threatening and crime laden' polite euphuisms for a rowdy neighborhood. The firehouse monopolizing this little slice of Beulah Land handles slightly more than eight thousand calls a year, almost evenly divided between the two companies calling it home—Engine 50 and Truck 105—and when you find one of those companies neatly typed on your GCA35, you get recognition rivaling celebrity status. That's when it begins to sink in that this job is more than just a paycheck and face time on television. You can take that acclamation and burn it, because most of the vermin living in that neighborhood don't care about heroes and wouldn't care if they did bodily harm to one. Most importantly, you've got some heavy hitters working in that firehouse, firemen who haven't been with any new guys for decades. The past months in the academy have been fun, but now your real learning curve begins to cut in.

You want to make a good impression on these veterans. Most of them have been working out of the Fort Avenue firehouse an average of eighteen years. More unit citations have been awarded to each of these two companies at Fort Avenue than at least a third of the rest of the fire departments combined. Three members of Truck 105 currently rank among the most decorated firemen in the entire city and two of the men on Engine 50 are not far behind. Nobody is going to be awed by some newby from the academy, but in a sense *you know you've arrived* when you show up to introduce yourself a week before your first trick is official—four distinct events occur.

First, the company to which you've been assigned hands you your own '35 Key', the key that unlocks the front door of every firehouse in the city. Next comes the front piece for your helmet; a piece of stiff leather embossed with the company number that is affixed to the front of your 'lid'—your protective headgear—and marks you as an 'official' member, the key to your own personal locker at the firehouse and finally, the officer flips you a bright yellow can of Teflon spray. With a straight face you are told to use the spray liberally around your backside, because, . . . "it will ease the pain from working your butt off."

You find out the fires to which you'll respond come steadily and consistently, all types of fires. Because of the age and design of the districts demographics as well as the somewhat preternatural location of this firehouse, you're going to see every kind of fire in the books. They include big multiple dwellings with four or five families cramped into filthy living conditions, row upon row of vacated dwellings unfit for human occupation, but ideal for wandering dopers and crack hounds who use empty space as shooting galleries. Also still standing multi-storied warehouses abandoned after being slated for destruction under the guise of urban renewal, yet still standing years later and because of the proximity to city government there is the midtown array of office buildings in clusters of modern skyscrapers teeming with lawyers and business. In short, name the type of structural fire that's been written up in the fire engineering texts and you'll find it in spades in the 15ᵗʰ Battalion.

Of the burning and general destruction much sociological observation has been made by professionally educated scientists who speak in terms of lack of education among the citizens, socio-environmental factors and the poverty, always the poverty. In the firehouse, sociologic theory is reduced to stark realistic observation that follows simple laws of nature and genetic predisposition.

"These people," Jerry March explains with a wave of his hand in the general direction of the neighborhood, "need something to burn." Gazing out over the mottled landscape of what remains after years of arson and general ignorance, the pump operator recognizes the prerogative attributes of the Creator. "And in His great wisdom, God brought them all here to the 15ᵗʰ Battalion."

Until someone else is assigned to 'The Fort,' you'll remain ". . . that Newby." To the veterans it won't matter if you've been there one year or five—every new man is just that; 'the Newby.' You wont be considered a member until *they* say you are. The arbitrary decision is, of course, mere tradition, but such tradition lies at the core of the companies at the firehouse. Take the East Side Lightening logo, the same icon worn as a tattoo by the veterans. When a Newby has finally been accepted, permission is given to wear the tattoo. You'll eventually get one—if you last long enough working there—but not until the other guys reach some degree of approval that you might be possessed of some scintilla of potential. Acceptance must be earned, slowly.

So after that first day, with each succeeding trick behind you, the process continues inexorably. Somewhere along that process—there is no mystical date or time—you discover you don't work this job for anything or anyone except the approval and acceptance of the Brothers, your second family. And yes, there's going to be a lot of times when family priorities get reversed, when those loud, brash men become closer to you than your real, flesh and blood family. You stroll up to the door of the firehouse and use your 35 key and walk inside. That ego gets left on the sidewalk and the notion that this is some heroic job has long since been flushed down the toilet. What you are and will eventually become starts in the firehouse.

Due to its sheer size and architecture, the firehouse stands in stark contrast to everything within several blocks. The surrounding neighborhood bears an eerie resemblance to old black and white photographs of similar places at the close of the war in Europe—The Big One—WW2—except those cities, even with the wartime devastation so recent, were already undergoing some degree of renewal and rebuilding. In this 'hood' those words, 'renewal and rebuilding,' means new sheets of plywood are appearing over empty windows and doors.

A now infamous candidate for vice president created a media firestorm with the observance that . . . "if you've seen one ghetto, you've seen them all." The statement was a colossal blunder in terms of its political correctness. Even the brain deads of a ghetto have civic pride, its basic honesty was on the mark.

Known locally as 'Central City,' the neighborhood is better referred to as 'The Penny;' due in large part to the generational habit of it's residents to drop the second syllable until everyone, everywhere simply said 'Cent City' from which the identification with the common penny was eventually derived. Its prevailing hue is a jagged blur of earth tones interspersed with the varying shades of gray and brown overlaid with nondescript grime.

Along 'the avenue' neon signs indicate the current sociology, bars, tattoo parlors, bail bonds offices and is a quaint juxtaposition of good and evil, 'The All Saints Temple of Jesus the Redeemer,' faces directly across the pot holed surface at the garish entrance to 'Reggie's All Nude Revue.' Once past the ramp to the Cross City Parkway, the enduring collections of weary two and three story storefronts continue, sagging reminders of dreams since vacated, others a testimony to septuagenarian 'businessmen' with too many years of a depressing battered life already invested to admit failure. Packed behind this rank of doomed ventures are row upon row, street upon street of low income and mostly vacant housing. It is from those narrow, cramped rowhouses which bear witness that life in a neighborhood is more than a collection of wood and bricks. Something of a retrograde Welcome Wagon manifests itself on opposing street corners as the homeboys gather in trios and quartets to jive rapid-fire and threaten anyone with the temerity to pass within a few yards of their turf.

The firehouse on Fort Avenue is almost a century old. A two story monument of solid, rough hewn granite and neat lines of red brick, rolls of razor wire along the perimeter of the flat roof and steel bars bolted over every window are mute acknowledgement that times and values show more than change with succeeding generations, they also mutate.

Barred and barricaded windows became a necessity after the firehouse had been burglarized a third time. While men and vehicles were absent on a call, the color television, microwave oven, kitchen equipment, radios, and an assortment of personal property owned by the firemen were 'relocated' to a pawn shop nearby. By the time firemen and police tracked stolen goods, more than three quarters had been sold. Now, in addition to the steel-barred windows lining both sides of the firehouse, six-inch bolts anchor every movable fixture of value, even the television isn't simply bolted in place, the doors of the TV cabinet itself are chained and padlocked.

Along the roof, razor wire does more than prevent an intruder from gaining access to the firehouse; it prevents the wide, flat, surface from becoming an impromptu garden for marijuana. Just a year ago, flying routine patrol over the city, a police helicopter swept low enough to recognize long rows of healthy flora benefiting from the unobstructed sunlight. Fortunately, the police observer maintained his presence of mind, thoughtfully notifying the firehouse of the discovery before filing a report with his supervising sergeant. The offending plants disappeared immediately, with the subsequent explanation that marijuana could have been cultivated on the rooftop by any one of a thousand locals, an explanation as believable as the Loch Ness Monster or the Theory of Atlantis.

Further rooftop agricultural endeavors never materialized, influenced by the knowledge that a keen eye was being kept on the plantation site and reinforced by the tactful announcement from Dan Kemp that privately tended 'gardens' atop the firehouse would be met with dire consequences.

Despite its imposing outer façade, the interior of the firehouse, especially the apparatus floor, is surprisingly claustrophobic. Arranged abreast across the front of the auditorium sized room are the three department vehicles assigned here; Engine 50 and Truck 105 flanking the chief's red car, all facing fort Avenue. Plymovent hoses and battery cables hang from the pressed tin ceiling, connected to the apparatus collecting fumes and providing power to motors when not in use. Radiators run the length of both walls with tables, chairs, rows of lockers, work benches and small mounds of equipment filling any open space and shrinking the side of the main floor, creating a man-made maze through which only the well initiated successfully—and rapidly—navigate. Built in an era when fire department apparatus was much smaller, the otherwise big room is quite cramped. Barely fifteen inches separates the rear of Truck 105's tiller cab from the back wall.

Immediately behind the red car and slightly elevated atop an 8x8 slab of concrete is the watch desk, government-issue gray, solid and heavy, with its matching government-issue wheeled desk chair. Surrounded on three sides by large sheets of plexiglass forming a sharp-angled 'U,' the watch desk serves as the communications center in the house. Six long brass poles are strategically positioned at equidistant points on the cement floor, reaching up through the high ceiling into the second floor bunk room. These are the poles down which each man slides when taking a call.

Throughout the entire firehouse, but particularly on the apparatus floor, is that peculiar and singular combination of odors, wet canvas, the sweet-sour smells of diesel exhaust mixing with clinging, pungent smoke and stale sweat; instantly identifiable to any fireman in the world. And despite its job-related equipment and tools and gear, with signs and decals signifying everything as belonging to the city fire department, the apparatus floor is, essentially a big garage.

Regardless of the time of day, the inside of the firehouse is cloaked in shadow. Although a double row of fluorescent lights run along the pressed-tin ceiling, the only actual illumination is provided by a solitary goose-necked lamp sitting on the top shelf of the watchdesk, an electric eternal flame. When an alarm is received, the fluorescent lighting comes to life for a few moments before the electric timer shuts them off. High on the front wall, directly over the exit door for the red car, the big firehouse gong, slightly larger in diameter than a hubcap and encased in a handcrafted oak case, is an enduring relic to tradition. There was a time when the companies were called to an alarm by the urgent and ear-splitting *clang* of the bell activated by a toggle switch at the desk. Now the same gong is controlled by the Fire Communications, set off electronically with the announcement of every alarm. Immediately below the gong is the wide, gray plastic radio 'horn' transmitting all announcements to the firehouse. Even when muted, the constant sounds from the radio creates an echo around the inside of the firehouse because of the high ceiling.

There were thirty men divided among four shifts assigned to every fire company in the city. Although each of the four shifts—red, white, blue and green—will comprise about eight men on any given day, the demands of vacation, holidays, scheduled time off and personnel details across the city invariably means only five men will actually be on duty during a particular tour. Each company is commanded by a captain and three lieutenants, scheduled so that no shift is left without a supervising officer. The companies are autonomous. The captain of Engine 50 does not control the operation or personnel of truck 105 and vice versa. In addition to the two companies at the Fort Avenue firehouse, the chief of the 15th Battalion maintains an office.

Twelve men are always on duty at the Fort, five for the engine, five for the truck, and the chief and his driver. On Blue Shift they are called Fat Man, Crazy Horse, Ramjet, and Pear . . . names that have evolved with meaning only to the men themselves. None of the firemen live here, none would ever want to be identified with this eyesore.

Ask a member of either company in the firehouse why they chose this cesspool and the answer is invariably accompanied by a shrug, indicating the obvious. "Because it's the busiest . . ." is the honest reply. Sam Killen, the senior member of truck 105 has worked here for seventeen years, Bill Burger, for nineteen years. Both men share a visceral distaste for this small portion of the city and travel forty-five minutes one way from homes in the surrounding suburbs to keep the distance between themselves and this modern-day metropolitan outhouse.

It is a large urban civilization in arrested decay, an accurate, concise term considering its legal-cultural weave of citizenry. Consider the case of John Bailey, the senior man on White-Shift, Engine50, who keeps small plastics of candies in the cab of the engine for the kids in the neighborhood. They call John 'Mr. Bags' but twice a year for the past ten years Baily goes to juvenile court to confirm to the presiding judge that "Yes Your Honor, my headlights and mirrors were broken again by the defendants . . . yes, Your Honor, they were shot out while I was at work."

This is a septic system where you are hugged, kissed, patted on the back and praised as heroes when you save 'Momma', invariably an obese matriarchal figure ruling over three extended families crammed into a two bedroom rowhouse lit off like a torch. You are called back a little later on a Medic Assist and be shot at because you're trying to save the life of 'Little Chips' who, in turn, was shot for selling burn bags in front of the same house.

The people living and having their being in 'The Penny' find no apologist in Sam Killen, the shift's only black fireman. Killen's values are not restricted to allusions to human life with fast food. Like when Jaavon Tuttle, the doper from the projects got shot in the chest arguing over the last piece of crispy chicken on the platter at the KFC on Grugen Street, or the smart-mouth who got his throat cut demanding the last rack of baby back ribs from Old Bull's down on Vicker Street. Any accumulation of time working at Fort Avenue proves skin color has no bearing on mentality. The 'US versus Them' mindset. All humanoids no matter the color, not wearing Fire Department Blue are definitely 'them.'

There is a disconnect between these men and the 'hood'. In many instances the answer is a resounding 'yes'. A cultural chasm exists, a deep gorge created by the multiplied numbers of thugs, homeboys and dirt-bags, who act as predators in the midst of sheep. There is an abiding distrust and antipathy between the men in the firehouse and those sullen, angry people who believe they are owed a living at no expense to them, and resent any divergent views. Those are the violent 'bloods,' the flippant, aggressive females who can care less about their femininity as long as their self-indulgent lifestyles can be maintained at minimum personal cost.

Unfortunately the ebb and flow of this 'hood' seems to be determined and steered by a minority of the inhabitants, the males whose idea of masculinity comes from either the end of a gun, knife or genitalia and their female companions who enjoy their attention and protection.

What can be easily overlooked and more easily forgotten after years of skin-thickening exposure to the human debris littering the streets around your firehouse, is that vast sea of ordinary people who live in daily fear that tomorrow is never a guarantee. Maybe their economic straits are self-induced, perhaps the consequence of being brought into a world they never sought, but it becomes easy to ignore the fact that they like you are ordinary people sharing the same fears and maybe the same hopes.

So you climb through a room full of debris with fire rolling over you, flames moving like liquid across the ceiling, in a filthy hellhole you would never imagine existed outside of a Third World dictatorship, and drag out a kid, boy, girl, it doesn't matter. Or maybe you find an adult, probably the mother since ninety percent of the 'families' in your district have only one parent, barely alive, limp, and usually unconscious. You don't see a face color. What goes through your mind most of the time is that you've become responsible for another human being, for better or worse. Sometimes depending on the occasion, you see your kid's face, the same one you just went to a PTA meeting for, or whose little league game you helped coach last week. When it's an adult, for whom you are breaking your back and risking your life, you see a sister, mother, or grandmother. It gets real personal in the middle of a smoking, blazing dwelling, sort of up close and personal.

You do the dirty, nasty work without complaining, not because of some storybook definition, but because it is what this job is all about. What it has always been about and fifty years from now will *still* be about. When it is convenient, some political suit that needs a vote will call you a hero and refer to those around you as heroes. The media will consider you a darling, after the tragedy has already hit and the funerals are being planned. The best chance you have of getting your name and picture in the paper will be in an obituary notice. You are tired, exhausted and the only people who know and appreciate your work are those you work with and the people who are alive because you did your job. Don't think some media-type is going to come down to where you work, the story is not worth that much to them. The only time political suits show up is to speak some one dimensional words about the tragedy or death is because it represents loss of a vote.

Be sure you realize, you won't make the front page when you wake up in a cold sweat, remembering how you just missed being toasted in that fire ten years ago, the one where you bailed out five seconds before the whole room lit-off. Post traumatic stress is something they discovered for solders not firefighters, even though you've sugared through it for years. And you can bet the farm nobody is going to see your tears when you cradle the frail limp body of an infant at three in the morning because nobody reported the fire until too late. No media-types have the guts to go where you *MAKE* yourself go, so don't expect a camera flash during a dramatic moment.

When you kneel beside a tiny body bag in the alley behind another burn-out, helmet in your hand, eyes closed and tears leaving clean tracks on your smoke darkened face, you think some TV channel is going to see that? Or see the other four men with you kneeling in a semi circle, their immediate task completed, taking time to pray because they don't just see a tiny body bag . . . they see their own children safely asleep at home and, because they are parents too, feel that tearing sensation of loss and grief.

Yeah, you're a hero, by any definition of the word, a convenient one, but you didn't take this job for convenience or because someone might think you are a hero.

CHAPTER 3

WHO GETS THERE FIRST

"We ready?" Howard and Loughlin exchange glances over the roof of the red Jeep Cherokee.

"Yeah Ken," Loughlin replies in a clipped voice. "I don't want to be out all day." He opens the passenger door and slides into his seat.

Howard pauses a moment and looks back at Jerry, rolling his eyes and scowling before pinching his nose between two fingers. Abruptly the big man slides behind the wheel of the car and starts the motor, waiting for March to hit the button allowing the exit door to roll upward. As the door rattles and creaks, Bill Burger saunters to the desk from somewhere at the back of the firehouse. Loughlin's voice sounds over the radio, informing Communications he is out in the district for inspections.

"I saw Ken hold his nose," Bill shoves his hands in his pockets. "I take it Loughlin is still conserving water?" He has a bland, empty expression on his face.

"It's only the second day," Jerry laughs and brings his feet down from the desk.

Inside the red car Ken Howard has not driven two blocks before becoming aware of the powerful, pungent, sour odor filling the Cherokee's interior and shakes his head, glancing at Loughlin from the corner of his eyes. The chief stares impassively out the window, observing the same dreary scenery he has viewed for the past eleven years as the shift's chief. He sits silent, oblivious to the noxious environment around him.

Tom Loughlin can be moody, he demands every officer under him to properly prepare and submit their paper work in a timely manner, often returning reports with corrections in red ink and written admonitions concerning grammar and spelling. He is a prince on the fire ground and inside the firehouse. Do your job, make Loughlin look good and you'll never have to deal with reports about napping during day-shift, 'longitudinal therapy' after a night spent inside a bottle—or changing into tee shirts or job shirts before seven o'clock on night shifts. Hell, knock down a general alarms for Loughlin and he'll sit in the lounge and be a Chatty Cathy with everybody. Loughlin allows officers leeway in running their companies without interference. Some chiefs micromanage the activities of every company in their command. Some battalion chiefs will have you on report and up on charges for not having your collar pins on your uniform shirt. And most chiefs sure wouldn't put up with Greenstreet's habit of pasting skull and crossbones on the tiller cab—tracking the number of fire fatalities the truck has experienced.

Freedom from inane consequences comes with a price, however. In addition to his leadership acumen, Tom Loughlin enjoys a robust relationship with personal body odor. Regular bathing seems a hygienic undertaking alien to Loughlin's lifestyle. Bill Burger once bet twenty dollars the battalion chief didn't own a deodorant—a bet won after Mark Hagan picked the lock on the chief's personal locker and half the shift examined its contents not finding as much as an advertisement for deodorant. Two weeks later, while helping Loughln add a deck to the rear of his Hamden Valley townhouse, Nick Miller unobtrusively rifled the chief's bathroom without finding even an empty wrapper from the stuff. Acknowledgement of Loughlin's preference for aged, natural body scents led to the discussion concerning the survival of Mrs. Loughlin during their thirty years of marriage. It was left to Ken Howard, suffering the longest and most frequent exposure to the chief's *lassez faire* view on body aromatics, to note Loughlin held a European view of bathing—a twice a week occurrence, needed or not. Ken suggested that, perhaps Loughlin utilized a deodorant unknown to anyone at the firehouse and named *'Eaux d'Gymnasium'*.

It would be a long day for Howard, knowing the chief is blissfully unaware and unaffected by his malodorous condition. *Maybe I oughta shove some Vick's Vaporub up my nose,* Howard scowls and cracks his side window an inch. *I gotta get a dozen of those damned car deodorizers,* he reminds himself, thinking his best bet is to hang them around the entire interior of the car like garlic to ward off vampires. *Maybe wearing a surgical mask would send a subtle message.*

Loughlin's battalion is large—five engines, three trucks, a squad engine, a regular engine equipped with rescue equipment, the division's heavy duty rescue and three ambulances housed in six firehouses. The day's inspection will consume two hours and Howard knows that it will require luck, several recitations of the Rosary and innumerable veiled suggestions if they are to stop and lunch somewhere in the battalion. He envisions one of the huge seafood sandwiches from the sprawling Jefferson Market at the southern-most boundary of the district. More than fifty vendors occupying a massive open air market selling everything from pizza and spaghetti to frosty health shakes made from one hundred percent fruit and served in quart-sized cups. Most of the proprietors at the 'Market' expect payment for their goods however and another of Tom Loughlin's idiosyncrasies was a death grip on his wallet, making Ebenezer Scrooge appear philanthropic. *The chief's tight,* Howard reminds himself, the image of his two pound sandwich evaporating.

By the time truck 105 returns to the Fort Avenue firehouse, Engine 50 has had three runs, none fire related, consisting of a trio of 'medic assists'—manpower to paramedics in the battalion's ambulances—runs viewed by the firemen as odious necessities. To their admittedly biased perspective, the department's Emergency Medical Service is an unwanted stepchild to the city's fire service.

"We'll end up in the top busiest companies in the city" Burger complains loudly, "simply because of the farcical calls." He lathers his hands at the sink at the rear of the firehouse. Rinsing them he observes cynically, "Eighteen years at this job and I gotta go look at some moron layin' in the gutter 'cause he wants to shoot up and then call for help 'cause he overdoses." Drying his hands with a wad of paper towels, he hook-shots the wad into the trash can. "And then the medic' give 'em a shot of Narcan to reverse the crap in their veins and the sons-a-bitches get up, wave to us and stagger off."

"You need to stop holding in all that aggression, Bunk," Michael Greenstreet pats Burger on the shoulder as he passes the big man. "Let all that anger out sometime, huh?" Nick Miller—'Filthy Nick' - replaces March at the throne at the watch desk. His shirt hangs out of his pants, a patchwork of faded stains of undefined origin and chemistry. Nick's hair and thick moustache are prematurely silver and unruly—a Phil Donahue from Borneo—highlighting bright blue eyes. He slumps in the high backed chair at the desk, a matchless prophet of fire, a seer forecasting the substance of a call based not on examining entrails but, on his imagination, and an instinctive sense about every call the company receives. "I got a hot one," Miller guarantees a "crapper".

Nick is a ten-year veteran in the firehouse after working in the Boston and Los Angeles Fire Departments. He answers to the nick name 'Filthy Nick' and like 'Pig Pen' in 'Peanuts,' fame attracts dirt, grime and assorted mixtures like a magnet in a box of iron filings. Nick may report to work respectably attired, but within a few hours his shirt works its way from his pants. A total stranger can identify the fires involving Engine 50 and any other natural element within close proximity to the firefighter simply by assessing the assorted splatters and stain on Miller's clothing.

Nick is also known as 'The Peerless Pyro Prophet' by anyone working more than one day with him. Courtesy of Nick's ability to announce, en route, whether or not a fire is a disaster or a 'common run', the descriptions occupying opposite ends of the firefighting spectrum. A disaster, by any definition a fire whose intensity and involvement drains a firefighter's strength and taxes his resources, a common run, however, ranges from any fire extinguished by' . . . somebody throwing a cup of water on it . . .' to responding to an odor of smoke or some poor citizen trapped in an elevator.

For the next hour Nick will be officially responsible for the watch desk, monitoring all radio communications and answering the departmental phone—that black, non descript, government issue phone, large and bulky. God strikes dead those allowing that phone to ring twice before being answered. God will not only strike you dead, but will resurrect you and strike you a second time if the caller on the other end of the line is Division Chief Gregory Ryan, 'The Predator.' And if you have not been struck dead after two rings of a Ryan call, the Division Chief assumes the role of God and metes out similar punishment. Those companies under his command—every company in the First or Eastern Division—debate whether Ryan has already lost patience with the Almighty and assumed His mantle unannounced.

There is a second telephone at the watch desk, a bright red phone hanging from its receiver on the side of the desk. It is called 'The Bat Phone' and its eerie warbling always guarantees a run of substance. The phone is a direct link to the Communications Supervisor's desk and never activated unless one or both companies need to be alerted to a serious emergency. Regardless of color, red or black, both phones are answered on the first ring.

From the wall speaker the warbling, rising-falling tone seems to explode and the brass gong rips out its triple *Clang . . . Clang . . . Clang* as the teleprinter at the desk buzzes and clatters printing out the alarm assignments in triplicate. The radio on the front wall even sounds louder as a dispatcher's voice drones in a demanding monotone:

"Engine fifty . . . Engine ninety-six . . . Truck one . . . oh . . . five respond . . . report of smoke in the dwelling . . . Conver Street . . ." the rest of the announcement is lost in the eruption of movement. Blue shirted men materialize from all over the firehouse. Jerry March slides a brass pole that lands him on the far side of the engine, Paul Gulfee slides a brass pole that brings him to his door on the truck. Mark Hagan makes three long strides and disengages the exhaust venting and battery cable from the side of the big apparatus before stepping up behind the steering wheel of the truck. Feet are shoved into boot tops and suspenders hoisted over shoulders allowing bunker pants to be fastened.

The interior of the firehouse is rocked with the deep rumble of diesel motors and hollow metallic slamming of doors. Dan Kemp stands beside the open door on his side of the engine, turnout coat over one arm, helmet in hand. Red and white lights are already pulsing and swirling around the inside of the house. Truck 105 is the first to depart in a loud hiss of brakes. As if cued, Kemp steps up into the front seat and slams his door and Jerry March eases Engine 50 through the rising door.

The alarm is technically known as a 'two and one', the result of communications receiving a phone call from a duly concerned citizen mumbling in a halting mush about smoke seen coming from a rowhouse. This less than succinct information was entered into ninety-five million dollars worth of electronics, the computer assisted dispatch—CAD, in use for less than a year. With mind numbing speed, the system took into consideration the time of day, location and vague contents of the report and displayed the companies to be sent to the location.

Rocking and jolting inside the cab of Engine 50, Dan Kemp leans his considerable bulk back in his seat and glances at the three firefighters slouched in the jump seats behind him. None express any signs of excitement or anticipation, looking like bored adults trapped at a children's party. Gone are the days when firemen rode on the back step of the apparatus, often hanging on for dear life. OSHA regulations required that every person riding emergency apparatus be seated in an enclosed area. The regulations had the right idea—safety—but accidents continue—like the poor fellow on Engine 22 who leaned against the door of the cab during a run only to have the latch break, sending the shocked firefighter headlong into the street at thirty miles an hour. OSHA didn't foresee faulty doors.

"This ain't nothing," Nick Miller finally complains, shifting in his seat. His head rolls back and forth as they rumble over cracked and broken streets, "I ain't even got butterflies."

"Well that settles it," Billy Burger lifts both arms in a dramatic display of frustration. "No butterflies, no fire." Filthy Nick has spoken, his pronouncement more sure than the Delphic Oracle, though the Delphic mystery received no assistance from any physical prognosticator.

"Beat me to tears," Nick adds his personal *coup de gras,* a verbal *finis* to the authenticity of this call.

The engine arrives first turning onto Conver Street and slowing to allow Terry Buck to exit the cab, trot to the rear and pull off the water supply line to be coupled to the hydrant. March guns the motor slightly, pulling away from Buck, hose leaping from the hose bed to land in the street, laying in a gentle, curving line as the engine moves closer to the fire. With no water supply on the engine which, in turn supplies water to the attacking hose line, the pipe man is reduced to invective filled prayer and spitting on the flames.

Smoke rushes from the second floor window of a structure considered a dwelling in name only, a more apt description would be 'hovel.' Robinson Crusoe lived in better conditions. The smoke is light gray and though it flows quickly from the open window on the second floor, whatever might be burning inside is still in an embryonic stage.

Jerry is careful to bring the engine slightly past the front of the dwelling, allowing room for Mark Hagan to steer Truck 105 in behind and parallel to the curb directly in front of the fire. Mike Greenstreet, in a display of agility shocking for a massive accumulation of adipose, is out of the tiller cab and helping Sam Killen pull a twenty-four foot ladder from the side of the truck and position it at the window—'throwing the ladder.'

There are men in motion everywhere, that choreographed chaos alien to the casual observer. Even as Greenie and Sam are throwing their ladder to the second floor, Hagan has set the brakes, engaged the truck's power to the turntable and jumped from behind the steering wheel to place chocks against the massive tires of the vehicle. Climbing the side of the truck, he is already lifting the big aerial ladder, the 'stick' from its bed and rotating the turntable, bringing its tip to the roof. Richard Simms, imposing in his mask and breathing apparatus, brandishes a halligan tool and six foot ceiling hook and climbs the smaller ladder placed by Killen and Greenie. His first act ascending the ladder is to smash the first floor windows to assist ventilation. As Rich moves up the rungs, Killen, also masked up, waits on the sidewalk to follow. Overhead, the fat bulk of Greenstreet, hauling a chainsaw, clambers up the steel aerial to the roof where he will cross the flat surface, get on his belly and break out the top windows at the rear of the structure before opening the roof, all to vent the smoke and heat building inside.

Paul Gulfee has opened the front door of the decrepit shamble posing as a 'dwelling.' Behind him, Burger and Miller have pulled off several lengths of the smaller hose to attack the fire from the interior. Supplied with water from the engine, the two men work the hard charged line from the truck and up a stairway to the second floor.

There is a heavy, 'gauzy' appearance to the room—a kitchen judging from the old stove against one wall and, in the middle of the floor, a broken table surrounded by four equally broken chairs. Simms and Killen have broken out the windows along the second floor and hears the sound of Greenstreet's heavy footsteps, like a jolly green giant stomping ants, thuds overhead. In another era the men would have entered a room like this without breathing apparatus, the worst consequences are burning eyes and raw irritated throats. Working in such conditions was the 'manly' method, OSHA prevents the practice in the modern fire department. Masks are worn every time a firefighter goes into a building until the environment is confirmed to be safe. The regulations automatically add an additional sixty pounds to each man's burden. The trade-off is in longevity in working and living.

"Engine Five-Oh to communications," Kemp is standing in the doorway of the long abandoned kitchen. "Engine Five-Oh. Truck-One-Oh-Five will handle a small fire in the kitchen. Return Engine Ninety-Six . . . Engine Five-Oh has the card." The captain, as senior officer, automatically becomes 'incident commander' and accepts 'the card', the responsibility for securing this scene and making a report to contribute to the mountains of paperwork rising daily in department headquarters. The news is welcomed by Engine 96, sitting out on Conver Street opposite Jerry March and Engine 50. A short blast of their air horn draws a middle finger from March and the second engine returns to its firehouse on Cathedral Street.

Burger opens the nozzle of the hose, the one and three quarter inch line used for all interior work, and the rush of water blasts against a large pile of rubbish, old newspapers, broken two by fours and an assortment of flammable material, gathered in one corner of the room. The force of the stream blows small embers into the air, drowning the body of the fire and extinguishing the embers as they descend into the man-made lake forming across the cracked and peeling linoleum floor.

There is no evidence the fire has been extended elsewhere in this crumbling inner city dwelling, but Killen and Simms content themselves with yanking down the ceiling and pulling out large chunks of the walls. Aging joists and supports and exposed electric conduits that will later be stolen by some of the community's appreciative citizen and sold for drug money, a small part of the larger, ongoing saga between the firemen and dopers. Set a fire in some abandoned, vacant dwelling, let the firemen come and tear apart the interior of the place and return to rip out and otherwise confiscate any material with a resale value to fund an increasing need for narcotics—crack, heroin, speed or whatever toxic combination can be concocted and ingested.

Paul Gulfee has climbed the narrow stairway and pushed past Kemp. The captain leans against the doorframe slowly shaking his head and surveying what is left of the room.

"How long you think this hole has been vacant Paul." Kemp asks with pure disgust in his voice.

"Legally?" Gulfee laughs. "Somebody was obviously here a little while ago." He waves at the pile of sodden debris along the far wall. "But actually living here?" Gulfee looks around the room. "This isn't my idea of 'Home Sweet Home' but probably a couple months ago." He shrugs and watches Richard Simms prepare to pull down a section of ceiling.

In Richard's hands, the six foot ceiling hook looks like a toy, its working end is set with a sharp steel spike and, at a right angle to the spike is a large, curved hook. As Simms moves to steady himself, Gulfee suddenly grabs the huge man's arm and forcefully yanks Rich backward.

"Whoa big fella," the lieutenant yells abruptly, causing everyone in the steamy, smoking room to turn in Golfer's direction. "Looky here," he frowns and points to a drenched, filthy rug lying on the floor where Simms was about to step. At first glance the rug appears to have been haphazardly discarded onto the floor. Using Simms hook, Paul pulls the sodden piece of cloth to one side exposing a jagged hole in the floor, large enough to have swallowed Richard's leg to his groin or, perhaps caused the big man to fall through the first floor.

"What the hell!" Simms facemask is off, dangling from the webbing of his breathing harness. He stares angrily at the hole. Although its edges are jagged, there is no doubt among the men standing in the room the hole has been purposely created to cause injury.

"A little surprise from the scum we get paid to protect," Paul purses his lips and shakes his head. "Once that fat leg of yours went through that hole your whole body weight would have probably taken the rest of you all the way down."

"A slimy set-up." Dan Kemp walks to the edge of the hole. Looking down he can see the first floor. "A rotten piece of work. They figured you'd be so caught up puttin' out the damn fire nobody'd notice the rug and step on it."

Simms is fuming, the hole in the floor becomes a personal attack on him. "Anybody wanna tell me why some dirt-bag would go to the trouble of doing that?" He gestures at the hole, seething.

"For fun," Gulfree shrugs.

"Ain't no television around," Burger comments wryly. "Gotta get entertainment anyway you can when you're working on a low budget." He carefully moves the still hose around the room, giving wide berth to the exposed booby trap.

"Shoulda let the damn place burn," Simms declares, still angered and a little shaken over what might have been.

"We done here?" Nick Miller inhales deeply on a cigarette and blows out smoke rings. Kemp gives the stripped and burned out room a final, visual inspection.

"Let's get the hell home," the captain nods toward the stairway.

"A lousy booby trap. An ambush." Richard is repeating to Sam Killen as the two men sit in their seats in the truck's cab. Both companies slowly return to the Fort Avenue firehouse, this time without sirens and lights. "Cops are one thing," Richard continues as Killen listens with a sullen expression on his face. "I mean, y'know, the cops can tic you off. They hand out tickets, they carry guns, they intimidate people." The big man is angry and frustrated, trying to rationalize what cannot be understood. "But a *fireman*? Gimme a break, okay? You got an emergency, you call the fire department. We come and stop a fire, save somebody's house . . . save somebody from getting' toasted." He pauses. "And we get to the scene faster than any other city department you can call for an emergency."

Richard's observation is part of an age old truism spelled out on a smaller banner draped over the doorway of the firehouse lounge. It reads: *Call for the Police, Call for a Pizza, Call for the fire department—see who gets there first!* As first noted by Dennis Smith, that poet laureate of the fire department, you can call your plumber and have some confidence he will eventually get there, you can call the police and know that they will eventually get there, but every time you call the fire department or yank the handle on that fire alarm box, you can be sure beyond any doubt those fire engines will be there within minutes.

CHAPTER 4

CONFRONTATION AND RECOGNITION

A fearful anticipation has been mounting in the city government. An ongoing political confrontation has been carefully documented by the newspapers and television reporters in a city run by an intensely partisan mayor demanding that the state's governor (from an opposing party) provide school funding. Both men have taken diametrically opposed positions, publicly swearing there will be no retreat from their published and private positions.

According to published reports from the city's newspapers, the school budget is operating with more than a seventy-five million dollars deficit. Accusations run rampant of over priced administrators, highly salaried secretaries, administrative assistants paid three and four times the national average, exorbitant over time pay, and at least three vacant positions each receiving one hundred thousand dollars annually, in addition to several questionable contracts let to bidders with inside contacts to the Board of Education.

Under normal circumstances, the fight over educational funds would be viewed as the usual political tug-of-war between city and state. For the men sitting in the firehouse kitchen, however, and a few thousand of their fellow department members, the battle is far more personal.

Claiming a crisis in the city's finances, the mayor has, for the past couple of years, become actively engaged in reducing costs among agencies—hardest hit is the fire department. Assisting him in targeting budget reductions, the mayor appointed a committee of businessmen, large contributors to past mayoral campaigns, 'The Greater Metropolitan Commission.' Acting on the advice of his hand-picked commission, the mayor 'requested' the fire department to submit an annual budget reducing costs thirty-five percent. To 'guide' the department's rank and file, the department's administration, headed by a now retired chief of the department, held up its figurative hands maintaining the mayor's executive order held the finality of divine fiat. In turn, the mayor pointed to the findings of his select commission and placed responsibility on its recommendations. This Pontius Pilate washing of hands, placing the ultimate responsibility on his commission was hollow and disingenuous. The city's police department received a mandate to reduce costs by eight percent and even the sanitation department reduced costs by only twelve percent.

The truth, as surmised by most of the firefighters, lay in the fact that few, if any of the department members voted for the mayor and both unions, the Officer's Local and the Firefighter's Local, endorsed the mayor's opponent in the last election. Paybacks are the proverbial hell. Faced with an eviscerated budget while witnessing the Board of Education squander funds serves to kindle and maintain deep-seated animosity between the mayor and the fire department.

Publicly the mayor is opportunistic, often seen on the fire ground shaking hands and backslapping 'his' firefighters in photographed displays of pride and encouragement. During such 'photo-ops' the mayor, with his award winning smile, invariably wears a dark blue baseball cap with the fire department insignia and a dark blue windbreaker emblazoned with the Maltese Cross. These Judah's Kisses, as they have become to be known, serve to further alienate the department members.

"The Nit-Wit sure slashed our budget like Attila the Hun," Burger observes. "He don't get our vote so he skins us good." He runs a hand through his sparse brown hair, "Just proof that the stinky brown stuff always flows down hill.'

"There's gonna be a million of those television vans and reporters crawling over the streets," Jerry March slumps in his chair. Glancing at his wristwatch the pump operator sighs. "You know it's gonna be a bitch trying to drive anywhere near Cromwell." The street feeds the

East-West Expressway, the fastest, most direct route home for Jerry when his relief arrives. It also sits close to the boundary between the 15th and 12th Battalions in the department's eastern division.

"That's City Hall," Dan Kemp declares, reaching into his pants pocket. "How much is lunch?"

"Depends on how much the hospital charges to pump our stomachs in a couple hours," Nick Miller suggests.

"Hey Fatso," Burger calls to Greenie, "are you actually gonna charge us for this meal?"

"Double price for you, you big eagle-beaked, dumplin' shaped goon," Mike Greenstreet spits back. He fills three huge bowls with beef stew and hands them to Hagan. Four large baskets of warm bread line the center of the tables.

He inhales the fragrant steam. Greenstreet is a good cook, regardless of the constant complaints.

Three loud, sharp *clangs* rip from the gong on the apparatus floor, followed by the familiar warbling alert. "Damn, I felt that one!" March announces in a loud voice.

In the controlled melee of men emptying the kitchen, the voice of the communications dispatcher takes more than the usual amount of time to inform the firehouse of the alarm. The litany of assignments brings an intuitive response from Jerry.

"I think we got something this time," he calls out.

By the time Jerry has disconnected the battery cable and plymovent and settled behind the steering wheel, Dan Kemp sits in the officer's seat and is anxiously tapping his foot, more than ready to depart.

The lengthy recitation of companies alerted for the alarm is the first indication the call is of consequence; four engines, two trucks, the division's heavy duty rescue, two ambulances and the chiefs of two battalions—Loughlin and the chief of the next closest district. A fifth engine company is also being sent, a combination pumper and mini-rescue—a 'Squad'—carrying specialized rescue and extraction tools. Each division is assigned two squads to respond as a Rapid Intervention Team—RIT—to every fire occurring within its assignment area. The RIT company arrives on the fire ground and immediately positions a pair of two man teams at the front and rear of the fire scene to rescue trapped and injured firefighters. Each squad carries two large blue bags of equipment, RIT bags, filled with extra breathing apparatus, ropes, a five pound maul, halogen tool and high intensity flashlights. The moment a department member is reported trapped, it is the RIT that moves to rescue the would-be-rescuers.

Engine 50 rolls out of quarters first, bouncing and rocking as Jerry makes the wide turn on to Fort Avenue and an indication of the fire's intensity becomes evident.

"I got a belly-ache!" announces Miller.

"GEEZ, look at that . . ." Jerry's loud voice blends with Nick's revelation. The men's heads duck as they bend to peer out at the skyline ahead. In the distance a tall plume of black smoke forms a thick, rolling pillar that continues to ascend and intensify without slowing or dispersing in the steady breeze.

"I hope that's just a car fire," Kemp shouts, instinctively knowing otherwise.

"Kiss my butt!" Nick's comment is hurried. The trio in the rear pull protective hoods over their heads, buckling coats tighter and tugging gloves on their hands. As they begin sliding their arms through the shoulder straps of their breathing apparatus, Kemp leans forward to check the screen for the identification of the companies responding lists order in which they should arrive at the scene. Between the two blocks of data, the specific location of the fire hydrants nearest the fire flashes repetitively.

"We got a real crapper!" he shouts at March. From the radio a rush of static makes Dan wince.

"*Battalion one-five responding from Lafayette Park . . .*" Tom Loughlin's voice is calm, a soft monotone, like he's calling in for pizza. Half his battalion could be burning and Loughlin will sound the same. The chief and Howard are at the Lafayette Park headquarters of the division, an old, ivy covered building almost hidden among the trees. The two story, brown brick structure holds the offices and meeting rooms for division Chief Gregory 'The Predator' Ryan, the chief of the division's Emergency Medical Services—the paramedics, the SCO—Special Operations Command and the division's Fire Investigation Bureau—the arson squad.

"Keep a lookout for Nineteen Engine," Jerry is yelling over the noise of the air horn and siren. "They're liable to pop up out of one

41

of these side streets before we see 'em." He begins weaving in and out of traffic along Fort Avenue, some vehicles pulling left, others to the right and the occasional nut stopping in the middle of the street like a deer caught in headlights. Most dangerous, however, are the drivers whose one-celled brain challenges them to make a quick run in front of the fire engine and navigate the intersection while all the other 'nerds' aren't moving.

Although the column of smoke clearly marks the fire's location, it's a long drive from the fire house—'way out there'—a generic category including . . .'East Elsewhere or North Nowhere.' Where time matters and long scenic rides create frustration and the accumulation of gastric acid considering that two firehouses, three full companies of equipment and men, have been closed and disbanded. Fifteen months ago this run—an assignment—both Engine 50 and Truck 105 would have taken on the second alarm and two years ago, *third* alarm. It is a recurring scenario producing increasing physical and mechanical stress on both men and apparatus, overcome only because the firemen work twice as hard and first-line vehicles are repaired and re-tuned from breakdowns never anticipated when ordered from the manufacturers.

March drives in a maddening series of feverish slow-down, accelerate, tap the brake, weave left, slow down, and turn back to the right, movements. Following the engine, Hagan runs the same gauntlet of vehicles, keeping close behind the engine in a nerve-fraying, follow-the-leader. A fast paced game causing Ken Howard to swear he will never drive the red car between the vehicles. "Too damn scary," he says shaking his head.

The two vehicles pass Mount Street, slow at Montgomery and once past Makin Street, the traffic has sufficiently parted and they have a straight shot down Fort Avenue. All the while they are watching the thickening plume of black smoke, like the Israelites of Exodus following the cloud preceding them. After what seems an eternity of driving, Jerry makes a wide turn on Anne Street, one block from a news conference.

"Damn, a press conference," March yells in frustration. Clusters of television trucks and vans fill the street. He brakes and weaves between two of the trucks before accelerating again and turning left. At the street corner a group of people point and wave frantically. Kemp can see the fire ahead of them, people have already massed in the street and along the sidewalks.

"Damn," Kemp swears long and loudly and speaks into his radio. "Engine Five-Oh on location . . . working fire." His report to Communications will bring a third truck company, one of the department's safety officers and the Air-Cascade Unit, a specialized vehicle to maintain the breathing apparatus worn by the firemen.

Large three-story row houses sit back several yards from the curb; houses once owned by middle-class families who sold them to the highest bidder during the decades of 'white-flight' from the city. At the far end of the block is the source of the rising column of smoke—one of the largest dwellings at the end of the row is sending out that thick, soupy, black cloud from the second and third floors. Ugly, tightly, bunched clouds with heavy, rolling orange tongues of flame curling inside.

March slows the engine to allow Terry Buck to jump from the cab. He pulls further down the street to give Truck 105 the room to slide in closest to the fire. By the time the engine has come to a hissing halt, Buck has made the hydrant connection. The gathering crowd, despite its size, stays on the opposite curb. A safe decision since Hagan has followed the engine so closely that anyone in the street would get run over.

Sirens and air horns continue in the distance and fire department vehicles arrive at intervals, seconds apart, water supply hoses stretching down the street, across the street, criss-crossing each other to form that familiar tangle of 'spaghetti.' The whine of hydraulics accompanies aerial ladders lifting from their beds and telescoping upwards, their turntables rotating in the direction of the fire.

Killen and Gulfee, in a scuttling crouch, enter the first floor of the burning house, each man carrying his tools, the halligans and ceiling hook and axe. For an instant, both men are framed by dark gray smoke swirling at the front door before they disappear inside. Rich Simms and Greenstreet have already thrown a ladder to a second floor window as Hagan positions the aerial ladder at the roof.

Burger and Nick Miller control a hose line, sending a powerful stream of water into another second floor window before temporarily shutting and following Sam and Paul Gulfee through the front door.

Spectators increase, curious bystanders and worried neighbors who shout and cry and offer advice and instructions. Their numbers are augmented by the herd of reporters who anticipated the boredom of another political speech but find themselves witness to high drama. Satellite vans begin inching along the street as drivers cautiously search for the nearest location to the action, ignoring pedestrians and fire department apparatus alike; competing with engine and truck companies for precious space. Television camera crews wander back and forth across the street and around the corners, vying for the best angles.

"Battalion one-five on location . . . confirming a working fire. Battalion will assume command." Tom Loughlin signals his presence on the fire ground.

The interior of the house is inky black, its atmosphere heavy and suffocating, enveloping within it. Within that pitch shroud, men are moving on hands and knees, on their stomachs with arms extended performing bulky, exhausting breast strokes, jostling and bumping into each other. "Big Ed" lights hanging from chest straps are of little use, the blanketing darkness swallows the beams of light, limiting vision to inches in any direction. Progress is made by touch, the instinctive feel of a familiar object—furniture, a television, a lamp stand, blind men identifying objects around them.

Sounds became absorbed in the heavy smoke; the shattering of windows, the ripping, crunching sound of walls being torn down. The biting whine of a chain saw can be heard, muffled by smoke and distance as each man forces his way through this black pudding. Muted shouts between men are the only means of communication giving a distorted sense of direction within the black heat.

Dan Kemp is pressed against the two men in front of him who control the hose. They attempt to navigate a stairway to their right, steps to the second floor. Above them, fire seems to pour down out of the smoke, rolling through the flowing clouds and forcing the trio to huddle on the steps, heads down. With the nozzle of their hose directed up into the roaring, groaning cauldron above, the water turns into steam descending and enveloping the men, soaking their turnout gear only to be vaporized again by the heat, recyclable scalding. No retreats from the stairway, they have moved together as a single unit and the fire causes them to press together as one. Nobody moves out of sheer will—what one endures, they will endure together.

The heat on the stairway is agonizing; it cannot be quantified. A fire started in the center of a room will create a ceiling heat of one thousand degrees within five minutes, steel begins to destabilize at fifteen hundred degrees. A single stream of water, even at a hundred seventy gallons per minute is like urinating on a fire like this and all three men hunched together on that stairway know it.

Outside the house, in the rear, the chief of the Eleventh Battalion is carefully watching the progress of the fire. Heavy smoke blankets the entire rear of the row of dwellings; thick black clouds pushing out from the second and third floors and spreading further down the block. Arriving at the scene from the rear, a third engine company has already stretched a big, two and a half inch hose into the small, concrete area that passes as a 'backyard' in this neighborhood; the volume of fire demands it. The line opens on the second floor and as the heavier stream of water blasts into the smoking, swirling flames, the dark clouds immediately begin turning gray, then white. From the third floor however, fire continues to roll in quick, powerful spurts through the cloud that seems as thick as gravy.

On the stairway, the fire reaches down toward the men huddled behind the pipe, the heavier hose line opening up in the rear of the fire at them. As if alive, the fire retreats along the path of least resistance, in this case, toward the smaller hose.

"Damn it!" Miller is cursing loudly behind his mask. "This damn thing is super hot!" Shove your face into a heated ceramic kiln and you get the idea.

For a moment Kemp considers backing out, moving away from the flame thrower at the top of the stairs. In the seconds it takes to move a booted foot to steady himself, the captain becomes aware of the bulk of more men joining them. Muffled shouts over his head are suddenly drowned into a sudden roar, a second line opening inches over the officer's helmet. Another company has joined them on the stairway. Instantly the small group disappears in a massive swirling cloud of gray-white smoke.

Sam Killen has completed his first search of the ground floor, finding no one. He emerges from the back door exhausted and empty handed. To his left, a ladder has been extended to the upper floors and Killen ascends its rungs, aware of the rush of water nearby, courtesy of that third engine in the rear of the rowhouse. On the roof Mark Hagan is working at cutting a hole, the chain saw he operates makes Sam think of a logging operation. Mark and two other firemen work furiously to vent the smoke and heat built up inside the top floors. Their position is precarious and nobody knows how long this fire has been burning, how long the flames have been eating away at the beams supporting the roof. The men become obscured in thick, rolling smoke, only the continued grating of the chainsaw marking their approximate location.

Terry Buck follows Killen up the ladder. It is not Bucky's immediate task to scale ladders and do search and rescue, but with the other members of the engine company inside the home and the murky interior of the house, Terry uses his own initiative to 'double-up' with Killen.

"I got a body," Sam is already grunting from the exertion of lifting a small body found just inside the window. He is aware another fireman is behind him, not knowing it is Terry. The frail little body is passed from one man to the other and then out the window. In the heat and smoke there is little time to affect a 'fireman's carry.' Terry reverts to the time-honored method best described as 'anyway you can as fast as possible.' Atop the ladder he hears Sam inside, thumping and thudding around and through whatever was in his way.

Killen recognizes the outline of a second victim, limbs entwined with those of a third. "*God, it's the whole damned family!*" The thought races through his mind. Like a collection of dolls, there is a jumble of arms, legs and prone bodies. As the big man works quickly to separate and arrange this collection of barely breathing humanity, the warning signal on his breathing apparatus begins its high-pitched, pulsing screech. The warning indicates about five minutes of breathing air left in the air bottle, but in actual working conditions in a fire, it is more like three.

Dan Kemp has gotten to the top of the stairway, crouching behind Burger and Miller, no longer forced to kneel and take a beating from the heat. The fire is driven back, heat and smoke venting up and out through the openings cut by Hagen and others on the roof. As the men on the nozzle, the 'pipe,' progress further, visibility changes. Layers of filmy gauzy white smoke hang in the air exposing charred and charcoaled wood throughout the second floor. The rooms resemble blackened cubicles strewn with smoking remains of what had once been furniture—beds, dressers, a woman's make-up table, a child's desk. Tongues of fire lap intermittently from behind broken walls or through jagged holes in the ceiling. Truckies will be through each room, boots crunching on broken glass and debris that had once been a families household possessions, to rip and tear with ceiling hooks and pry bars, pulling apart whatever remains to hide the lurking fire. Those flames and the embers that accompany them, will be drowned in a rush of water—a final wash-down—leaving this big house a smoking, blackened skeleton.

"Battalion One-Five to Communications," Tom Loughlin's voice sounds from the radios of nearly a dozen fire department vehicles in the surrounding streets. *"Place this fire under control . . ."* The high tide of excitement passes. Faced with the smoking hulk of what remains of the house, the mob of spectators begins dispersing, their interest dissipated, except for giving thanks that this was not their own home. Whatever takes place now occurs inside the scorched walls of the row home, with it's shattered windows and gaping holes in its roof. There is nothing outwardly visible to hold their interest.

A flow of wet and sooty firefighters wearily return to their apparatus for a moment's respite before retrieving and packing away their equipment. A shout rises above the throb of diesel motors causing heads to turn. A hundred faces stare anxiously, for a moment, at the skeleton of wood. Cheers break out accompanied by applause, scattered at first, but rising to a mini crescendo. People, who moments before, had been walking away from the scene with arms folded and heads shaking, are streaming back to previous vantage points. Television cameramen, followed by sound technicians carrying microphones on long booms, begin jostling for position while field reporters quickly scout the surrounding ground for the best backdrop.

Walking slowly from the house, Sam Killen summons his last reserves of energy, vaguely aware of paramedics surging toward him, of fellow firemen scrambling to his side. Sam's air mask dangles from his chest, his helmet is skewed in an awkward position and his face is covered with a mottling of dust, and dirt streaked with sweat.

The big man moves stiffly, awkwardly, advancing a few feet with each effort. Under his arms he carries a small body, another tiny victim hangs over his shoulder and he carries a fourth in his ham-sized hands. When Sam steps to his right, Terry Buck—Bucky—comes into view with two more children in his arms. Like Killen, Terry is the picture of abject exhaustion, his face drawn and filthy with soot and grime. Drawing closer, Terry's eyes stand out as white marbles in a smear of black soot and in seconds both men are mobbed, relieved of their burdens and escorted to the back step of Engine 50.

Camera lenses form a small semi-circle around the two, microphones and small hand held recorders are thrust between the cameramen, unintelligible questions shouted from all directions.

"Just get the hell outta here," Jerry March interposes himself between the gaggle of reporters and the exhausted, dazed firemen. Jerry is scowling, big arms flailing, pushing at the cameras and sound devices. "You guys want a medic to look at ya'?" he shouts the question at Killen and Buck.

Sam is too drained to answer. It hurts to shrug his shoulders and slide the padded straps of his breathing harness down his arms. He accepts a bottle of cold water, tilts his head, opens his mouth and literally pours the iced water down his throat; stopping enough to empty the remains of the bottle over his head.

Terry Buck sags back against the engine, too weary to further exert himself. His mouth and throat feel as if he had gargled with heated sand, his tongue is swollen, clinging to his teeth and gums. Despite the press of humanity and the shouted questions, Terry becomes aware of a suit, a three piece suit, to his left. The suit is joined by another, the two suits acting as blockers for a third.

"These are what are known as heroes," an enthusiastic voice shouts the words. "These are the kind of men who dedicate their lives to the city. These are the men who make me proud of my fire department." The mayor wears a dark blue windbreaker with 'FIRE DEPARTMENT' emblazoned in large yellow letters across the back. The opportunistic politico has also procured a navy blue baseball cap with the fire department logo on its front and as he proclaims the virtues of 'his' fire department, the mayor looks directly into the camera lenses.

"What's your names fellas?" he asks, glancing back and forth between the two exhausted men and the lenses of the cameras. He wears an awkward smile, a tortured mix of pseudo-concern for the firemen and a forced grin for the reporters. The mayor has yet to offer to shake either man's hand.

"Firefighter Terry Buck," Terry manages to mumble. He tilts his head to his right in Killen's direction. "Firefighter Sam Killen."

"Engine fifty and Truck One-Oh-Five," Jerry March interjects, sliding between the two dirty men and reporters.

"These are men worthy of the word 'hero'," the mayor becomes a veritable cliché machine among the media. He seems unaware and unaffected by the continued movement of firemen around him. A few feet from this impromptu media event, Dan Kemp and Mark Hagan stand with hands on hips.

"First time I've seen him on a fire ground," Mark comments, his trademark smirk has returned to his face.

"Ahh," Kemp shakes his head in disgust, "the jerk was here to find out what the governor was gonna say, that's all."

"Yeah, but where'd he come up with the department jacket and hat?"

"He probably keeps a supply of uniforms in his car and between us and the cops he has a case covered when he needs it on a scene like this. I bet if there was a scene with a Sanitation Department he'd have one of their jumpsuits to put on."

A small space is finally cleared at the rear of the engine. The presence of the mayor forces the mass of reporters to question him. There are no questions asked about who closed the two fire houses just blocks away. The old hose tower of one building, the antiquated tower used to dry and store wet hose in another era, could still be seen rising above the roofs of nearby row homes.

"You think maybe I oughtta yell something about 49 Engine and 62 Truck being closed . . . just five blocks away?" Hagan laughs at the thought but knows Kemp wont have the guts to allow it.

"Hell no," Dan glances back at the smoldering house behind them. "Maybe if Sam and Terry hadn't pulled the kids out alive."

"We're ignored either way," Mark recognizes the futility of their position. Do a good job and it's expected. "Do a great job under duress and nobody notices because they can't tell the difference."

"You got officer potential," Kemp replies, hoping Mark realizes he is being facetious.

Another 'suit' interposes it's way between the media and the back step of the engine. "Are you two men from the same company?" The question is polite.

"No," Jerry March answers. "Different companies, same firehouse." His tone is softer. "Engine Fifty, Truck One-Oh-Five," he identifies the two once again.

"And you are?" the suit asks in a professional, measured tone.

"Pump operator Gerald March, and you?" Jerry shakes hands with the civilian.

"Paul Garret," the suit doesn't attempt to wipe his hand after shaking Jerry's. "I'm an aide to the governor . . . we watched your operations from nearby." Buck and Killen turn their attention to the gubernatorial aide.

"The governor would like to extend an invitation to your companies," Garrett explains in a somber voice. "What was demonstrated today," the aide motions toward the burnt-out house, "warrants special recognition. I assume there are channels through which the invitation should be directed?"

March's chest expands, assuming the role of arbiter, giving Paul Garrett the address of the firehouse. "But all communications goes through department headquarters," the pump operator explains in an off-the-cuff reference to the department's hierarchy.

Paul Garrett has a small smile on his face when he nods at Jerry. "I'm sure," he allows in a quiet voice. "The governor wants to recognize the efforts of these men . . . probably at the State House with dinner or something similar."

Killen and Buck regain their energy and composure to edge from the pumper's back step and begin a slow retreat from the media. The party is over.

"We're heroes?" Hagan frowns at Killen. "Gimme a break."

CHAPTER 5

FIRE AND POLITICS DO NOT MIX

A dangerous shell game is being played in the city; unannounced and unpublicized—a Russian Roulette series of decisions practiced on a daily basis.

In the fire department, on every shift, at least twelve companies are officially listed 'OOS'—'Out of Service'—unavailable to respond to an emergency. Personnel from the companies are temporarily absorbed into the ranks of adjacent companies; returning to their own fire houses at the beginning of the next trick.

The choice of the companies rendered OOS appears random; no rhyme or reason or pattern is discerned. Worse, mere twenty-four hour notice is given to the affected members—the optimum agreed upon by the city and department hierarchy. At least the fire department gets twenty-four hours; the public, dependent upon the fire department for its safety, doesn't get a ten second radio spot. An attentive neighborhood gets a flyer taped to an exit door on the darkened firehouse. Inside that darkened building, apparatus sits unattended. The building's doors are locked and for twenty-four hours the existence of both firehouse and vehicles is a fiction. Tell that to Mr. Smith banging on the door of the fictional firehouse at two in the morning because his home is on fire and his family is trapped inside. If the flyer taped to the door hasn't been torn off or blown away by a strong breeze, Mr. Smith might read that this same firehouse he'd visited a day earlier and spoken to real, live firemen, isn't 'working' while his home burns down. There are no directions to the closest 'open' firehouse. Foresight is in short supply in municipal governments.

On the rare occasion an irate, tax-paying citizen remembers the correct phone number to contact city hall about the closed firehouse at the end of the block, he is shuffled through a half-dozen agencies before a bored, but polite desk clerk informs him the best agency to contact would be to call 911. If this concerned citizen still possesses a semblance of sanity after the electronic wild goose chase, he finally contacts a polite civil servant at the department's Public Information Office who assures the caller the company in question does, indeed, exist but is . . . "temporarily out-of-service in order that the members attend 'Enhanced Training' to better meet the needs of the community. There is no real threat to the safety of the neighborhood." The explanation goes on to tell any caller tenacious enough to pursue the issue, "the needs of the area is adequately covered by the other companies within moments of any emergency."

The assurance is pure rubbish, a less genteel public would call it a lie. It is not revealed, for example, that 'Enhanced Training' does not occur at the Fire Academy at night, nor is it revealed, or noticed, that firehouses close to City Hall are *NEVER* 'Out of Service', nor do those companies in the first alarm areas of the members of the City Council undergo such 'Training.' Those companies in the city's most prosperous community's evidently need less training. Companies responsible for property values in the upper six figures are seldom if ever closed. Instead, the larger percentage of darkened firehouses occur in neighborhoods needing the services most, but without the political influence to keep them open.

This 'dirty little secret' has borne tragic consequences. Truck 105 had two fatalities in the Heights—a couple of addicts died while sleeping in a vacant dwelling. Two blocks from the fire, ninety seconds as the fire engines drive, Truck 12 sat in a deserted firehouse. There was an occupied dwelling in the second Battalion where an eighty year old man was trapped by fire and died, his wife was grabbed by the guys from Engine 6, a company responding from fifteen blocks away. Unfortunately, the firehouse three blocks away, the company responsible for—search—and rescue in a dwelling fire, was out-of-service; they would have pulled both octogenarians from the burning home, while

Engine 6 put the fire out. As it turned out, everyone from Engine 6 was involved in the rescue attempt while the fire grew in intensity.

Over in the west where run totals are beginning to escalate exponentially, Truck 3 responds to an assignment it normally takes on *fourth* alarm because the two closest truck companies were already out and the next due company is a 'rotated closure.'

Maybe the simple fact that *anyone* being rescued and property saved is a tribute to the firemen. In an effort to overcome the deficit placed on them by this reduction of available resources, firemen are exerting twice the energy to produce the same results. Unfortunately this is not a city whose recipients of such service do not recognize their liability or probable flammability. In the bowels of City Hall, the people crunching numbers and authoring efficiency reports lack the genetic code allowing for the recognition of the physical and mental cost on personnel and the wear and tear on equipment involved with doubling or tripling the effort to achieve parity just twelve months prior. A collective dedication to excellence is lost in the quest proving reduction in funding doesn't affect outcome. Besides their reasoning maintains, who really cares if some normally healthy firefighter across town suddenly develops a cardiac problem, or a twenty-five year old firefighter shows all the back and spine ailments of a man three times his age? It's a budgetary no-brainer that a replacement entering the department at the beginning pay scale costs less. Attrition can be City Hall's best friend.

In a quintessential display of buck-passing, City Hall insists the fire department's policy on temporary closures should be determined internally—a matter of 'plausible deniability'—the mayor can always claim, truthfully, the availability of fire service is a decision arrived at by the department, not City Hall. All city agencies are ultimately responsible to the mayor so any policy affecting the city as a whole must give passing deference to Hizzoner. Politicians live and breathe for one solitary purpose, re-election, a process requiring lies, deceit and charm. Managing a large city in the throes of a dwindling tax base which, in turn, limits budgetary considerations, the mayor effortlessly robs Peter to pay Paul, bequeathing financial life support to one agency while denying it to another; the real expertise comes in doing so with a smile.

Most firefighters view the primary tasks of government to be the support of business and suppression of crime. Fighting fire falls somewhere in the latter category without a specific clarifying clause. Any budget consideration given the fire department is subject to the whim of whoever controls the political helm of the city, in this instance the mayor.

The mayor's ascendance to office is the result of solemn promises to revitalize the city; a Herculean task for an experienced elder statesman, much less a young lawyer. Slender, clean-cut with an affinity to Brooks Brothers suits and oxford weave shirts, he is not yet forty years old. He speaks with passion and enthusiasm, using skills honed persuading reluctant juries. The neat appearance, along with a rhetorical style and dimpled smile, gives the impression he truly believes what he says. As one disaffected, former staff member revealed in a moment of honesty, "He'll say whatever he thinks the people believe . . ." a revelation that appeared in print early in his administration creating the subsequent warning from the mayor that . . . "any future reports of similar content will result in expulsion of the offending media member from City Hall *in perpetuity . . ."*

One large group thought initially the promises were for the fire department. The mayoral candidate promised a 'New Camelot' tantamount to raising the legendary city on a slag heap. But his was a new face, young and personifying hope for the future. Part of his election effort emphasized courting the unions representing city employees. With the fire department, the approach was done straight faced, asking the unions to 'believe' in him, in his heartfelt efforts and know he was a 'man of his word.' Like most unions, the firefighter's local, and it's sister organizations representing fire officers, tend to lean heavily Democratic. The Mayoral candidate had backing from the party's national committee, and somewhat grudgingly, both unions threw their support behind the young attorney, believing his promise that if the department members accepted one year without a pay raise, the city could solidify it's financial base and their loyalty would be rewarded in the administration's second year with an eight percent retroactive raise.

Six years after that initial request to 'believe' years including his re-election, the city's several thousand firemen continued to work with no raise, retroactive or otherwise. The tepid interest in the fire department unions was conspicuous during his second bid for office. He found the police department more supportive of his agenda and, consequently, the police department found itself the recipient of City Hall's largesse, along with the Board of Education and the Department of Sanitation.

Historically, an uneasy tension exists between city agencies and the occupant of the mayor's office. For five years relations between the mayor and 'his' fire department had been tension filled. City firefighters were the only metropolitan employees habitually failing to applaud the mayor at public functions, most refused to rise from their seats. At best 'his' fire department was viewed by the mayor like a harried parent of a pedantic child; the department had become a 'thorn-in-the flesh'.

"Who the hell even names their kid 'Myron' these days?" Jerry March complains loud enough to overcome the other conversations in the fire house lounge. He is sprawled on one of the big sofas that fit along opposing walls, a large bag of potato chips rests on his stomach and rattles each time he digs inside. On the television screen the mayor is delivering an impromptu speech commemorating the opening of a new middle school. "Impromptu? Is this guy for real, bet he had that speech ready for months."

There is no answer to Jerry's question; the other men continue their discussions unabated. At the rear of the room Dan Kemp sips his coffee, standing with one hand in his pocket. Instead of answering March's question, the captain arches an eyebrow in classic fashion and suppresses a grin. "I know he has a nickname; . . . 'Chip'."

The name causes Jerry to twist on the couch, spilling the bag of potato chips onto the worn carpeting. "You're kidding?" he focuses on the captain. "You're serious?" he pauses. "Chip?"

"Can't be," Dan shrugs and allows the grin to tug at the corners of his mouth.

"Well well," Jerry retrieves the bag from the floor and resumes his position. "Next time I see the Ol' Chipmeister on a fire ground, I'm gonna remember that. It'll gimme a chance to get close and personal with him."

"You hear how much that new school cost?" Kemp remains at the rear of the room, like a Colossus holding his coffee mug and nodding at the television screen as Mayor 'Chip' concludes his remarks.

"With the education the kids get," Sam Killen interjects, "I'd say about fifty million too much." He searches through discarded sections of the newspaper Burger has been reading. "Hell!" he frowns at Bill. "How long does it take you to read that part of the paper?"

"There ain't no pictures," Burger wears half-glasses at the end of his nose and peers over the tops at Killen, dramatically rattling the paper. "And the words are kinda big so I read slowly," he sniffs in autocratic disdain.

"A product of the school system?" Kemp uses his half-filled coffee mug as a pointer in Burger's direction. "Just so you know," he adds.

Comparing the educational budget with the fire department's is a dangerous endeavor. The fiscal restraint of the Governor flies in the face of the financial beggary that has epitomized the city leadership for decades. Heading the city's list of financial needs is its school system. A monolithic behemoth consuming millions of tax dollars annually with little to show for it's efforts. In contrast, the fire department is spoon-fed money and commanded to demonstrate its efficiencies; part of the mayor's conscious effort to reward sympathetic voting blocs and to remind antagonists who controls the literal cost of recalcitrance. While the fire department is told to operate with its budget reduced by eighteen percent, the beleaguered, debt-ridden school system is suddenly gifted with an increase in its budget; compliments of the 'discovery of funds.' This leaves a noticeable impression on the public. The mayor has the quiet confidence of a lion in its own den. This is *his office* with the oak paneled walls, deep plush wine colored carpeting and heavily padded chairs. Mozart plays softly in the background.

Schools are an ever present accomplishment. The fire department on the other hand tends to remain 'out of sight' until called, sort of an 'as needed accessory.' Other than Fire Prevention Week, most of the department's vehicles stay in their firehouses.

Sitting in a high-backed leather chair, the mayor tells this to the Chief of the Fire Department, Thomas Callahan who is wearing his dress uniform, four gold stripes around each cuff of the dark blue jacket, starched white shirt and black tie and gold collar pins engraved with five crossed trumpets; symbols of his rank. Callahan is ramrod straight in the chair, white cap resting on his lap. His eyes warily watching Hizzonor's movements.

Callahan is a thirty-two year veteran, entering as a firefighter, promoted to pump operator, rising through each rank—lieutenant, captain, battalion chief, division commander and finally to become deputy chief of the department. His appointment as Chief of Department at the beginning of the mayor's second term in office had been initially welcomed by the members of the department. Tom Callahan is the recipient of eight medals of valor as well as a handful of citations of merit and including a half dozen unit citations awarded to companies he directed in major fires.

Thomas Callahan makes a commanding presence. An impressive specimen, stands well over six feet tall, broad shouldered with close-cropped dark hair, strong jaws and intense brown eyes. 'Chippy' insists Callahan remains seated during their meeting so the diminutive mayor isn't force to stare at Callahan's chest. The two men can be photographed shoulder-to shoulder only if the mayor is standing on a stepstool.

"With all due respect," Callahan takes a deep breath. He has been listening to a lecture for fifteen minutes and his clenched jaws are aching. "I can't close any more stations to reduce the costs." It is the quarterly sparring session between the two men. The mayor openly reasons why the department should reduce the strength as Callahan patiently parries each suggestion and explains the fire department's resources are stretched to the breaking point. "We're at the critical level right now in terms of the size of the city and the minimum requirements needed to protect it."

Myron can't concern himself with recommendations from the International Fire Protection Agency, if the IFPA doesn't have to piece together an annual budget and account for the needs of a dozen different agencies vying for the same dollar pool. He is focused on public relations imagery and re-election; the 'smoke and mirrors' of politics. "Tom," he fixes Callahan with a level stare, "one of the reasons I appointed you as my chief was because I figured you were smart enough to juggle the numbers and allocate costs. I don't give a Tinker's damn if some hundred year old firehouse has to be closed or some of those shiny new fire engines get sent back to their maker . . ." Myron gives a small grin, "or gets sold off somewhere. You weren't appointed just because you're a decent firefighter." The insult is overshadowed only by the former attorney's arrogance.

In addition to Callahan's impeccable record, the chief possesses a graduate degree in business management and recently completed the course work toward a similar degree in Physics. Mark Hagan observed that "Callahan arranges the department budget by splitting the atom."

Despite his resume, professional and academic, Callahan is guilty of one particular venal sin—one negative notation in his private personnel folder preventing a closer association to Myron; Callahan belongs to The Other Party. Worse, the chief has close, personal ties to the state's governor. In point of fact during his transition to the State House, the newly elected governor had indeed hoped to put him in a position in the state.

"Tom," the governor had to concede, "the best advice I can give you is to stay in the city. I can't come close to matching your salary and position, and I won't offer you anything worth giving up what you already have."

Callahan accepted his appointment as Chief of Department realistically, aware of the antipathy between City Hall and the fire department. Before taking the oath of office, he visited every firehouse in the city, promising that he would resign before allowing another closure or disbanding another company. That promise had been warmly received, since the previous chief had almost blindly reduced the department. Thomas took command of a professional fire department so poverty stricken its members were not even afforded traditional uniforms. Callahan's appointment proves that opposing political views are still capable of success.

The day-to-day operation of the fire department is the responsibility of it's chief, the holder of that office being familiar with it's duties and requirements. The department as an agency, however, is supervised by the three member Board of Fire commissioners, none of whom have any background in the fire service. The Honorable Alan Feldman, serving as president of the Board, is given the title 'Commissioner' and brings to his office all the knowledge and skill that can be garnered by visits to the neighborhood fire houses when he was between the ages of eight and fifteen.

Within a few months of Feldman's appointment, a large maroon colored Mercury sedan began appearing on fire grounds across the city. Sporting red-and-white strobe lights on it's roof, a second set spasming behind it's grill and a dashboard mounted emergency light flashing through the windshield; the big car is festooned with enough radio antennae to rival an NSA telemetry transceiver. It's license plates leave no question about the vehicle's importance; large red letters on the white background spell: FIRE ONE. Not satisfied with his uniquely audacious transportation, Feldman announces his presence on the department radio with a personalized call sign—'*Fire-Com-One.*'

Enthused and energized and sporting to a large office on the top floor of the fire department headquarters in Lafayette Park, replete with detailed scale models of apparatus, it's wall lined with the portraits of former commissioners and plaques listing the names of heroes, living and dead, Alan Feldman disdains sitting at the massive desk to leaf through reports. Instead the immaculately dressed businessman prefers cruising the city streets comfortably seated in the rear of 'Fire-One' directing his personal driver—a real, live fire department EVD, to any number of private, previously determined locations to confer with a variety of department support personnel, communications workers, file technicians public affairs officers and the like, ostensibly receiving reports on critical issues. As if the life of a public affairs officer in the city fire department or field technician is crowded with critical issues.

The pre-selected locations are listed in a five page memoranda developed by Feldman, the secrecy guarded with a tenacity envied by a cold-war spy. It never occurs to him that the close-knit society within the department has distributed the secret memo to every watch desk in every firehouse moments after it came off the photocopier. As the maroon dreadnaught moves along city streets and its radio announces, '*Fire Com One approaching location nineteen . . .*' bored faces in a hundred firehouses glance wearily at the neatly typed sheet of paper tucked inside a plastic page protector and note that Feldman is cruising down Madison Street heading north. Only when 'Fire One' approaches within a block or two of a firehouse will the brass gong clang and a shouted 'Commissioner-in-bound!' warns of a potential 'surprise visit.'

Pepto-Bismol is a nutritional supplement to Thomas Callahan; he often considers ingesting the pink stuff prophylactically at the mention of conferring with the fire commissioner. The chief of the department—technically there is no article in the title—has toyed with the idea of creating, large slabs of anti-anxiety medication to be torn off and chewed, like beef jerky during his weekly meeting with Feldman. The discussions could be meaningful if both men share reasonably similar training and experience, but Callahan views Feldman as a kid sitting at the controls of a set of toy trains, without the directions. The fire department Callahan truly loves is nothing more than a play thing to the clueless real estate entrepreneur.

"I have an idea," Feldman informs Callahan. Monday luncheons in the commissioner's office are the setting for each weeks 'brainstorm.' The chief has politely picked through the better part of his lobster salad watching the commissioner wolf down an impressive chicken cacciatore, both meals delivered weekly by one of the catering businesses owned by Feldman. Delicately dabbing his chin with a linen napkin, Feldman gulps a glass of water. "Sprinkler trucks."

"Sprinkler trucks?"

"Yeah," Feldman bobs his head excitedly, "I guess there's a technical name for them," he shrugs unapologetically. "I saw a picture of one in a magazine." The man's eyes are bright with excitement. "I think the city could really use 'em; they look keen and could be beneficial."

Tom Callahan has heard many descriptions of apparatus in more than three decades of service; 'keen' has been a rare adjective. He remains quiet while Feldman opens a desk drawer and withdraws a glossy trade journal, noisily flipping through pages until he finds a dog-eared photo in the middle of the magazine.

"Here," Feldman turns the magazine to give the chief a better view. He stabs the center of the photo with a finger. "I call it a sprinkler truck."

Tom Callahan moves subtly in his chair, jaws tensing and relaxing. The cost of one piece of fire apparatus can vary between four hundred to seven hundred thousand dollars. He has spent the last two years scraping together every extra dollar he can find; haggled, begged and contacted every dealer, distributor, manufacturer and municipality in the western hemisphere to modernize the department's fleet. He is sitting across the desk—a desk covered with expensive catered food—from a man, technically his 'boss,' who wants Callahan to expend more money on a fire engine because it is 'keen.' "I see" the chief murmurs, wondering if Feldman can see the color draining from his face.

The vehicle in question is nothing more than a pumper with a telescoping boom affixed to a turntable atop it's rear. The tip of the boom projects over the cab of the engine and has a large nozzle attached. Water reaches the nozzle through supply piping and the boom can be raised and extended over a fire to pour hundreds of gallons of water onto the blaze without exposing personnel to heat and smoke.

"What do you think?" Alan looks anxiously at the chief.

"The trade name is 'Squrt' or 'Telesqurt,'" Callahan remarks dryly. "They've been an industry norm for a number of years." The words 'sprinkler trucks' keeps repeating in his mind.

"Can we get some?"

"I can certainly look into it," Callahan inhales deeply and hopes he sounds sincere. He isn't certain who is more pathetic—a fire commissioner who doesn't know a nozzle if he tripped over one, or a chief for committing to even considering this empty suit's suggestion.

Thirty minutes later Tom Callahan sits in the passenger seat of his own vehicle—a glossy, black Grand Cherokee, department logo on the front doors and gold-leaf lettering along each front fender 'Chief of Fire Department.' He also has his own chauffer—a full fledged captain with twenty years experience—John Williams.

"So how'd it go this week?" Williams asks without looking at the chief. He will spend more time with Callahan than anyone else in the department; arriving at the chief's home in the upscale community in the county every morning at seven, driving the chief to headquarters and home again each evening at six. In between, during the course of the day, it is John Williams who will absorb Tom Callahan's thoughts and opinions as he drives the senior officer wherever the schedule dictates. And there are days when the two men arrive home an hour or two later than usual after sharing a drink at the tiny bar four blocks from Callahan's house.

The chief draws another deep breath, staring straight ahead. "John," he speaks softly, but with resigned commitment to the inevitable, "One of these days you're gonna drive me home and I'm gonna tell you not to pick me up in the morning . . . ever again.".

'Wish Lists' centered on 'keen' equipment form the least of the department's problems with it's new commissioner at the helm. It is Alan Feldman who convinces Chip that modern business methods, driven by technology, are the ideal tool for quantifying management assets in the fire service.

"Information data . . . compiled, collated and codified will give you the precise numbers you need to see just how efficient the department is," Feldman lays out his concept of a massive computer database. "Every company, every day . . . the officer in charge enters the day's activities. Whatever it is they do—inspections, fires, fire prevention. It doesn't matter." Feldman taps the computer schematic. "It all goes to a central database and can be accessed anytime you want."

The Mayor sees the benefits immediately; the concept enhances his image of an aggressive, new breed mayor. "Those guys seem to have the time on their hands," he agrees, nodding

"We'll call it 'Metropolitan Strategies,'" Feldman explains. "'Metro-Stat' for short. I've used it business-wise and have seen the modules for larger scale planning. You don't have to worry about accepting junk. You get everything by the numbers."

Within a fortnight every firehouse, every company, in the city fire department received the official memorandum from City Hall Office of Management. All functions—yes A-L-L, functions undertaken by every active company in the department—training, inventory, inspections, smoke detector installation, staffing and, oh yeah, that firefighting thing—will be entered into the database known as 'Metro-Strat' at the end of each shift. In addition, keep your butt glued in front of that computer keyboard because the city wants to know just how *many* hours in each category is being spent. How much hose did you use on that fire? How long were you out of service? What was your weekly consumption of fuel?

Michael Danning, a fresh-faced, three piece suit stooge-in-training is designated as the MetroStrat liaison. The added tasks inherent to MetroStrat are not only deemed a waste by firemen, the new system serves as a warning that City Hall has no intent to become fire department friendly. MetroStrat is designed to track efficiency!

The collective groans rising from every city firehouse results from one more intrusion into the job by 'suits' alien to the 'Brotherhood.' Computers in firehouse offices do not translate into faster response times, better equipment, or technological advances in fire science; the first concern of the rank and file. But the mayor now holds the one tool that he will hang like a 'Sword of Damocles' over *his* department. He will possess raw data generated by the department itself, to force whatever concessions he may desire. It is known that to increase the department's workload and the department 's inability to match that increase underscores the need for further 'streamlining'. Mr. Feldman may not be the most qualified commissioner in this city's history, but his contribution will be its most political.

It is inevitable that Alan Feldman becomes the terminus for the firemen's frustration and anger. In the fire house on Fort Avenue, Jerry March holds court at the watch desk, leaning back in the chair; feet propped on the top of the desk. Around him, crowding the small cubicle, Burger, Killen, and Donald Holland wait with barely controlled impatience for their evening relief to arrive.

Holland, the assigned EVD for Truck 105 on this shift is a burly, stocky man with a thick mass of curly gravity-defying hair and wire framed glasses forever ending millimeters from the end of his nose. Donald is another of the FOG's who form the aggressive core around which this firehouse and this shift in particular is built. He's also a genuine 'buff'; his adolescence spent chasing fire engines and watching firefighters at work. At the tender age of twelve, Donald borrowed two dollars from his mother to catch the bus downtown in order to watch a three alarm fire. Although Holland views the world through dust speckled lenses, his focus on the department is crystal clear. Before entering the fire academy, Donald had memorized the location of every fire alarm box in the city and even after boxes and been removed from the street corners under advanced technology, Holland still recites the precise box number and assignment from memory, when a call is announced over the radio. Between alarms the EVD moves with slow, sauntering stride; that harsh triple *clang* of the gong and grating warble of the tones transforms him, like the opening starting gate for the thoroughbred, into a study of focused, boundless energy.

Jerry watches the numbers on the digital clock slowly blink a new minute. At this hour, late in the afternoon, shirt tails hang from pants, the shirts unbuttoned and each man has one eye on the small entrance door at the front of the firehouse waiting the sign his relief has arrived; the other eye watches the inexorable movement of the clock mounted into the desk. The voice of the communications technician echoes softly through the high-ceiling apparatus floor.

"Fire Com One to communications . . . request Fire Investigators meet me at location two."

"Location two?" March frowns and searches for the cheat-sheet of Feldman's not so secret location.

"Yeah," Holland pushes his glasses back from the edge of his nose for the hundredth time. "Dickey's Garage on twelfth Avenue."

"You're kidding me!" March stares at the EVD. "You got locations memorized?" March worries that Holland at times is like an idiot-savant.

"I kid you not," Donald pretends offense and taps the side of his head. "A veritable bear trap of numbers and locations," he reminds Jerry.

Killen stretches his tree trunk sized arms expansively. "Damned commissioner sounds like a jet pilot." he snorts in derision. "I'd half expect him to have a call sign like 'Foxtrot' or something dynamic."

"Foxtrot?." Burger murmurs.

"He's squirrelly," Jerry shakes his head, a final act of disgust in the waning hour of the last day shift.

"Donald?" Killen asks grinning and glancing at Holland.

"Hell no," Jerry waves at the secret location sheet. "I'm talking about the squirrel we got as a commissioner." The front door opens and heads turn expectantly, but relax when they recognize Albert Skalinsky, the senior on Truck 105, for the next shift. He will be working as an 'Acting Lieutenant.' The shift's actual lieutenant, Kyle Turner is recuperating from a broken leg; courtesy of a working fire three weeks ago in the Heights. Skalinsky is Paul Gulfee's relief and pauses briefly at the desk scribbling his name on the evening roster.

"Paul's up in the office," Killen informs the 'acting man.'

"Catch much?" Skalinsky asks, almost disinterested.

"Nada," Holland shakes his head. "A couple calls out on the road no action."

"We'll catch 'em tonight, then," Albert shrugs. He scans the clipboards that hang along one of the Plexiglas sheets enclosing the watch cubicle. There are four battered boards, each labeled with a different heading: Engine, Truck, Battalion, Battalion Division notices and memoranda, written communications needing to be read and signed get shoved on an appropriate board for dissemination. Seeing nothing new, Skalinsky checks the roster again to see who is working with him. He will take the names and assign fire ground responsibilities for each man . . . right step, left step, etc. Names and subsequent assignments will be scrawled on a Dry-Erase board informing each member of their role that night. When Albert makes his way back to the spiral staircase in the left corner of the apparatus floor, the conversation resumes.

"Feldman's a squirrel," Burger affirms. "Like we don't have enough problems in this department without him flyin' around the city."

Jerry March sits up in the chair so quickly the other men half expect an alarm to be announced. "Rocky!" Jerry announces, slapping his hand on the top of the desk.

"Huh?" Donald Holland pushes his glasses back again.

"Rocky," March declares, the epiphany crystallizing in his mind. "Y' know, like the cartoon . . . 'Rocky the Flyin' Squirrel!'"

Few titles and still fewer nicknames enter the lexicon with such suddenness and gain immediate acceptance as did the one given Commissioner Feldman. Within ninety-six hours of uttering those four words, Alan Feldman, business man, financier, Fire Department Commissioner, enters the living legends of the fire service across the city as 'Rocky.'

And thanks to Rocky, the mayor, awash in hard copy reports from the fire department, reports that keep the LaserJet printers in City Hall's MetroStrat offices humming, begins calling attention to the fact that most of the activity of fire companies spread over 'his' city comes from the west side and a small wedge on the east.

Nobody within shouting distance of 'Chip' has the nerve to tell him he doesn't need a multi-million dollar computer system to show how busy the companies in those areas have been. A dozen fifth graders can produce the same data by sitting on street curbs and counting the number of times those 'shiny' fire engines speed past.

Chief of Department Callahan slowly massages the bridge of his nose with two fingers. He has watched the evening news on television and read the newspapers for two weeks now. The mayor is campaigning again, not for political office, but certainly to produce bales of political 'hay'. Callahan understands he is in the proverbial hot seat but not because he has contrived reports or hidden facts. Fire fighting companies in poverty-stricken neighborhoods, high crime areas, and many low-income communities, are always busier than those assigned to neighborhoods with elevated socio-economic environments.

Callahan knows and understands realities that the mayor refuses to acknowledge. They are the simple realities, most are. Books are written, speeches delivered, entire lives are dedicated to explaining the reason behind the phenomena of busy, ghetto fire companies. Tim Bridges, young, college educated and maybe the most well-read fireman at the Fort Avenue fire house searched for an answer when he was initially assigned to Truck 105. After weeks of prodding other members for insight, Bridges received an answer, one distinctly outside the generally accepted rationale of the usual deep thinkers and social academicians.

After asking for the thousandth time why it seems fire companies like his . . . Truck 105 . . . and by extension, Engine 50, remain so busy with real fire, property-consuming, life-taking blazes while similar companies in say, Orangeville, consider themselves to have a busy year when they hit twelve hundred runs, it is Bill Burger who brings the younger man to the front of the firehouse where both men admire the crumbling, prehistoric panorama along Fort Avenue.

"You know why all that is out there, Bunky?" Burger's hand makes a sweeping arc at the dirty facade and scorched fronts of half dozen buildings.

Tim has no idea, of course, but Bill is about to give answer to the question bugging him. "I dunno," he shrugs.

Burger nods with a wise knowing smile. "I didn't think so," he winks. "At least you admit you're dumb." The big man slowly turns and points to the small toilet stall at the very rear of the firehouse, behind the apparatus floor. "They put that back there," Bill explains in a professional tone, "because the builders knew that you and me will always need it." The words cause Bridges a moment's pause; making the connection between scatology and the fire service.

"Okay."

"Well," Burger turns back to the pathetic sights of Fort Avenue. "These buildings and stuff got built 'cuz these people around here need something to *burn."* A contented smile crosses Bill's face. "It's all about people having needs and being able to meet 'em . . . to get 'em satisfied." Social insight, firefighter style. No fee.

"That's it huh?" Tim isn't really sure Burger is being funny.

"You reduce people to the lowest common denominator," Bill assures him. "Cause and effect, these people," he nods in the direction of a boy shuffling on the other side of the street, "see a building, find a match and gotta burn it."

Tim appreciates this unique application. The question is never raised by him again.

Tom Callahan's dilemma, however, involves more than primal needs. His promise not to close any more firehouses or disband any more companies is now on the line. Unlike 'Chip,' the chief must deal with more than just numbers; he has to evaluate the importance of his word.

"Chief?" the tone of the mayor's voice is almost comical. This little man in the spiffy suit was lining up in a school cafeteria with his lunchbox and thermos when Callahan was winning his first medals for valor in the fire department. The young mayor is leaning over the gleaming surface of his desk and looking at Callahan. "What are we going to do about these numbers? We're talking about expenditure of funds. We're talking funds that are real hard to come by."

Callahan must choose his words carefully. Crossing the mayor at this juncture, riding the crest of omnipotence, invites termination. There must be a means by which the mayor's own vanity can be made beneficial to Callahan's case. "Mr. Mayor," the chief maintains an even tone, "discrepancies between companies are common. There have been neighborhoods that require more service than others ever since cities have been built. Simply because a particular company isn't the busiest in the city doesn't lower the property values of the community. When a fire happens to occur in one of those communities and it is without fire protection, a rapid response, even a few minutes' headway becomes catastrophic." *Not to mention political suicide if you have personally closed firehouses in that neighbor, you arrogant twit,* Callahan thinks.

"At the same time," 'Chip' lifts a handful of MetroStrat reports, "we have quantitative evidence that time and manpower are underutilized. These slower firehouses as you call them, still need electricity, utilities and the like. We still pay salaries and benefits for personnel not fighting fires." It's always a numbers game for City Hall. Government bureaucracy for that matter, is reactionary; for thought is not part of the job description. It's the reason traffic signals are never erected until a bus filled with kids is broadsided in the middle of an intersection already known for potential danger,

Callahan is aware he is gripping the arm of his chair so tightly his knuckles are white. "Most of those firehouses have been neighborhood fixtures for half a century or more," his tone remains calm, slightly short of miraculous given the volcanic activity in his gut. "Whole neighborhoods have grown up around those firehouses believing they are fixtures in the community."

"Then we have a serious problem," the mayors forehead wrinkles in an ominous frown. "Neighborhood tradition or not," he shrugs, "we either cut the companies across the board or we start closing those firehouses." The handful of reports rattle again. "We can show they are statically out of the loop and totally under-utilized."

In an isolated portion of Tom Callahan's mind, he begins seeing the images of himself placing uniforms in garment bags, sealing them for long-term storage. He is as aware of the numbers contained in the MetroStrat reports as the mayor, but, unlike the mayor, the chief understands the numbers, their context and practical significance. The uneven spread of fires and emergencies in every town and city is a shared reality in the fire service and Thomas Callahan's management acumen, combined with some small talent for creative thinking, has helped prepare him for this moment. He has known before how the mayor will view the numbers and that foreknowledge provides for a planning scheme.

A small poster hangs in a corner of Callahan's office, nondescript and rarely noticed by the average visitor. It reads: 'First class people hire first class people, second class people hire *third* class people'. It is a basis for success in life and business. His belief in that policy motivated

Callahan to appoint Geoffrey Kennedy as his strategic planning director. It is Kennedy's sole priority to think 'outside the box' and design a particular strategy to counter every attempt by City Hall to affect a negative impact on the fire department. On his first day in the office Thomas Callahan drew up the absolute minimum levels of strength and staffing for the department, underscoring each category in red ink. "Nothing less," he had instructed Kennedy, handing him the information. "Your sole function will be to come up with manageable plans, fact not theory, to keep the fire department at or above these levels. Figure every angle, every tactic, every concept, and detail the strategy and how to make it work, period."

Callahan shifts in his chair, steepling his fingers as he leans slightly toward the mayor. "I can offer an immediate suggestion," he tells the mayor.

"I'm listening," Chip's face is expressionless, but he enjoys this ability to display power.`

"Rotational closing," the chief quietly announces. It is the last thing 'Chip' expected to hear, if he ever contemplated such a concept in his wildest machinations.

"Rotational closings?" Chip straightens and takes a step back.

Callahan nods. "We examine the numbers carefully. We target shifts that show consistent and repeated down time and, for the duration of these shifts we close the firehouse, not the company. And the closing is strictly temporary," he is quick to add. "We keep the apparatus and other equipment in quarters, but for the specified amount of time both firehouse and company would be considered out-of-service and unavailable for any response. Any gaps created can be filled by the next available companies."

"We can do this? Make it happen?"

"Definitely," Callahan feels the mayor is warming slightly. "All alarms are assigned and dispatched by computer," he gives the most cursory of explanations on how fire alarms are handled. "By tweaking the software slightly we can automatically by-pass any fire house we rotated closed."

"Explain."

The chief speaks rapidly, there's little sense for philosophic ramifications of The Decalogue to a mental retardate. Any time an area of the city is left without it's first alarm protection due to multiple alarms or other emergencies, the department's Prometheus Computer system automatically identifies and assigns the next-closest companies, fill ins, to cover. The system allows Communications immediate assignments to provide coverage up to ten alarms before the dispatchers begin 'creative' adjustments.

Myron closes his eyes for a moment, considering the potential. "So you're saying these rotational closures will positively affect the department's budget?"

"Yeah," that image of storing away his uniforms begins to dissolve in Callahan's mind. "What is saved on utilities, manpower and the like will offset actual working costs in the long term."

The mayor really does not care about long term considerations; the soul of local politics imagery. The slight of hand getting voters to believe one thing is occurring while the actual accomplishment takes place else ware. "We do not publicize the fact that a completely useless firehouse is sitting in the neighborhood. There needs to be something to make these closures seem equitable to the ethnic communities."

You mean the blacks, Hispanics, and Asians can't see themselves as victims unless they have a real powerful proponent in the City Council. I wonder if Caucasians are included in his ethnic category. "Yes sir," Callahan answers.

"Formulate a potential schedule, Tom," he nods at the chief.

He wants me to come up with a schedule so he can always deny any part in all of this, if something happens, the little SOB!! "We can come up with something equitable," the chief nods. "It'll accommodate any projected temporary closing." Callahan emphasizes the word 'temporary.'

"That'll work." the mayor nods in agreement.

"Will the city at least notify communities that a particular fire house is only temporarily out of service?"

"No." the answer was swift and firm.

"Huh?"

"That would be suicidal," the mayor explains, his tone condescending of Callahan's naiveté. He laughs ruefully. "Can you imagine the commotion in the streets? I'd have every neighborhood rioting." He flashes the chief an incredulous glance and thrusts his hands deep into his pockets.

Probably searching for his head, Callahan thinks. "I would have thought just the opposite, for general safety." Frightened people beating on the door of a closed fire house, apparatus in full view in a darkened, locked building creates another image for which he'd rather not be held accountable.

"No. no. no." Myron removes his hands. The smaller, slender man sits on an edge of the desk and gestures. "If the people know a fire house is closed . . . say for a day . . . don't you see what an invitation that is to start fires or create some other hazardous emergency ?" He shakes his head. "No . . . we'll keep things under wraps."

The plan and the agreement on its implementation presents a tactical victory for Callahan. Further disbanding of companies and the permanent closure of firehouses has been averted for now. There's going to be howls of anger and accusations of disloyalty from the firefighters and their unions; the chief can accept that as a fact of life. He'll be candid in describing the alternatives and, for some, he will have gained a measure of respect. For many of the department hardliners Callahan will be viewed as another chief who caved in to 'Chip' Even the union representatives will pitch the proverbial bitch in high drama, whether or not they agree it is the very best the chief can wring from 'Chippy." The job of the union presidents is guarding the best interests of the firemen and officers, personal opinion aside. However, Thomas Callahan can honestly affirm he has prevented further disaster as he promised, and he makes a mental note to get a gift certificate from the Steak House for Jeff Kennedy.

Myron has gained a strategic victory. Any fallout from this plan can be directly laid at the doorstep of the fire department; it was Callahan suggestion, right? If some hovel burns to the ground because the nearest fire station is temporarily closed, Myron just shrugs and points out the department came up with the idea. But if there can be an actual positive showing that converts to dollars, he can make the announcement that MetroStrat works and be the recipient of a grateful city's best gift . . . re-election.

Another category buried within the constant flow of paperwork to Michael Danning, who gleefully challenges the land speed record relaying data to the mayor, is far more troubling to the mayor than budget implications, racial disparity. Despite obsequious lip-service to the ideals of personal achievement, he is keenly aware that much of his ability to remain in office rests on the shoulders of the city's black community. In a city with more than a two thirds black majority it becomes critical that the black voting bloc senses he is a 'sensitive' man. In contrast to the mayor's casual arrogance and haughty condescension over budget costs in the fire department, Myron becomes absolutely militant at the mere whiff of racial tension.

"Have you checked out the new Fire Academy class?" he addresses the issue with Callahan without polite preliminaries and superficial cordialities. It is the second time within three days the chief has been summarily ordered to meet with the city's highest elected official.

"I'm aware a new class just started a few days ago." Callahan makes the offhand remark without considering the implications. He has barely had time to take his assumed position sitting in a chair when meeting in the mayor's office.

"So you haven't seen the new hires personally," he stands erect behind his desk, hands on hips.

"Not personally," the chief notes the icy edge to Myron's voice.

"Maybe you better." the statement is testy.

"Am I missing something?" Callahan frowns.

The question allows Myron to punch at a pile of papers with a forefinger. "You're missing a lot of color. The entire class is white," he identifies the problem like he has discovered a diseased body part in an otherwise healthy body. "Sixty recruits and not one person of color in the entire class."

Thomas Callahan steels himself. Nothing draws Myron's finger to the nuclear trigger faster and with knee-jerk surety as racial issues. "The recruits are hired through the city's Human Resources Department," he explains. "The fire department simply gets whoever makes the list."

Accepting applications and determining qualifications is the task of the Civil Service Commission; a function blind to color and focused solely on the neutral position of numeric scores on the examination for the firefighter and subsequent background checks and criminal records. It is a tried and true tradition that has channeled decades of worthy applicants to the Fire Academy and prevented a decidedly criminal element from joining the ranks. When the City interferes in that process for politically motivated reasons, the system collapses.

That same collapse occurs at each point along the line of promotion; tradition-be-damned.

'The best man gets the job . . .' a recognized dictum of little practical worth in the fire department. The question is not whether a black man is as good a firefighter as a white man; as if skin color translates into ability. At the core of the issue is whether an applicant to the fire department becomes a firefighter and can advance through the ranks as a result of skin color.

Every three years the city gives its civil service test to applicants interested in employment in any of its myriad of agencies. Each testing period finds over a thousand hopeful individuals filing into the cavernous Civic Arena to take the two-hour written examination for 'firefighter.' Under the auspices of it's Human Resources Agency the test is designed to be specifically gender and racial neutral. Examinees completing the written portion of the recruitment process are subsequently placed on a list according to their score, highest to lowest. Background checks are generated on each name on the list. Those names with criminal records, a history of drug use, questionable motor vehicle driving or who reside beyond the city limits are immediately disqualified. It is a winnowing process that usually reduces the number of potential hires by fifty to seventy percent. This second, smaller list is delivered, through channels, to the medical department where the remaining applicants undergo an hour of physical and medical examination eliminating a further ten percent. At that time, personal interviews and a physical competency test are given by the fire department and the final scores dictate the actual 'hire' list. Usually the list remains in effect for three years whereupon the entire process begins again. Ostensibly the most cherished employment opportunities lie within the fire department and it's brother in blue, the police. Of the two, applicants to the fire department outnumber police hopefuls two-to-one.

Throughout the entire process the potential city employees are known only by social security number. Race and gender identities are zealously guarded by Human Resources until the final phases of hiring take place. No city agency has any real input on the position of any applicant on it's particular list. The cautious approach to employment is due to lawsuits entered by both white and black applicants claiming racial discrimination. In the case of white applicants, the complaints centered on the issue of quotas and the city's practice of identifying minorities and awarding 'cultural points' to their final score in order to elevate their position on the hiring list over Caucasians whose scores without cultural 'augmentation' consistently placed them at the top positions to be hired.

The black applicants on the other hand, complained the entire testing process was skewed towards an 'ethnocentric bias' placing the whites in a far more favorable position due to general education, background, and a past history of prejudice in hiring for the city government. Court decisions flew back and forth until, under the direct supervision of the Federal Government Office of Economic Employment Opportunity, a test was designed, studied, changed and otherwise denuded of any possible ability to determine race or gender. In short, years of legal battles, consultants' input and public scrutiny resulted in clean, neutral examination taking the selection process out of the fire department's hands. The city fire department simply accepted whoever Human Resources declared qualified.

"Sixty recruits," Myron repeats, again using a manicured finger to punch the top sheet of a stack of papers. "Sixty. And every damned one of them is ivory white."

It is an issue that cannot totally be blamed on Danning. Unknown to the mayor, a coterie of black, former firefighters and officers had been quietly informed by the three black instructors at the academy that the incoming class was missing some color. Remembering the horrific days and racially tense era when blacks were forced to sleep in segregated beds in the firehouses and never allowed positions of leadership, the cadre of black ex-members flexed political muscle and contacts within the community to protest the recruit class.

"I have no response," Tom Callahan can only stare back at the mayor. "You know, yourself, the department has absolutely no control or input on who walks through those academy doors. It's an issue with Human Resources, not the fire service."

But Myron regards the issue as a personal affront. His relations with the former chief Malachy, had been cordial; mainly to Malachy's willingness to let the mayor dictate how the department should be run. Myron, however, fostered that he and Malachy were of one accord, a crafted image that helped the mayor during re-election. He will not allow that inroad to the black community to be altered regardless who may be responsible. "It doesn't matter now whose fault this is," he replies tersely. "The issue has to be addressed and addressed quickly and thoroughly. One thing I don't want and won't tolerate is the faintest notion that we are running a racist fire department and look like we're taking a huge leap backwards about fifty years."

Thomas Callahan is dumbfounded. Of all the issues Myron can raise about the fire department, the hiring practice is one over which the chief has no control whatsoever. In fact, the issue is one within Myron's own area of responsibility, the nine supervisors of the Human Resources Agency were mayoral appointments, six of them black.

Racial diversity doesn't begin at City Hall. Ninety-two percent of the mayor's senior staff is white, the sea of black faces filling the offices of the huge City Hall building belong to clerks and mid-level supervisors. Although much of Myron's pre-election rhetoric involved promises that his administration will be representative of the city's demographic, the most casual observer at any of the mayor's advisory meetings is surprised at the white's sitting at attention around the table. There are few malcontents, however, because of his lavish expenditures; like the education department and policy that most down trodden, hapless, societal dregs have the same access to city services as high society. It elevates 'Chip' to the status of political icon. This inordinate leeway provides him the latitude and opportunity to blithely ignore the stark, simple reality that six *black* Human Resources advisors agreed with three whites to accept the all-white-all sixty-applicants to the fire academy.

Manny Rojo and Larry Koznell see through the vapor-thin veneer Myron uses. "The department ain't got nothing to do with new hires," Rojo thunders, eyes narrowed in anger.

"Yep," Callahan agrees, it is a fact. "But Myron is accusing the department of some conspiracy to throw things back under Jim Crow law."

"Jim who?" Koznell, confused, frowns at Rojo.

'HEYDAY OF THE KKK," Rojo, the president of the Officer's Local quickly explains. Koznell shrugs, satisfied with the answer. American history starts with World War Two for Larry; the war his father fought in France. Rojo is focused back on the chief. "We take what Civil Service sends us."

"Uh huh," Callahan responds dully. Sitting behind his desk, Callahan drums his fingers on it's surface. For a moment he glances around the room, portraits of every former chief hangs on the walls. Behind the desk is an enlarged photo of the Monumental fire, taken from a helicopter at the height of the conflagration. The photo is so dramatic it can pass as a movie poster.

"So what is the little dictator gonna do?" Larry Koznell cuts to the point.

Tom Callahan looks directly at Larry, silent. Then "You're gonna be impressed," he finally answers.

'Chip' appreciates the power of his office. Early in his legal career the soon-to-be mayor had been given a paperback resulting in a change in the diminutive man's entire business philosophy. Entitled 'Machiavelli and Management' the book's author underscores parallels between Machiavelli's The Prince and current management principles. One major theme that stays with the mayor is the idea that whoever may be in charge of an organization must have the power to perform 'public executions,' to hurl lightening bolts, establishing who is in charge. The display of power must be sufficient to convince everyone else under his authority that the 'boss' can continue to hurl lightning bolts; thereby maintaining the intimidation factor. The mayor understands he must choose these moments of power carefully and the fire academy situation provides that moment.

"I'm personally stepping in to act on this atrocity," he informs Callahan.

To the chief's mind, terms like 'atrocity' are reserved for heinous crimes, mass murders, animal-like behavior. The appointment of sixty white recruits to the fire academy by a Human Resource Agency, hardly qualifies. "Stepping in?" Callahan scowls. "In what way?"

The mayor takes a deep breath, expanding his chest and assuming the pose of a stern headmaster about to lecture a recalcitrant pupil. "I intend," the mayor's voice lowers several octaves, "to freeze the hiring list after this recent class enters the academy. There'll be no further hiring or appointments to the academy until I . . . with my staff . . . have examined the list of applicants and determined which members of that list would best mirror the racial face of the city." He lifts a single sheet of paper from his desk; the imprint of the mayor's office on its letterhead.

"I'm issuing an executive order within the hour that places the freeze in place. I am directing Human Resources to provide me with the department's recruit list as well as all the background data on each name on the list." He smiles thinly. "The next class of recruits will come from a listing generated by *my* office." He recognizes the exasperation etched on Callahan's face.

"Tom," the mayor says evenly, "I'm going to bring the department into the new era, the new *modern* era. And I'll do it if I have to drag it screaming and kicking." He pauses, making sure the bigger man across the desk has absorbed his meaning. "Tradition has its purposes, some good, most outdated. But I can promise you this city will have a modern fire department that includes *more* than just new fire engines."

Rarely does tradition run afoul of the laws of the land. Politicians seeking votes in a city comprised of an ethnic majority interpret laws through the lens of personal ambition, an interpretation that throws daggers at the heart of tradition. Political harvesting of voting in the city doesn't end with mere applicants to the fire department. The system of promotion bears the same taint. Factor into that political influence, the natural inclination to illegally influence the promotional system and the entire process becomes suspect.

It had been one of the City Council Presidents and a black activist, who demanded the fire department elevate a specific percentage of it's black firefighters beyond the rank of Firefighter 1st Grade. The department, more than willing to acquiesce to the Council President's demands, made the request that said promotions be based on the result of the traditional promotional examinations.

Tests for the title of 'Pump Operator' were scheduled to be given within three months and the department, with the blessing of City Hall and the Civil Service Commission, began arranging tutoring classes throughout the city; held in churches, in schools after hours and in libraries. Television and radio advertisements highlighted the department's 'need' for black pump operators and high schools in predominately black neighborhoods were turned into evening academies on water flow and hydraulics.

Concurrent with these accepted avenues of success was an enterprise designed by a trio of firefighters out of the 3rd Battalion to ensure high scores on the examination while profiting financially from the endeavor.

In an operation that can only be called 'black box,' the enterprising firefighters, two black and one white, gained entrance to the department's personnel office and obtained copies of the anticipated examination from a locked file cabinet. The heist was worthy of Hollywood. Entering the Lafayette Park building through the roof, ski masks, surgical gloves and pencil flashlights held between teeth, the locks were picked, files rifled and examination papers copied with originals replaced. Although the theft went unnoticed, underground circulars made the rounds of every firehouse in the city indicating copies and answers for the test could be obtained for the relatively small fee of one hundred dollars.

The evening classes in the high schools experienced a sharp decline in attendance. A sense of unexplained confidence began manifesting itself in men who just weeks before, had been anxious and studying hard for the upcoming test.

Rather than selling test copies outright, the three geniuses of the 3rd came up with the brilliant scheme of placing the test answers on plastic wristbands; the same type used in hospitals for identifying patients. An underground industry sprang up transferring the answers to two hundred questions on transparent bands with the subsequent in-service how these bands were to be used.

Three hundred sixteen men gathered to take the exam, held in the city's huge Civic Auditorium. Two hundred twelve wore matching wristbands with the test's answers printed on them. The originators of the grandiose scheme pocketed a little over seven thousand dollars for their efforts and took their seats with the examinees. In the relative quiet of the large room, the officers who proctored the test paid no attention to more than two hundred participants constantly checking their pulse or staring at their wrists. The test took ninety minutes to complete.

Great anticipation accompanied the wait for test results to be posted. Thirty days after the examination had been given the scores were posted; one hundred sixty-two men failed the exam, miserably. Of the men who posted passing scores and were high enough on the list to be promoted, none of those who'd used bracelets were among them. In the resultant uproar following the posting, the logical consequence of shelling out one hundred dollars for a guaranteed passing score and then failing, it was discovered the three rocket scientists who'd engineered the 'wristband scandal' had stolen the wrong test and had furthermore, incorrectly listed the right answers in correct order even if they'd stolen the *correct* examination.

Faced with the embarrassment of a cheating scandal involving an almost exclusive ethnic minority, the city exacerbated the crisis and its trustworthiness by canceling any promotions from the list that scored the highest. In addition, the city demanded, regardless of further legitimate tests, at least forty percent of any promotions were to be men of color.

"If the city and mayor would just stay outta the fire department's business," Paul Gulfee repeatedly says, "there'd be no problem. The minute some suit gets involved in something they know nothing about, there's gonna be resentment and everybody gets blamed for everything."

"Is this for real?" both union presidents chorus. Both men have scanned the written order from City Hall.

"Not only is it for real," Callahan assured them, he rests his chin in the palm of one hand, elbow on the desk, "but it is an *Executive Order* from the City Hall notifying the civil service folks that the current waiting list for the academy is now null and void." The chief lifts a solitary sheet of paper in front of his face and holds it stationary.

"He can't do that," Larry Koznell's face is crimson.

"Not only can he do it," the chief arches his eyebrows and allows the paper to drop to his desk, "he already did." Callahan is as mad as the two union leaders facing him. He has already received verbal reports from instructors at the academy. This was probably the best and brightest they've worked with in several years.

"The civil service is all based on merit," Manny Rojo continues to argue.

"The best man gets the job," Koznell adds, sitting on the edge of his chair. Larry has fought the battles before. He has warred with the civil service commission since the geniuses created the concept of 'culture points' in a moment of intellectual dysfunction. A half decade before

Larry generated the lawsuit against the city that banned a racial practice, one that found the proctors for the department's written examination instructing the applicants to indicate on the top of the page their 'race'. About five seconds later and with a straight face the same proctors assured one and all that identifying their ethnic background would have no influence on test scores. A vast majority of those taking the test got a whiff of something very rotten in the Civic Arena and a protest was lodged whose mounting strength caught the civil weenies without a bun.

Manny Rojo's face has gotten two shades darker with anger. "So now there is a couple hundred guys totally qualified to enter the fire service and are just outta luck?"

"That's what happens when politicians go looking for votes," Tom Callahan observes.

"I never . . . ever . . . figured I'd see this city sink this low," Manny remembers times during his adolescence when similar back stabbing and underhanded dealings would have been addressed with a baseball bat and chains. His school teachers, those severe omnipresent nuns, had assured him that violence was never the cure for betrayal, and in the adult other avenues proved more suitable. Sitting in the office, contemplating the news he's just received, Rojo fights the temporary urge to spend an hour in Wal-Mart's sporting goods section foundling aluminum bats.

"Incrementalism," Thomas Callahan comments, "a little push here, a nudge there; always keeping up the pressure, gradually increasing it a little at a time. Like putting the frog in the pan of water. If you drop a frog in boiling water he hops right out . . . but stick him in water and gradually increase the heat and it doesn't notice the change until you got boiled frog."

"I gotta remember these words," Koznell suddenly grins. "Jim Crow . . . incrementalism." He winks. If I keep coming here I'll have a whole new vocabulary.

"Somehow I doubt it," Rojo shakes his head.

"The problem isn't racial," Larry voices what the other two are thinking.

"Political" Callahan spit out the word like he's found something foul in his mouth.

"We're supposed to get the people with the top scores," Koznell states the obvious. The issue is already tired. In companies that remain busy there isn't time to worry about skin color; you either do the job or you don't. Regardless of circumstances everything revolves around 'the job.' Of the various labels and titles of derision and insult used throughout the department on a daily basis, none holds the disdain and complete disrespect as 'load'. To be associated with that one word description forever marks its bearer with a modern day 'mark of Cain'.

"He's a load." Forget it. Fellow members might sit and have a beer with you. They may speak to you if nobody else is in the room. But a discreet distance remains between a company 'load' and anyone else who may be working that shift. For the job, 'load' is more a slur than any epithet. The days of segregation are long past. By the time a member gets to the company level, it is peer pressure that shapes and molds the character.

Find yourself in a running company, one of the real hotshot companies and just do the job as a team member and any bias is shed at the fire house door. Black skin burns and chars as easily as any other skin color and the blood from a cut from falling glass or debris remains red. The insult to the profession has always been the intrusion of blatant political agendas.

"Well," Tom Callahan asserts, "the city gets federal and state dollars in subsidies to run this crap," he speaks bluntly with these men now, "so whatever the touchy-feely political fad might be at any given moment will also drive what happens in the fire department."

Manny Rojo and Larry Koznell nod in agreement. Not often will they find common ground with the department's hierarchy. Their mandate is to protect and push the best labor environment for the city's fire department union members, regardless of personal feelings. Many times both union leaders have agreed that one of the members of their local is an ass, but that ass is protected by the union. Wages, salaries, benefits, retirement, medical coverage, all important parts of the union leaders responsibilities. Even when department tradition is threatened, the union presidents swallow their pride and devote their energies to protect the unions. One with which neither man is truly comfortable, is women in the department.

"They're great as paramedics," Rojo is blunt in his assessment.

"And in communications," Koznell admits openly.

Yet despite the Fire Academy debacle, promotional exam scandal, the growing number of females suddenly wearing turnout gear and the big 'eye' of MetroStrat reporting every sneeze and belch, it is the rotational closures affecting the firemen most. In one profession where the race against time is the reality and not the lead-in to a late night movie, the extra miles and minutes it now takes to arrive at a fire brings the greatest frustration, the deepest anger. And it is felt on every shift at least once during any given trick.

The 15th Battalion is no different than any other of the fourteen in this city. Sam Killen pulls a five year old from the projects, dead from smoke inhalation. Four blocks away Truck 31 sits in the dark, unmanned. Terry Buck finds an eighty year old blind woman, burned in a row house fire. The first due truck is filling in for another truck company whose rig is out-of-service for 'Enhanced Training.' Mark Hagan can't get to a fifty-three year old man because the fire trapping him on the second floor is volcanic in strength and the engine company that would have covered Mark's entry into the dwelling sits in a locked fire house unmanned.

There is much candid debate whether any of the fatalities could have been prevented, outcomes altered, if the out-of-service companies had been available. But the bottom line in every instance is that chances for success would have been greater.

In the two weeks since Sam Killen's nationally televised rescue of the four children in the row house fire, both companies in the Fort Avenue firehouse remain busy. Donald Holland back from vacation isn't complaining about the fires he has missed or the whirlwind of fires he's experiencing since getting back to work.

Jerry March, Bill Burger and Tim Bridges, back after four days off, loiter at the watch desk. To make sure the younger man knows he has been missed, they make his life miserable.

Dan Kemp, the captain appears from the back of the firehouse, having descended the wrought iron spiral staircase in the far corner. He has been in his second floor office dealing with paper work and his sleeves are rolled back on his forearms.

"Hey Cap," the men greet Kemp. "What's up?"

"What's the paper?" Jerry notes the page in Kemp's hand.

"You aren't gonna believe it," Kemp promises them. "Even if I told you, you still wouldn't believe it. I gotta show you the proof." He dangles the single sheet of paper in the air.

"Proof of what?"

Kemp's large frame fills the entrance to the cubicle and just over his shoulder Ken Shaw stands with arms folded across his chest. "You remember Killen's fire?" the captain reminds them, seeing every one nod. "We got an invitation to meet with the governor at the statehouse."

"Everybody working that day," Jerry adds, glancing at Tim. "Not those who chose to stay at home."

"It was a day off," Bridges corrects the pump operator.

"Anyways," Dan Kemp continues, "the governor *did* extend an invitation . . . a written one."

"He did?" Bridges asks. The dramatic rescue, witnessed by several dozen television cameras, had caught enough attention of the national media. For three consecutive nights thirty second video clips broadcast the exhausted faces of Killen and Buck, the protective dramatics of Jerry and, in an inset on the television screen, the faces of the children who had been brought from the fire. Already impressed by the efforts of the firemen, the governor, prompted by the national exposure given the heroics, planned a statehouse press conference to make special awards to the men of Engine 50 and Truck 105. Two weeks had passed in total silence, no thought given the timing since the wheels of government move with agonizing slowness.

"Oh yeah," Kemp affirms. "A written invitation was sent; everyone was invited to the statehouse . . . last Tuesday."

Silence drops like a weighted curtain.

"Who told you that?" the question comes from Jerry. "Nobody here heard anything about it." He glances at the assembled men. Receiving shrugs and nods in response.

Dan Kemp rattles the single sheet of paper, holding between thumb and forefinger. "Seems the invitation went through channels," the captain informs them. "Starting with City Hall . . ." the inevitable screw-up begins to materialize. "As a courtesy, the governor sent the invitation to the mayor first . . . since we are city employees."

"You're kidding me," Jerry forcefully slams the palms of both hands on the top of the desk.

"It seems the mayor's office misplaced the invitation," the officer continues, extending the paper in his hand to give everyone a good look. "I got this notice in my mail. City Hall regrets losing the invitation."

"Lost it like hell!" Burger's chin juts out, eyes wide in anger. "That little man at City Hall is more worried . . ." his words are interrupted by the rapid, grating triple *clang, clang, clang* of the gong on the wall followed by the harsh warbling tone over the radio.

"*Building fire . . . Pickett Hotel . . . Nine hundred block Holiday Street . . .* the dispatcher's voice announces the alarm in a clipped Staccato cadence. In the scurrying melee that follows, men materialize throughout the firehouse. Gulfee, Buck and Nick Miller slide down the poles at the front of the apparatus floor, Holland and Greenstreet trot out from the lounge, while Hagan and Tom Loughlin descend brass poles at the rear of the building. Lights flash, diesel motors grumble to life and doors slam.

"The mayor is a disgrace," Jerry is shouting inside the cab of the engine. Siren and air horns combine with a constant stream of voice transmissions from the radio; creating a din within the confines of the front seat requiring shouts to communicate.

"Nothin' we can do about it," Kemp is snapping the clasps along the front of his heavy coat. "Maybe somebody'll let the governor know we never got the invitation. I'd hate for him to think we didn't show up out of disrespect." He glances at the computer terminal situated between himself and Jerry. "We got a full box," he yells across to the pump operator. "Must be the neighborhood."

From the firehouse, the route to the fire ground is relatively short. Traffic is heavy because of rush hour, but cars and buses eventually find room to veer aside, causing Jerry to slow, turn, stop momentarily and begin again. Off of Fort Avenue the engine turns left, a wide buttonhook left, and then a maddening series of weaves through business traffic competing to enter one of the ramps for the by-pass. Once past the crowded entrances the ride is a straight shot. The changing face of the surrounding buildings indicates the proximity of Midtown, the fringes of the business district.

The Pickett Hotel stands at the corner of Holiday Street, an aging, seedy, brown structure. At one time, in past decades the hotel enjoyed it's reputation as a clean, tidy, no-frills establishment with modest prices and easy access to the heart of the city. Now, however, the building has degenerated into a sagging, tired conglomeration of threadbare rooms where prospective clientele rendezvous. The only real occupants of the Pickett are bent broken men and women clutching their bottles of cheap wine in brown paper bags.

"Engine Five-Oh on location . . . smoke showing," Kemp's report is the first aired. As the engine hisses to a stop at the curb to the side of the building, light gray smoke rushes from the seams of a metal bulkhead door at street level. The kind of door built into the sidewalk to accept deliveries, the kind leading to storm basements in the Midwest. Truck 105 passes the engine and makes the left turn to halt directly in front of the hotel.

The bulkhead door is forced open and Nick Miller is engulfed by thickening smoke boiling up out of the opening. "Can you see inside?" Kemp is shouting to Miller. The captain strides toward the smoking hole, adjusting his air mask over his face. Concrete steps appear just inside the lip of the doorway leading down into the mass of swirling gray soup. Kemp pauses and steps back as Burger drags a hose line into the smoke, disappearing into the basement with Miller following.

Sirens and air horns signal the arrival of more apparatus. What the department calls a 'full tactical response' and the accepted assignment to the report that a hotel is involved. Within moments, at the height of rush hour, the streets in this little slice of midtown are filled with red and white vehicles, hoses being stretched as men move quickly to enter the first floor lobby and disperse to assist in potential rescues.

Bridges and Hagan enter the small lobby, masks dangling from their chests, the faintest layers of smoke hang suspended in lazy ribbons in the air. The carpeting, once a rich red color, is worn and threadbare and appears rust brown. In front of them is the check-in desk, and behind the desk a wide stairway leads to the upper floors.

Access up the stairway is impeded by the steady flow of heavily made-up women in too tight, too short clothing in a range of garish colors being led to safety by pimps. The two men navigate their way to the second floor where they find a single narrow hallway extending to their right. Cheap battered doors line both sides of the hall, each opening into a small, sparse bedroom, holding a single bed and night stand.

"Glamorous place," Tim mumbles. "Real five star accommodations here." He is pushing each door open along his side of the hall, glancing inside for any sign of humanity before proceeding to the next room. There is no evidence of burning material, no smoke or visible fire. The only sign that something is awry is the mass of fire department vehicles clogging the streets outside, sending loud radio transmission into the air.

The basement of the hotel is awash, literally. Water from three separate lines has accumulated several inches in depth over the concrete floor and is held in place to form small lakes by cement ledges along each wall that subdivides the larger basement into smaller rooms and the absence of any drains in the old floor. Smoke hangs in the air after the fire has been extinguished, a small, smoky fire that flared in one of the cluttered storage rooms in the depths of the building. More than a dozen firemen slosh about in the manmade lake of black, filthy, sooty water. Each movement of heavily booted feet sends small waves rolling across the flooring to break against the walls.

Tom Loughlin moves quickly through the basement, whipping the beam of his hand light over every surface, searching the low ceiling and having the men push aside old desks, chairs, and other old, discarded furniture. There is no lighting in the basement, at least none that seems to work. Any illumination comes from a dozen Garrity lights on the helmets of the firemen and their 'Big Ed' lights clipped to the outside of their coats.

"Any chance somebody's gonna get a couple portable lights down here?" Loughlin calls out the suggestion. "And bring in a couple smoke ejectors, too."

"You got it Chief," a voice calls out across the room.

"What the hell is down here?" Burger slogs across the cellar, water more than ankle-deep.

"Looks like all kinds of junk from the hotel," Nick Miller replies. "Junk they never got around to throwing out."

"That'd be most of their inventory," the observation comes from John Paul, a member of Truck 15, the famous '15-Hook', a company the men from Fort Avenue jokingly call . . . 'the *second best* company in the city.' There is laughter in the semi-darkness. "How many rooms are down here?" John is running gloved hands over the walls feeling for doorways.

"I got a real little place back here," Michael Greenstreet announces, "almost like a tiny closet."

"Well don't go in there, Fatso," John Paul shouts back. "We don't have time to pry your fat butt out of there when you get stuck."

"You can kiss mine," Greenie calls back as he edges his girth through the narrow doorway.

"Anything good in there? Something we can take home?"

"Damned if I know," Greenie complains. His hands move over the surface of an enormous, upright metal box. "I got something that feels like a refrigerator."

"What is a refrigerator doing down here?" It is Burger's voice.

"Lemme see, lemme see," Greenstreet plays his light over the surface of the monstrous object. It is painted black with no handles or knobs and Mike can find no hinges. His curiosity piqued, Greenstreet wedges himself along side the 'thing', remembering John Paul's admonition about getting stuck. There is a space of about ten inches between the wall and the back of the big box and Mike shines his light along the rear of what he is assuming is a container of some sort.

The beam of his light catches the surface of yellow paint over the black; information painted in a neat linear script. Greenstreet becomes more determined to discover what this big box is and what it is doing in the tiny room.

Pressing his round face into the ten-inch gap between wall and object, Mike reads each letter aloud. "D-A-N-G-E-R," three inches below, the words are smaller markings also in yellow paint like brushstrokes against the smooth black surface:

50,000 VOLTS

Greenstreet feels a chill run down his spine and he glances from the painted information on the back of the box to the ankle-deep water covering his boots. Sweat beads on his forehead, soaking the flash hood under his helmet.

Uh . . . you guys aren't going to believe what I just found," he calls in a high pitched voice.

"What, anything good?"

"How about a fifty thousand volt transformer," Greenie shouts back pulling his jowls from the wall. He takes a step back, finding the cement ledge of the small doorway and standing on it; both feet out of the water. He begins to laugh as the darkened basement behind him explodes in a watery flurry of excited firemen making long strides and high leaps to find a dry surface.

In the street, dusk falling, Jerry March shoves both hands into the pockets of his trousers and ambles around the front of the engine, sauntering as far as the corner of the street. In the distance, the great golden dome of City Hall gleams, caught in the last beam of sunlight. Around City Hall, lining the maze of streets forming the edges of Midtown, the big canyons formed by the high rise investment and banking buildings, the courthouses and trade centers and government agency offices show the fringes of 'downtown,' the heart of the city. Now that the sun is settling, those canyons are gradually being cloaked in shadow. Breezes caught there, gain velocity and create a chill enhanced by all the cement and concrete. Lights burning in most of the skyscrapers indicate people still at work in their offices, shuffling paper, making phone calls; some probably poring over MetroStrat reports.

The pump operator shrugs, hiking the woolen jacket up on his shoulders. His gaze shifts from the City Hall dome, spotlights now illuminating the golden surface with it's fifty foot spire, the crumbling, gritty façade of the Pickett Hotel where equipment is being placed back on the fire department vehicles, companies preparing to leave the scene.

"Whorehouses," Jerry mumbles aloud. "Two whorehouses with in sight of each other . . .

At least he tells himself, turning back to the engine, the ones working at the Pickett admit what they are doing is for money. City Hall, he reflects, does it for free,

CHAPTER 6

ENGINE COMPANY 10

Engine 50 is forty months old, not just the company; the apparatus, the rig, its engine. Don't call it a fire truck! Call it a fire truck and anyone within sniffing distance of the fire service will know you are trying to impress someone. A fire engine is an engine with hoses, pump, nozzles . . . you get the picture. A fire truck comes with ladders, big ones, little ones and the two terms, engine and truck relate to the two most important, but different types of vehicles used in the fire department.

The engine, the apparatus used by the company is one of two dozen identical models initially delivered to the city at the start of Thomas Callahan's campaign to modernize the fleet. Essentially, it is a chassis built around a powerful pump that, when maintained and monitored, can push over twelve hundred gallons of water per minute through its hoses for uninterrupted days on end. Of course, you add about a half mile of large hose for big fires and several hundred feet of smaller diameter hose for smaller fires; portable tools, lights and a dozen more specialties of the trade and paint it white-over-red and you are ready to roll.

In it's bay in the Fort Avenue firehouse, the engine sits parked on the gray-painted cement floor, the battery charging cable plugged in to the panel on its left, the wide yellow plymovent hose on its exhaust pipe to the right and umbilical attachments to the twenty-plus ton behemoth until an alarm is received. Everyday the five men scheduled to work each shift deposit their protective gear at, or near their seats in the big cab. Helmets and bulky coats are inside or slung over an open door, bunker pants and boots on the floor alongside.

Scratched and dented, accepted attrition from nearly fifteen thousand runs in it's relatively short life, the engine looks new at a distance; closer inspection reveals the beating it has taken on the city's streets. The men who ride it have developed a love/hate relationship borne from familiarity and adapting to it's quirks and strengths. At first delighted with the new apparatus, it is now referred to as the crap wagon, a reference that might bring protests from its Florida builder. But the wagon arrived in a first wave of deliveries that will eventually replace every engine throughout the department and secure Tom Callahan for the short term.

An engine company, however, is more than its apparatus; as a nation is not confined to its geographic boundaries and the church is not simply a building with a steeple. Although its 'rig' is it's most visible symbol, it is the thirty-odd firemen and the officers assigned to the company that comprise 'Engine 50.'

Jerry March creates the 'Fort Avenue Celebrity Look-Alike' contest in a moment of creative epiphany; energized by the uncanny resemblance between Dan Kemp and Brian Dennehy or, most likely, to get a few laughs at the expense of the men of his shift. Nevertheless, the names of each member of Blue Shift have been arranged on a sheet of plain white paper, photocopied and sent to each firehouse in the battalion. Members submitting winning matches are promised . . . "a McDonald's Happy Meal Toy to be awarded at some point in the winner's lifetime . . ."

Two entries in the contest proved such eerie matches, Jerry halted further submissions and posted the winning combinations. Tom Kelly, the youngest member of the company, his eternally fresh-scrubbed face, always smiling with carefully combed reddish-brown hair can be a twin for Howdy-Doody, without the puppet strings. The second look-alike became debatable since the matching character was not, technically a person. Barry Kramer, however, could not be denied the striking resemblance because of it's perfection. In fact, Kramer's match fit so well it subsequently became his nickname.

Kelly already responds to Tomcat, although the youngest and newest addition to the firehouse will be called a 'piece of garbage' until some less senior takes his place. Tom accepts his titles with his ever present smile and good-natured willingness to endure insults has helped him bond with veterans like Burger and March. Barry Kramer is a veteran fireman with more than a decade of experience behind him; although he is senior only to Kelly on the engine,

Barry isn't enthralled with his nickname, accepting it grudgingly and swearing he sees nothing about his appearance that would give him the name 'Fred.' But his somewhat short bulky body, mop of dark hair, and perpetual five o'clock shadow personifies the most famous citizen of Bedrock, Fred Flintstone.

Kramer possesses a certain *'je ne sais quoi'* that leaves lasting impressions. His forehead, heavy and protruding, gives him a decided Neanderthal look. In turnout gear, weighed down with breathing apparatus, his shoulders hunched forward, arms akimbo, 'Fred' Kramer projects the profile of the missing link; a potential poster child confirming all firefighters are not created equal. Where Tomcat Kelly does the job with a studied ease borne of natural athleticism, Barry 'Fred' Kramer struggles to attain mediocrity.

"Establish a water supply," Jerry March reminds every new face in the firehouse. At a fire it is the function of the engine company to locate the closest hydrant and connect to it-lead off-and provide sufficient water to attack the fire. March's dictum is simple. A function practiced so frequently at the Fire Academy, a two week recruit performs the task blind-folded. It is a responsibility usually assigned the junior member working on the engine during a given shift.

Upon arrival at a fire, the lead-off man exit's the cab and moves to the back step of the engine where a leather strap secures the hydrant connection. Taken from the engine, a three-inch diameter supply hose connected to its largest opening, the hydrant connection is fastened to the largest outlet on the hydrant. As the engine is driven closer, the hose plays out from the hose bed. Once in position, the pump operator breaks the connection with the hose played out from the engine, coupling it to the intake jutting from the pump panel. At that point the hydrant is opened and water flows to the engine's pump to be pressurized and regulated by the PO and sent on to the nozzle, a simple evolution and standard operating procedure in the city for over half a century. Barry Kramer takes that standard to the level of 'adventure.'

"I worry when Fred is the lead-off man," March will confide. "I mean, I really *worry!*" And, though Dan Kemp spends more time assuring Jerry about Kramer's ability than any other member of the company, the senior Pump Operator remains a skeptic.

"He might get the thing right most of the time," Jerry explains, "but somehow I just *know* that when things are tight he's gonna screw up, and I'm gonna be standing at that pump panel with nothing happening."

Just two weeks before this trick began, Kramer confirms the pump operator's fear. The fire is a classic crapper. Two second floor bedrooms are off and rolling by the time Engine 50 arrives, flames leap dramatically in and out of black clouds of smoke curling over the rooftops.

Kramer, assigned lead-off, makes it out of the cab safely, no stumbling or falling, and gets to the back step of the engine without directions. Barry intends to give himself enough slack in the hose and stands on the back step for a moment to slide a thick arm through a fold of the hose to make the carry to the hydrant easier.

Kramer's movement on the step causes his body to press the small button just under the hose bed sending a buzzing signal to the pump operator to proceed toward the fire. Jerry hears the signal and accelerates slowly, unaware that his lead-off man is precariously balanced on the back step with both arms flailing at empty air in an instinctual attempt to grab at the tightly packed supply hose in its bed. A hose that is rapidly emptying from its resting place.

Department policy requires every fireman to wear 'full protective gear' on the fire ground, especially the breathing apparatus strapped to their back; an added sixty pounds of bulky weight. With the advent of larger cabs on engines and trucks, the entire crew is transported to a fire in relative safety.

The interior seating arrangement includes brackets holding the air bottles and straps so firefighters are able to harness in route. Following the department's protocols, Barry Kramer has his sixty pound breathing pack on his back, totally subject to the laws of gravity.

Although the fire in the row house is dramatic, a sizeable collection of people in this grimy little section of the 'hood' find more entertainment in the awkward ballet performed by the squat, blocky-built fireman who, for a split second, hangs suspended in mid-air frantically clutching a hose that follows that peculiar law of physics demanding that . . . 'objects in motion tend to remain in motion.'

The suspension in air is, assuredly, temporary despite Barry-Fred's later assertions it lasted . . . "for at least thirty seconds." He lands in the middle of the street, a mixture of frustration, embarrassment and confusion; encased and confined by his turnout gear and breathing harness. Beside him in the street is the hydrant connection with a lengthening trail of hose leading from Kramer's midsection to the back of the departing engine. Further insult is heaped upon the prone fireman by a small knot of children forming a semi-circle, a respectful distance from Barry, giggling and laughing with open-mouthed excitement.

Barry-Fred's predicament intensifies when he realizes the weight of his breathing apparatus renders him almost immobile, a turtle turned on its back. Instead of rolling left or right, Kramer's momentary embarrassment further unravels his thought process reducing him to kicking his legs and straining to right himself using his outstretched arms as leverage. The potential for a community relations coup would be enormous had it not been for the inconvenience of the nearby dwelling being consumed by an increasing volume of flame and smoke.

Ken Shaw is left to place the scene in perspective. The red car slows to a stop a few feet from the struggling squirming Kramer. In the passenger seat Loughlin is grimly shaking his head. The chief's EVD slowly lowers the window and thrusts his head out long enough to ask, "Hey Fred, you need a lift to the hydrant?"

Barry curses in extreme unturtle-like fashion, though the adolescents surrounding use the same words in every conversation. The fireman lowers his chin to his chest, eyes following the long trail of hose down the street to its terminus in the vicinity of Engine 50. There, standing with legs straddling the far end of the hose, hands on hips in classic imitation of 'Rhodes Colossus,' Jerry March can only glare with his face contorted in anger, shaking his head in that manner revealing total surrender.

Barry is equally challenged when the lead-off process finds him at the opposite end of the hose. The pump operator of an engine company positions his vehicle on the fire ground and provides water to extinguish the fire, a simple job description. To provide the water, given the connection is made to the hydrant, the hose coming from the hydrant is attached to the appropriate intake on the pump panel. During that process a common practice is to supply the men on the pipe with water from the engines internal five-hundred gallon water tank. As water flows from the opened hydrant, the PO must change his water source from 'tank' to 'pump' closing the flow from the internal water tank and opening the discharge valve on the pump. Once the water is routed through the correct pathway, the PO adjusts its pressure accordingly, unless the 'Kramer Method' is utilized.

The restaurant fire on Flagg Street begins at the stove and climbs into the ventilation system. Jerry March is not working, his place taken by a confident Barry Kramer assigned as 'Acting Pump Operator.' Inside the smoky fire, Burger, Buck and Nick Miller are working with the hose used for internal attack. Charged with water from the engine's tank, the five hundred gallon should be sufficient for three or four minutes. Tomcat Kelly is the lead-off man and makes the connection easily, perfectly. Fred Flintstone Kramer proudly wears one of the red collar pins of 'Acting Pump Operator' even if temporarily until Jerry returns, and he stands in the street at the pump panel watching the lengths of hose filling and hardening as water rockets toward the engine. He feels secure knowing the three men inside the building are well supplied and takes time to tap a cigarette from the rumpled, twisted pack in his shirt pocket.

Taking a deep drag, the block-shaped fireman leans back against the pump panel and blows two perfect smoke rings into the air, gazing after the lazy, swirling blue-gray rings and suddenly becomes aware his shirt is getting wet, very wet.

In a job where timing is everything, Barry-Fred pushes himself away from the engine and turns at the precise moment a geyser of water erupts from atop the midsection of the pumper. Not an 'Old Faithful'-type geyser, but a dramatic and voluminous geyser nonetheless. Within minutes Barry's pacific bliss is shattered. Sheets of water cascade down the side of the engine creating a Niagara over the pump panel. This maelstrom of events escalates so rapidly it surpasses Kramer's ability to react intelligently. Dials, gauges, and levers on the panel suddenly transform into the console of a space shuttle, banks of data completely alien to Barry's comprehension. He yanks, twists and pushes, guessing at varying combinations of switches and throttles without having the slightest effect on the flood. In a last effort to bring this disaster under control, acting pump operator Barry Flintstone resorts to the time honored cure for whatever has gone wrong; he pounds on the side of the engine with his fists.

Water falls to the street creating a swift moving current back toward the hydrant, an ever-increasing, ever-widening torrent rushing down the gutters and overflowing the curb to inundate the sidewalk.

Tomcat, his face a mask of confusion, sees the watery cataclysm as he trots up the street towards the engine, arms extended in a perplexed gesture. He can make the lead-off connection in his sleep and, after opening the hydrant, hopes to get into the restaurant and get time on the pipe. Those hopes dissolve as quickly as he approaches Barry, the erstwhile 'Acting PO' whose eyes are wide in desperation, wet shirt clinging to his skin and rivulets of water running the length of his arms.

"Barry!" Kelly's initial confusion turns to outright rage and mortification, the closer he gets to the engine. Nobody comes to Barry-Fred's assistance. Mute observation of one of the inviolable rules of fire department tradition that no-one, *nobody, not your best friend, the officer of the company, not even the Chief of the Department,* touches another company's pump panel.

"You gotta' help me, Tom," Kramer's voice is a hoarse croak by the time Kelly arrives. Tom doesn't give instructions to the older men, peering through the sheet of cascading water at the engine's side to make sense from the gauges. The moment Tomcat diagnosis the problem, he begins making corrections.

"You didn't switch from tank to pump!" he yells, face splattered with water. "The tank filled with water from the hydrant faster'n you were puttin it out to the pipe, it overflowed!" Kelly makes adjustments as he speaks to Kramer, pulling one T-shaped lever while simultaneously pushing and twisting another.

Abruptly the flood ends. Scattered applause and cheers sound from other firemen pausing to witness the watery melodrama. The 'Kramer School of Pump Operating' has just been inaugurated, finding use for it presents a different challenge.

With the emphasis in any company being teamwork, there is a natural evolution, over time, from which various combinations of men, working together, seem to be more cohesive, a better 'team' within a team.

On Engine 50 the 'better' shift seems to be the Blue-Shift, not due to any inherent superiority at the job, everyone in the company knows the job, maybe because Kemp works Blue-Shift and shapes the group to his liking. Within the seven-member shift, an even more bonded group emerges, one that just fit's the scenarios on the fire ground best and whose inter-relationships are smoother.

The March-Kemp-Burger-Miller and Buck combination has a fluid, seamless character, the 'chemistry' so often alluded to about sports teams communicating without words, confidence borne from endless crises together. Drop Terry and add Tomcat Kelly and there is only the slightest change in efficiency but nowhere near the change when Barry is placed at any position within the group. Bill Burger is more than adequate as a fill-in officer for Dan, but that means someone else on the pipe and the inclusion of Barry or Tom, a well functioning combination but not at the same level of innate ability as the 'First Team' of March, Kemp, et. al.

Likewise certain combinations of firefighters within a shift seem to serve as a catalyst to fire gods, resulting in a frequency of runs and quality fires, alien to everyone else. White-Shift is on a rampage this year, averaging close to three working fires or additional alarm every trick. Red-Shift, on the other hand suffers through two and three tricks at a time languishing in the firehouse while every company around them seems to spend their lives on the street.

Blue-Shift gets their share of fire; the presence of Kemp, March and Burger evidently, a severe irritant to the Great Fire Starter in the sky. If however, one of those three is absent from the equation, the chances for a really good fire diminishes unless J.C. Somerville is working as the Acting-Battalion Chief, then all bets are off. There is no scientific reasoning behind the phenomena except that it exists to the degree one can simply check the roster and see who is working and be assured, within a ninety-nine percent chance of being correct, the shift will either be very busy or uneventful.

As far as he is able to shape the company, Dan Kemp is satisfied with the results, a satisfaction he will not verbalize to the men, but one manifesting itself in a more relaxed environment than what might be.

"Tell them I'm satisfied," Kemp will later explain, "and they will immediately assume they've reached the pinnacle and no further enhancement is possible. They'll figure they're as good as the job allows." The captain will smile, "I'll take my best crew, Billy and Nick and Terry, and go down in a volcano and they know it . . . but I won't tell them that. I'll just tend to forget some of the stuff I happen to see or hear, stuff that can easily cause them to lose a vacation day or something."

Kemp will bring up Bill Burger's name. "Bill's been around a long, long time and should've been a lieutenant years ago. When he or someone else skates by sometimes . . . he's smart enough to know it's because I let 'em and I let them because of how they do the job on the fire ground."

On Kramer, "Barry-Fred is the weak link, we all know it, including Barry. But in a company where performance is so high, even just an 'average' firefighter is gonna standout as the weak link. He's brave as a lion, he's just dense as a rock."

After working with Kramer for a number of years, Jerry March may have the best insight on the man. "Barry," the pump operator explains, "talks a good story and when somebody challenges him that he isn't as good as, say, some of the guys in this battalion or maybe over in the Twelfth . . . Barry takes it personal and figures the only way to prove it is to get in a really jumpin' company and do the job." And as March will confess to Dan Kemp and Burger, "When Fred leads-off I always have an anxiety attack until I see water comin' from the hydrant and know he made the connection right."

March's bombast, of course can be positive and negative also. "He's the best PO in the division," Burger is quick to defend his close friend. "He's self-confident and knows he does the job better than anybody else and he expects the guys around him to be the same."

Barry Kramer, however, sees March through a different lens. "The words, 'Jerry March' and 'humility' are never gonna appear together in the same sentence." A description to which Jerry quickly added-when he heard it . . . "and neither will Barry Kramer."

Despite individual lapses personified by Barry, the history and reputation of Engine 50 is storied and proud. The fire house was originally constructed solely for the engine company. The rest of it's space occupied by vehicles from a combination of other city agencies. When the disparate agencies subsequently vacated the granite structure, Engine 50 became the 'house company' and it's senior officer, the captain became the 'house captain', responsible for all daily functions and activities related to the building. It would be six months before Truck 105 began sharing quarters with the engine, but the 'seniority' of it's original occupant continues to elevate the captain of the engine as the ranking officer of the fire house. As a result of the company's location near Midtown in the addition to the immediate residential areas and surrounding small businesses, the variety of fires that ultimately greet the firefighters presents a continued challenge. One of the primary reasons men desire transfer to Fort Avenue. With the collapse of inner cities and subsequent 'White Flight', the neighborhoods began filling with subsidized housing, low income families and the accompanying crime and drug societies.

There is a waiting list of transfers to 'The Fort.' The half dozen factors involving manpower attrition, injuries, and changed staffing among them, translates into an average wait of four years for a vacancy to occur. Engine 50 is not the busiest company in the city, a distinction held by a handful of units in the west, but the numbers and quality of fires, in addition to the broad range of type, serves as its primary attraction.

Attached to the outside wall of the watch desk cubicle, the side facing the engine, are two large dry-erase boards, one labeled for each company, 50 and 105. The boards are hung on the lower half of the wall, the waist-high wood paneling supporting the upper Plexiglas. Prior to the beginning of the shift, the officer of each company lists the names of the men who are working and the member's duties at a fire. On Engine 50, fire ground responsibility dictates seating on the apparatus. The Pump Operator and officer always ride in the front seats. The 'pipe' as the job is designated, sits in the jump seat directly behind the officer, the 'lead-off' directly behind the PO. By tradition the senior man on the shift always has the pipe. The least senior member always leads-off. With luck Truck 105, however, assigned seating dictates fire ground function.

The EVD listed first on the board drives the truck, automatically relegating the second EVD as tiller. On the fire ground it is the truck's driver who secures the vehicle in it's place, sets the stabilizers and operates its aerial ladder, the 'stick.' He will ascend the ladder to ventilate the roof. At the same time, the tiller man assists in stabilizing the truck and 'throwing' ground ladders to the lower floors. Whoever is assigned 'right step' is first up the ground ladders, breaking windows for ventilation as he ascends. Being first into a structure doing search and rescue, the 'left step' assists his counterpart as the officer forces entry at ground level for the engine company. Tradition rules. Even the terms 'right/left step' is a throwback to the days when men rode the side running boards of the long aerial ladder trucks.

Terry Buck sits at the watch desk, the large exit doors in front of him are rolled up. The fetid smell of Fort Avenue carries into the quarters, the unmistakable stench of decay in progress. The boredom of sitting watch alone is oppressive, the inactivity broken only by the stream of radio communications echoing uninterrupted through the fire house. Bucky feels put-upon of course. A stack of run sheets is piled neatly in front of him and must be arranged under new categories dictated by some faceless creature occupying a nondescript office being paid twice the salary of a fireman for coming up with ideas to fill Terry's day.

The litany of communications serves as background noise, an ever present almost rhythmic flow of sound so familiar to Terry, his mind automatically gathers information and arranges it in a mental hierarchy of priorities.

"*Engine nine in service in the district for hydrant inspection . . .*"

"*Fire maintenance three en route to quarters of Truck Thirteen . . .*" probably an electrical problem on the truck . . .

"*Battalion One-One in the district for inspection . . .*"

"*Truck Seventeen in service en route to the shop . . .*" they have that thing in the shop again?

"*Fire Com One on the air . . . location two . . .*" Rocky is parking his car at Lafayette Park . . .

"*Medic Six . . . Engine Twenty-Four clearing King Avenue . . . units in service . . .*" a medical assist . . .

The scratch of leather on cement draws Terry's attention. The source is a small, emaciated man, red-rimmed eyes, gold-toothed grin on his face, wearing a belted raincoat. Seeing he has been noticed, the shuffling, nodding street person gently pats the breast of his raincoat. "Would you be interested in purchasing some quality meats fo' yo' private usage . . ." the sales pitch begins; an opening inquiry repeated a minimum of ten times weekly when the fire house doors remain open.

"What you got?' the fireman lapses into his accented street lingo.`

"I gots prahm beef, I gots all them steaks you can eat . . ." top quality, high grade meat courtesy of the local supermarket whose manager will be reporting the loss to the police in a few hours. Terry tries to keep a straight face.

"All that meat still in its original wrapping?" he asks, nodding at the bulk under the raincoat. The sun is shining of course. Most street business is conducted by men in raincoats, whether the product is food or tools; the ersatz vendor invariably wears a long raincoat.

Three rapid *clangs* and an abbreviated warbling tone momentarily freeze both men. When the radio echoes in the firehouse this time Buck listens for all of five seconds before shouting loudly, "Truck goes!" spinning the chair around to tear off the glossy run sheet ratcheted out by the teleprinter behind him. He stands in the cubicle and hands the glossy to Donald Holland as the EVD walks briskly on his way to the cab of Truck 105.

Terry and the street pirate wait until the truck has left the fire house before resuming their brief bartering. "How much you charging for the stuff you stole?" Buck asks, looking at the traveling salesman with a bemused expression.

Taken aback by the insinuation his goods have questionable origins, the gold toothed man casts a suspicious glance over both shoulders; glances as authentic as any Hollywood spymaster could muster. "Oh man," there is no hint of guilt in the man's voice, "I ain't tryin' to shine you muh man . . ." his hands move back and forth between them. "I'm axin' you 'bout this offer ma' respeck fo' da' job you do . . . see what I'm sayin?"

Buck knows very well what the man is saying, better still, he knows what is going on, as he enters the discussion as much for entertainment as for stocking his freezer. Two weeks ago it had been Terry and Paul Gulfee engaged in idle conversation with one of the 'street girls' LaJulia, about employment in the fire department. Their exchange occurred in front of the fire house.

LaJulia, whose prominent mammary glands pushes triple digits, inquired about becoming a paramedic. "I'm real good workin' wit' people," she confirmed to the two men, a claim hard to refute.

"You gotta pass a drug test," Paul is able to keep a straight face, although his attention tends to return to the upper part of her body.

"I ain't worried 'bout no drug test," the 'lady' is confident. "I'm kerful 'bout what goes in my body," Neither Paul nor Bucky dares glance at the other. LaJulia likes the department T-shirt worn by Terry, a dark blue with 'Fire Department' across the back in bright-red script. "I look good in 'em," she points out.

Familiarity with the mass of humanity packed into this neighborhood is a matter of continuing education for the men in "The Fort.' During the last night trick, Engine 50 had the call on Lehigh Street, a narrow, dirty little stretch of asphalt scented with wine and littered with empty wine bottles, syringes and refuse; escapees from the large black plastic trash bags that serve as dumpsters in the neighborhood near the Projects. The call is broadcast as . . . "strong odor of smoke in a vacant dwelling . . ." Communications dispatched the requisite 'two and one' with Engine 50 arriving on the location first. Dan Kemp informs the listening audience that *"Engine five-zero is on location and investigating . . ."* and as Jerry sits in the engine in the street, Kemp, Miller, Barry-Fred Kramer and Tomcat Kelly enter what seems a vacant two-story row house at the end of the block.

The men are forced to move slowly through the darkened building. A dozen different areas inside are significantly charred, evidence that fires have been set numerous times by transient occupants in an effort to warm themselves while they fill their bodies with mind-altering toxins. Milk cartons litter the floor, emptied of the original contents to serve 'other' purposes such as human excrement.

There is, indeed, a strong odor of smoke but no by-product of usual combustibles. Gauzy ribbons of gray hang in mid-air at the top of the second floor stairway, becoming thicker and heavier as the firemen near a large room once the master bedroom, in another life. Garrity lights on their helmets and the Big Ed's hanging from chest loops on the coats create sharp, defined beams cutting through the blackness, bobbing as each man moved. When Dan pushes open the door, they find it filled with clusters of human debris. Junkies entwined, propped against each other and all at different levels and depths of consciousness staring vacantly back at the firemen observing them. "Geeezzz," the soft murmur comes from Tomcat.

"Yeah," Kemp acknowledges, "the people we protect. Take a good look. The captain gestures toward the semi-conscious bodies, "One of these days you're gonna risk your ass tryin' to save these worthless dregs of humanity." Kelly gets a cynical grin from the captain. "Makes you damn proud to be a city firefighter, don't it? This is what the city pays you the lowest possible salary for . . ."

"So what do you do now?"

"Hell," Kemp shrugs. "There ain't no fire here." His voice lowers. "But keep your eye on 'em Tomcat. One of those blockheads might think we're gonna call the cops and end up cappin' all of us." The fireman glances around the roomful of human debris. "They think we're gonna tell the cops of this secret location," Kemp comments with a shake of his head.

"Maybe all of 'em'll OD," Tomcat suggests, a hopeful note in his voice. The darkened room alive with the beams of lights from the Garrity's whipping about sharply.

"We'll be back here sometime," Dan observes as the four tread heavily down the stairway. "One night these useless fools are gonna fire up their rock candy and end up lightin' off this whole place. Take it to the bank."

By the time they reach the street, their heads are swimming, a vague giddiness envelopes them, the consequences of breathing second hand smoke from crack pipes.

"Every body breath deep," Kemp orders, "maybe we should have had a medic unit respond so we can suck up some oxygen." He checks to make sure each of the men accompanying him is taking deep gulps of fresh air, not that the fetid air on Lehigh Street can technically be considered 'fresh.' The odor of sweat, urine and garbage that hang in the air are less toxic than the harsh cocaine residue hanging suspended in the house.

"Dopers?" Jerry asks from behind the steering wheel of the engine. The other two department vehicles, the second engine and a solitary truck assigned to the box, slowly depart the scene, the sharp rumble of diesel motors cutting through the night.

"About a dozen," Kemp replies, climbing into the seat next to Jerry.

"To hell with 'em," March shrugs. "You gonna call it in?" glancing at the captain's profile in the darkness.

"Nah," Dan shakes his head, "if one of the beat cops stops by the firehouse sometime soon maybe we'll let 'em know what's goin' on. But they aren't gonna do anything anyway." The priority of the police officers seems one of keeping the drug problem out of sight. Shoot all you want to, just not in front of a cop or when the mayor is touring the neighborhood. That seems to be the working thesis. But since 'Chippy' has a better chance of sauntering into a lion's den, buck naked with a sixteen ounce porterhouse hung around his neck than making a walking tour of this small slice of the city, the lolling half-conscious addicts spaced out of their drug-baked brains are quite safe from the intrusive arms of the law.

"So how are the wife and kids?" Jerry March's question startles Buck, who has resumed reading MOP's at the silent watch desk. With the truck's empty bay, their voices cause a haunted echo around the fire house walls.

"Same old story," Terry shakes his head, "she doesn't like the idea of me working a lot of nights . . . thinks I oughtta trade 'em off for more days." Buck closes the binder he has been reading and sinks deeper in the chair, "The kids figure daddy is gonna go ride fire engines again." He smiles at the idea of a child's simplistic view of the world.

"Nights are where the action is," Jerry remarks. "Best education in the world."

Most wives of firemen share a deep-seated uneasiness at their husband's absence at night and develop a personalized means of dealing with their angst. Jerry's wife, Trisha, swears she has never slept completely through a night when March is working. She keeps a department scanner operating all night with an extension speaker on the night stand by her pillow. Bonnie Burger has her sister spend nights with her when Bill works, the two not going to bed until three in the morning. In turn, their husbands are sensitive to the anxieties at home.

Jerry telephones Trisha after every run, day or night, since joining the fire department. Dan Kemp makes sure his wife knows he has returned safely to the firehouse by insisting she listen to the scanner in their bedroom so she can actually hear him on the department radio.

"Truck One-Oh-Five in service returning," Paul Gulfee's voice fills the large room.

"Paul's bringing back lunch," Jerry comments, digging in a shirt pocket for a cigarette, lighting it and inhaling deeply. Next to his head is a sign on the cubicle panel: NO SMOKING!!

"From Goldman's Deli three blocks away from the run they took," Jerry confirms. A firehouse version of 'Meals on Wheels,' it's been two years since Killen and Simms worked their way through a murky, smoky fire in a one room apartment to rescue Sadie Goldman, the owner of Goldman's Deli. He sends three humongous trays of deli sandwiches to the firehouse every two weeks in gratitude for saving his wife's life. On the appointed day, Truck 105 finds time to wend it's way into the cramped, Jewish community to pick up the free food prepared personally by Walter and Sadie Goldman.

"Gotta run some errands," the voice of Ken Shaw causes both men at the desk to turn in time to see Tom Loughlin and his aide making their way to the red car.

"Paul's coming back with lunch," Jerry dryly informs Shaw.

Tom Loughlin's face splits into a wide grin. "We'll be back in time . . . save me some."

I bet you will as tight as you are, Jerry keeps the thought to himself. "Hey Chief," the pump operator calls after Loughlin, "you gonna play golf next week with us?" Seeking a competent fourth, Killen and Burger have been pressing Jerry to include Loughlin.

"Damn it," Killen argues, "we pool our money and pay his greens fees, okay?"

"But why Loughlin?" March can think of three or four other men he'd rather play with, men who'd pay the fees with their own money.

"Because it's a good chance to get the chief to give us some inside info," Burger makes his point. "With these rotating closures and crap, nobody knows what's going on at Lafayette like Loughlin."

Jerry knows he will never see the thirty dollars he will pay for Loughlin's greens fees, he's more surprised the chief hasn't asked to borrow clubs. "I'm looking forward to the golf," Loughlin nods and smiles. Over the chief's right shoulder, March sees Howard pinching his nose together, the chief and soap are at war again.

"Tee time's at seven-thirty," March reminds the older man. There is a pause. "Any truth to the rumor floating around we got a torch working the area?" Tom Loughlin looks at Jerry like he'd been asked to reveal military secrets.

"There's been evidence," the battalion chief nods slightly. He glances at the faces around him debating how much information he should share. "I don't think the guy is a pro or anything," he allows. "All the fires being investigated seem amateurish." Loughlin gets a wan smile on his face. "Nothing like when we had 'Ronnie the Torch' running around, remember?" Loughlin suddenly relaxes into a fatherly attitude. For a moment there is the anticipation the chief will elaborate but the idea of coming back to the firehouse to huge trays of three-inch thick sandwiches is powerful motivation to complete the task at hand. Loughlin gets into the passenger seat of the red car without further revelation on the possible arsonist or nostalgic details on the days when Ron Kovalchek almost single handedly burned half of Midtown.

To the men who experienced Kovalchek's campaign, the seven months are known as 'The Days of The Blaze.' A multiple alarm fire occurring at least twice a week, monstrous fires that escalated by factors of two and three. Jumping from a one alarm to three and then to six in a matter of minutes. Ron Kovalchek was never apprehended for the massive conflagrations although his M.O . . . Modus Operandi . . . marked every fire so well he could have erected a billboard claiming credit.

The midtown buildings being torched were always vacant and slated for eventual razing; their fiery end coming so propitiously with great devastation. As always, rumors were rampant, the arsonist was a pro, the arsonist was an amateur. The arsonist was on the city payroll for demolishing old buildings to make room for new ones, the arsonist had a grudge against the city and was exacting revenge, and on and on the rumors went. Whatever the truth had been, a construction boom was the end result and whoever the arsonist was, he was good . . . very good.

Nobody could say, authoritatively, that the first fires were related, but, when arson was confirmed as the cause, a reward was offered for the arrest of the pyro. It was during the second month, within hours after a nine-alarm fire had utterly destroyed the old Hammerman Warehouse near the docks . . . a fire that kept some companies on the scene for three days. Alan Feldman originated the idea of allowing off-duty firemen to patrol Midtown in department sedans to help catch the fire starter.

Three or four firemen would pile into a red, reserve officer's car, usually a hand-me-down Crown Victoria and cruise the prime target area, a forty block square known as 'South city.' Some nights found so many of the reds on patrol they'd end up following each other, criss-crossing South City in ten hour follow the leader mode. Such an orchestration naturally drew it's share of cynicism and within thirty-six hours the project became known as 'The Rat Patrol.' In retrospect, it was obvious the torch knew he was the subject of the red car madness, and the fires suddenly stopped. The sudden cessation of fires caused a false sense of security to fall over the city. Powerful enough that the 'Rat Patrol' was reduced to two cars in addition to the city's arson squad unit and the fire department's Fire Investigation Bureau and a single officer assigned to coordinate further patrols. Despite the surety the arsonist was still lurking about, a full three weeks passed without that ominous orange glow somewhere on the city horizon and the wailing sirens in the distance.

But the torch possessed a sense of drama as well as humor. On an unseasonably balmy Friday evening in October, three and one half weeks without a fire of any significance, the two cars of the diminished Rat Patrol rolled back and forth though a small section of Midtown bordered by Hamburg on its north and Key Avenue on its south. Within this area were two prime targets, an eight story book depository and an adjacent six story supply warehouse once utilized by building contractors. Both vacant, but whose surrounding neighborhood was the quarters of Engine 5 and Truck 55, a fact considered a deterrent to the arsonist who, previously, never lit anything within fifteen blocks of a firehouse.

That warm Friday night, however, marked the birthday of Jerome Gentile, the EVD of Truck 55. Gentile's wife had baked two large birthday cakes and delivered both to the firehouse. As the evening deepened with no sign of the arsonist, not so much as a fire alarm had been received for South City. The two cars bearing the remnants of Feldman's patrol was parked in the rear of the firehouse at the invitation of the two companies to wish the birthday boy well.

"C'mon you guys," Gentile himself had persuaded the erstwhile arson hunters, "fifteen minutes tops. Watch me blow out the candles, get a slice of cake and then go back to drivin' around.

Each member of the patrol grudgingly checked their watches and agreed that fifteen minutes couldn't hurt, they'd not stay one second beyond fifteen minutes though. The careful timing and solemn was unnecessary, however. Gentile had barely finished slicing the first slice of cake when an eerie glow became apparent through the tall, narrow, windows along one side of the firehouse. Where ever the torch had been, he'd watched the Rat Patrol. In the time it took to walk from the firehouse, take ten steps to the street corner and peer down Hamburg, fire was through the roof of the book depository. Engine 5 was the first company on the scene, the officer in the front seat looked at the wall of flames in front of him and calmly requested a fourth alarm. When the chief of the battalion exited his quarters, he could see the dull orange glow undulating against the low-hanging clouds sixteen blocks away and asked for four additional alarms.

The fire eventually rose to ten alarms, gutted the book depository as well as the warehouse, and resulted in the disbanding of the Rat Patrol. Alan Feldman could boast that the Fire Department was ready to meet any challenge given it, on-duty or not, although all mention of birthday cakes was absent from his public statements. As abruptly and suspiciously as they'd started, the fires ended. Investigators later surmised the arsonist had either moved on or most likely became bored with the ease with which this city burned. Ronnie Kovalchek was named 'Arsonist of the Year' by the Fire Investigation Bureau, courtesy of the signature accelerant used to create the destruction and the final consequence of 'Ronnie's Inferno,' the massive campaign that reshaped Midtown.

When Engine 50 returns to quarters and the delicatessen lunch absorbed, Dan Kemp announces that Engine 50 will be out-of-service in order that maintenance can be performed at the fire department shop to correct the detailed list of deficiencies that have been reported by the companies four pump operators during the course of the last three months. The quarterly visit to the sprawling maintenance and repair shop is never a cause for celebration. This particular venture, however, will encounter one true department legend and help create another.

The Fire Department Maintenance Shop is a sprawling fifteen acre complex in the 8th battalion, a thirty-five minute drive over the Cross-Town Expressway and in the heart of the small industrial district of Monroeville. Until a company experiences a mechanical emergency with its apparatus, visits to 'The Shop' are routinely handled with quarterly, scheduled appointments. Even so, an appointment, with the mechanics is just that, an appointment, time on the clock, no promises made on the length of stay, no promises made that the real problem can be fixed. Routine maintenance, oil changes, light bulbs replaced, electrical wires connected, has more certainty of timely completion. A complex issue, given that no guarantees exist beyond the quarterly 'tune-ups' requires real faith-based 'hope' and belief in metaphysics; as if proximity to tools to broken parts will heal them, untouched by human hands.

At the shop, the main garage and central mechanical terminal is three acres in size, situated fifty yards off the street. Sole access to the entire complex is only through the main doors of the terminal. The surrounding acreage is ringed with a twenty foot chain link fence topped with rolls of razor wire. The temptation of driving off in a stolen city fire engine is not absent in Monroeville. Other buildings within the protective fence are task-specific, the paint shop, motor repair, transmission, and a few others, but the central garage serves as the general purpose shop for all scheduled maintenance. It is a two story building. The cement floor is painted a light gray and colored with arrows pointing the way to the different work stations and out onto the yard to the other buildings. The main garage, its work floor open and spacious, is ringed with yellow-lined head in parking spaces each supplied with its own workbench and tools. On any given day, there are at least a dozen fire department vehicles being attended to in the various bays. Engines on hydraulic lifts six and seven feet off the floor, aerial ladder trucks secured in place with cabs tilted forward and motors exposed, officers cars, Jeep Cherokees, Chevy Blazers, older Crown Vics or newer Chevy Caprices are on jacks with wheels removed. The sound of pneumatic tools rip the air in conjunction with the echoing metallic reverberation of the favorite companion of mechanics everywhere, the hammer. Above it all are the shouts and laughter of the shop workmen.

Jerry eases the engine into the assigned bay, guided by a tall, lean mechanic waving and pointing before disappearing completely the moment March turns off the ignition. "Take a break," Kemp grunts climbing from the cab, "who knows how long this agony is gonna last?"

Red and white department rigs are being inspected, repaired or augmented on this afternoon. Extra tool compartments are added to the three engines, seating re-arranged on three trucks and several ambulances have their hoods open for engines to be tuned. Across the wide expanse of gray-painted floor, on the far side of the terminal, two trucks, rear-mounted ladders extending forward over the cabs, are being examined by a trio of white-hat officers in dark blue dress coats, gold stripes around the cuffs. Neither of the apparatus is painted in the city's scheme and, although from the same builder, both trucks are at least fifteen year-old models. They will be carefully and strategically disassembled, thoroughly inspected and repaired before being sent to the paint terminal for a fresh layer of paint, matching every other department apparatus and then reassembled. The trucks will be renumbered and re-lettered for the city and driven to the east section of the complex, to the fleet depot where both will be added to the reserve fleet.

In the department's tasking order, the Deputy Chief for Administration is responsible for the Maintenance Shop. The day-to-day operations of the shop are supervised by a harried captain who remains Super-glued to the desk on the second floor of the main terminal. Inundated with an ocean of paperwork, the officer has no time to leave his desk. He is responsible for the registration of every vehicle in the department that can conceivably be placed on the street, and the reports on the street-worthiness of each vehicle, the maintenance schedule and records for every piece of equipment that moves. He maintains the parts inventory in addition to reviewing the work schedule of the thirty men under his command. There is little physical harm in the captain's job, not counting paper cuts and the occasional stapling of a finger, but the mental toll is exhausting. As a direct result of bearing the paper-load on his shoulders, much as the Atlas of mythology bore the world, the captain has willingly abrogated all responsibility with it's accompanying authority, to one man who becomes the *de facto* head-of-maintenance. The Chief Mechanic of the Fire Department and true honest-to-God department legend, Elmer Rawley.

Rawley is fifty-seven years old, a short man, barely five-feet six inches tall with a pot belly, sloping shoulders and spindly legs. Elmer's eyebrows are thick and graying, and so bushy they give the appearance of a silver and black caterpillar glued across his forehead. His face is weathered from his constant frown and the outdoor work he does. No one has ever seen him smoke the stump of a cigar that he constantly moves from one side of his mouth to the other while he is thinking aloud and scratching his head.

Regardless of his unique appearance, Elmer is a god in the maintenance complex. There is no court of appeal, no second opinion, or matter of recourse. There is only Elmer, and it is the Chief Mechanic/missing dwarf who strolls across the open floor in the center of the garage to greet Jerry March. While the pump operator and mechanic discuss needed repairs on the engine, Kemp and the other three men climb metal stairs to a small, brightly lit conference room on the second floor overlooking the work area where they will have soft drinks from the room's vending machine and munch pretzels from the snack bar. The small, portable television on a tabletop is playing cartoons, suitable, though slightly heady entertainment given the audience.

"Pump Operator March," Rawley has his hands on his hips, greeting Jerry as he approaches. "What did you bring to my shop today?" His eyes dart back and forth, almost suspiciously. Jerry recalls the enduring rumor, never proven, that Rawley actually knows how to use every tool in the cavernous shop, although nobody can remember personally witnessing so much as a screw driver in his hands. Elmer's self-professed forte is diagnosis and he has a simplistic approach to rendering advice: ask and ye shall receive. Both dispensed in a quick rapid fire manner with a thin nasal high-pitched voice. "Pump Operator Jerry March," the short man repeats the greeting and question again, "what did you bring to my shop today?"

The slightest hint of a smile tugs at the corners of Elmer's mouth as that stump of a cigar flaps up and down; his head is level with Jerry's shoulders. He stops a few feet from March, squinting up at him, tracking slowly back and forth on the balls of his feet. Feet that are shoved into heavy, black work boots.

"Elmer," Jerry nods at the other man, "how are things going today?" A gentle, kindly, bond exists between the two. Both grew up in the same Northtown neighborhood, only blocks from each other, although Rawley is nearly twice as old. Jerry moved from his parent's home after graduation from the fire academy but, during each visit to his widowed mother March never fails to walk the short distance to the row house where Elmer continues to reside. The two empty a can of beer nuts, polish off a six pack of Budweiser and talk about the fire department until time and an impatient Trisha force Jerry to leave.

"I'm still standin'" Elmer shrugs, "and I ain't assumed room temperature . . . so all things considered I'm doin' alright." The cold cigar is flapping in time with the caterpillar eyebrows. But the older man is undaunted. "What have you brought to my shop today?"

"We need to hug more," Jerry grins and steps toward Elmer, who backs away, arms raised in defense.

"Damn boy," the mechanic scowls "don't you pull that around here," he squints harder at the taller man, "you goin' queer on me?"

"I was just thinking how I missed you," March shakes his head and glances at Elmer's hands. "I'm relieved to see those hands untouched by mechanic's tools."

Rawley fixes Jerry with a steely squint and puts a finger in the bigger man's chest. "You just made the list," he emphasizes the words with a jab accompanying each word. Every Emergency Vehicle Driver and PO in the department has been relegated to Elmer's list at one point in their careers. It is an imaginary list that says "Your apparatus will be the last thing fixed after the moon turns blue." Elmer's way of telling the guilty party, this is *his country and he runs it his own way.*

"C'mon Elmer," Jerry slaps Rawley's back, "you know you love me."

"Yeah, yeah," Elmer's reply sounds more like a duck quacking. "I love my old lady too," he fires back at Jerry, speaking so rapidly the sentence blurs into a single high-pitched explosion, "but when the witch makes 'the list' she gets slapped and thrown in the closet and fed Slim Jim's under the door." The two men have maneuvered around to face Engine 50. Elmer folds his arms across his chest. "So what we got here?" he asks.

"When I get in the cab and hit the starter button," March explains, using hand movements demonstrating the problem, "the motor starts, but won't turn over . . . not right away I mean. Sometimes I gotta wait and try again.

"Uh huh." Rawley begins a slow walk around the engine, peering at the vehicle like a predator after it's prey. "Everything else sound okay?" he has not acknowledged Jerry's presence since examining the apparatus.

"Just that the motor won't start right away when I hit the button."

Elmer strokes his chin for a moment. "Okay," the chief mechanic nods. "I bet if you hit that starter button . . . maybe about a hunnert times real fast," Rawley punctuates the advice with a pantomime of hitting the starter on the engine, "that motor will start right up."

Jerry's face is blank, "huh?" He cannot think of anything else to say.

"Yeah," Elmer's arms wave in front of him as he repeats the pantomime again. "You get behind that wheel and hit the damned button about a hunnert times like I just said, maybe a little less . . . then again maybe a little more . . . and I bet the starter kicks right in." He shrugs, ask and receive, case closed, problem solved.

"Are you actually paid by the city for this?" Jerry follows the little man as they walk closer to the big apparatus.

The question is lost on Elmer. The man is already thinking on another plane; maybe another reality. "Anything else?" he shoots a glance over his shoulder toward a perplexed pump operator still visualizing himself stabbing the engine's starter button a hundred times with Dan Kemp glaring at him from the next seat.

"Well," March thinks of the braking problem, considers asking about it and wonders about the odds of getting similar advice, "when I hit the brakes, it's like the engine swerves a little to the left," he takes the plunge. "I mean, if I hit the brakes hard, y'know, turning a corner or comin' up on something I wanna miss."

"Yeah, yeah," Elmer quacks again, nodding. His hands go up to his hips, "try lightening up on the brakes," he replies, "don't hit 'em hard." He bends to examine a front tire, and his pants drop far enough to expose the waistband of his boxer shorts.

"You sure?" Jerry makes a mental note that Elmer wears boxers.

"Not really," Elmer shrugs, standing up. "But give it a try anyway." A quick glance at March, "anything else?"

"Why were you looking at the tires?"

Rawley arches the caterpillar over his eyes several times. I been getting some feedback from other companies," he explains. "Everybody's complaining about getting' bounced around." He bends and examines the opposite set of tires at the front of the apparatus. "I ain't sure if it's the shocks or the tires." Elmer runs a hand over the deep treads of the front tire.

"So what do you think?" Jerry isn't sure how Elmer will answer; anything from mechanics to a theory on Atlantis.

"The tires" Rawley says finally, standing and kicking the heavy hubs. "They're losing their . . . uh . . . rubberbility." Not quite an Atlantis theory, but still beyond Jerry's grasp. Elmer's command of picturesque language defies Webster; perhaps anything outside Rawley's own world.

"*Rubberbility?*" March frowns. "Does that happen?" Rawley is now walking down the side of the apparatus, his squint intensified as he studies every inch of the big vehicle. Jerry isn't sure what the mechanic is talking about. Tires, electrical systems, apparatus workings in general have special designations in the short man's mind.

"All this time," Elmer's arms wave in the air, "I seen it over and over."

"Rubberbility," Jerry repeats the word quietly, looking back at the front tire.

"What about overheating'? You got problems with overheatin'?" Elmer is bent at the waist again examining the pump panel.

"Overheating?" March frowns.

"All them new engines overheat," Elmer glances at Jerry, glad to have shared a small secret, at least one March hadn't heard.

"This isn't a new rig," Jerry replies, unaware of this information and wondering if it is true. "It's almost four years old."

Rawley straightens again and gives March 'the look', an expression falling somewhere between disappointment and exasperation that the pump operator could be so naïve as to doubt his word. The caterpillar rises and falls several times matching the movement of the cold cigar. Elmer removes the stogie from his mouth and sighs. "March," sadness in his voice, "I been doin' this for a long time now. When I tell you a new engine is overheatin' I know what I mean." He turns slightly to wave an arm around the interior of the shop. "See all them apparatus?" he asks. "Newest one came in yesterday, six months old," he pauses and lifts his chin, ". . . overheatin'." A stubby finger points at Engine 50, "and this comes from the same manufacturer. I'm just checkin'."

"It's not overheating, Elmer," Jerry argues, wishing there was beer in the conference room with Kemp and the other guys.

"Power?" Elmer runs a hand through the shock of wild hair, discovering his glasses, patting them and leaving them in place in that mass of black and silver hair. "No battery problem?" He eyes Jerry suspiciously, as if expecting the pump operator to lie to him.

"No problems at all," Jerry swears, "none."

The short man is pensive for a moment. "We'll keep it on the battery charger anyway," he advises

"Just keep it on the charger?" March is not sure of Elmer's reasoning.

"Yep," Rawley grunts with authority. "When in doubt just keep it on the charger." Jerry remains mystified, the mechanic's advice coming like rain from a clear blue sky.

"You see March," Elmer gestures again at the array of apparatus along the perimeter of the terminal, some on the hydraulic lifts, and others with cabs tilted forward and motor housing removed. This is Elmer's kingdom, his fiefdom and Rawley reigns over the complex as surely as any feudal lord ruled his lands during the middle ages. "For the first time since I been here, the first time," he continues, "we got all the rigs in the department uniform." Something vaguely resembling a grin tries to appear on Elmer's grizzled features; facial muscles unfamiliar to the task battling nerve impulses demanding their movement, the final result looking more like Bell's Palsy than an expression of happiness. "All them engines," Elmer reminds March, "come from the same builder, everyone of 'em. All the trucks come from one maker too," he says. "Whether it's a tillered job or a rear mount or even one of the Tower Ladders, they all came from the same factory. You got any clue how much easier that makes my job?"

Easy as what? Jerry smirks, *Rubberbility?* He thinks of the word again. The two men slowly cross the open work area and climb the step to Rawley's office.

"Things are damn easier," Rawley says. "We need a ladder? We call out to Wisconsin and they got it, whether it's for Truck 10 or Truck 22, same ladder for both."

His sloped shoulders rise and fall with a shrug. "Same with engines, I need a throttle control? I call Florida and I get one I can use in either Engine 9 or 96 . . . it don't matter." They've reached the office of the Chief Mechanic. Below them, two bored mechanics begin preventive maintenance on Engine 50.

Rawley's work space is cramped. The walls are yellow and the floor is green linoleum. Elmer uses an ancient wooden desk jammed in one corner of the room, time and use has rendered the wood a sickly yellow appearance. Heavy, government-green file cabinets line each wall with charts. Calendars and fire service advertisements hang above them. Secured in place by an assortment of tacks, nails, and staples and a grated, fluorescent light in the ceiling keeps the office brightly lit. Seated behind Elmer's paper laden desk is an officer with dual trumpets on his collar pins.

Ron Doohan, captain of Engine 15, is thumbing through a worn, well-used magazine, and looks up when the other two men enter the office. Like Engine 50, Doohan's apparatus is being serviced in one of the work areas. Giving March and Rawley a grunt and wave of his hand, Doohan returns to an intense examination of an anatomically impressive female pictured across two pages.

"Don't sit in my chair," Elmer barks rapidly. Doohan quickly raises himself from the seat and steps aside as Elmer takes his place and scoots the chair forward. "I don't like that," Rawley warns the captain, direct and without deference to the officer's rank. His candor is a prerequisite of being nearly indispensable. The only man who can manage the big maintenance complex without developing an ulcer, the frankness of a true legend in the department. The caterpillar angles forward in a

scowl. "Sit in my chair and you make the list . . . the *real* short list."
March and Doohan exchange a glance and a wink.

"Hey Jerry," the officer greets March and receives a nod in return.

"Okay March," Elmer Rawley roots through the extensive litter on
his desk and discovers a yellow legal pad; it's top sheet covered with
enough brown coffee rings to form the Olympic symbol. The mechanic
grasps a stubby pencil in equally stubby fingers and begins to print in
large wavy letters. Unconcerned with the decorative stains on the sheet
of paper, Elmer makes a written list. "I'm gonna write out what needs
to get looked at on your wagon, got it?" he talks as he writes. "And you
do what I told you to do with that engine, got it" I don't wanna see
that piece of junk in here again until time for the next inspections."
The pump operator nods and marvels at Rawley's scrawl; something
resembling Sanskrit fill most of the page.

"Problems?" Doohan asks.

"Little things," Jerry shrugs and then utters the words that will lead
to the making of another fire department legend. "Nothing that would
keep us from knockin' you out on 15 Engine." Doohan's eyes narrow
at the challenge.

"Oh yeah?"

"Yeah," Jerry replies with typical bombast. He shoves a hand deep
into a pocket, withdrawing a thin fold of bills. Peeling off the three
topmost and placing them on the edge of Rawley's desk, "I got fifty
bucks sayin' we can knock you guys off on any box where you guys run
with us."

Although Doohan's company and Engine 50 are in separate
battalions, they share half a dozen locations where both companies
respond to an alarm. In each instance, Engine 50 must travel further
than Doohan's company, but Jerry remains undeterred.

"Name the box," Jerry offers first choice to the captain.

Doohan, fifty years old, balding, with thick glasses, considers
March's offer and grins. From his wallet the captain withdraws several
bills to match Jerry's and places them atop the money on Rawley's desk.
"Corner of Pluskat and Beane," he names an intersection one block
from his own firehouse. "It used to be that Five-One-Nine-One box,
remember?" With the advent of the department's Promethus CAD
system, there was no longer the need for numbered fire alarm boxes on

the city's street corners. When dispatching companies for emergency, however, it is not uncommon for Communications to identify the location using the old box numbers.

Jerry blushed and grins sheepishly. Doohan's choice, while only a block from Doohan's firehouse, is at the furthest point southeast of Battalion 15. When the department still responded to box numbers, 5191 had Engine 15 assigned as the first due, the closest company and Engine 50 the fourth, the last due. The streets leading to the intersection are narrow and run through block after block of small businesses where traffic seems to remain at a standstill.

Doohan knows he has Jerry. "Is it a bet?"

"What the hell," Jerry shrugs. Since the whole thing was his idea there's no way he can back out and save face. "Yeah, okay," he finally agrees with a tight-lipped smile. Looking over at Elmer he asks, "You wanna witness this?"

The mechanic looks up from the legal pad filled with his Sanskrit lettering. "What's the bet now?"

Ron Doohan slaps March on the shoulder. "Jerry here says Engine 50 will beat my company to the intersection of Pluskat and Beane, or where that Five-One-Nine-One box used to be . . . for fifty bucks. Hearing the scope of the wager, Elmer's eyes widen. Getting from his chair, he walks to the far wall to study the map of the city spread over a six square foot section and highlights the location of every firehouse. Rawley squints at the intersection of the two streets and looks over at the pump operator.

"Hell March," he circles the cold cigar in his toothless mouth. "Ain't no way." He emit's a sound resembling a cackle. "But I'll witness the bet." He ambles back to the cluttered desk, finds another soiled, blank sheet of paper and writes down the bet. Both Doohan and Jerry attach their signatures and watch as Elmer leans over his desk, tip of his tongue protruding past his lips and signs his name.

Rawley collects the hundred dollars on the corner of the desk and folds it inside the signed, witnessed bet and places the folded page in a locked drawer. "Okay," he bobs his head, "it's a formal bet now." With a mischievous grin, Rawley hands Jerry the page on which he has noted the work to be done on Engine 50 while it is parked on the work floor below. "We'll get the stuff done," he assures March, "and you can wait over in the conference room with everybody else." There is a pause, "I'll make sure it's done before the end of the shift," he promises with a wave of his hand. "If I gotta do the work my own self."

The mention of tools and Elmer in the same sentence is unsettling to Jerry. "Don't put yourself out, Elmer," he says reluctantly. "Just as long as we get outta here with the same engine we came in with." Rawley glares at March's finger.

Friday night, last night of the four-day trick, coincides with the formal end of Fire Prevention Week, a seven day period during which the department's Public Relations Office attempts to reach out to a general public whose interest can me measured in angstroms. The climax of this Fire Prevention Week, however, is different from those in the past; Alan (Rocky) Feldman has ordered a special, city wide event to culminate this week's aggravation.

Not content with a week-long open house, where hordes of children wearing red, plastic fire helmets wandered through neighborhood firehouses beyond the control of exhausted, harried teachers and parents, 'Sparky the Fire Dog' visits every firehouse. 'Rocky' Feldman successfully orchestrates a city 'Fire Drill' that will, Feldman anticipates, involve every family in all the communities across the city.

In Feldman's grand plan, each of the city's engine companies will pull out onto the driveways, the cement aprons, of their respective firehouses at six o'clock in the evening. At precisely six, each engine is to sound their siren and air horn for a period of thirty seconds; the signal for every family in the surrounding neighborhood to practice their own, pre-arranged drill to escape their home from an imaginary fire.

"You gotta wake these crack heads out of their dope dreams first," Jerry March is complaining loudly, checking his wristwatch and wandering toward the front of the firehouse sipping from a can of juice.

"There might be some people here who actually have fire drills in their homes," Sam Killen injects the idea innocently, waiting for Jerry's reaction.

"Yeah," March nods and scowls, "all six of 'em."

"Thing of it is," adds Burger, leaning against the watch desk cubicle," only neighborhoods that have the brains to read the flyers we sent out are going to know what's going on. Like maybe the people in South City and Homestead and maybe Little Italy."

In preparation for this fire drill, the city distributed over a million flyers detailing the event and how it will take place. The hope is that enough people have read the flyers and understand the contents. Better still, once understanding the contents, the same people actually care and participate.

"Well that makes about one-fifth of the city," Jerry observes dryly. "I wonder how many vagrants around here," he gestures toward the front of the firehouse, "have a clue?" The three men turn at the sound of Dan Kemp strolling up front from the lounge.

"You gonna take the wagon out at six?" Kemp asks his pump operator.

"On the dot, Cap," March nods vigorously. "I'll hit the siren for a whole damned minute if you want."

"Thirty seconds'll be fine," Dan shrugs. "I doubt most of the people around here are even gonna know what's happenin' and if you go more than thirty seconds, we'll get complaints about the noise." The captain taps his wristwatch, "I just want to make sure we get out and do our thing," he adds. "I'll be up in my office if anyone wants me." Dan lingers for a moment before heading to the spiral staircase.

"I wonder," Burger muses aloud, "if anyone would complain if they didn't get a chance to go through that fire drill." He studies the faces of March and Killen.

"Like who?" Sam's eyes narrow and he crosses those massive arms across his chest.

"Oh," Burger grins malevolently, "like those folks in South City." His brow furrows with intensity. "Like maybe if Engine 17 didn't signal? You think anybody would call in and complain?"

"So how we gonna do it?" Jerry slides into the chair behind the watch desk and leans back, stretching his arms. Bill's idea is appealing in concept.

"I'll think of something," Bill purses his lips and nods.

Engine 17 and Truck Company 22 share a Kensington Avenue firehouse in the heart of South City, an enclave of white middle and lower class blue collar families. It is a close knit neighborhood and, as a result, neither company in the firehouse comes within shouting distance of being 'busy'. Victims of that socio-economic phenomenon of the inverse ratio of fires to income. Consequently, lack of fire diminishes the number of runs which, in turn, dulls the razor edge of personnel. Even the circumspect Loughlin confesses his reservations about the companies.

"To tell the truth," the battalion chief once confessed in a rare moment of candor, "if I have to go down there in South City on a call, I don't count either company as part of the assignment. I'd just as soon put in a special call as to depend on those two." But that assessment is not appreciated by the firehouse's surrounding neighborhood that prides itself in involvement with city activities. There are big plans for this night's fire drill.

Barry Kramer shuffles toward the watch desk, his square fleshy face set in a menacing scowl. "The front of Barry-Fred's shirt is wet; an oblong water mark stretching down from his chest to his stomach. "Anybody know if Hagan has been around?" his voice is thick with anger.

"What's up?" March and Killen shrug.

Barry speaks through clenched jaws. "That jerk put a cup of water in my locker tilted against the door. I opened the door and got water down the front of me." He runs his hands over the front of the drenched shirt.

"No shower needed this weekend," Jerry declares.

"I just noticed," Sam cocks his head at an angle, examining Kramer. "You don't have a neck."

"Do too," Kramer reacts Immediately, defensively.

"Nah c'mon," Killen puts a finger on Barry's shirt collar. "Your head just kinda sits right on top of your shoulders, no space between your chin and chest." The observation causes Jerry to rise from the chair and peer down at Kramer's chin.

"Damn," March nods, "you're right Sam."

"I have a neck," Barry protests loudly.

"I heard about this disease," Sam gestures grasping is neck with both hands. "It's like a gradual disintegration of the vertebrae, they just sort of crumble internally over a period of time and your head gets lower and lower until it rests right on your shoulders." Killen peers at Kramer once more. "I think you got it."

"You're knockin' me," Barry grumbles. He backs away from the watch desk but pauses to run a finger around the inside of his shirt collar. "I got a neck," he declares, "I can feel it."

"The hell you can," March declares. "Hey Nicky, c'mere," he beckons to Miller who has appeared on the other side of the engine. "Look at Barry and tell me if you think he has a neck."

Filthy Nick walks over to Kramer and bends slightly at the knees, going through the motions of searching. "Nope," Nick declares straightening, "nothing."

Sam points at Kramer's collar a second time. "If you buttoned the top button of your shirt, you'd cover your chin."

"I take a size eighteen neck." Barry remains defiant.

"More like a size eighteen chin," Miller corrects with a twitch of his mustache.

"Six o'clock, Jerry!" Bill Burger is standing in front of the firehouse and shouts back in to March.

"Damn," the pump operator drops his head and shakes it. "Well," he sighs. "This will be quick." Leaving the cubicle Jerry takes his time walking to the engine and climbing into the cab. For a moment the firehouse is filled with the roar of exhaust and hiss of brakes and Jerry rolls the apparatus onto the driveway. For a solid thirty seconds the siren of this engine screeches, rising in volume as March keeps his foot on the pedal.

Sitting in the cab March spies Bill Burger hunched over, one hand over, one hand against his ear, speaking into the phone. The big man is animated as he talks, head bobbing and nodding. "Is this the fire department?" A pause. "Well . . . weren't you gonna sound a siren so we can practice our home drill?" Billy turns and sees March watching, raising a finger to his lips. "Well I thought so too," Bill continues in a high-pitched voice, nasal and affecting the slightest hillbilly drawl. "But my whole family . . ." he pauses and audibly counts to eleven, . . . there's eleven of us . . . well, we've been waiting all week for this drill." Another pause. "My little girls are crying and the boys are disappointed." Glancing back at Jerry, it is all Burger can do to maintain a straight face. "I'm in South City," he says into the phone. "I just live one block from that firehouse on Kensington Avenue . . . you know the one that has the big hook-and ladder in it?"

Jerry watches in amazement as Bill continues. "That's the firehouse, yes, that's the exact one, we waited and waited and they never sounded the siren and now it's too late and my whole family, there are eleven of us you know, my whole family is just really upset." Another pause. "Well I don't know what to do because everything is ruined because of those firemen. I just wanted to call and say something because that firehouse isn't doing its job . . . and I am a taxpayer!" Burger listens quietly for a moment before closing the cell phone, a triumphant grin on his face.

"You're crazy!" Jerry shouts from the open window of the engine as he backs it into quarters. He jumps down from the cab, slamming the door, just in time to hear the radio come to life.

"*Engine Seventeen . . . Engine Seventeen . . .*" the voice of the officer at *Communications* sounds unusually loud. "*Engine Seventeen please follow General Order Nine-Oh-Nine of this date and comply with the Fire Commissioner's Home Fire Drill Order!*" Gathered around the watch desk, Burger, Miller, March, Killen and Kramer stare at the radio, imagining the confusion reigning at the Kensington Avenue firehouse.

"*Engine Seventeen has complied,*" a voice sounds from the speaker.

"*Engine Seventeen,*" the dispatcher sounds again, "*On Orders of Deputy Chief Monroe, please sound your engine's siren for the required thirty seconds.*" A split second later the speaker comes to life.

"Oh damn," Miller giggles and looks at Burger. "You think they'll get in trouble?"

"What do you think?" The older man shrugs and points to the radio speaker on the wall. "Sounds like somebody called and complained."

Dan Kemp buzzes down on the bitch box, "You guys hear that?"

"Hear what, Cap?" Jerry presses the speaker button and replies.

"Sounds like somebody complained about Seventeen Engine didn't take part in the fire drill." March is forced to wait several seconds before answering. He is trying to control his laughing.

"Glad it wasn't us, Cap." he says. "I hope you heard me outside with the siren."

"I heard," Kemp assures March, there is a hint of suspicion in his voice.

For nearly an hour there is silence from the department radio. At Lafayette Park, Deputy Chief of Operations, Todd Monroe, is listening to the sputtering, halting explanation of the Acting Lieutenant of Engine Company 17 who is swearing on the grave of his mother that the company did, indeed, comply with the fire drill. Monroe maintains a stern exterior . . . he believes the company probably complied . . . but interaction with the public is a critical issue within the department now, given the mayor's view the department needs to become more visible. Todd Monroe, despite his taciturn aloofness and well earned reputation as a bastard, understands practical jokes and is sure one has been played on the South City firehouse. Lacking absolute proof, however, he will hold Engine 17 accountable. The apologetic and apoplectic Acting Lieutenant is ordered to have the men of both companies in the firehouse canvass the neighborhood and collect three hundred signatures and addresses verifying complicity with the fire drill. It will take several hours to comply with Monroe's order and disrupt the quiet evening the firehouse has anticipated, but their other option is being drawn on departmental charges for failing to obey orders from Commissioner Feldman, himself. Instead of enjoying a sumptuous fried chicken dinner and a movie that night, ten angry firemen will be going door-to door collecting proof about their participation in the drill.

By nine o'clock Engine 50 has had three runs, a dumpster fire in Lincoln Heights and an odor of smoke in the projects, requiring less than half an hour out of the firehouse. The third call, however, a report of a kitchen fire on Juniata Street, held the promise of actual work. Two blocks from the listed address, the engine slows to a complete stop at the intersection. It's progress is impeded by two police cars pulled across the route, blue strobe flashing. There is no way around the cars unless the company can find bicycles and, adding insult to injury, the uniforms assigned to the cars are nowhere in sight.

"What the hell is this?" Jerry throws up his hands in disgust. Beside him in the seat, Dan Kemp is blasting away on the air horn. The sounds echo up and down the narrow street lined with cars bumper to bumper. Ahead of them, both men can see the flashing red lights of a second engine . . . 24 . . . in front of the address . . . getting to the fire and beating Engine 50 to the scene.

"If that turns out to be really good," Kemp shouts "these creeps are in some deep trouble." He is looking left and right for some sign of life, some movement indicating the police officers are in the general vicinity. A high pitched tone from the radio fills the interior of the cab. Seconds later the voice of the dispatcher informs Engine 50 can return to quarters, Engine 24 will handle the scene.

As if cued, two uniforms dart from the shadows and are caught in the engine's lights. Two police officers climb in there respective cruisers, throwing them in reverse and backing away from each other, creating a gap for the waiting apparatus. March guns the motor and the engine slides into the gap before jerking to a halt again. Yanking furiously at the window, Jerry leans out to glare at a white faced, wide eyed officer standing next to one of the cars.

"You guys get taught that at the police academy?" he shouts venomously.

"We didn't hear you coming," the reply is accompanied by a weak shrug.

"Give me a break," Dan Kemp joins in berating the policemen. "You got a twenty ton fire engine full of flashing lights with a siren and horn blasting away coming down a one-way street and you don't know we're comin'?" He shakes his head in anger and slumps back in his seat.

"You're getting soft in your old age Dan," March carefully brings the engine around the block. "Two years ago you'd have been out of the cab shoving his night stick up his nose."

Kemp squirms uncomfortably in his seat, features shadowed by the green glow of the lights along the instrument panel. "I'm trying to be kinder and gentler," Kemp agrees.

"I thought there was going to be a big fire tonight," Bill Burger addresses March as the men climb from the cab. He pulls off his heavy duty turnout coat and drapes it over his empty seat, drawing his feet from boots and turnout pants and arranging them on the floor beside the open door.

Guess your man missed it, huh?" Barry-Fred shoves his helmet atop the compartment next to his seat opposite next to Bill.

"Hey," Jerry holds up both hands. "I'm telling' you what Bob Hannah passed on to me. He said all the charts and graphs show we were due for one helluva fire during this night trick." The pump operator pauses to plug the cord for the battery charger into the socket on the side of the engine. "Hannah ain't perfect," he admits.

"I got the watch," Jerry calls loudly, reaching the wood and Plexiglas enclosed cubicle and dropping his backside into the chair. Except for the glare of the solitary goose-neck lamp arced over the desk, the apparatus floor is dark and quiet.

For a moment, a shaft of light appears and a rush of noise burst from the lounge as Burger opens the door and enters. In an instant the door shuts and silence and shadows return to the apparatus floor.

Nick Miller hangs around the desk, lighting a cigarette and lowering himself to sit on the concrete slab. "It's been slow," he complains.

"We're due," March assures the other man, lifting his feet and resting them atop the desk.

Forty minutes later, neither man has appreciably changed his position. On Fort Avenue the occasional car passes, tires humming on the asphalt. Even the radio stays silent, as if the city itself has buttoned itself shut for the night. A ghostly silence hangs over the shadowy apparatus floor. An atmosphere heavier than normal and both Nick and Jerry feel it, though neither can describe the feeling.

At the desk, the numbers on the digital clock morph into parallel "1's" and Nick dozes off twice since the police car incident. His dark blue tee-shirt hangs out of his pants. With luck and the scientific advances in laundry detergents, the myriad stains on Nick's shirt will be washed clean as new for his next trick.

One by one the other men in the firehouse gradually evacuate the lounge and trudge up the staircase to the soft metallic click marking their passage. The second-floor bunkroom is covered with green and white linoleum tile, the same green and white flooring in every firehouse bunkroom, probably a pricing deal the city received from the manufacturer. Single steel bunks line opposite walls, head first, leaving a wide space down the center of the room. Facing Fort Avenue, the three offices have their doors closed, Loughlin has his cot in the battalion's office. Gulfee and Kemp use beds just outside the doors of their company office.

Spaced at even intervals along the second floor are the brass poles the men slide when an alarm is received. Each wide circular hole in the floor has a double brass railing encircling it with a narrow opening for access to the poles. The railings are a safety addition in the event someone can't figure the potential danger of accidentally falling through the hole to the concrete apparatus floor below without a solid grip on the pole.

The bunkroom is dark. Dim light shines up through the pole holes from the first floor and the only sounds are the snoring of sleeping firemen. Burger, whose bunk is three down from the engine company office, forms an amorphous mountain in the bed, with a blanket under his chin, he reminds one of a large stuffed teddy bear. Two bunks down, Barry-Fred's deep snoring sounds eerily like a snorting bull. His blanket is a gift from his wife . . . baby blue with yellow smiley-faced firemen across it's surface.

March yawns and contemplates hitting the sack. Since losing the bread and butter route and becoming unemployed, his wife Trish, has come to expect an outpouring of creative energy remodeling their home; a level of energy beyond Jerry's scope of thinking. A good night's sleep would be beneficial. The kitchen floor is scheduled for replacement the next morning. If he doesn't find a second job quickly, Jerry knows he will soon find himself actually working for a living.

A loud sudden *BING* from the small bell at the watch desk causes Jerry to jerk upward. From the smaller speaker at the desk comes a long, softly muted tone, the signal for an alarm received in another, adjacent battalion. March, already bored, reaches across the desk to adjust the volume on the speaker.

"ADT for Box Ten-Seven . . . Boston Park Street and Industry Dock . . . Harcourt Licorice Building . . ." something in the announcement triggers a reaction in the pump operator. Miller still sitting on the concrete slab, dozing off and on, is also conscious of the signal.

"What was that?" Nick's voice is groggy and he rubs his eyes.

"ADT Box," Jerry replies, yanking open the right hand drawer of the desk.

"Damned automatic alarm," Nick yawns. "Water flow . . . somebody flushed three toilets at the same time and the system picked up the water flow . . . set off the alarm."

"It ain't automatic," March corrects the drowsy man, "it's a hand-pulled box." That means somebody had to *pull* it. The information causes Nick to sit up. Jerry flips through the old assignment cards in the desk drawer, finds the card tabbed for ADT Box 10-7 and separates it from the rest.

"We on it?" Nick asks sleepily.

"We got it on the third," March examines the rows of companies, each row signifying an alarm. "Truck takes it on the fourth." The building is located in the Seventh Battalion, near the edge of the harbor, nine stories in height and abandoned for the past eight years; a brick and wood eyesore looming over the old cobblestones of Boston Park Street. "This has a chance of being something," Jerry comments, laying the card on the desk.

Nick is standing now, entering the cubicle and looking over Jerry's shoulder. "Who's first due?" He lights a cigarette.

"Engine 57 and Truck 19," March murmurs, "about ten blocks down from Boston Park." He fidgets with the volume control knob on the small speaker and shoots a glance at the clock. "We ought to hear something soon."

A burst of noise comes from the speaker, a harsh combination of siren, air horns, and male voices in the background calling excitedly to each other. Nick moves to the side of the desk, listening.

"Engine 57 Nineteen to Communications!" the voice of the officer borders on hysteria. When the dispatcher replies there is no response, only an enduring silence. Jerry glances at Nick and arches his eyebrows in succession, his best Grouch Marx imitation.

Finally, *"Truck Nineteen to Communications!"* the same officer, same hysteric tone. A second attempt to raise the officer on the radio is again met with silence.

"They got something," Jerry nods, "I told you this night could be something." His smile is smug.

Three times the dispatcher tries to get a response from the truck company without success and Nick Miller is counting off the seconds before Communications tries a fourth. Before the dispatcher can speak however, the excited officer is back on the radio shouting above the din of sirens and horns.

"Truck Nineteen to Communications, gimme a fourth alarm on this box!" March jerks is head in Nick's direction.

"Judas Priest," he hisses, "what have they got?" The dispatcher makes contact with the chief of the 7th Battalion, informing him of the truck company's request. There is no discernable break between the dispatcher's relay and the chief's response.

"Go to fourth alarm. Communications, I am three blocks behind Truck Nineteen and see fire through the roof . . . fully involved building . . ."

Nick is already trotting to the engine as Jerry reaches for the manual alarm key, flipping it up and down three-four-five times, each up and down toggle resulting in a loud *Clang* from the house gong magnified through the silent apparatus floor. Lights flash on illuminating the big room in a brilliant burst of fluorescent light.

"Fourth alarm, Harcourt Licorice," Jerry calls to Kemp whose descent down a brass pole lands him between the watch cubicle and the engine. "The Chief and the Engine take it on the third . . . truck on the fourth." Jerry turns and rips the teleprinter sheet from the machine and leans from the cubicle to hand a copy to Donald Holland and Ken Shaw. Greenstreet clambers up into the tiller cab, already buzzing Holland is ready. Killen and Hagan stand on opposite sides of the truck's cab pulling on turnout coats as Paul Gulfee slides down a pole on the far side of the truck.

"I was just startin' to sleep," Bill Burger is grumbling, adjusting his flash hood over his head and grabbing his helmet.

None of the vehicles in the firehouse can respond until the dispatcher sitting in the Communications-East alarm center announces their respective alarms. March and Kemp are curious about the size of the fire and walk under raised exit doors to stand in the nighttime darkness and the sight is impressive . . . a huge undulating, pulsing hemisphere of orange-pink seems to press upward against a dark, dimpled canopy. Both men know the dimpled canopy is a blanket of heavy black smoke hanging over the buildings, reflecting the glow of the fire back to the ground.

"Holy Cow," Dan runs a big hand through his rumpled hair and looks at Jerry.

"You know the fastest way, Jer?" Behind them the warning lights of the truck are already fluttering.

"Got it," Jerry nods as the two men do a quick walk-skip back under the exit doors. "We'll come in west, right off Patton Avenue. There's a hydrant sitting right on the corner, maybe a hundred feet from Harcourt. It's a little off to the side so it might get missed, but there's a second hydrant a block from Front Street. If we get there just right we'll have our choice." The pump operator's precise knowledge of the fire hydrants in a third alarm district is noteworthy, some guys still need directions to hydrants in their own districts.

Dan has one booted foot up in the cab when the wide gray radio horn on the front wall begins blaring. *"Third alarm . . . ADT Box Ten-Seven . . ."*

The fire ground around Boston Park Street is, literally, a surreal scene to the casual observer. Partially illuminated by the building fire, the surrounding streets are further highlighted in the blaze of halogen light from the nearly three dozen fire department vehicles; an eerie, manmade brilliance of blue-white lighting turning night into day. Towering above the street level, the Harcourt Licorice building belches heavy smoke skyward, its insides a solid wall of yellow orange fire with flames blowing out of every window, sending a steady stream of embers rocketing into the air.

As far as strategy is concerned, this is your basic 'surround and drown' scenario. The size of the building and volume of fire dictates the obvious. Consider a stream of water, two hundred and fifty gallons per minute, propelled through one nozzle, pouring into one broken window on the building's eastern exposure, vaporized instantly by the incomprehensible heat inside. Multiply that reaction by twenty and you get some idea of the enormity and intensity of a really large fire and appreciate the vivid description of trying to extinguish such a fire with too few hoses as ". . . spitting on it." So you surround the fire with as many hose lines as you can, make yourself as comfortable as possible and, literally, just pour all the water you can into the building until there is no more fire.

Along the front of the building and bracketing either side, truck companies have raised their big aerials, their sticks and the hundred foot jobs, with large diameter nozzles attached. Each of these 'ladder pipes' is fed by hoses stretching down the rungs to an engine pumping away in the distance. Seven hundred and fifty gallons per minute cascading from each ladder pipe into the heart of the fire, in addition to the handheld lines doing the same from street level. Added to this deluge approach are tower ladders; truck companies with ninety-foot telescoping booms, insulated baskets at the business end holding two firemen directing dual five hundred gallon per minute pipes. Because the baskets are manned, their streams are better directed into specific areas and, using their handie-talkies, the firefighters high over the site give a constant narrative of what they see and the direct effect of the attack on the fire. In short, thousands of gallons of water are being dumped into this fire every minute and it continues to burn. But Rome was not built overnight either.

Jerry March has Engine 50 next to the hydrant on front street, supplying three large hose lines. The side of the engine, where the pump panel is located, looks like a small octopus with it's tentacles splayed toward the ground. Each line snakes off in the direction of the fire, where men kneel in the street directing their water into the building, watching the stream disappear into a solid body of yellow fire.

The pump operator stands alongside the engine, a cigarette hanging loosely from his mouth, occasionally glancing at the gauges of the pump panel. He is wearing a navy blue woolen jacket, it's collar upturned against the chill of the night and he will stay with the engine all night, guaranteeing the three lines he supplies will have a steady flow of water. It will be a long night.

Adjacent to the Harcourt Building is another structure three stories tall. It is separated from the fire by about fifty yards and it's flat topped roof is caught in the fire's illumination, casting long shadows across the surface. Around the perimeter of the roof is a waist high railing of rusting iron pipe and it is to this roof that the firemen of Engine 50 will have taken their hose.

Bill Burger holds the heavy nozzle, the pipe, against the top of the railing. Behind him, Kramer and Miller support the thick, rock hard hose, their faces lit by the flames of the nearby building rising an additional six stories above them. Dan Kemp walks back and forth in a slow, measured pace, just to the rear of the three men, watching the fire and then at the heavy stream of water rushing from the hose. The position is ideal. The railing provides perfect support for the back pressure of the nozzle and Bill has securely tied off the hose to the top rail, directing the water into a fourth floor window.

"You think we're gonna need to move this?" Bill shouts back to the pacing captain.

"Not right now," Kemp replies, walking to the railing and surveying the mass of flame and brick. "At least, not until this bastard gets knocked down a whole lot more than it is." He shakes his head. "This blaze was off and rolling fast." His glance catches Burger. "Makes you wonder if we ain't got a case of "Jewish Lighting"."

"No big surprise," Bill shrugs. Like everyone else connected with this fire, the men accept it will be a long night for them.

Across the street from the fire, Thomas Callahan and Todd Monroe stand together, white helmets reflecting the lights and fire. Gregory Ryan, The Predator, and Roland Peete, the division deputy immediately subordinate to Ryan, stand a few yards from the Chief of Department, impressed by the size and scope of the fire. Supervising the immediate periphery, half a dozen battalion chiefs move about, silhouetted against the flames, directing men, adjusting the direction of water and relaying information to the big bosses across the street.

"Todd, where's the first truck company?" Callahan scans the upraised tower ladders and aerials; water cascading from their nozzles falling in wide arcs into the flames.

"Truck Nineteen," Monroe answers quickly.

"I know *who* it is," Callahan replies evenly, "I want to know *where* they are."

"Well," Monroe shakes his head, looks at the ground and then squints across the street, "they were first in, called for the additionals and seems like they got off the truck and disappeared."

"Disappeared?" Callahan turns at the word.

"Look over there." Todd Monroe edges closer to Callahan and directs the chief's attention to the right exposure, street level. Caught in the flickering gleam of the fire, Truck 19's apparatus is parked at curbside, no ladder is raised.

"They haven't done anything." Callahan fumes.

"They need chewing out," Monroe agrees, Torquemada planning his next inquisition.

Callahan sets his jaw firmly. He will not spend time allowing the truck's inactivity to distract him, there's a fire to put out. "I didn't expect that from a good truck company," the chief sighs and turns his attention to the hulking burning building.

CHAPTER 7

TRUCK COMPANY 105

There are not a hundred and five truck companies in the city fire department. Truck 105 is an historic anomaly, evidence of city, county, and state legislative agreements and deals of the past gone wild.

During a period of land annexation from it's surrounding county, the city acquired property holding Sussex Hook and Ladder Company #105, a volunteer group whose history and ties with the county extended a hundred years past. The president of the company was the brother of a powerful state legislator and married to the sister of the then governor. Such hue and cry attended the announcement that the horse-drawn ladder wagon was to be abolished. The protests grew so great the governor, himself, entered the fray. Legislation was introduced through the State Senate and lobbied for its successful passage. Despite indignation from the handful of city representatives in the senate, the governor's bill was passed speedily and with overwhelming support. State archives show that no bill past or future was voted into law faster and with such enormous support as that dealing with a fire engine. A grudging city agreed to the declaration that 'Hook and Ladder Company #105 shall presently and for all perpetuity be a recognized and continuing company of the city fire department'. The law further forbade the city from forever changing the designation of said company so it will always bear the number '105'.

In actuality there are less than half the number of trucks in the city, one would surmise from the triple digits assigned the apparatus. As time and history are wont to do, settled acceptance of the company's existence evolved into the current status as one company never to be disbanded.

Three distinct types of 'truck' are in service throughout the city. Most, like 105, are tillered, essentially, a tractor-trailer with a second steering wheel at the rear to guide the back wheels. In the last two decades 'rear mount' trucks began to increase in numbers in the department's fleet, a straight chassis with the hundred foot aerial ladder mounted on a turntable at the rear of the vehicle. The ladder itself projecting forward over the cab. It also became fashionable to include 'elevating platforms' as truck companies. Trucks with either telescoping or articulating booms with baskets or buckets attached to provide a secure base for firemen working at higher elevations for rescue or delivering water through large diameter nozzles. The city fire department availed itself of this last category of truck design, designating them as 'tower ladders' and incorporating them, operationally, as truck companies.

To the chagrin of many, some of the companies were assigned the rear mount designs, and tower ladders. Since both are built on a straight chassis, an ominous fault presented itself; a distinct inability to maneuver along and around narrow streets. With tillered trucks you can almost make a ninety-degree turn, regardless of the street. Try going into Little Italy or Monroeville with their tiny streets and suffocating intersections or try making a turn anywhere in Lafayette Heights or around the East Side and you are out of luck. Bouncing one of those big rear mounts up over the curb on a turn and you risk taking out an end house or maybe three cars parked closest to the end of the street. You end up having to park that spiffy-looking rear mount five or six blocks from the fire and walking to the scene, lugging all your equipment with you. The same is true with those tower ladders, but you have to get there first, and the tower ladders have the same problem as the rear mounts. You want to make a turn in Little Italy? Good luck, because you're not driving a Fiat and the same rule holds in other ethnic parts of the city. Some of the streets might be five feet wide if there is nothing parked on them. Even delivery trucks take half an hour to negotiate that one turn on Gold Street, you think you can do it in a twenty-plus ton fire truck with no control over those rear wheels?

That tiller cab is no lap of luxury either, though basically a rectangular box welded to the rear of the ladder bed with a steering column stuck down to the rear axle. There's no heat in the cab, no brakes, just you, that steering wheel and a seat that might have an inch of padding to it and once Greenstreet sits on the cushion, you can forget the padding. It wasn't until later that the tiller cabs were even enclosed. There were no windshields so you didn't have wipers either.

There's an old adage that you could tell the weather just by looking at the company's tiller man. If the guy was all bundled up and had a blue face, it's cold. If he is all bundled, blue and wet in the winter, it was common for the tiller man to be wearing his turnout gear, a heavy muffler around his neck trailing behind him like the tail of a comet, earmuffs the size of birthday cakes over his ears and a pair of snow goggles protecting his eyes. But even the advent of the tiller cab was no real gift. You sit in the tiny bucket seat bolted to the floor without shock absorbers and God save you going over the cobble streets in South City or those pot holes on Fort Avenue that could trap a brontosaurus. Cobblestone streets look pretty in a Currier and Ives painting, but going over them in a tiller cab and your dentist can retire after fixing your chipped teeth. Remember Dave Boone on Truck 15 ? He was one helluva EVD, maybe even the best around until 15 Hook went over a pot hole on Thames Street and the whole rear assembly cracked. Boone started bouncing up and down in that tiller cab like he was on a pogo stick. His head hit the roof about a dozen times and when he got back to quarters, he complained about a sore neck until his lieutenant finally sent him to the medical officer. It was discovered Davey's sore neck was actually *broken.* The poor guy got total disability just by *driving* to the scene of a fire!

For all it's inherent problems the tiller's ride, however, was the closest thing you'll get to a free carnival ride. Perched in the cab, the tiller sees way out in front of everything and when the driving EVD turns right, the tiller goes left and then swings right. Swinging that big end of the truck out and then aligning again with the front of the vehicle, was a fun ride and the city paid you for it.

The truck in service with 105 was not quite ten years old. Built by the big manufacturer in Wisconsin, the apparatus has endured almost a decade of playing bumper cars along the city's street. Although its main attraction is its one hundred foot aerial telescoped in four sections in the ladder bed, the apparatus is also a traveling truck. In addition to the smaller ground ladders resting length wise in compartments under the main 'stick', the truck carries power saws, axes, sledge hammers, and ceiling hooks, a wrecking crew's dream wagon. There is everything needed to pull apart a building, make holes to ventilate heat and smoke and tear down walls, floors, and ceilings in search of embers escaping the water that has extinguished the main body of fire.

Like it's firehouse counterpart, the cab of the truck is large enough to carry it's crew and the men who comprise the company, in relative protection and comfort. At least there's no more standing on the running board or side steps during torrential downpours. Each seat in the cab has brackets holding the breathing apparatus and harness and there's heating and air conditioning.

As with the engine, Truck 105 has its combinations of shifts and groups within it's shifts that engender more fires, bigger fires and, conversely, longer nights of uninterrupted sleep. In the truck company, it is it's Blue-Shift that commandeers the busiest times and seems to be presented it's hottest fires. Lacking a notable 'Weak Link' as personified in Barry Kramer, any shuffling of the roster doesn't bring corresponding inconsistency of performance.

Holland—Gulfee—Killen—Greenstreet and Hagan are very good, add Tim Bridges instead of Hagan and there is no change other than Hagan's ability to tiller and drive. Put Rich Simms in place of either Hagan and Bridges and there might even be a slight elevation in the teamwork. Many of the FOG's have a stock answer. Paul Gulfee's insistence on the need for a truckie to think and work independently means the grouping of the same types simply enhances existing superior efforts. After finishing a detailed annual review of Tim Bridges' work, Paul concedes there is, candidly, no discernible drop in company performance. "He's hungry," Gulfee has explained, "and he's something of a natural. Not only does he love the job he's doing, but he loves the work . . . it's spooky in a way." About Hagan, the lieutenant rocks back in his chair, smiles ruefully, "You give me four more Marks on the fire ground and let me deal with the off duty stuff privately and I can retire with that."

In return, Paul's leadership style engenders the performance of his men. "Paul don't mess with your head," Greenie will say, "he's not gonna tell that you did a good job on a fire and then turn you down for time off or write you up for some minor infraction."

Even Mark Hagan, the 'Pecks-Bad-Boy' of the company blushes red when discussing his lieutenant, and admits, "If I was with any other shift, much less any other company, I'd probably be in jail," he laughs. "Gulfee will beat my ass at times, but the minute that gong hits off, everything is forgotten, even after the fire. You wanna get Paul Gulfee off your back? Do a good job on the fire ground."

Mike Greenstreet, he of the perfectly symmetric body, is a good tiller, the guy might be fat, but he's a mean S.O.B. inside that tiller cab. Coming down Fort Avenue, returning to quarters, Greenie whips the tiller around so the entire truck rolls down the street sideways, adjusting the wheel ever so slightly he stops dead on a dime in front of the big arched doorway lettered over it's top 'H&L 105.'

Tim Bridges is in a frustrating position. He is preparing to qualify as an EVD and tiller, but his chances of getting assigned that position is like trying to win the hundred meter dash in the Olympics with both legs in a potato sack. Donald Holland is the assigned EVD and Greenie is the tiller, both men have been with the company for over twelve years, and even if both men were off-duty the same shift, Mark Hagan, Rich Simms and Killen are all qualified in front of him.

Each trick Bridges strolls into the firehouse and checks the dry-erase board hanging outside the watch desk cubicle, the board where Gulfee or whoever is Acting Man has posted the running assignments. Tim is an optimist about his chances as tiller, but he is also the most junior on the shift. A position at the bottom of the totem relegating him the permanent 'right step man.' The moment 105 arrives at a fire, Bridges grabs a ceiling hook and halligan tool and, depending on the type of structure burning, will get an assist from the 'left-step man' pulling ground ladders from the truck's rear rack, either a twenty-four or thirty-six foot ladder. Thirty-sixes get thrown for a three story building, twenty-four for anything less, and the work begins.

A number of slogans accompany truck work, and it can be the perfect job for anyone harboring a destructive personality or streaks of vandalism. 'Breaking glass and kicking ass' is a popular phrase as well as 'Truckies make bigger holes' terms descriptive of what companies do best. Heat and gas build inside a burning structure creating a toxic, potentially explosive conditions to the guys on the hose. When the heat and gas can be vented, either by breaking windows or creating holes in the highest point of the building, smoke and heat escape to make the working conditions better, even if only slightly, for the men on the pipe. The danger in the job is that you're working above the fire, trusting that whatever you might be standing on hasn't been so weakened by the flames below it won't collapse under your feet.

It's happened everywhere, a guy cutting vent holes atop a burning building suddenly falls through the roof. Fire weakens the support structures and you don't know how long those supports have been burning, you get 'a feel' for the consistency of a roof or floor. If it feels 'spongy' or 'mushy', that is a sure sign it is no longer the firmest of foundations. So you avoid putting any weight on it. Anything that has any 'give' to it, avoid. You pay attention to the hole you're making and how quickly it fills with smoke. Is fire coming through it the moment it opens or you notice how long that black smoke has been rolling out from under the eaves of the roof you are standing or kneeling on?

Tim Bridges is good at rescues, he has already made three by himself, a second function of truck companies, search and rescue. You get into a smoky, hot dwelling and crawl on your belly through accumulated trash, looking under beds and in closets, anywhere someone might run and hide from sheer terror. The heat builds and gets to you, makes you wonder what genetic defect made you so stupid you wanted to be a firefighter, much less work in a truck company. But it is part of the job and you do it. Heroism is a retrospective view from people probably too smart to do the job. Unfortunately the city doesn't pay you a hero's salary, the category doesn't appear in the MetroStrats reports.

The first day of the trick finds the natives restless, unusual when the sun has risen. Even with the volume of the radio turned down, the apparatus floor continuously echoes radio communications, responses from the companies in the street and announcements from units on the scene of an emergency. Engine 50 is out in the battalion on those God-awful inspections. The number crunchers at MetroStrat center want data to justify their existence. The empty bay makes the apparatus floor seem bigger and Tim Bridges leans back in the chair at the watch desk reading the morning paper.

"We gotta run to the shop," Paul Gulfee materializes from nowhere, walking briskly to the truck, a clipboard in his hand. Tim welcomes the relief from sitting behind the desk and joins the other men who are working this day shift as they climb into their seats. Holland is driving with Greenie at the tiller. Tim climbs into his familiar right step seat as Hagan slouches in the left.

Donald Holland has been complaining, the big turntable on which the truck's aerial is mounted, jerks and grinds when he attempts to swing it to the left. A truck handicapped with a one-way ladder tends to be problematic and Gulfee has scheduled a quick trip to the shop.

Holland and Gulfee huddle with Rawley, identifying potential problems with the truck. Holland is asking Elmer not to assign a reserve apparatus as 105 is being checked out.

Overhead a high-pitched squeal and warbling of the alarm systems cuts through the terminal, "*Report of a fire, Nine-Zero-Nine Barker Street . . . Box Alarm Five-One-Nine-One . . .*"

"Ha!" Elmer cackles, his opened mouthed grin shows nothing but gums. "I was wonderin' when that would come in . . . March is going to get his rear waxed." The idea of Jerry losing his bet animates the mechanic.

Jerry March harbors no thought of getting 'waxed.' Engine 50 lumbers down Americus Avenue, near the farthest boundary of the battalion. The company has endured two hours of door-to-door interviews ensuring each household has a working smoke detector and the pump operator is bored to tears.

"Cap," he complains loudly to Kemp, "how much longer are we gonna keep up with this aggravation?" Jerry is forced into stop-and-go traffic, weaving in and out of slower moving cars.

"Til we get in enough to keep the bosses happy," Kemp answers his PO. He is hardly happy with the data collection, but realizes, unlike March, there is nothing to be gained by overturning the dictates of Lafayette Park. The engine comes to a heavy squeaking, hissing, stop at the traffic light at Highland and Ashland.

"Damn," Jerry ducks his head and stares out the windshield at the street signs. "We're a long way from where we oughta be." He turns to make a point to Kemp, mouth open and index finger raised when the radio interrupts with a staccato burst.

"*Engine Five-Oh-Available . . . ? Battalion One-Five . . . available . . . ?* Kemp and March exchange a glance as the captain informs communications that Engine 50 is, indeed available.

Engine Five-Zero, be informed that we are transmitting a report of fire at Nine Zero Nine Barker Street, cross street location Pluskat and Beane . . ."

Box Five-One-Nine-One . . ." Jerry echoes back the dispatcher's words.

Kemp reaches to his left and begins pressing a bank of buttons on the engine's console, the lights atop the engine flash on as the siren rises in volume. Jerry whips the engine along Highland, weaving in and out of traffic while the men in the back seats begin donning their gear. "I been waitin' for this ride," he shouts to Kemp.

The engine makes the wide turn at Highland on to Macon and a quick left on to Beane Street. With air horn blasting, engine 50 speeds past the firehouse of Engine 15, it's door wide open and crew in the process of climbing into the cab.

"You see Doohan?" Jerry yells to Kemp.

"Yeah," the captain nods wearily, "I saw him . . . he's there."

"Fantastic!" March replies, hitting the brake and turning on to Barker. A small crowd has gathered at curb's edge and Jerry swerves the apparatus toward the group easing to a stop while Kramer and Nick Miller join Kemp in investigating the call.

The ride back to the fire house seems interminable to March, he drums his fingers against a thigh, driving as rapidly as traffic and the speed limit will allow. At two intersections Jerry turns on the emergency lights, gives the air horn a couple of toots and slides effortlessly through the traffic. It is one of those rare moments when the pump operator is anxious about backing into quarters, a by product of his impatience.

While the other men make their way to the lounge, Jerry strides triumphantly to the watch desk, lifting the black department telephone and punching the Centrex number for the fire house of Engine 15.

"Hey Babe," he speaks loudly into the phone, "is Cap'n Doohan available?" He waits, "Okay, can I speak to him?" Jerry is on a mission, he is on a roll, nothing could deter him from making this call.

"Cap?" his voice rises when Doohan answers the phone. "Cap," March continues, "I just wanted to make sure you knew," he grins widely, "that wasn't any ice-cream truck you watched knock you back a little while ago!" He doesn't wait for Doohan to respond, letting the phone drop into it's cradle from a height of ten inches.

Across town Elmer Rawley listens to the radio, hearing Engine 50 arrive at the scene first. "I'll be damned" he mumbles, rubbing a hand across the back of his neck. "I never would have believed that."

"I also got a problem with the warning lights," Donald Holland continues to get Rawley's attention to the list of problems on the clipboard.

"What warning lights?" Elmer glances at the EVD.

"On the truck Elmer," Donald waves a hand in frustration. "I get in the cab and start the truck and get a bunch of warning lights flashing on . . . then they go off."

Rawley frowns, one hand rubbing his chin, the other pulling on the gnarled pencil behind his ear. "It's a malfunction," the mechanic finally announces. "Ignore 'em."

"Ignore them?" Donald stares down at the shorter man.

"Malfunction," Elmer says confidently.

"Damn!" Holland scratches his head.

It is the ground ladders that receive the most use from a truck company. The first due truck ladders the front of a structure, and the second assigned truck takes the rear, invariably using it's ground ladders. Paul Gulfee is concerned about the rotating closures. The significant gaps left in the districts leaves 105 second due on the first alarm to locations the truck would usually be called for a second or third alarm.

On the first night of the four day trick, Paul studies the list of rotating closures handed down from the brain trust at Lafayette Park. Walking stridently from his second floor office, the lieutenant wraps an arm and leg around the nearest pole and slides quickly to the apparatus floor. At the watch desk cubicle he tapes the list of closures to the center of one Plexiglas wall. "Look at that," he waves a hand at the list.

Leaning over the desk, March, Burger and Hagan study the companies listed as being out-of-service for the night. "Sonofa . . ." Hagan shakes his head in surprise and disgust, "they put 15 outta service?" He glances from the list to Gulfee. "It's not like it isn't a busy company or something," his voice dripping sarcasm.

"Uh huh," Paul nods, "so now we're coverin' their area west of Brooklyn Street and all of the north." The absence of truck-15—creates a wide corridor for which Truck 105 will be responsible as the second due truck. "Frankly," the lieutenant remarks bitterly, "I just don't understand those people."

"Just have to roll faster," March shrugs and sits back in the desk chair.

"We still got to cover all that ground," Hagan complains, waving outside the firehouse, "God help us if we catch a crapper anywhere north of the City thoroughfare." The mention of the area draws nods, a slice of heaven, home to welfare families packed into subsidized housing; two families sharing a two bedroom apartment that most folks might confuse for a large closet, and addicts whose minds have long since fired their last synapse.

"At least they only shut down the truck company outta the battalion," Gulfee notes soberly.

"Uh . . . I notice there aren't any shut down near City Hall," March comments wryly. The observation further kindles Gulfee's anger.

"And you can bet your butt there aren't any closures around neighborhoods with City Council members in them either," he snorts. "Miss Coronada," Gulfee spits out the first name coming to mind, an outspoken supporter of 'Chip' Sprague openly calling for more police cars in the streets than fire department vehicles. "Might support a lower fire department budget, but you better keep two companies in service around the neighborhood she represents." Paul's anger energizes him and he paces outside the watch desk cubicle.

Jerry glances at the clock. "I thought we were getting a twenty-four hour notice on closures?"

"Kemp had the list in his office," Gulfee explains, "and I just saw it a minute ago."

"Hell," March laughs, hands behind his head, "I'm glad Engine 50 wasn't on the list . . . we'd been sittin' here all night wonderin' why we didn't catch a run not knowing we were out of service."

Gulfee's concerns manifest themselves shortly before midnight. The fire is in an occupied dwelling, a full assignment is dispatched but Truck 105, as the duly assigned second truck, has a much further distance to travel. Holland, behind the wheel, is cursing from the moment the truck hits Fort Avenue, wanting to beat the first truck to the scene. Beside him, slumped in his seat, Gulfee wears an expression telling the world "I knew this was going to happen . . ."

The truck approaches the fire from the rear coming down Kelly Street and seeing the flat roof of the row house in the glow of the flames boiling out its front windows to expand back over the top. From the rear windows a viscous billowing smoke is pushing out rapidly as if being propelled. Holland brings the long truck against the curb at the entrance to the alley that runs along the rear of the dwelling.

Greenie and Bridges have a ladder pulled, stumbling through the darkness to the backyard of the house. The alley is strewn with debris, old furniture, overturned garbage cans and even some unmentionable items. Maneuvering through this maze of man-made filth and debris they find the gate to the backyard and enter quickly. A small awning projects out from the back of the house, partially obscured through the free-flowing smoke. The two men throw their ladder to the awning.

Gulfee and Hagan follow right behind Greenie and Tim carrying a second ladder. Mark climbs over a discarded sofa in the alley and guides the ladder into the backyard where he pauses a moment to pull his protective hood over his head. In that interval Gulfee tries to place the ladder closer to the house. There is a sudden sizzling, popping sound followed by an explosion of blue white light and the sharp odor of ozone. Against the dark sky, made darker by the volume of smoke, nobody sees the electrical wires strung from the utility pole in the alley and coming into the back yard. The ladder Paul is handling bounces into the power line.

The lieutenant grunts loudly and his body is hurled against the chain link fence along one side of the yard. His helmet tumbles to the ground and for several seconds the officer sits sprawled, without moving, against the base of the fence.

"Wow!" Mark is the first to react. "You okay, Loo." He bends over the semi-stupendous lieutenant who is just beginning to open his eyes. Paul squints at Hagan with a ' . . . who are you?' look as Bridges and Greenstreet rush to their officer's side, their arms digging under Paul's.

"You okay, Loo?' Greenie asks a second time. Gulfee yanked his arms from the grasp of the two men trying to assist him, nods his head and reaches for his helmet.

"Damn!" he shakes his head, "that was a wild ride!" Looking at the men clustered around him he grins sheepishly. "I feel great!" a wild unsettled look in his eyes.

Tim turns from the officer and begins ascending the ladder. In the swirling smoke ahead, he sees a woman leaning from a rear window on the right. In her arms she carries a large bundle of cloth. *What is she doing? Trying to save bed linens?* The thought rockets through Tim's mind. It is more than bed linens.

Lost in a swirl of dark smoke, the woman makes a loud squeaking sound and drops the armful of linens from the window. Bridges glances down to check his footing and makes a leaning stretch to his right, attempting to intercept the drop.

"Hey!" he yells at the woman momentarily framed in the smoke, the whites of her eyes bulging wildly. She looks right through Tim as the bundle of cloth in which she has wrapped her infant son sails inches from Bridges fingertips. Tim shouts in a combination of anger and sheer frustration. *You dumb bitch!* he is raging at her in his head. *I was right here damn you!!*

The thick wet sound of impact is heard as the bed linens and infant strike the ground. Grass, soil, anything associated with a 'yard' is an alien concept in this 'hood.' A 'backyard' consists of a ten by ten square of poured cement surrounded by a five foot high chain link fence demarking the boundaries of one yard from another. Although he is perhaps eighteen feet above the ground, Tim can glance down and see the expanding halo of dark blood against the lighter background of cement. When he turns back to the window, the woman has disappeared into the depths of the house. Hagan is up the ladder now, handing tools to Tim and together, both men enter the second floor.

In the alley, an engine company has arrived and a line is stretched into the backyard. Gulfee has been shouting for a paramedic the moment he sees the infant take a header out the window. Despite the lump of unmoving linen on the ground, the men of the engine company manage to drag their hose right across the little boy's body and it is Paul Gulfee who kneels to lift the charged line and remove the dead infant from further abuse.

Tim is first in the window, dropping to his stomach and feeling the floor in front of him. Hagan enters the room, smoke and heat oppressive enough to drive both men into the prone position. Bridges, in the lead, breaststrokes his way through an opening he assumes is a doorway. Each sweeping movement brings him into contact with empty plastic bottles, garbage bags filled with refuse and whatever other debris has been strewn across the floor. There is no vision, both Tim and Mark move by sense of feel and are easily swallowed up into the inky, black toxic soup flowing so heavily around them. Sounds filter through the smoke. The wheezing, creaking groan of the fire 'talking' to them, beckoning them, waiting for them like some predator waits on it's unsuspecting prey.

Hagan moves faster than Tim, pushing up against him as they move along a narrow hallway, splayed arms brushing perpendicular walls, breathing and gritting their teeth against the heat; always that heat that just builds and presses them flat. You move a few feet and swear you can't go further, but you don't stop because you can never stop when you do this. There is no backing out, because you've silently committed yourself to go after that hysterical mother who in desperation dropped her kid to it's death and you know will die too if someone doesn't get to her.

Damn! Tim is wincing. The protective hood he wears really works, but gives a false sense of security. There is a reason the body feels pain; *it's a warning you're in danger!!* But the hood, that piece of cloth that makes you look like a knight in chain mail, lures you deeper into the fire because it shields you from the intensity of the heat.

"You got anything?" Mark is yelling, his voice sounds miles away.

"Nothin'!" Tim grits his teeth and replies as loudly. He slides forward another few feet and both feel a knife rip their gut when a sharp, crackling, tearing noise is followed by a dull roar and smoke suddenly whips around them and the floor becomes visible. Smoke lifts slightly. It's actually possible to see around them for a few feet but then comes that sound, those words that kick every fireman on earth into a sort of overdrive.

"Firefighter down!"

The RIT goes into high gear, it's the reason for their presence here; a mad scramble up the ladder at the front, two guys with the RIT bag, a large tank of breathing air attached to an extra-long breathing circuit and mask. Two hundred feet of rope and a set of tools rescuing the rescuers. Every 'tactical box' is assigned a fifth engine company, usually one of the division's Squad Engines, serving as the Rapid Intervention Team. Two men with a RIT bag take the front of a fire and another duo covers the rear.

Steve Piscatelli from Truck 11 is down, coming through the roof. Tim knows Piscatelli, not personally, but from union meetings and parties, but, maybe more importantly, Steve's brother, Santos, works White Shift on Engine 50. While working above the fire Steve finds his footing becoming sloppy and before he can move away the roof caves. A shower of sparks and orange-tinged smoke belch upward through the hole and that instant ventilation causes the smoke inside the dwelling to lift.

Tim and Mark move faster, forgetting everything and everyone else, you got a brother down. As Tim gets into a front room he can see the sharp beams of Garrity lights on the helmets of guys coming through the front windows. There are shouts, "Steve, hey, Steve!" The windows themselves are backlit from all the apparatus in the street and huge silhouettes loom in that back light; a guy from an engine company and another one working the RIT, then the glass shatters.

Wooden beams and plaster board hang at odd angles in the room, an eerie light filters around grotesque shadows and, despite the shouting and noise, Tim can hear groaning, Piscatelli groaning somewhere to his right. An instant later, Piscatelli's PASS goes off, his personal safety signal, an electronic warning device worn by every fireman. It activates automatically if it's bearer remains motionless for thirty seconds. The screech from Piscatelli's PASS is incredibly grating, an ear piercing shriek, pinpointing the fallen man's exact location.

"I got him!" Bridges makes contact with the bulky body of the other truckie and a split second later Hagan joins him, both of them lifting debris and trash from Piscatelli. A Big Ed light shines in the fallen man's face. His eyes are wide with fear wanting to get the hell out of that smoky, broken hole.

"Be cool, Bud," Bridges repeats over and over, an attempt to calm the other man, to keep him from instinctively lurching for safety and further injuring himself.

"We got you, Steve," Mark's voice has that goofy, muffled sound behind the air mask. More gloved hands and arms of turnout coats appear; the RIT bag is there.

"We got him," a helmet with 'S40' on it's front piece says.

With Piscatelli in good hands, Tim and Mark back from the room. Smoke is rising, visibility is better and the two men are able to maneuver more freely. Both firemen know that somewhere in this house should be a very large woman, but neither Mark nor Tim can figure where. The second floor is a shamble. Blackened and crisped walls, charcoaled furniture and unidentified objects are agglutinated by the heat until it is impossible to guess what it might have been.

Mike Greenstreet, in the rear bedroom where Tim and Mark entered, uses a ceiling hook to pull down huge chunks of wallboard overhead. A strong thrust upward lets the curved hook catch and then a heave downward is accompanied by falling debris leaving the fat man's helmet and turnout coat covered in white, chalky material looking like moon dust. He is overhauling' that strenuous and exhausting job of tearing out the interior of the roof to check for any extension of the fire, to reveal potential burning embers and 'open up' walls and ceiling. By the time he is done, Greenie will resemble a grimy Pillsbury Doughboy and he will have shredded walls and ceiling in order that one of the engine men on the pipe can open up and 'wash down' everything until it looks like sooty gruel.

"What the hell happened to that woman who dropped the baby off the roof?" Donald Holland is standing in the street beside the truck, pulling off his breathing apparatus. He glances over at Hagan, standing nearby, bent at the waist and breathing hard.

"I don't know," Mark's coat is open, his shirt is soaked and stuck to his blue tee-shirt which, in turn has become his second skin. "I was inside with Tim," he jerks his head in the direction of the house. "We saw her in the smoke and then she just disappears."

"Nobody found her?" Holland shakes his head. "That's weird."

Paul Gulfee is talking to a paramedic, hands moving rapidly in the air as he describes the woman's actions and the descent of the child onto the cement pavement below. "Straight on it's head," Paul ends his gestures with a fist driven into the palm of his hand. "And then a couple of our geniuses bring in a line and run it right over the kid," he screws up his handsome face. "Geez, it's head. It was bad enough the kid is dropped and dies like that, but when we got guys who don't even stop to check and see what they're running over!"

Charred furniture, bedding and debris is tossed out the second floor windows, crashing to the ground and splintering. Thin eddies of wispy smoke drift lazily from blackened openings that had once been windows. Beams of light move across the darkness as firemen go room to room opening walls, sifting through the aftermath of the fire.

"How'd Piscatelli make out?" Bridges asks Greenie. The two of them work the same room, stripping it completely with the detached professionalism of a surgeon slicing a dinner roast.

"He got banged up," Greenstreet brays loudly. Even if it were possible for the man to speak in a whisper he wouldn't. The only question is who *doesn't* hear him. "I was talking to Marty Sledgeski on the Squad. He says Steve hurt his pelvis bad, the way he came down."

Tim shakes his head and warily eyes the ceiling above.

"Paramedics took him to University," Mike continues his work. "He's a good truck man, a hard worker." There is a pause. "What happened to that woman who threw her kid out the window?"

"Don't know."

"What the hell?" Greenie pauses to look over at Tim.

"Hey," Bridges shrugs, "me and Hagan were comin' in after her and then Piscatelli drops in from the roof." The short explanation satisfies Greenie. He wonders if he will need two stickers for the windshield of the tiller cab or only one.

Mike Greenstreet's body mass fills the interior of the tiller's cab as he labors diligently to precisely align a pair of skull and crossbones sticker's inside the lower left-hand corner of the cab's front window.

Mark Hagan stands on the apparatus floor, hands in pockets, looking up at Greenie's decals. "Two?" Mark asks. There is a short horizontal line of identical stickers already in place along the window.

"Yeah," he mumbles. The confines of the cab tax Mike's range of motion. When he emerges, he glances at Hagan. "The woman who dropped her kid from the window at the fire last night? Well, Dean

Bruschi on Truck 3 told me she was found dead on the first floor. Smoke inhalation must have got her. She was running from the window and fell down the stairs in all the confusion . . . not bein' able to see through the smoke."

Hagan purses his lips. "Maybe," he suggests, "she dropped the kid and was runnin' to catch him before he hit the ground." A moment passes while Greenie actually considers the possibility. A deep rumbling laugh erupts from him and his face reddens.

"Oh hell," he says with a wave of his hand. "Maybe it's just poetic justice after sendin' that poor kid down the way she did."

Mark watches intently as Greenie makes his way down the side of the truck, always intrigued how he can be so limber. "Me and Tim were all over the second floor," he gives a shrug and the two men saunter back into the firehouse lounge.

They pass the spiral staircase and through the open doorway just behind it. The room is a product of the firefighters' own labor, decorated and furnished at their own expense over a period of time. In addition to the sofas facing each other along opposite walls, two overstuffed arm chairs sit at the near end of the room facing the big screen television at the other end. Carpeting in a nauseating shade of mustard brown covers all but the outer inch of the cement floor and is thinned and worn from years of tramping and stomping. It's walls are paneled three quarters of the way up, the remaining space is painted a light green, a color that was on sale and too good to pass up. A row of fluorescent lighting goes down the center of the ceiling. Two floor lamps bracket each sofa and a single large, heavy coffee table sits in the middle of the room, and, at the end nearest the kitchen doorway another oval table has two more upright chairs. The room is littered with dog eared magazines, mostly automotive, racing, hunting and fishing periodicals and a few day old newspapers folded and discarded.

At the front of the room, the television is on, playing some wildlife program dealing with the way animals treat their young. Donald is sprawled in one of the armchairs, a newspaper crumpled in his lap, glasses at the tip of his nose.

Holland complains that "the damned animals are more protective of their young than some of the potheads around here." He is disgusted and waves a hand in the direction of the television. It isn't quite five thirty and Donald's shirt is already unbuttoned and he is shoeless.

"You are far too critical," Rich Simms accuses straight-faced. The big man, hands behind his head, is watching the TV, lying on his back on one of the sofas. He looks like a huge bear, overwhelming the furniture. "Poverty is the problem Donald . . . poverty."

Holland lifts himself slightly to better see the TV. "Look at the animals, Rich, I'm not real sure but I'll bet none of them get welfare checks or has a bank account but they sure don't give up on their young."

"I've always admired your tolerance and understanding," Simms laughs.

"Anybody stop by to see Piscatelli?" Hagan asks in a loud voice. The question brings a moment of silence.

"I stopped by on the way to work," Donald answers, shaking his head. "The guy has a cracked pelvis and femur. He's gonna' be out for a while." It is a sobering thought . . . *serious* injury . . . is simply part of the job. Every man in the room knows other firemen who've been badly hurt or worse . . . You don't dwell on it, it is a fact of life and there isn't a need to dwell on accepted facts unless you are one of the gloom and doom people. As the adage observes so eloquently: Shit Happens.

"We're taking up a collection for Steve's wife and kids," Mark informs them. "I think I heard a union rep say the family will need about twenty-five hundred a month to help out and both the officers local and the firefighters local have a goal of giving them a two to three month buffer."

"Good move," Greenstreet says. There is, perhaps, no closer, more tightly knit group of people than those in the city's two largest agencies, the firefighter and police officers. Although each group is quick to accuse the other of having less important jobs, no other agencies in any city have ever been conferred with the titles 'Bravest and Finest'.

On the wall by the doorway is an intercom and it *bleeps* twice. "Where's Tomcat detailed tonight?" Jerry March inquires from the watch desk.

"Engine Seven," Simms answers loudly from his prostrate position on the couch.

"Gotcha," the intercom switches off.

"What's for dinner?" Ken Shaw enters the lounge and spies Greenie moving in the small kitchen on the left.

"Cornish game hen," Greenie replies, pots and pans banging. He yanks open the door of the refrigerator and pulls out the game hens, dropping them into two large metal pans, forming equal rows, and begins liberally basting them with marinade. "Somebody going to set the table?"

"Isn't that Tomcat's job?" Holland calls back lazily.

Greenstreet laughs sarcastically, "Howdy-Dowdy still doesn't know where the plates and cups are." He opens the door of an overhead cabinet, one labeled: 'Nasty Happens' underneath which someone has scrawled in black magic marker: 'When Greenie Cooks'. Scanning the contents of the cabinet, Mike slams the door and reopens the refrigerator, wiping his hands as he examines the stocked shelves.

"What's the cost for dinner?" Barry Kramer wanders into the room and asks the question innocently. Immediately, heads turn in his direction.

"Huh?" Greenie is caught off guard. Barry-Fred's 'tab' on firehouse expenses rivals the national debt of some of the smaller Third-World countries. "You gonna' *pay* for a meal?" Mike examines Kramer with a suspicious look, like the Fred Flintstone-twin is a pod creature.

"Yeah." Barry nods, a wounded expression on his face, as if the concept was not a wildly abstract flight of fantasy.

"Ha!" Greenie mutters loudly . . . everything audible from Mike is loud. "Hey," he shouts into the lounge, "somebody call Jerry at the watch desk and ask him to bring the digital camera back here." The request brings a flush to Barry-Fred's face. "I want a photo record of this event."

At the watch desk, Pump Operator March is engrossed in a highly sensitive electronic project, one that includes Bill Burger. "I think it'll be a hoot." Jerry says, examining the schematic diagram he's just completed.

"What did Dan say?" Bill peers over March's shoulder and agrees the plan is workable.

"I asked him and he didn't say no," Jerry admits.

"But what *did* he say?"

"That I was crazy," Jerry giggles, "but you know Dan Dan the Idea Man! I figured it was just his lovable way to say he liked it." Both men pause as the radio comes to life for a full two minutes of communication between units in the street. They have been working on the diagram during a constant blizzard of calls and dispatches serving as an echo of background noise.

The plan, as conceived by March, is to integrate a personalized sound system, one of his own making, into the electrical system of the engine's siren. Across the top of the engine's cab, the apparatus emergency lights and siren are contained in a long cylindrical bar, or tube. Both siren and lights are powered electrically from the fuse box under the front console and Jerry's design incorporates a bit of extra wiring and the subtle placement of a miniature digital player under the console. The project poses no great challenge and, besides, Burger is a whiz with all that electrical stuff and what Bill didn't know, his brother-in-law over at Engine 3 does.

"So you got the hardware?" Bill finally asks when the radio falls silent. He continues to study March's hand-drawn schematic. "Bought it all at Radio Shack," Jerry nods. The intercom interrupts him.

"Jerry," it is Hagan. Greenie wants the digital camera back here . . . Fred wants to pay for the meal tonight."

"No stuff?" March replies. "I'll be right back."

"Stretch your neck," Hagan is posing Fred Flintstone.

"Go to hell," Barry growls at the younger man behind the camera. In one hand Kramer holds a handful of bills as Greenstreet reaches for them. There is a flash of light and Mike grabs the money on the chance that Barry-Fred might have second thoughts.

"Now if I can get Loughlin to pay his tab," Greenie comments, folding the wad of money and tucking it into a pants pocket.

"Forget it," Ken Shaw laughs.

"Anybody check the list to see who's closed tonight?" Donald Holland calls loudly from his armchair. He now has a leg draped over one of the arms, wiggling his toes in his sock.

"Truck 20 . . . Engine 45," Shaw reports. "Doesn't really affect anybody here unless somebody pulls a deuce." The tall balding man pours orange soda into an ice filled mug and watches the fizz.

"Yeah . . ." Rich Simms lifts his head, twisting and looking at Shaw, "only problem is that 20 Truck is in Calvin's battalion so you *know* you're gonna at least have a second alarm in there somewhere," he pauses at the chorus of agreements, "and 45 Engine is in the adjacent battalion. Either side, engine or truck . . . we get stuck." The rhyme and implication makes the man giggle. "I like that," he compliments himself.

Donald has other concerns. He slumps in the armchair, "I think we need one of them GPS systems installed in the wagon, y' know?" He is disgusted. "I was just figuring we'll end up covering for anything on the back end of the Fifth Battalion with 20 Truck out and then you figure we gotta be runnin' to cover for everybody else who's running to cover for 20!" The EVD shakes his head and shoves his glasses back up the bridge of his nose. "Anybody got one of the little ADC maps of the city?" he asks sarcastically. "I need to start memorizing street names and directions all over again."

The men begin drifting into the kitchen when Greenstreet announces dinner is ready. Tom Loughlin's arrival causes March to call to the chief.

"Hey chief, is the arson task force still lookin' for that possible torch?"

Tom Loughlin scowls and shrugs noncommittally. "Somebody's lighting off stuff," the chief allows, "but nobody thinks it's a pro. We're finding lots of little things but no real pattern." He slides into a seat at the end of one of the long tables and glances at the board to check the meal's cost. "Nice meal for the price," he observes. Glances are quickly exchanged around the tables with smirks and nervous coughs.

"I hear the city is buyin' some more apparatus," Greenstreet starts in. He holds a pair of large tongs, using them to transfer a crisped, browned Cornish hen to each man's plate. "A little birdy told me the city's buyin' six new trucks and eight new engines. True?" He doesn't look at Loughlin.

"A birdy?" Gulfee grins.

"Mike's been talkin' to himself again," Hagan says, piling a mountain of rice pilaf on his plate. "It's the littlest birdy he knows."

"From what I understand," Loughlin answers, "there's a request for bids." The topic of new equipment is keen in every firehouse. The mere mention of the sighting of a different model or mention of new apparatus sets off a firestorm of rumor and investigation, men hunting down other men who might be better informed to confirm or deny new acquisitions. "There's two rear mounts being rotated through the city now," the chief continues. "Lafayette Park wants to get feedback on how they operate."

"All the new ones going to be rear mounts?" Greenstreet asks quickly, he has a vested interest in the models involved.

"All but one," Loughlin concedes. The issue involves more than just the design of the apparatus, a rear mounted truck requires only one EVD; that translates to a loss of four EVD's per truck company since no tillers are needed. That becomes, then, a union issue regarding labor, job titles and a host of other incidentals beyond a shiny new fire truck.

"I'm gonna be unemployed," Mike groans, finished serving the hens.

"You get no sympathy from me," Jerry mumbles around a mouthful of chicken. "Join the club."

"I'm a craftsman, an artisan, with what I do," Mike continues, squeezing into a chair at the table.

"You're fat!" Dan Kemp growls from the other end.

"Yeah, but you're ugly, Cap," Greenstreet retorts, face red with delight. "An I can always lose weight."

"Oh man," Jerry laughs out loud, "that was a dagger to the heart."

"Hey Mike," Dan is smiling at the fat man, "I'll admit it, there *is* one thing you can do that I can't."

For an instant there is an electric tension that freezes time.

Clang, clang, clang, clang; the triple gong goes off, the warbling alarm tone lost under the very loud and distinct voice from the radio: *Dwelling fire, Eighteen-nineteen Glenetta Street . . ."* echoing thunderously through the apparatus floor and simultaneously, the speaker in the lounge.

"Sonofa . . . ," Greenstreet's head drops, thinking of the dozen hens he has meticulously prepared. Chairs scrape on the floor, bodies disappear through the doorway and by the time Greenie lumbers toward the rear of the truck, March has the motor of Engine 50 rumbling.

Doors slam as Mike trundles up the small step ladder to the tiller cab. "Damn fire department," he mumbles angrily.

It's the front of one of those big row homes on Glenetta Street that is 'off and rolling.' A once solidly upper-middle class neighborhood has undergone radical changes in the last twenty years. Each of the houses along the street is huge, three floors with wide deep, stone porches and plenty of interior space to pack in three and four families, an accepted rite in this neighborhood. Pool the money for a down payment, list the home under one name and within a week of settlement every member of the extended family from great-grandma Smith and her sister Thelma to the father of Tarita's second child, Jerome, whose cousin Fariq and his pregnant girlfriend Michelle have been needing a place to stay . . . have moved in, human parallel to the proverbial can of sardines.

Orange flames roll dramatically from two front windows on the second floor of the house near the end of the block. Deep, black scorch marks surround each window and heavy, dark, smoke is pumping rapidly from them and puffing from under the eaves running the entire width of the home. The evening's entertainment firmly established, a large group of emotionally charged spectators gather a safe distance from the fire to watch the proceedings.

Glenetta Street sits at the outermost limit of the companies' first alarm district. The run is a long one, time consuming even at night with relatively little traffic. The importance, however, is the location and assignments of companies to the fire making Truck 105 the 'second due' truck company, taking the rear of the fire scene.

Hagan and Simms work the back of the house where, unlike the cramped enclosure of the previous night, the backyard is wide and spacious. Grass and other organic material is still found in vacant spots. Everything remains cement in these yards, although painted the right color green, the surroundings would look quite nice.

"No wires?" Gulfee shouts good-naturedly. There is no smoke or fire facing the men in the rear and Paul glances around briefly to ensure there isn't going to be a repeat of his shock of the previous night. Because they are coming in from the rear, Gulfee's first responsibility is to make sure all power, electrical, gas, and/or everything else is shut off. Hagan riding 'right step' is still first up the ladder to the second floor windows. Beneath Mark, kneeling on the ground to 'mask-up,' Rich Simms will follow. The two men will ventilate the windows and enter.

To Hagan's left, a wide, peaked roof shelters a back porch on this house. Mark reaches the second story window, halligan in hand. Glass shatters in one window and within seconds the entire frame is yanked apart, fluttering to the ground. Almost immediately smoke begins bleeding from inside.

The work is swift and sure, the footing on the porch roof is firm and movement is easy. "Take the other window," Hagan calls to Simms, who moves past him toward the farthest window. Smoke blowing from the gaping hole in the outside wall is thicker now. Engine companies at the front of the dwelling are pushing the fire back into the house. "Where's the engine covering our rear?" Hagan shouts down to Gulfee.

"Who knows?" the lieutenant responds as loudly. "Holland was flying here like a bat outta hell so I'm not surprised we beat anybody else here." The engine assigned as the third on this fire is responsible for the rear exposure and is only just making the turn at the corner to lead-off. Mark is momentarily reluctant to enter until he is sure there will be a man on the pipe to support him.

"I got a hell of a lot of smoke blowin' out here now," Hagan shouts down, bending over as he prepares to enter the window. "I think they're pushin' this stuff in from the front." In the split second Mark swings a leg over the bottom of the hole in the wall, his attention is arrested by a sudden movement from Simms.

Rich opens the far window, forced to stand at an odd angle attempting to maintain balance. Using his halligan to tear away the framing, Rich yanks on the bar and transfers his center of gravity. The shift in weight is enough to cause his loss of balance and in that instant he has fallen onto the cement 'yard' below.

"Somebody check on Rich!" Hagan shouts, removing his leg from the window and shuffling to the edge of the overhang to peer below. "He okay?"

Gulfee and Greenstreet kneel on either side of Simms; Paul speaking rapidly into his radio. "Get inside," he finally yells up to Mark. "Greenie will be with you." The lieutenant glances at Mike, "Go on in Mikey," he says. "I'll stay with Rich."

Responding to Gulfee's call, two paramedics hustle into the yard with a stretcher, followed by a cluster of firemen. Among the sudden onslaught of personnel is the engine company covering the back of the fire. Despite the size of this house, the yard suddenly becomes very cramped; the prone firefighter, Simms, his officer, the paramedics and stretcher and the crew from the engine company vying for position and still keep out of each other's way.

"How you feelin'?" Gulfee is speaking loudly to Rich Simms.

"I feel dead," he moans and inhales sharply as a paramedic probes his body. "We gotta' get him on a stretcher," the second medic remarks. He looks at Simm's bulk and his eyebrows arch. "Is this guy normal or is he some kind of freak of nature?"

"He's a normal freak of nature," Gulfee explains. "We're gonna need some extra hands."

"How 'bout a crane?" the first medic suggests.

One of the medics nods, "He's going to be okay as far as I can tell. We'll put him on a headboard and keep his neck immobilized. His vitals are good and his neurologicals are good." The small group parts briefly as a third paramedic approaches with a long, solid headboard used to transport all potential head and neck injuries.

"We got a second ambulance pulling around back," the third paramedic informs everyone.

"Can you feel your feet, Rich?" Gulfee squats beside the fallen man's head.

"Yeah," Simms grimaces. Hands support his head as his helmet is removed and strips of tape are wound over his forehead securing head and spine in alignment. Rich is breathing loudly through his mouth, most of his features obscured by heavy foam blocks on either side of his face. Around them, more firemen are moving into the yard. A second hose line runs up the ladder and into the house.

"Hey Loo," Simms mumbles.

"Yeah?" Gulfee cocks his head and brings his ear to Rich's mouth.

"Can you get me outta' here before Hagan and Greenie start overhaulin' and throwin' things out on top of me?" Paul grins and looks at the paramedics.

"Yeah, man," he pats the big man's arm, "we'll get ya outta' here."

At the firehouse, two hours later, it is learned that Richard is not the only casualty sustained at the fire.

"Barry got it too," Dan Kemp tells the members of the truck company. He is drying his hands on a paper towel from the big sink at the very rear of the apparatus floor. Donald Holland and Greenstreet still wear their turnout pants, the heavy bunkers, suspenders hanging at their sides. Gulfee and Hagan exchange glances.

"So what happened to Barry-Fred?" Paul waits until Kemp executes a clumsy hook shot into the waste can.

"He got burned," the captain shakes his head. "We're advancing the line up into one of those big front windows on the second floor and Barry goes through the window . . . he starts screaming and grabbin' himself. He's bailin' outta there and I told him to check with the paramedics and then with Loughlin."

"Sounds like the department is taking a real hit these last two nights." Paul shakes is head.

"Sounds like Rich got it a little worse than Fred," Dan remarks. "They took Kramer to University in the back of the ambulance, but at least he wasn't on a damned backboard." There's an unsettled tension among the group, injuries are commonplace in the department but not in this firehouse. "At least Barry'll report back here, I don't think Rich'll be discharged, do you?"

"I'll check with Shaw," the lieutenant says as the group begins to disperse. An injured firefighter taken to University Hospital is treated and the fire department surgeon is notified as well as the department Safety Officer assigned to the division that shift. In turn the chief in whose battalion the injury occurred is notified and the information is passed down the chain. If the injured member is to be discharged and returned to duty, there's about three pounds of paperwork to be completed. If the injured firefighter is kept overnight and then released, add two more pounds to the bureaucratic load. Bring a wheelbarrow for the required paperwork should that injured firefighter remain in the hospital, wheel the papers to the red car and dump them in. Ironically, the least amount of paper is needed if the member dies. There is no trade-off though, the minute amount of paperwork never offsets the heart-breaking burden that is carried a lifetime by the surviving brotherhood.

"You got the shift covered?" Kemp asks the truck's lieutenant. It is a question between friends. Kemp has no actual authority over the truck company despite being the 'house captain'. Truck 105 is an entirely separate entity with it's own command structure.

"It'll be fine Dan," Gulfee replies wearily. "The worst thing to happen would be for Bridges and Sam to work together." He laughs wickedly at the thought. "But it would be kinda' fun, huh?"

There is no actual enmity between Sam and Tim, if you discount the usual suspicion, protection and veiled malice a loving father directs toward any male showing interest in his daughter, much less date the girl. Tim and Leeann are consenting adults, their decisions are their own to make. Of course, you have to factor in Bill Burger and Jerry who, in the very special case of the Bridges/Killen relationship have their own *raison d'etre.*

With Rich Simms hospitalized, there will be a good chance that Sam Killen and his daughter's steady boyfriend will be sharing seats in the truck's cab. Paul Gulfee has reason to smile wickedly as he considers the roster.

Cold dinner has to be scraped and cleaned from the dishes. Fortunately, a Cornish hen can be eaten cold as well as hot; only bones and gristle remain when the men finish eating.

"I shoulda' known something was gonna happen to Kramer," Greenstreet complains.

"How so?" Nick Miller fits plates in to the dishwasher. "How could you have known?"

"He paid for tonight's meal, Mike replies, "it was a sure sign."

"You got proof he paid?"

"A photo," Greenie nods.

Burger's voice breaks in over the intercom, "Hey, Kramer's back from University." The announcement brings men trooping to the watch desk.

Barry-Fred is in uniform, his turnout gear is being brought to the firehouse by a union representative. He winces in pain and moves stiffly around to each man, shaking hands and accepting their condolences at his injury. "I got two weeks medical leave," his voice is softened but still gruff, "and then I got vacation time already in."

"You timed it perfectly, Barry," March congratulates the injured man. "I'm not sure how you planned everything so well . . . I mean, just perfect. The important thing is it worked out."

"Yeah," Barry-Fred smiles weakly. "But I got something else I wanted to show you," Kramer reaches into a back pocket and withdraws three sheets of folded paper, holding them out to March. "I asked the emergency room people if I could have a copy of these," he explains.

"What is it?" Jerry accepts the papers, unfolds them and begins reading. In the interim Barry-Fred grins expectantly, looking from one man to another. "Oh for cryin' out loud," Jerry bellows, rattling the papers and shaking his head. He rolls his eyes and looks around at the other men. "You wont believe this," the papers rattle again.

"He got some award?" Miller asks.

"No," Jerry grimaces and looks once again at the papers. "This is the hospital release for Barry, the one he takes down to the department infirmary, okay?" He pauses, "So you wanna know where Kramer got injured?" Jerry pauses for effect and gives Barry that' . . . you are so pathetic look.'

"Barry got a second degree burn on his . . . *neck*," he finishes dramatically. "The nut actually came back here to prove he has a . . . neck!" Heads turn in Barry's direction and he blushes.

"I told you guys I had a neck," he wags a finger at the group and then points to the hospital report in Jerry's hands. "And that report proves it, okay? It's medical proof I got a neck . . . so no more talk around here about me not havin' a neck!"

Satisfied that medical science has vindicated his anatomical structure and averted further debate, Kramer slowly makes his way out of the firehouse where a car waits to take him home. Jerry and Burger stand at the watch desk, remaining silent until Barry is outside.

"Do you believe that?" March is grinning.

"I still don't believe he has a neck," Burger confesses. "I think we ought to start a rumor he paid off the doctor to write that." Around them the other firefighters are drifting to the lounge or the stairway to the bunkroom. "Yeah," March agrees with Bill's plan, "but for now I gotta' wonder who's gonna be detailed to the truck for Big Rich . . . and who we gonna get for Kramer." The two of them saunter toward the back, both men staring at the floor.

"You think they'll detail somebody here?" Bill wonders aloud.

"Who knows," Jerry replies as they reach the door to the lounge. "In the old days, we'd have enough guys to cover, but now . . ." he shakes his head, "with this clown running the city and the rotating closures . . . who knows what they will do."

CHAPTER 8

"Details, Fill-ins and Bare Spots"

Detailed firefighters are rare at the Fort Avenue firehouse. Vacations, scheduled days off and, as in the case of Kramer and Simms, illness and injury create temporary vacancies during a given shift which must be filled. When required manpower is not available from within the company itself, personnel from outside the company, sometimes outside the battalion are 'detailed' to bring the working shift up to the full complement of five. The trick, however, is to maintain the efficiency of the company receiving the detail.

Identifying a detailed firefighter can be relatively easy. The numbers on the helmet conflicts with those of the other men and, in the 'hood,' you simply look for the guy wearing clean turnout gear, the shiny black helmet, yellow reflective panels still crisp and bright, and both coat and bunker pants with that deep crisp onyx color. Compare that with those battered, grimy helmets around him with front pieces barely legible and turnout gear with that 'salty' look, faded, black streaked and spotted with grayish ash. Sometimes when you check the apparatus you find the gear of the detailed guy looking so clean and pressed that water beads on it. It can be embarrassing.

Someone from outside the battalion or its immediately adjacent districts, and most assuredly anyone from a company near the suburbs, detailed to Fort Avenue firehouse is considered from 'way out the road.' A certain amount of in-service is required to prepare this novice for immediate integration into one of the companies, engine or truck.

Traditionally, the first topic covered with a 'strange guy' is paperwork, the outhouse variety.

Along the rear wall of the apparatus floor is a single bathroom, and inside the door, placed at eye level when seated, is a sign in bold letters reminding the occupant to: **"TAKE CARE OF YOUR PAPER WORK FIRST!"** You go to the bathroom and before anything else, strip off about twenty sheets of toilet paper, folding them in one hand. Now you are ready for 'business'. Keep in mind, however, when that gong hits you do not take time to follow the Good Housekeeping Guidelines. You just close up shop, ram that pre-folded paper into your underwear and run for the wagon because they aren't waiting for *anybody.*

Details to Engine 50 always ride in the lead-off seat. Jerry March is never thrilled having a 'newbie' lead-off but then, anybody is better than Kramer so just make the correction and the rest will follow naturally. On Truck 105 the detailed man gets the 'right step' because the first ladder will be thrown by the 'left step and the detailed newbie grabs the tools and follows the officer.

Benjamin Henry is detailed to Engine 50 because Barry-Fred gets a doctor to officially state Barry actually has a neck and that neck was burned. Ben is an affable firefighter, probably a very proficient member of his own company, Engine 21, out in Glendyl. Glendyl is an upper-middle class community where grass actually grows in *front* yards as well as back, and not in the cracks of sidewalks. If trash is not picked up by mid-morning on Mondays and Thursdays then, by God, somebody downtown will get a *real* angry phone call.

Henry's company totaled a little less than one thousand runs last year, between two and three a day on average, and now he's been detailed to 50. A company more than four times as busy in a neighborhood so opposite as to induce culture shock. Henry's gear is pristine. His wife probably buffed his helmet every now and then and his turn out gear looks like the only smoke it has *ever* been exposed to is from the barbeque grill on a windy day.

Early into the first day of the four day trick, Henry and Kemp make swift rounds of the firehouse with Dan emphasizing the bathroom rules and the fact that the company turns out faster than any other . . . no need being left behind with his pants around his ankles.

"When we catch a run," Henry asks earnestly, "you want me to flag out?"

"Huh?" Kemp has a blank look on his face.

"Flag out," Henry repeats. "Get the orange warning flags and stop traffic so we can get out unimpeded." He explained that Engine 21 has three sets of flags at its exit door. You catch a run and a guy grabs the flags, stops the traffic and the engine rolls out, slowing down so the flag man can climb aboard.

"We don't flag out," Kemp grunts, arching that eyebrow and looking at Henry.

"Oh, okay," the detailed man shrugs. "You guys have the flashing traffic lights out front?"

"Not unless they've been installed since you signed in this morning," Dan comments dryly.

Incredible, the newbie thinks. "So who does the traffic control when you guys run?"

"The PO," Kemp mumbles, waving a hand in the general direction of the front doors. "When those doors open it looks like a rodeo rider coming out of the chute," he explains. "All sirens and horns and lights . . . they see us coming, trust me."

Henry doesn't recall MOP's covering that particular procedure. "Where you want me putting my gear, Cap?" He is following the officer as they walk the length of the wagon.

"Lead-off man sits behind the PO," Dan pauses briefly at the door of the cab where Ben will be seated. "Leave your stuff here. I'll have one of the guys set you up with a bunk upstairs for your nights here. Engine sleeps on the left, truck on the right."

Henry opens the door of the cab, stepping back and wrinkling is nose. "Oh," he clears his throat. "It stinks." Inside the door, two bench-type jump-seats face each other and Ben packs his coat on the seat facing forward and drops his helmet on the other seat. The whole interior smells of old sweat and smoke. "You guys ever use air freshener?"

Dan turns to answer the detailed man and changes his mind, the question tells him all he needs to know. "We got showers upstairs," he continues the brief spiel of a tour guide.

Twenty minutes later Henry rises from a chair in the lounge, "I got to hit the head," he announces.

"You know where it is right?" Bill Burger asks from the kitchen, pouring a bowl of Cheerios.

"I got it," Henry waves off the directions.

"This guy is too clean," Bill announces after Henry departs.

Killen is surfing the television in search of a program with content above fourth grade level, sixth grade would be acceptable, Sam is not that picky. "How often you think his company gets a fire?" He makes a face. "I'm betting they get maybe a dozen working fires all of last year."

Burger stands in the middle of the lounge spooning Cheerios in his mouth. He addressed Killen's issue, "I know what you mean, Sammy. We gotta get this guy salty, y'know? Give him a memorable visit to take back with him to wherever he came from."

"I bet they keep their turn-out gear hanging nice and neat on hangers along the wall of the firehouse." Sam discovers a Tom and Jerry cartoon and settles back in an armchair.

"They got a nice new engine too," Bill eats more cereal.

The plight of Engine Company 21 and the community of Glendyl became a publicized embarrassment for both the city and the fire department less than a year ago. For two decades the company had been assigned an ancient piece of apparatus whose fate it was to be repaired over and over instead of being replaced by a new acquisition. The firehouse on White Street had been quarters for the department's sole open-cab engine for almost twenty five years, rain and snow as much a part of its front seat as the pump operator and officer. Unfortunately for the residents of Glendyl, the community is not considered politically crucial to any of the mayoral elections. So what if the engine they have looks like it could have served pre WW2? Nobody complained, except the firefighters, the voters there had no impact on who sat in City Hall. If you want City Hall, you make sure Lincoln Heights and South City and Libertyville get attention. Don't forget the Projects either; those monstrous canyons formed by a dozen or so brick and cement towers packed with subsidized housing residents. You can bet those communities are represented by the most militant and aggressive black city council members. The type of support you need to get elected in a city with the majority of its populace being 'people of color.'

A television cameraman had gotten some candid footage of the men of Engine Company 21 pushing . . . yes pushing their wagon down White Street and popping the clutch in an attempt to start it's motor. That little piece of vintage camera work ended up as the centerpiece on one of the cable networks which, in turn became the genesis of a media blitz on the liabilities incurred by metropolitan centers who ignored the basic fire protection needs of their communities.

A miracle happened! Within six months of the media firestorm, the city's fire department issued a public announcement that the community of Glendyl had been scheduled to receive a brand new fire engine straight from the factory in Florida. A neighborhood block party was arranged with hot dogs, ice cream and balloons and with the media in full-blown coverage, His Royal Highness Mayor Myron with his entourage. With two dozen television cameras recording the event, 'Chip' stood on a brightly covered dais replete in fire department windbreaker and baseball cap to declare his concerns for the community needs and his relief the fire department eventually submitted to his reported demands to provide efficient equipment to this 'important' community.

Ben Henry knew the bacon, egg and cheese muffin he's eaten for breakfast on the way to this Godforsaken firehouse was going to make him sick. He can feel the food mass working its way through his bowels, and now seated in the small bathroom hopes he can rid himself of his burden. Tomorrow he'd get something lighter. Ben Henry forgets Priority One . . . the reminder on the inside of the door in front of his face.

The first hint that this particular call of nature was going awry begins with the sudden, gut-wrenching mind, clearing, triple *clang* from the brass gong . . . the sound that carries through the apparatus floor into the bathroom where Benjamin Henry sits unprepared.

"Smoke reported in the dwelling . . . Eighteen hundred Vitali . . . Building Number Three . . . Apartment . . ."

"Everybody goes!" the voice sounds like the pump operator, March, Henry remembers, the guy at the watch desk.

Damn, now what? Henry reaches for the precious toilet paper and hears doors slamming already for God's sakes! Hold on! Henry's mind works faster than his hands, he can't get enough paper off the roll. Diesels rumble to life, firehouse doors rattle upward, there is shouting. Henry gets the door open, his pants aren't buckled yet, he's slightly bent at the waist. Sirens crescendo and Henry finds he is standing at the rear of an empty firehouse watching the tillered end of Truck 105 making a right turn out on Fort Avenue.

There is no alternative but to accept the obvious and finish what he started. A somewhat lighter and significantly more relieved Ben Henry leaves the toilet stall minutes later with nothing to do but listen to the radio and wait for the return of the two companies and red car. He realizes he has had an auspicious beginning in this firehouse.

Images gleaned from the radio communications form a general picture of the scene. Henry sits at the desk mentally visualizing the activity.

Vitali East is a nasty place; there are no polite terms to describe the projects and be truthful. The multi-storied apartment buildings that comprise the Projects are packed, inside and out with families, some of whom were born, lived and died without traveling more than a dozen blocks from the subsidized housing. With the living spaces forming an inner 'core', each of the cement towers has open terraces around each floor's exterior . . . terraces that must be fenced now to prevent occupants from being thrown to the street below.

Engine 50, absent of it's detailed Benjamin Henry, arrives first, reporting no evidence of smoke and confirming that the engine and Truck 105 will be investigating. Another ten minutes passes before Battalion chief 15 informs communications the 'emergency' has turned out to be a pot of food left on a stove too long, all units are returning to their quarters. It is twenty minutes after Loughlin's report that Henry can hear the distinct sounds of the fire apparatus returning to the firehouse . . . a sound singular above all other traffic noises. He stands inside the cubicle while Engine 50 is backed into it's bay. Red-faced and nervous Ben waits for Dan Kemp to climb down from the cab; the officer fixing the newbie with that cynical glare.

"Got caught in the toilet," it is a statement from Kemp.

"Sorry, Cap," Henry is unsure how to address the mistake.

"Forgot your paperwork," it is Burger, the big pear-shaped man. He had a grin on his face while putting his turnout coat back on to his seat in the cab.

"I didn't figure you guys would tear out of here like that," Henry's face flushes deeper.

"Well," Kemp slams the door of the engine and turns to the detailed man, "You got your first mistake, no problem. It was a dumb run. But now you know how things work, don't let it happen again, got it?"

The officer's largesse is appreciated. Henry knows he could have been placed on report and subject to disciplinary action. He wants to fit in or at least become as inconspicuous as possible.

"You guys got traffic control flags?" Henry asks Jerry's legs. The pump operator is under the engine, lying on a creeper wheeling about inspecting the underside of the apparatus; only his legs protruding out along the floor indicates his presence.

"Flags?" Jerry asks, squinting at a maze of pipes, hoses and linkages. "You mean like using them to flag out when we get a run?"

"Yeah," the detailed man is relieved to get a better response from Jerry than the captain.

"Oh hell yeah," Jerry informs him. "If you can hold a second I'll go find 'em for you." The creeper moves silently along the length of the engine. "You gonna be the flagger?"

"That's just what I'm comfortable with," Henry admits. "We keep flags at the door at Engine 21."

"Uh huh," the grunt from Jerry is neutral.

On the second floor of the firehouse, Jerry and Ben Henry engage in a room-by room search for the flags that mean so much to Ben. In a storage room opening off the rear of the bunkroom, old lockers hang open, boxes and file cabinets have been rifled and the floor is littered with their contents. The flags have not been found. The two men have already conducted a thorough search of the first floor without success and, having rummaged about on the upper floor the options are dwindling.

"I know they gotta be around here someplace," Jerry mutters, digging through more trunks packed with memorabilia and artifacts that have gathered dust for a quarter of a century. Fire prevention banners, old jerseys from the firehouse flag football team and an assortment of moldy smelling old tee-shirts and cleaning rags. March, arms filled with the wrinkled bunched remains of too-small sweatshirts bearing the company insignia, peers into the very bottom of the trunk. "Found 'em," he announces.

The flags are bright, Day-glo orange squares mounted on twenty-four inch handles. Two of them are in pristine condition, wrapped together and secured with a large rubber band. Jerry hands them to the newbie. "These look brand new to me," Henry examines the flags suspiciously.

"Probably are," Jerry agrees. "I don't ever remember them bein' used."

"Ever?"

"Not since I been here," Jerry swears.

"I'll take them downstairs." Henry is happy, he has a purpose now, his presence in this firehouse has meaning.

Although well intentioned, the use of warning flags on Fort Avenue to halt traffic has draw-backs. Nobody in the firehouse has ever used them and, because flagging traffic is not a familiar, habitual practice, nobody in the firehouse knows how to react to their appearance.

Pleased with the new-found signals, Ben Henry leans them just inside the door at the engine's bay. Within seconds of an alarm he can swoop them up, trot to the middle of Fort Avenue, halting all traffic and be picked up by the engine as it rolls by. The imagery in Henry's mind is vivid, it is also illusory.

Firehouse routing during the day can become slow and monotonous, even with the pressing, life-and-death efforts of inspecting smoke detectors for the MetroStrat database. The rotation of the second hand on the wall clocks seems to slow, the changing numbers of the watch desk digital seem to freeze and each minute becomes comprised of a thousand seconds rather than the usual sixty. A few hours of inactivity accepted as commonplace at Engine 21 becomes a source of anxiety and frustration at Fort Avenue.

Shortly before noon, however, the toxic and angst-ridden boredom is suddenly broken when the gong trips off, lights flash on during the warbling tone and men who, moments ago lolled in frustration, trot to their respective apparatus with a welcome vigor. The address on Bond Street is familiar, both companies pay the neighborhood regular visits. Within three syllables from the dispatcher, the firefighters are moving in that more rapid than usual skip-trot.

An excited Benjamin Henry, anxious to demonstrate his unequaled skills with orange warning flags, is already trotting quickly into Fort Avenue while viciously waving his flags, closely resembling a desperate man signaling for help.

There are four cars using Fort Avenue at that moment and all four come to a sudden, unceremonious halt. Unfortunately the cars have no point of reference. The appearance of a man in the street frantically waving a bright orange flag is a first . . . there has never been a warning before. The unexpected sight of Ben Henry causes two cars to screech to a halt blocking one half of the firehouse driveway. Henry begins to pump his arm horizontally, the signal to reverse and give the fire department vehicles room to exit.

Ben scowls angrily at the two drivers who have dared to get so close to him, it never happened in Glendyl where everybody knows proper protocol. Well, he thinks, I'll make *sure* there's room for the apparatus to maneuver! His forcefulness is rewarded when the offending motorists edge their cars backward. Henry allows himself a moment of authoritative pleasure seeing there is plenty of room in front of the firehouse now. The self-satisfaction lasts about thirty seconds.

Firefighter Henry can only stand in the street, arms at his side, orange flags hanging, watching open-mouthed as Engine 50 rushes by patently oblivious to his presence, despite the fact that there is nobody else standing in the street wearing a fireman's helmet and turnout gear, turns and rumbles off in the distance. The rear of the engine growing smaller and smaller. At the moment Ben can't be positive and even a few months later, recalling the incident, he is still uncertain that Jerry March didn't sound an extra blast on the air horn for his benefit.

In the fire department, a vacant position on a shift is remedied by a 'detail.' When a vacancy occurs geographically due to a company or companies being out of service in their usual territory, the remedial replacement is a 'fill-in'. Consider when company A is unavailable to respond to a call within their normal territory, Company B must be notified to take it's place, or fill-in.' The absence of a company normally assigned a call is factored by the Prometheus system which automatically identifies the next closest company to handle the emergency. For the computer's binary system, the requirement involves the proper and instantaneous placement of combinations of '0' and '1'.

In terms of men and equipment, the consequences involve much more, with longer lasting and sometimes dangerous inclusions.

Do the math! Fewer companies mean longer distances to travel. When combinations of companies are working in tandem and unavailable, the next closest companies must travel two and three times the normal distance in an attempt to provide an equal level of service. The multiplication in distance advances wear on apparatus, fatigue in men, and overall stress to a system already struggling to cover territory made too big by diminution of resources.

The question of which firehouses to close and companies to disband resides in the hands of the Greater Metropolitan Advisory Committee. Computer models, data from other cities of equal size, demographics and advice from self-appointed experts are combined and fashioned into recommendations listing companies responding to the same locations. Would all such companies be just a duplication of services, and the city's firehouses spaced inappropriately too close to each other? What would be the expected cost-savings if certain, 'too close' firehouses are shut down?

Although the thinking and extrapolations have a logical flow, there is an absence of reality. But what if three truck companies cover the same, general neighborhood? Why include portions of the area covered by the disbanded company? Decisions were made and acted upon by individuals who never lived in the affected communities and who'd never been in the fire department. Maps, push pins and red pencil marks shaped a fire department and its personnel, diminishing it by one-half, without a word of argument by its chief, Malachy Martin, who accepted the bloodletting in silence.

For every action there is an equal reaction, so says scientific law. There is, also, the existence of the 'Law of Unintended Consequence.' Both laws, not computer models and committee decisions, collide head-on over the city's restructured fire department. City 'planners' determine there are more than enough public telephones that can be utilized to report emergencies and all fire alarm boxes are removed from the street corners. The public utility company responsible for the telephones decides the use of cellular phones is so widespread there is little need for public phones and, almost overnight there is no general reporting system for fires, medical emergencies or other calamities.

Paramedic services are added to the fire department's responsibilities requiring apparatus formerly utilized almost exclusively for firefighting to also engage in emergency medical services. During that same time frame, fires throughout the city increased by three hundred percent; said increase now fought by a department reduced by half

Finally, in an effort to suppress fires by a massive first response, the first alarm assignments are changed. The numbers and type of apparatus increased in order to overwhelm a given fire at it's genesis. The philosophy is sound and it's general application is successful, but in a department cut in half, the reality translates into longer run times with labor-intensive efforts requiring twice the energy to accomplish the same results. The finished 'product' of this effort is a city silently ignorant of precariously teetering on the edge of disaster, leaving even the slightest informed observer to question what the city's 'planners' had planned.

With the general public ignorant of the fact that on any given night, the firehouse down the street, the one they'd seen in business just twelve hours ago, has a fire engine or two sitting in darkness. Behind the closed and locked doors with nobody at home, not a fireman is in sight of it's brick walls. It is the ultimate catch-22. A department with half it's former resources must work twice as hard to maintain it's previous success which, in turn, proves there was no real need for a larger department to begin with at all.

On the first night of the trick, the ominous indicators of a memorable shift have already begun to emerge. No sooner has Bill Burger scribbled his name on the night shift roster when Jerry March calls from the doorway to the lounge.

"Hey, Bunk," Jerry shouts, "you better get yourself right on the wagon."

What's going on?" Bill's equipment locker is the third one down in a row that begins several feet from the engine's back step and stretches thirty feet back toward the rear of the apparatus floor. He is already in uniform and works the combination on the locker's handle. Yanking his bunker pants and their boots from the bottom of the locker, Burger drapes the sooty, grimy turnout coat over one arm and pulls his battered black helmet from the top shelf. Opening the rear door of the cab, Bill tosses the helmet atop his seat, checks the pockets of his coat for gloves and hand tools. He makes sure his Big Ed light is fully charged before draping the coat over his seat and arranges the turnout pants on the floor beside the engine. The waist and suspenders are pushed down past the tops of the boots so he can pull everything on in one motion. The pipe man is ready for the night.

"Eugene!" shouts Jerry to Gene Hill, the day shift 'pipe', "Burger's on. Get outta' here."

Hill, in the lounge behind March appears in the doorway and spies the looming figure of his relief. "You got it, Billy." When Burger waves, Gene Hill gives a sloppy salute and walks quickly up past the engine. "Air masks are all checked and filled," he relays the information to Burger. "We had five runs . . . nothing worth talking about." He passes Bill with a slap on the shoulder on his way home.

"We got a whole load of area to cover," Jerry leans against the lounge door. "As of right now everything south of Federal Street and east of Lancaster Square is wide open. We're the only engine company in service between Lancaster Square and Federal."

Burger scowls, "What happened?" He joins Jerry in the lounge, marking him for a soda.

"Fifth Battalion's got a second alarm going up past Fellowes Avenue and they already special-called another engine and truck." Jerry is ticking off the events on his fingers. "Eleventh Battalion has a working fire down on Thurgood Marshall Avenue, fully involved. I think they said it was an antique shop or something," he shrugs, "but anyway, Chief Marriott gets there and reports a working fire, fully involved and through the roof." Jerry makes an upward slashing motion with is hand, "and two minutes later he's asking for an additional engine and the next available tower ladder." Finished with the litany of fires, the pump operator smiles ruefully. "That leaves us in the middle of a big, big bare spot."

The conversation is interrupted by Mark Hagan's entrance into the room. He nods quietly to the other men and drops into one of the couches, his hands immediately cradling his head. "I got a headache that's killing me."

March scowls, "You go out drinking last night?"

Mark sprawls along the couch, an arm over his eyes now. "Yeah," he gives a resigned sigh. "I couldn't help myself, it's a weakness, a disgusting, perverted moral weakness."

"Where'd you go?" Burger sits on the sofa opposite Mark, enjoying a sadistic delight in Hagan's agony.

"I ended up at 'Boots'," Mark groans. The strip bar sits in the middle of the city's red-light district.

"You dumb jerk" Bill sits back on the sofa and stirs the drink in his cup. "You deserve to suffer."

Jerry looks disgusted, then turns to Terry Buck. "You got your stuff ready to go? We're the only engine company in-service for about forty blocks."

"I heard all that on the radio," Buck nods, "I just threw everything on the wagon as soon as I got here." He pauses. "How's the detail guy?"

"Engine 21," March doesn't need to add more.

"He's good with flags," Burger quips.

Paul Gulfee enters the lounge, white shirt starched and pressed, his appearance is unexpected and Burger and March stare at him for several moments. "Dressed up for the ball?" Jerry grins.

"No," Paul strolls to the television, glancing down at Hagan on his right, "my wife got this out for me, said I never wear anything ironed to work . . ." He nods at Mark, "What's with him?"

Jerry rolls his eyes. "He spent the night at Boots' Bar and then comes in here feeling like hell." Hagan augments this with a soft groan.

The lounge begins to fill now, Holland, Greenstreet and Killen file into the room, the shift has officially begun.

"Dinner at seven-thirty," Greenstreet declares, stepping into the kitchen to examine the contents of the freezer.

Each transmission from the radio echoes through the firehouse and is reason to cause the two companies to remain the sole protection for more than three dozen city blocks. With every announcement, the men grow quiet and listen, the odds are overwhelming they will get a call, *some* kind of call.

"Damned spooky," Terry Buck admits to Benjamin Henry as the two men share the watch desk cubicle, "Just thinking that the only thing around here is us."

"I never ran with a busy company," Henry confesses. He likes Terry, there's a quiet, unassuming charm about the guy. There's certainly no animus from the other men, but Buck has a youthful openness, an infectious laugh that makes Henry feel comfortable. He sure as hell feels intimidated by the big guy Killen. That guy is like Goliath and he doesn't smile much except when he's hanging around March and Burger.

"Well," Bucky sighs, "we're in kind of a slow period now," he shrugs. "Not sure why it is but we're not catching the working fires we usually do. Terry considers asking this newbie how many fires he's actually been in and opens his mouth to speak. He's interrupted by the triple *clang* and the staccato-voiced dispatcher.

"*Engine Five-Zero respond to . . .*"

"Where the hell are we going?" Kemp is shouting at Jerry. The pump operator is weaving through nighttime traffic, making the left turn up Kennedy Street.

"Kile Terrace," Jerry shouts back his reply, "one of them big apartment buildings . . . odor of smoke."

Everything else being equal, Engine 50 would not make this run until at *least* the third alarm had been requested. Tonight however is not a night of equality.

The streets seem bathed in a bright pink glow from the mercury vapor street lamps. Traffic is steady enough that Jerry must work the engine in and out of the lanes, weaving wherever there is an opening. He makes the right turn on Casimir Pulaski Street, named for the Revolutionary War Hero, a three lane avenue with more than enough room for March to accelerate toward the intersection with Patterson Avenue. Inside the cab a bored silence dominates. There is no indication this run will produce anything but a walking investigation of the premises in question, locating the source of the smoky odor. Turnout coats remain buckled, helmets rest on laps and the men rock gently back and forth in their seats, staring impassively at the buildings and cars as the engine passes. This is the classic 'fill-in'. The companies nearest Kile Terrace are working elsewhere, leaving the neighborhood without immediate fire protection. With the adjacent companies also out-of-service, the Prometheus System prompted Engine 50 as the next unit in order to answer this call, compliment of the Greater Metropolitan Committee.

At the intersection of Pulaski and Patterson, the traffic light shows red, two lanes of traffic on Patterson Avenue are lined up at a green light. Jerry has to make a left turn off Pulaski on to Patterson, and he's glad the traffic is halted at the light. He can make a wide sweeping turn at the intersection. Once on Patterson it is a straight shot for about ten or twelve blocks to Kile Terrace.

Dan Kemp is giving short blasts on the air horn, *one-two-three* and glances briefly to his right, out the window. Jerry, turning the engine's big steering wheel, also gives a quick look to the right and in that instance notices that several of the cars idling in the line on Patterson are angled slightly to the right; drivers pulling aside to make way for an oncoming emergency vehicle. Jerry's foot eases off the accelerator as he goes into the left turn, when from the corner of his eye, there is movement. The unmistakable movement of a very large object moving very fast.

"What the hell!" the shouts from the five men seated in the cab come together as one, loud, chorused exclamation.

Truck 15, all twenty-three tons of it, from grill to tiller, red body, white topped cab and a crazy zigzag streak along it's sides, flashes through the intersection so quickly there is no time for the brain to receive neural transmission from the optic nerve, analyze it and respond. There is no sound of braking, no deviation from it's route and for five seconds the two vehicles, Engine 50 and Truck 15 parallel each other on Patterson Avenue. Just one inch exists between the side mirror on Jerry's side and the mirror on the officer's side of Truck 15.

Jerry will swear later his heart stopped beating during those five seconds and Kemp says his stomach was suddenly filled with a ball of lead weighing ten pounds. The three men in the seats behind them became as statues. Jerry doesn't even take his eyes from the street in front of him, terrified the slightest movement in any direction will influence his handling of the engine. Beside him, Dan's neck is locked in place holding his head turned to the left, facial features frozen. He vividly remembers the very white face of Captain Francis Somerville, pressed against the door window of the truck and then nothing. The rear lights of Truck 15 disappear into the distance ahead of the engine.

Truck 15, also responding as a 'fill-in,' had been running up Patterson Avenue for ten blocks already when it came to the intersection with Pulaski. The cars Jerry sees angled to the right on Patterson were moving from the path of the oncoming truck. Like all good companies, '15 Hook' has taken the call and proceeds to Kile Terrace like the proverbial 'bat out of hell . . .' intent on arriving first and beating Engine 50. Similar to their friends on the engine, the members of the truck experience that definitive moment when lives flash before their eyes before their apparatus outdistances the competing company. The driver for 15 will later shake his head and reveal that Somerville was so terrified he was unable to annunciate his classic exclamation . . . his mouth moving with only the first syllable . . . Je . . . Je . . . Je . . . ," repeating itself the rest of the way to Kile Terrace.

Jerry's foot has yet to come near the accelerator and as Truck 15 separates further from the engine, March simply groans loudly and sags slightly behind the steering wheel.

"Where the hell did *they* come from?" Dan a dazed expression on his face, looks at Jerry. The captain's heart is thudding in his chest and his mouth is dry as cotton.

"*Units responding to Kile Terrace . . . Box Six-One-Two-Three assignment . . . Truck One-five on location investigating . . . Truck One-Five will handle,*" The voice from communications transmit's the message from Truck 15.

"Let's go home," Kemp mumbles.

The fill-in at Kile Terrace takes it's place in the pantheon of Fort Avenue legend; singular events prompting a dramatic reflexive act of contrition. Jerry literally jumps from the cab to tell his wife, Trisha, and describe the event in graphic detail. Dan Kemp performs a very *UN*-captain-like thanksgiving rite, climbing down from his seat to kneel, still in his turnout gear, and kiss the cement floor. Burger and Buck stand beside the engine, hands on hips, shaking their heads, while Ben Henry remains in his seat in the cab, a stunned bewildered look on his face, he later describes it as ". . . having just seen the death angel."

"You think maybe Somerville is cleaning himself?" the captain asks in a loud voice, slowly rising from the floor and wiping his lips. "When I was lookin over, all I could see was a white face pressed against the window."

"You should have seen the tiller man," Terry Buck adds, his shaky voice revealing a still unnerved young man. "I think there was maybe a layer of paint between us."

"So much for closures, rotating closures and fill-ins," Kemp mumbles and his voice becomes louder. "I need a beer."

By ten o'clock each company has logged five runs none of which were of consequence and all but one resulting from the absence of everyone around them at fires burning elsewhere in the division. It seems like the restless denizens in this part of the city have decided that two good fires meet some unspoken code and as night deepens it is time to relax.

On the second floor, light shines thinly beneath the closed door of the battalion office where Thomas Loughlin reads his reports. Although fairly early by firehouse standards, the men begin heading to their bunks slightly after nine. Trudging up the black spiral staircase, through the second floor locker room and into the bunkroom. Some men like Henry and Terry Buck, quickly shower before going to bed, while others like Greenstreet and Burger, just climb into the sturdy bunks and pull dark woolen blankets over them. Everyone, however, has carried their turnout pants and boots bedside for immediate access.

Cloaked in semidarkness, Loughlin's office light and whatever illumination gets up through the pole openings give the big room a dark gray overcast, the sounds of cars intermittently passing along Fort Avenue are all that can be heard.

"I miss my mommy," Burger whimpers out of the darkness; there are assorted snorts and giggles then silence.

"I miss Uncle Stanley," Hagan adds, "he always would tuck me in and tell me a story." Once again giggling and then silence.

"I love you, Mikey," Holland calls to Greenstreet.

"Shut up Donnie," Greenstreet calls from under his blanket.

Lordy, Henry thinks pulling his blanket higher and tighter under his chin, *these guys are looney.*

For a moment there is complete silence. Benjamin Henry feels an uneasy tension building and an abrupt, anonymous "Oh hell." The sound of a very faint click is barely audible and within a split-second the bunk room light flashes on, illuminating the entire room. The brass gong downstairs is hitting off and the voice of the dispatcher sounds as though his mouth is next to your ear rather than rolling across the apparatus floor.

"Truck One-Zero-Five respond . . . Dwelling fire . . ." Most of the firefighters who've worked night shifts can attest to the eerie phenomenon of actually hearing dead silence that ensues just before an alarm is sounded. In many cases those same individuals will swear they 'hear' that faintest 'click' of the gong triggering itself to sound. No logical explanation can be found for this auditory sensation except to admit to the existence of a highly developed sixth sense. Before the bell has sounded twice, blankets are thrown back, men sit up in their beds and shove feet into boot tops and stand to yank up their turnout pants before heading to the brass poles.

"Don't be long, honey," March calls to the group.

From the bunk room the exit door at the truck's bay can be heard rattling open and diesel fuel motors rumble to life. Moments before the apparatus rolls into the street Donald Holland hit's the air Horn twice, two thundering blasts in reply to Jerry's farewell.

Paul Gulfee peers at the glossy teleprinter sheet in his hands. He grimaces and shakes his head. "We gotta go right past 9 Truck." The daily schedule of rotating closures has listed Truck Company 9 as out of service, while the company attends 'in-service-classes' like you're going to believe the Academy is supposed to be open at this hour.

"Better than that," Holland skillfully wends his way through traffic along Fulmon Avenue, "not only is 9 Hook closed, but 11 is already out, and so is Truck 24." Donald laughs grimly and glances at Paul. "This is third . . . maybe fourth territory for us."

Gulfee slaps his knee and glares out the window.

"Units responding on Box assignment Nine-One-Eight be informed . . . a signal fifty is being transmitted by Battalion . . ." Donald, always the alert fire buff, glances over at Gulfee again.

"Hey Paul, what's this new dispatch crap?" He indicates the radio in the cab. "Sounds like we're getting half CAD dispatches by location and half box locations by number . . ." The EVD lets the observation hang in the air.

In matter of fact, Donald's observance is on the money. The multi-million dollar computer system was designed and purchased to identify emergencies and dispatch equipment without the slower and tedious method using electromagnetic Gamewell alarm boxes. The number on each Gamewell box corresponded to a specific street corner around the city. By recording the number of bells sent by the box, the dispatchers checked the assignment cards, found the box number and alerted the companies listed on the card. Now, however, the Prometheus system is supposed to do everything simply by typing in an address, there is no longer a need for 'box numbers'. Besides, companies knew their first alarm box numbers so well there was little need for an address to be given or the specific assignments announced. The moment the box number was given, firehouse gongs were activated.

Change can be anathema to organizations steeped in tradition. As a stop-gap measure and in response to complaints by firefighters, communications has agreed, sometimes to 'augment' the Prometheus dispatch with a back-up dispatch utilizing the old fire alarm box number for the same location. It is expected, however, the next generation of city firefighters will be further inclined to enter the new technological age divorced from the traditional dispatches. It is a nodding acceptance that old ways die extremely difficult deaths.

Paul Gulfee turns to glance in the rear seats. Killen and Hagan have heard the call, the department's technical numerical 'ten-code' for a working fire. Obviously the battalion chief on the scene enjoys doing things by the book. In some firehouses entire conversations have centered around whether the ten-codes have more syllables, on average, than everyday English. In many instances the entire ten-code has been recited using fingers to track the syllables, the same method is utilized to compare everyday language. In the end it is agreed the ten-code sucked, because the system was hard to memorize and commonly used English far easier to understand.

Killen and Hagan are already sliding their arms through the shoulder harnesses of breathing apparatus and pulling their flash hoods over their heads. No sooner does Paul turn back around, when he sees the glow of fire above the long, flat roofs of the row houses in front of them. "Okay, Donnie," the lieutenant sighs, pulling on his own hood, "we got the rear, let's see what this is all about and show 'em how the boys from downtown do it, right?"

The truck arrives upon the scene of a media circus. Television crews, alerted by their scanners are already at the fire, reporters with cameramen in tow search for the best backdrop or the most dramatic imagery possible. Halogens mounted on apparatus already bathe the front of the dwelling in bright light revealing two engines have led off from the hydrants, their lines stretched in the street. "We're gonna get on television," Donald laughs cynically at this buzzing of reporters. A camera crew catches the arrival of Truck 105 but, having no idea the truck is assigned to the rear of the house, loses the apparatus when it passes by en route to the back. There's plenty of fire, the windows on the second floor front have flames rolling from them and smoke pours from the eaves.

Sam and Mark are already moving when the truck jerks to a hissing stop. The first ladder is thrown while Donald illuminates the upper floor with the halogens carried on the vehicle. The men's movements are caught in long shadows against the outside wall. Mark is the first up the ladder, tumbling into a rear window and orienting himself inside the room. Smoke forces him to his knees and then to his stomach. Debris is strewn over the floor and Hagan is fumbling with every forward movement.

"Fire department, anybody here?" the eternal call of the searching firefighter. Mark's Garrity light and Big Ed cut through the dense soupy mix bunching around him and he sweeps an arm under a bed and feels his way to a narrow closet, yanking it open and feeling through the mounds of dirty clothes inside. Every few moments he glances overhead and sees flashes of orange swirling with the smoke. Huge flakes of ash and charred paper wheel crazily inches from his helmet.

"I got nothin'," he yells back to Killen who has followed Mark through the window. Mark pushes forward, his glances upward becoming more frequent. Even in the protective equipment he feels the heat building, the smoke thickening. 'Swimming' to a doorway Hagan feels along the edge of the wall to orient himself again. Whatever is burning around him must really be rolling; Mark is thinking, chunks of ceiling plaster fall on his shoulders.

If this was on television Hagan would be upright or at least bent over slightly, and stroll through this inferno, finding victims of all shapes and sizes huddled in plain view awaiting their rescuer. Mark pauses, already feeling fatigued. Reality is far different than Hollywood, as if people actually knew. Terrified children hide themselves from danger with a fatal expertise, whatever drives their security, also seals their doom. Adults, who should know better, how many dollars are spent annually repeating the litany of life saving practices, expose themselves to the toxic contents of smoke. The plastics and synthetics used in making everything from socks to tables breaks down into airborne poison when oxidized by heat. The story repeats itself so often, the results so commonplace, that it is no longer a thought process to Hagan. His recurring question, the constant refrain echoing in his mind in these fires is why these morons cannot keep a house clean! He encounters so much trash and debris, mounds of it, his amazement is that something has not lit off before.

Mark pauses once more, breathing hard. It's like climbing into a ceramic heating kiln at high cycle and closing the lid. He thinks he has heard a sound, soft, almost inaudible, but human. A cough? Wheeze? The roaring and creaking of the fire increases and, simultaneously, the smoke whispers past, dense and drifting slowly, a silent killer.

There! Mark can feel an arm, thin as a rail, short, a child. He sweeps a gloved hand under a bed frame, snagging the tiny arm by it's wrist. "Got one!" Hagan shouts. The body is very light and limp and he kneels beside the bed cradling the child in his arms. The child's head rolls back, mouth open, foamy saliva drooling around the chin, no small bubbles indicating breath. "Oh God," Mark shouts through his mask at the little form, c'mon kid, be alive!"

"I got you," Sam's voice is close, maybe a few feet away. "Keep comin,'" the big man continues calling, an audible tracking on which Hagan can fix for direction.

Mark collides with the massive bulk that is Killen. Smoke has effectively created the total blackout, but Sam suddenly looms from nowhere, huge hands sweeping over Mark. A body search by Braille, until they locate the child he holds. Mark passes the body to the other man.

"Go check again," Sam urges loudly, headed back to the window through which they'd entered, sliding along the floor grasping the little victim.

Overhead, creaks and bangs and dull thuds an be heard, some so loud and heavy the house seems to shake. Mark stretches back to the approximate area where he had found the child. It is a guess, there are no points of reference other than the immediate space he has occupied. He feels a second body, "Damn," he shouts to himself. *How did I miss this one?* And like the first, this body is a child's, it feels smaller if possible, maybe younger.

Flames reach lower, rolling in with the smoke, almost level with Mark's shoulders when he is on his knees. Twisting, Hagan places his own body between the lapping fire and reaching the child on the floor. It is at this point the firefighter's mind almost begins operating on two very conscious levels. The rational logical thought processes scream for Hagan to get his stupid butt out of the house, nothing more can be done. It is a constant screaming now, echoing through his head, but it is that second, smaller, steadier voice that urges him to check his instincts step-by-step, don't rush, don't panic. You are trained and experienced with this, you got time, not a lot, but you got it.

Carrying the child is like transporting a small pet. There 's no life in the body and it sags in his arms, limp. Arms and legs splayed out like a small body of jelly. Mark edges toward the window remembering the path he'd used before. Heat is palpable on his back and neck and a few more steps from the window he hears a rumble and a tearing noise from behind in that thick blackness. Part of the ceiling gives way, dropping fire and embers on the very place Hagan has just vacated. Timing is everything.

Hands reach for the body, big hands, strong ones. Mark is too fatigued to move further. Once he has delivered the child into Sam's arms, the younger man simply leans over the sill, lifting his mask and sucking air. His face is red and contorted, the veins in his neck stand out and there is a wild desperate look in his eyes. Over his head, smoke continues to pour from the window. Sapped of energy, it becomes a matter of will to lift one leg over the sill and fit a heeled boot on to the rung of the ladder. The tank of air on his back feels like a thousand pounds and the straps of it's harness dig deeply into his shoulders. Mark is exhausted.

"Coffee wagon is around front," Holland informs them. The EVD has been inside on the first floor pulling out the ceiling and working on the walls, his face is smeared with soot.

Sitting on the sideboard of the truck, Mark is bent over, face between his knees, long strings of saliva and vomitus stretch from his chin and sway back and forth. His hair is matted and wet, either glued from his forehead or sticking up in the air.

The fire buffs, men and women whose consuming affinity involves everything associated with the fire department, own and operate two state of the art recreational vehicles customized into mobile canteens. Both vehicles bearing the department's red-and-white color schemes are equipped with warning lights and electric sirens and are staffed by the fire buff organization, 'The Third Alarm Association', on a voluntary basis. Officially the department recognizes the vehicles as 'Unit 400' and 'Unit 500' and allows both full radio communications. One or the other of the vehicles are automatically dispatched on a second alarm or by request of the commander on the scene. Unit 400 covers the east side of the city and Unit 500 the west. Unit 400 is housed in the 4th battalion, sharing quarters with Engine 1, and its members and operators are accepted by the fighters as one of their own. A dozen men and women assigned twelve-hour shifts voluntarily drive to their assigned firehouses when requested and respond whenever needed.

Unit 400 is usually staffed by four buffs wearing dark coats or jackets bearing a large Maltese Cross on the back with a unit number in the center; they wear ball caps with the same logo. The unit has serving windows along both sides of it's length, the interior brightly lit. The buffs move rapidly about the microwave ovens and coffee machines fastened to shelves. A gas powered stove heats huge pots of soup, waist-high chests of ice are filled with drinks, water, soda, tea and fruit juices. Sandwiches, hot dogs and burgers are readily available . . . free of charge to any fireman or emergency worker on the scene. All expenses are underwritten by the Association itself. The entire operation is a labor of love and the bond between weary firefighters and any unit staffer is unbreakable.

Mark forces himself off the side board of the truck, flexing his shoulders, and turns up the collar of his turnout coat. He walks slowly, like an old man, around the corner of the street, locating the big red and white Unit 400. One of the staffers, an attractive middle aged woman he has spoken to often and who he knows only as Maggie, greets Mark with a smile and hands the tired man two icy cold sodas. Hagan downs one drink immediately and wanders back to Truck 105.

Falling instep beside him, Sam Killen nudges Mark's shoulder, it is like pushing a bull.

"Good job," Killen rumbles.

Hagan fixes a dull stare on Sam's massive, craggy face, like looking at a mountainside the color of a Hershey bar. "How the hell did that fire get rolling so fast in there with those little kids?" It is a rhetorical question. The issue is not about the speed of the fire's expansion, the laws of physics do not stop at the doorway of the still smoking house, the question is one of timing, the amount of time required to get to the scene. Resources in the department are always spread thin and the added burden of filling in for companies closed for the night adds a time factor impacted by distance. Mathematic equations, however, cannot suffice for the loss of two children.

"Hey," a familiar voice causes the two men to turn sharply. Paul Gulfee nods to them, his coat is open and the once crisply starched white shirt is loose and soaked, wrinkled with streaks of black soot. Paul's blue eyes narrow and he directs Sam and Mark to focus their attention to the right. "Look," Paul says tersely.

Myron Sprague wears his navy blue windbreaker with it's fire department logo on the back and a dark blue ball cap on his head, a Maltese Cross identifying it as another prop. Surrounding the Mayor is a cordon of City Hall 'suits' in overcoats, others in sweaters and sport coats. Everyone's attention is fixed on the charred and scorched exterior of the dwelling. Heads nod, shoulders shrug and hand gestures cut the air occasionally. Two television news crews wait patiently, standing a respectful distance from Sprague as he goes through the motions of being briefed by his advisors. The reporters and camera crews glance nervously in Sprague's direction, similar to puppies waiting for table scraps.

"Those are the MetroStrat guys," Paul identifies the suits in overcoats. Each with a hand-held computer, their Palm Pilots, furiously pecking with stylus in the other hand recording data. "They're calculating response times with how many lines are in use, total man hours . . ." his voice trails off.

"Kiss my ass," Sam's voice is venomous. "S.O.B's keeping' tabs on every damn thing we do on the fire ground, where two tiny babies been killed and they're responsible for shuttin' down the fire house just down the block!" his rage builds.

"Y'know?" Donald Holland explains to Gulfee on the way back to the firehouse, "we were second due on that fire and had to drive almost three times as far as the first due." He checks the rearview mirror to see Greenstreet in the tiller cab. "Both those little girls died in that back room and it wasn't lit off when we got there, y'know?" Donald's glasses have slipped to the end of his nose.

"I keep thinking that," the lieutenant sighs, trying to get comfortable in his seat

"We had to come by two separate truck companies, either of which was even closer by half again as we are." Holland's curly hair is askew and errant strands slowly wave back and forth. "You just cannot convince me that that would not have made a difference tonight, Paul." Donald's head is bobbing earnestly as he speaks, the disturbed passion in his voice energizing the man. "I'll go to my grave swearing those little girls could have been saved if either of those truck companies was in service tonight." There is no reply.

Paul Gulfee stares sullenly out the wide windshield, eyes darting to the small mirror over the front of the console. Inside the cab, the men's faces are caught in the faint green hue given off by the dials and gauges. Each man sitting alone and quiet as he wrestles with his inner thoughts, gently rocking backing and forth as the truck rumbles over cobblestones and pot holes. Nobody turns to look at the darkened firehouse of Truck 9, the big rear mount sitting impassively behind closed, locked doors, it's company unavailable because of 'training.'

Death presents an equality because of it's finality, it's inevitability. There is a vast gulf, however, between preventable deaths and those who simply can't be helped. Gulfee has joked about 'toaster doodles', deaths that have eliminated some dope addict who fired heroin into their veins or took one too many hits off the coke rocks. There is no rationalizing however, the deaths of two little girls directly attributable to a group of well-dressed pieces of dung, who happen to push buttons on a computer keyboard. Two little girls . . . sisters . . . die of smoke inhalation! The paramedics say they were three and five years of age. The guilty parties don't push drugs or smoke crack, they push buttons. Buttons that compile data that is then translated into the notion that two truck companies housed too close together in a neighborhood, aren't worth the cost and so one is disbanded. The second is temporarily closed for the same reason . . . cost. And now a shattered family must also deal with the cost that cannot be remedied by punching a Blackberry.

On live television, in the aftermath of the fire, 'Chip' Sprague praises the dedication of 'his' firefighters. In the background the scarred, scorched façade of the row house gives mute testament to the mayor's words. Cameras focus on Sprague's face, solemn and sober, while he remarks about his true concerns for the welfare of this community. Nothing is said, and there was no camera to record the two small bodies zipped in black bags lying side by side at the rear of the empty dwelling or the two firefighters squatting on either side of the body bags, heads bowed and lips moving in a short, silent prayer.

Truck 105 gets it's own detailed man, the consequence of Rich Simms' accident and injury. Bill Carr works out of Truck 4 in Homestead, a bastion of academies planted midway between the city-county boundary and the first clusters of antiquated row houses, marking the beginning of lower income neighborhoods ringing the downtown business district.

William Carr is pleasant, friendly and a five year veteran of the department, but brings with him certain impediments to acceptance in the firehouse and more so with the truck company. In order of immediate importance, Bill sports an earring in each ear, this among a group of men whose extreme limit of tolerance in male jewelry are rings on two fingers, making eyebrows arch and a ponytail. Carr's turnout gear remains in pristine condition, a rich deep black, as though it has just been dispensed form the department's supply warehouse, all that is missing is it's plastic wrapping. Less significant, but important is the fact that Carr talks big for someone coming from a company barely making a thousand runs in the past year. His misplaced braggadocio is rendered, 'big hat, no cattle.'

"You always keep your gear so immaculate?" Donald Holland watches Carr empty his equipment bag, placing his coat and helmet in the rear of the cab while positioning his pants and boots on the floor beside the cab's open door.

"Try to," Carr nods and answers quickly, "We think it looks professional."

"We?" Donald leans against the side of the truck, sucking a tootsie roll pop.

"Yeah, Truck 4," Carr affirms. "The captain figures if we look professional we'll act professional." He folds the large equipment bag into three sections and puts it under his arm.

"Mmmm hmm," Holland arches his eyebrows and follows the detailed man to the lounge.

Carr receives nods of welcome from the men gathered in the room. Tim Bridges, fresh from four days off, is wolfing down a monstrous breakfast in the kitchen and Hagan, tillering for Greenstreet is already on the couch thumbing through a magazine. He grunts a "Hey!", to the new man and turns a page.

"You guys catch much fire in Homestead?" March asks, the morning paper folded under one arm and a cigar clamped between his teeth. He has to tilt his head back slightly in order to see Carr through the cigar smoke.

"We catch our share," Carr nods. "Last month we caught a deuce over on Ashbury Street. We held it," there is a hint of pride in his voice.

"A deuce, huh?" Jerry nods and glances at Holland. The two men exchange a wink.

"Bill's got right step," Donald announces.

"Thank God," Bridges speaks through a mouthful of scrambled eggs. "My rear is starting to conform to the curvature of that seat"

"So how do you guys run?" Bill accepts a cup of coffee from Terry Buck, who pours a second for himself.

"Right step and tiller will throw the first ladder," Holland explains the company's particular evolutions on the fire ground. "Twenty-four footer for two stories, maybe three, definitely the thirty-five footer for three stories. Right step takes the halligan and axe, maybe halligan and six foot hook . . ." Carr is nodding through the recitation.

"How much first-in fire you guys catch?" Bill Carr sips the hot coffee, wincing slightly.

"I don't know," Holland shrugs. "How much Mark?"

Hagan pauses, captivated by a picture on page sixteen. "Probably forty percent, we get first fire."

Carr swallows with difficulty. "Forty?", he swears.

"Hey," Jerry puffs his cigar, "we be the beasts of the east."

The discerning eye picks out a newbie on the fire ground like a lioness picks out the crippled or newborn wildebeest in a herd, naturally, instinctively and immediately. Surrounded by men with dirty, battered helmets, the gleaming lid atop William Carr shines like a beacon in a dark cave.

"He's way too clean," March comments to Paul Gulfee. Both companies have been dispatched to a smoldering mound of rubbish in an alley behind Toole Street. Like most accumulations this size, fully four feet in height, the contents are an eclectic mixture referencing its contributors. Dirty diapers, household rubbish and always a large accretion of waste literally that has eluded the proper placement. Smoke rushes from the stinking mound and excavating the foul-smelling hill, falls to Bill Carr and Tim Bridges, who using ceiling hooks and rakes, break open the solidly packed refuse so Bucky can inundate whatever insists on combusting.

As Carr and Tim poke, probe and separate, the other members of the companies relax and watch with vague interest.

"I know," Paul replies. The two men lean against the side of the engine. "And with all that spick-and-span cleanliness, he's gotta have them damn earrings and ponytail," the lieutenant grimaces. "He'd look much nicer with shorter hair."

"I can do without the earrings." Jerry admits.

"There's just something about that spiffy turnout gear," Paul pulls a cigarette from the pack in his shirt and lights it.

"You're gonna have to do something about that," March warns, "he could set a trend."

"Worse still," Gulfee adds, inhaling deeply and sending a cloud of smoke rising around his face, "is that he'll go back to his company all clean and pretty and give us all a bad reputation."

The contents of the stinking mound are scattered and littered around the alley and, indeed, in the middle of the pile is a small plastic bucket filled with feces. Spying the bucket Carr glances at Bridges. "Is that feces?"

"Sure is," Tim grins.

"I mean the real . . . stuff?"

"Yep," Tim nods, "the waste of life."

Bill Carr's life experiences have just been augmented. "You get this a lot?"

Tim shrugs, "Yeah. Don't ask me why . . ." he laughs, "but it seems like a lot of the folks living around here have a habit of just using a bucket or a milk carton." Both men step back when Terry waters the scattered contents.

"I've never seen anything like that," Carr shakes his head.

Nothing survives the torrent of water Buck directs over the debris, leaving a sodden mass of filth. There is little else to accomplish in the alley and the companies prepare to depart when the radio crackles to life.

"Engine Five-Oh . . . Truck One-Zero-Five . . . Available?"

On Hunt avenue a five story building contains small apartments occupied on a short-term basis by a rustic and forgettable mix of some of the city's less steadily employed citizens. Located in the middle of the block, the building is a sad, dirty place.

The glass door of it's entrance is propped open with two concrete blocks and from a tiny window on the fourth floor a thin stream of light gray smoke ekes skyward.

"Fourth floor," Dan Kemp slides from his seat and stands on the sidewalk, hands on hips looking up at the smoke. Men from the truck company hustle past him while Terry Buck and Nick Miller stretch the hose from the engine. "Nothin' ever happens like this on the first floor," the officer complains.

Inside the entrance, a concrete stairway is partially blocked by an impressive collection of empty wine bottles, beer cans, a pile of discarded newspapers and an eye opening pile of other used items. Kemp uses a big booted foot to sweep a navigable path through the debris and begins the slow climb to the upper floors. Several steps ahead of him Gulfee, Bridges and Carr thump upward, banging and rattling tools that scrape over the concrete walls.

"Hell!" the exclamation escapes from Gulfee, who is first to reach the fourth floor. There is no mistaking the smell of a burning mattress. At the fourth-floor landing, a quartet of apartment doors form a squared semi-circle and, after considerable banging on doors Paul identifies the last door on the right as the entrance they want. He shoves the unlocked metal door hard and it bangs open loudly.

Now's the time to gag, that deep industrial-sized, throat-aching gag reserved for those really memorable moments that will last a lifetime. A narrow hallway leads from the door into the interior of a very small apartment. It's living room holds a small television atop a cardboard box and a single armchair. An adjacent bedroom has it's door wide open and is the source of the overpowering stench held in several layers of gauze-like smoke hanging in mid-air.

"Fire department!" the lieutenant's voice is loud. "Anybody home?" He steps into the bedroom followed by Bill Carr and Tim. A single mattress lies on the bare floor with a single twisted sheet gathered over it's top. The walls of the apartment are green-painted concrete and are bare except for the velvet painting of Christ in Gethsemane set in a broken frame above the television.

Buck and Miller arrive with the hose, bringing the line up the four flights of stairs and through, as to be expected, brown grocery bags of refuse. Tim and the detailed man are already at work tearing open the mattress, exposing glowing embers deep inside. At their contact with the air, those embers flare a brilliant orange and burst into small flames. Water from the hose turns the filthy stained mattress into something slightly firmer than a rectangle of oatmeal.

A soft low groan turns the attention of the assembled firefighters back to the living room, where, on it's far side a small door is ajar, exposing the rail-thin legs of an elderly man seated on the toilet. Kemp and the two men from the truck walk to the door and gently push it open.

"Huh?" a single, surprised grunt from the frail, white-haired man greets the firefighters. "Who are you?" his voice is high-pitched and he is drunkenly swaying unsteadily. A paper thin bathrobe is draped over bony shoulders, it's belt lost long ago and the robe hangs open.

"We're from the fire department," Kemp introduces the spectators in a loud voice. The words seem to register a few seconds later.

"Fire mans?" the old man's eyes open wide. "Is there a fire?"

Bridges stifles a giggle, "Not any more old man," he also speaks loudly.

"Well . . . what was on fire?" the old man looks from face to face.

"Your mattress was on fire," Bridges answers, "did you know that?" Not answering, the man struggles to rise from the seat.

"My mattress?" the words are finally absorbed and genuine concern fills the elderly man's voice. "Damn," he shakes his head, "I was just layin' on it, it weren't burnin' when I was in it." The claim makes the firefighters struggle to keep straight faces.

"Really?" Tim asks, taking one thin bicep in his gloved hand. "Then you got an arsonist loose in your house." Bridges gently guides the man from the bathroom. There is a moment of unsteadiness and the old man stumbles against Bill Carr.

"Damn!" Carr looks down at the spray of yellowish-green urine that now covers the lower portion of his turnout coat.

"What happened?" the old man examines his surroundings through red, watery eyes.

"You got me all wet!" Carr's teeth are gritted when he complains.

"I did?" the man looks at the others for confirmation. "Are you sure?" Tim and the detailed firefighter support the old man across the living room floor. "Whazzat smell?" he wrinkles his nose. "Your mattress," Carr hisses.

"I didn't set it on fire," there is a sense of urgency in his voice. "I swear I didn't. I woulda known if I did." The trio gets across the room without further incident, stopping at the doorway to the bedroom. "What is that?" pointing to the mush that had once been his bed, the old drunk squints at the mattress.

Mark Hagan has joined the group, standing in the bedroom beside its only window. "Gotta dump this," he tells the trembling apartment resident.

"My bed?"

"That ain't no bed no more, partner," Hagan points with a smirk.

"What am I gonna sleep on?" the old fellow pauses, raises a bony finger to his chin. "I gotta idea," he squeaks. "Can you firemen just leave it on the floor?"

"The floor?" Kemp is grinning, "Why on he floor?"

"Cause I can just wait 'til it dries out and use it again," the logic is crystal clear.

Bill Carr, arms held parallel to the floor, away from his coat, hustles down the stairs as quickly as he can. Behind him, the others troop along, grinning at the newbie's panic.

"Hey Bill," Mark calls loudly, "we can drop the coat at the dry cleaners."

Unfortunately for William Carr, his detail to Truck 105 takes a more distinctly negative turn that day.

Within an hour after being drenched with urine, both companies have responded to a fire more substantial than a burning mattress. The two story vacant dwelling on Castle Street isn't the classic 'crapper' it might have been, but the first two rooms downstairs are off and rolling by the time the first alarm assignment arrives. Within twenty minutes the fire is out, leaving a smoky scorched interior filled with that shifting, sifting white mass that burns your eyes and makes your chest hurt after you walk around without a mask.

Paul Gulfee runs a hand over the charred walls, blistered, cracked and shiny black. The ceiling is in similar shape and thin threads of smoke trail out and drift along the surface. The lieutenant glances at Kemp who stands in the middle of the room.

"Gotta be a torch job," Dan shakes his head and looks at Carr and Hagan, who stand on either side of Gulfee. "Might as well strip it all out." he says. "Somebody wanted this place to burn and if we don't really open all this up we'll be right back here in an hour."

Bill Burger stands behind Kemp, hose draped over his shoulder. He glances at Gulfee, "Okay Loo," he pulls the nozzle, "Open 'er up and let's flood the thing."

"Go ahead and take it," Paul motions to the men with him. As Gulfee steps back, Hagan follows suit, leaving Bill Carr to begin work with his ceiling hook, stabbing, circling and spearing huge chunks of wallboard, yanking hard and bringing down blackened, smoldering pieces. He moves over the surface quickly, working steadily, becoming lost in the clouds of dust and sooty powder.

Kemp moves out of the room, giving Carr plenty of room to work. Paul and Hagan retreat further back, as far from Bill Carr as they can. Burger, with Terry Buck behind for support, wait for the appearance of each glowing ember or the flaring of fire, created by the detailed man.

Bill Carr is shouting above the roar of the water. Filthy, disgusting torrents are cascading over his body, soaking him in grayish-black goo.

"Good job," Paul calls from the periphery of the waterfall. "Open that ceiling just a little bit more." Under the torrent of water and slushy debris, Bill Carr is unable to see the grin on Paul's face. "Get that far wall too, okay Bill?" Carr struggles to see through the cataract of water and dirt falling around and on him, as though Burger has been using the damned pipe for hours. Slogging about in a growing lake of black gloop, the detailed man is working on the blackened walls opening more gaping holes that are immediately blasted with water.

The coup de grace occurs so easily and naturally, it could not have been choreographed. Debris accumulates in the swirling filthy water around Bill Carr's boots, raining down under the determined prodding and pulling of the truckie and the pressurized blasts from Burger's pipe. His attention devoted to the ceiling, Carr is unsure of his footing and, at a most awkward moment, his foot twists on a section of ceiling covered by the sooty pond on the floor.

Bill Carr lands face first in the water, ceiling hook splashing down a few feet away. He remains prone for only a few moments. Gulfee and Hagan slog forward to help him upright; the damage has been down, however.

There is a moment of silence in the burnt-out shell of the room. Buck is the first to giggle, that high-pitched, infectious giggle that spreads to Burger and then to Hagan. Bill Carr blinks rapidly, arms extended perpendicular from his body, his first steps are stiff-legged and jerky . . . resembling Frankenstein's monster. Kemp and the men on the hose line step aside so the dazed firefighter can lurch past and stumble from the row house.

Carr emerges from the front door of the dwelling and into the sunlight. Bedraggled, his once pristine turnout gear has undergone a radical transformation. Bill Carr has morphed into 'Pig-Pen Charlie'. The once rich ebony coat is dripping dirty gray covering, soot and filth smear front and back, bunker pants caked with gray, muddy sludge, creased at the knees and thighs. The detailed man's soul has been seared. His face is a mass of gray and black streaks, soot and dirt drying and clinging to his skin. The neat blue uniform shirt is soaked and blackened, smelling awful and clinging to his body. Sludge is caked around Carr's neck and chest, covering his face and the circles of clean flesh around his eyes adds to the impression the man wears a dirt mask.

The detailed newbie walks slowly down the sidewalk, past Engine 50 where Jerry March observes his progress. Jerry, arms crossed on his chest, puffs a cigar and smiles. Bill Carr does not smile, he stares straight ahead, attention focused on the intersection a short distance away. He wears a wide-eyed stare, an expression of primordial shock as he walks past Truck 105. Donald Holland steps from the side of the truck and peers into Carr's face.

"You okay, Bunk?"

Carr pauses, swallows hard and nods. "I gotta know something," he manages to croak at the EVD.

Donald watches Bill walk haltingly, to the street corner, and step off the curb. Looking up at the green street sign, Carr steps to the other side of the steel pole to examine the cross-street. Satisfied at identifying his location, the filth-caked firefighter staggers back up the side walk with an air of resignation, gradually lowering his extended arms in a sign of surrender. Holland offers Carr a cigarette. The detailed man accepts the smoke and bends his head to light it in the flame of Donald's lighter.

"You know," Carr finally says, straightening and blowing out a rush of smoke, "I needed to know the exact address of this place." He speaks with a tone of finality. Rising up and down on the balls of his feet, Bill Carr looks vacantly at the sky.

"Oh yeah?" Holland asks.

"Oh yeah," Carr affirms with a glance at Donald and a dramatic nod of his head. He extends his dirt-caked arms again, offering them as evidence of his sorry state of existence. "I don't ever want to drive by this intersection," his jaws are clenched in fierce determination. "I don't even want to think of this damn intersection. This ain't fighting fires, this is a slop contest." He glares at Holland. "I don't even want to dream about being anywhere near this garbage dump of the world."

His declaration made public, the filthy, humbled firefighter trudges slowly back to the scene of his fall from grace. It is well he faces the burnt-out dwelling, his back to Donald Holland. He cannot see Donald laughing so hard his shoulders are heaving.

CHAPTER 9

"TRADITION"

Reb Tevye, the leading man in "Fiddler on the Roof", places his faith, his security in 'Tradition". Like Tevye, the fire department holds it's tradition in a perspective nearing theological treatises, that which serves as the foundation to all that is good, the unshakeable foundation of everything that has passed and encompassing all that is yet to come. Tradition, has no written roots. It is engrained from generation to generation, an oral passage of universal law meant to protect a noble profession from the heresy of change. FOG's still routinely peruse MOP's,they change and become updated from administration to administration. Those same FOG's recite tradition half a century old from memory, but can forget a grocery list from home within twenty-four hours.

Like the platoon sergeants in the military, it falls to the FOG's to pass along and enforce tradition. In most instances the company officer is younger than the company's oldest members and that officer will depend on his most experienced men to 'shape' the company, especially in the really busy companies with a heritage of citations, medals and awards for the fire ground work beyond what is expected.

Communications, despite its quantum leap in technology, is still bound in traditions. Witness the evolution from the red fire alarm box on every street corner to computer aided dispatch, CAD. Although today's dispatcher will announce the address and type of alarm being given, in addition to the assigned companies, there are still the preceding words 'Box number . . .' information including a numeric designation. In the city, it is common place for the dispatcher to include the number of the little red fire alarm box that had been identified with the general location of the fire for decades, lip service at best but still recognition for tradition. The instances are innumerable, daily, when Communications seems to have just overlaid the new Prometheus system on the former Gamewell system, the gong clangs and the radio announces, "Dwelling Fire, 100 East Alerado Street . . . Box . . . 5-5-2 . . ." Despite the fact the red fire alarm box 552 ceased to physically exist six years ago, the companies are dispatched to the scene compliments of the newer CAD Prometheus. That same iron-clad tradition is evidenced a dozen times daily when a battalion chief, be it Tom Loughlin or Alva Lemon or Calvin Redd, sounds plaintively over his radio, "Transmit Box_____ at this location . . ." and even further descending into tradition requesting ". . . second alarm be struck out on this box." This hearkening to the time when a chief used a special Morse key to literally 'strike' or 'tap' out the electric signal for an additional alarm at a specific fire alarm box.

Like the old beat cop with his call box key reporting his rounds to headquarters on the hour or half-hour, knowing the location of the boxes throughout the city but intimately familiar with his own, the fire house FOG's listened closely to every radio transmission for the sound of bells in the background of the Communications dispatcher; bells indicting an incoming signal from a fire box on a street corner. The yell of "I hear bells!" was an indication the observant FOG had picked up the rhythmic cadence of signals from an alarm box in the company's first alarm territory. Some veterans were so familiar with the system, they could tell what battalion was receiving an alarm simply by noting whether the rhythmic *'pingpingping . . . pingping . . . pingpingping . . .'* of three-two-three was loud or soft. A loud ringing meant the bells came from the main alarm circuit directly behind the radio dispatcher and was picked up by his microphone, an alarm in the Second Battalion. During a particularly busy period, a time when Communications seems to be dispatching companies hither and yon throughout the city, Jerry March sits at the desk listening to the assignments and locations echoing endlessly through the firehouse.

Gathered at the desk are Burger and Holland, each impressed with the escalation in activity even among the usually busy districts. "Damn," March observes as yet another group of companies is sent out, "they're banging out the boxes tonight."

"They're hittin' off all over the city," Donald Holland agrees.

"And it don't matter what they get," Burger shrugs. "Communications had to send the box just in case the calls for real . . ." Each instance of action, whether it refers to a 'bang' or a 'hit', goes to that not-so-long ago time when the signal of bells sounding at the fire alarm office represented a call for the fire department.

Even the collar pins worn by the officers are bound by tradition—the 'trumpet', originally used in the real old days as a megaphone to relay orders, indicates rank from lieutenant upward, a single trumpet for a lieutenant, parallel trumpets for captain, three crossed trumpets for battalion chief, etc. When an officer is unavailable, vacation holiday, injury, it is a combination of tradition and union/labor agreements that dictates the position be filled albeit temporarily by seniority.

Seniority in most companies is further sub-divided, by tradition, into seniority in the department and seniority in the company, two different categories. Barry-Fred Kramer has twice the number of years in the department as Terry Buck, but it is Bucky who has been a member of Engine 50 longer. In practical terms it means that, when both men are working the same time, it will be Barry-Fred leading off as the junior member, March's anxiety to the contrary. The same is true regarding the 'First-Acting-Man', a title given the oldest member of the company making him officer-in-charge of the shift when the lieutenant or captain of that shift isn't working.

On Truck 105, Killen is the First-in Acting-Man. On Engine 50 it is Burger and in the absence of Gulfee and Kemp, respectively, the other two are viewed as 'Acting-lieutenants'. The tradition of inner-company seniority will determine who will be an 'acting EVD or PO or tiller. The pecking order is always in terms of company seniority, although the debate within Engine 50 leans toward more confidence in Tomcat Kelly than Barry-Fred, who has more than a decade's jump on Tom.

One may deviate ever-so slightly from department tradition, but advances in technology force such changes, a sign of contemporary culture. Departure from fire house tradition is viewed as blatant apostasy, a heretical act worthy of reinstatement of the Salem trials. They are 'Old School' ways, a litany of unwritten laws rigorously applied to all new guys in every fire house and as inviolable as The Decalogue.

In the fire house on Fort Avenue, a primary rule of tradition states no first year firefighter, regardless of age, is allowed entry into the lounge, excepting passage to the kitchen for meals, for a period not less than six months. An adumbration to that primary rule constrains said 'rookie' to the immediate watch desk area, the apparatus floor and bunkroom. The rookie in question is further limited to his activities in those areas. The watch desk is to be used for studying and memorizing the MOP's 'memorization' of it's company's first alarm assignment by address, accompanying companies and former fire alarm box numbers. The apparatus floor is to be used for memorizing the exact placement of every piece of equipment on the apparatus and cleaning and maintenance of said equipment. The bunkroom is solely for sleeping. In most fire houses the slightest, minute deviation from those strictures results in a veritable hail of invective, insult and humiliation designed to reduce the guilty offender to a shell of his former humanity no longer fit for the noble career of a fire fighter.

Tradition guides the rites of passage. That body of observable action and skills which must be undertaken, experienced and successfully performed by the newbie; taking up space in this fire house before the scepter of acceptance is extended. Said acceptance conferred by permission to get the 'East Side Lightening' tattoo inked into one's body parts and relaxation of the geographic limits imposed by the primary rule. The circumstances remain optional until the next rookie arrives, but the trade-off is the accepted member is now *called* a member of the company.

Terry Buck endured a particularly nauseating rite during his first six months. A mattress fire in The Heights prompted Bill Burger to suggest to the eager first-year man that he'd make a good impression on the other veterans if he took off his air mask and extinguished the small, but smoky fire, *mano y mano*. Years later Buck still remembers the aftermath, on his knees with his face shoved in the toilet, still clad in his turnout gear while his stomach lurched and rolled and spasmed as a result of only a few moments breathing the fumes of the mattress.

He admits he had an idea the human stomach could knot and heave as his proved capable. Propelling it's contents with such impressive force that the episode provided talk within the company for weeks.

Burger, the FOG instigating Terry's initiation, stood directly behind the kneeling newbie, arms folded across his chest, observing the ritual. "Just keep your mouth open and let everything out." Lined up behind Burger, peering over the big man's shoulder were March and Miller. "Let your stomach do the talking.'

"Just let her rip, kid," Miller cheered him on.

"Never give your tools to anyone else," is another traditional rule. Tim Bridges, four months in the fire house, experienced the consequences of a slight infraction of that tradition and never relinquished a tool again. Overhauling the interior in the aftermath of a foundry fire, Bridges was approached by a member of Truck 12 who, wanting the experience himself, talked Tim out of the ceiling hook he'd been using. Although the hook was out of Bridges' hands a total of seven minutes and Tim's eyes never left the other man, Paul Gulfee materialized from nowhere with a roll of duct tape, securing the ceiling hook in Tim's hand until it felt as though it's handle was grafted to the young fire fighter's body.

Occasionally the first-year man is given trivial information to be remembered and recited at a later date and time. The trivia is always fire department related, unexpected bits of knowledge such as the placement of firehouses in the 'old days', locations that often lasted decades despite changes in technology and mechanics. A central fire house was erected and the distance was carefully measured where the horses pulling that wagon grew exhausted during an alarm. At that spot, a new firehouse was added and the procedure began again. Better get the answer correct, because that's why you see so many firehouses so close together now, ergo MetroStrat changes.

Rarely will the senior firefighter on an engine company not have the 'pipe', the nozzle of the attack lines, the tradition is too strong. Conversely, the most junior man on a given shift will always be leading-off . . . Barry-Fred to the contrary. Tomcat Kelly grabbed the nozzle of the hose during a small kitchen fire in the Pulaski Projects, Bill Burger simply stepped on the line as it rolled out and jerked Kelly backward five feet. "Don't try that again," Burger warned with a smile, not concerned with the kitchen fire as much as the tradition on the pipe.

On Truck 105, the right step is an eternal seat for a rookie. Tim Bridges once took his position in the left jump seat and found Mark Hagan standing on the apparatus floor, holding the cab's door open, waiting for the new guy to get in where he belonged.

Tradition had formerly motivated companies to respond to the report of a fire in a 'Damn the torpedoes, full speed ahead,' fashion that was ostensibly designed to arrive on the scene and save lives and property. Eventually it became a source for fist fights between companies wanting the victory over the fire for themselves.

Speed in responding remains imperative, but actual competition to arrive first is discouraged now by the department's administration. At one time the dispatcher announced the number of the fire alarm box whose signal was being electrically received, followed by the address of the emergency and companies assigned to 'the box.' But, because a primary requirement in the firehouse was memorizing all alarm box numbers in their area, just the number of the alarm box was given as the company was turning out. A company assigned to arrive third, by virtue of distance, could 'get the jump' on the two companies listed ahead of it and arrive first, being aided along the way by edging past the posted speed limit.

So that responses were carried out as designated, the department dispatched using addresses first, but competitive companies had the addresses memorized also. As a last resort, Communications began dispatches with the company numbers and identified the location of the fire last, preventing any apparatus from leaving quarters without first knowing it's destination.

A side issue involved with turning out for an alarm was donning turnout gear prior to responding. In the effort to be first on the scene, many companies simply got on their wagon and took off, putting on their gear along the way. Once again the department hierarchy viewed this speedy approach 'unsafe' and a new set of procedures was added to the MOP stating ***all members had to be fully clothed prior to departure from the fire house!***

But even the advances in sounding an alarm is fraught with tradition. The Prometheus system references specific addresses and lists the companies to be dispatched rather than the number and address of the little red fire box closest to the site of the emergency. To bridge the jump in technology, the department's communication Bureau uses it's new Prometheus as it's primary guide, but as a security blanket, occasionally utilizes the decades-old 'box' numbers. Thus, it is not uncommon for companies to be selected and dispatched via the new age electronics and be supported by old era information.

Another dwelling fire in Jefferson Heights is a case in point. The alarm was received shortly after nine o'clock in the evening, the triple *clang* of the gong and attendant warbling alarm tones had everyone scurrying to the apparatus. The address is given as Tapswing Street and zips from the teleprinter in the same format. When the alarm is repeated over the radio a second time, however, the dispatcher augments the transmission:

"Dwelling fire . . . Eighteen Fifty-two . . . Tapswing Street . . . Box Five-Seven-Nine-Seven . . . Tapswing Street and Harlen Avenue . . . *Engine Five-Oh . . ."* despite the fact the little red fire alarm box that had formerly been located at that intersection had been removed and absent for years. Whether the practice is a final, parting nod to traditional dispatches or, as many FNG's complain, another concoction by the older members to force rookies to stay at the watch desk and memorize their first alarm district, it is an overt example of blending the old and new allowing a tradition at the Fort Avenue firehouse as well as several dozen others in the busy neighborhoods. Over time with the number of runs to the same general areas, the men of both engine and truck are able to receive an alarm and be out of the firehouse in less than a minute. Part of that ability is due to Prometheus, the rest to natural desire on the part of the firefighters.

With the Prometheus system, communications is able to send an alert and dispatch to specific companies. No other gongs will sound, no alert warbles in any other firehouse not assigned on a call with either Engine 50 or Truck 105, and vice-versa. As a result of the new procedure, the time between the initial sounding of the bells and announcement of the location is taken 'gearing up', receiving the location almost becomes secondary. There are dangers remaining to this newer version of response however.

During a particularly frigid winter, the hardcore alcohol besotted blockheads living on the streets in the districts developed the survival tactic of taking refuge from the biting winds and cold, by huddling close together inside deeply recessed archways of the firehouse exit bays. With temperatures hovering in single digits or less, it was not uncommon for three or four shattered souls, examples of humanity lowered to the bottom rungs of the vertebrate chain, bundled beneath ratty blankets, reeking of alcohol, propped against one of the large red doors at the front of the firehouse.

On a bone chilling Saturday morning, with stars shining brilliantly through icy air, the noteworthy survival tactic came to an abrupt end. The alarm came in for a dwelling fire over on Circle Park Street with the additional information that the initial report of fire was questionable, an alarm however, is an alarm.

From his seat, Jerry March waited impatiently for the exit door to raise high enough to bolt from the firehouse. He was already in the process of releasing the brakes when he saw the first dolt fall backward into the firehouse, sprawling on the cold cement floor, semiconscious and unaware that he lay less than six feet from a twenty-plus ton fire engine with it's motor running and a madman behind the wheel.

"What the hell?" Jerry leaned forward, trying to look over the front of the engine as Dan Kemp stared, open-mouthed, at the lower half of a second body sprawling backward beside it's former partner. Truck 105 had already rolled out of the firehouse and Jerry was coming to the realization they faced a collection of stiffened insensible drunks claiming squatter's rights on the firehouse doorway.

"Get the hell outta my firehouse!" an enraged Jerry March slid from his seat, hustling to the front of the engine, to begin lifting and throwing emaciated derelicts left and right. "You pieces of worthless trash! You drunk, frozen ice balls of human debris!" Jerry's ranting was punctuated by the dispersal of sprawled bodies on the floor.

Sadly, the greatest tradition under assault is the time-honored, but unspoken law that a fire department's vehicles be . . . 'fire engine red.'

"You can't always see a red fire engine at night," is one complaint.

"Emergency vehicles require higher visibility," states another.

"Good grief," Donald Holland, firefighter and fire buff extraordinaire is shaken to the core with the idea that his beloved fire apparatus requires higher visibility simply because it is red. "We got a million lights and sirens and air horns" he complains bitterly, angrily reacting to the report from City Hall that the city has decided to experiment with alternative colors for it's apparatus. "That whirring sound you hear is Ben Franklin spinning in his grave." He slumps in an armchair in the lounge after referring to the accepted 'father' of the modern fire department in America.

"What color they talkin' about?" Burger is sprawled on an adjacent couch reading the sport pages.

"Lime green and yellow," Holland groans.

"Well that ought to be real nice," Bill murmurs contentedly not looking up from his reading.

"Fire engines are meant to be red," Holland crumples the report into a ball and throws it at the corner trash can. "I mean, for God's sakes, Bill . . . it's a color itself, fire engine red."

Paul Gulfee has entered the lounge, catching the end of Donald's diatribe. "You saw the report, too huh?"

"Damn right I did," Holland responds bitterly. 'We been using red fire engines for a hundred years in this city, with no problems and now it's not good enough."

"Lime green is a highly visible color," Gulfee shrugs, pouring a cup of coffee and wanting to exercise his EVD further.

"Looks like a garbage truck," Holland shakes his head.

"I think sanitation trucks are a darker green," Burger sniffs innocently from the couch. "My sister's husband has a garbage truck and it's forest green."

"He has his own garbage truck?" Gulfee looks up with interest.

"He has a garbage route," Burger clarifies the issue.

"Oh . . . well . . . that's different," Paul grins. "Sounded like it was a family vehicle."

"It could be," Bill concedes after a moment's consideration, "It'd be appropriate."

"You guys aren't taking this seriously," Holland protests. "They're foolin' with the oldest tradition there is."

"Nah," Gulfee sips his coffee and examines the cup, "Some have white and red."

"They used to be white and orange," Burger adds. "But went back to white and red. They went to the orange thing after buying a big batch of equipment from Seagrave."

"White and orange?" Donald Holland sees the end of the world on the horizon. There is no color for a fire engine except red.

"Bright orange," Burger adds to Holland's apocalyptic distress.

"Hey Donnie," Gulfee calls to the EVD, "even New York went green on a couple of their rigs. I saw it in Firehouse Magazine."

"It just don't make sense," Holland grumbles.

"My brother-in-law is in a volunteer company," the lieutenant mentions, "and they voted to paint their rigs blue."

"Oh save me," Donald sinks deeper into the chair.

The issue remained volcanic within the department for the better part of the year. In September the department took delivery of five new engines, each painted in the lime green color scheme and assigned to the 5th battalion. In honor of the memorable event Jerry March, Holland, and Mike Greenstreet drove to the quarters of Engine 24, one of the new arrivals, as its pump operator backed it into it's bay.

March was shaking his head, "That moron looks worse than I thought. My neighbor has a baby whose dirty diaper looks that color." The three men stood just inside the firehouse door, seventy years of fire department experience between them, in red fire engines.

Holland has to turn his back and stare at the floor. "I feel ill," he mumbles.

"Hey Bobby," March calls to the PO of the engine as the man climbs from it's cab, "What do you think?"

Bobby Taylor, eight years a pump operator, tall, slender, with long thin sideburns and a genuine flattop, glances at Jerry and then at the new apparatus. There is a moment of silence. "My kid had diarrhea a week ago," Taylor shakes his head, "and I swear the inside of his diaper was the same color."

Jerry turns to Greenstreet and Holland. "I told you," he commented.

People will see you better," Greenie remarked sarcastically.

"That's why we put all the red and white lights on it," Taylor makes a face like he is nauseated.

"What's your captain say?" Jerry asks.

Taylor only shakes his head again. "He's ordered brown paper bags for everybody in the company," he replied. "We're gonna cut holes in 'em for eyes and noses and wear 'em when we get a run."

Maybe somewhere, some place, the traditional firehouse of a Norman Rockwell painting sits in the middle of the neighborhood, it's doors are open and the men are sitting outside in those little, low-backed chairs, talking and laughing with the people in the community in a spirit of friendship and neighborhood involvement. It is a picture worthy of Rockwell. One that motivates such an artist to grasp paintbrush in hand and capture that snapshot of Americana.

On Fort Avenue the reality is a stark departure of the kind producing culture shock. There are no idyllic scenes and the only tradition is a memory from decades ago. Dopers cruise back and forth along the street, passing crack and heroin, crank and China White. Street pimps like Mauritius 'D-for-Divine' Smith keep careful watch over their 'girls' and the 'girls' keep watch for any cars moving less than twenty miles per hour to that potential john who can stand upright and inhales twelve times a minute.

The new paradigm, the current tradition, for Fort Avenue and Central City, 'The Penny' is the felons and junkies gathered at the corner with hands in pockets fondling the grip of their nine millimeters solemnly scrutinizing anyone passing by, especially nervous 'boys' who appear only when the sun is up.

If you work out of the firehouse here, The Fort, tradition demands you answer every call you receive with the same sense of urgency as though your own house is burning. Tradition here, at the firehouse, means excellence, no second-place efforts allowed or tolerated. Tradition means you deal with whatever comes your way, from dealing with memorizing those MOP's and enduring every insult thrown at your inexperience. At this firehouse, and almost everyone like it, means you throw yourself into every call like it is a prelude to Armageddon. Whether it's a fire set in a vacant dwelling with holes intentionally cut in the floors to injure you or helping a paramedic crew treating a gunshot victim, all because you're trying to save the life of a cokehead lying in the gutter.

You do all that because it's part of the job and the job has it's traditions. You do it and then wonder later if maybe your deficient

DNA hasn't predisposed you to continue doing stupid things normal people wouldn't dream about. But you also know that, a couple years from now someone will look at you and wonder how you made it and will question the same traditions you question right now. It all evens out and you realize how necessary it is.

At the firehouse, the crap you put up with, is all a long, historic, continuing tradition of 'the brothers' that bonds you to them. In this job it is sometimes all you have because you know that once you pass beyond the door of the firehouse, once you wade into that sea of unwashed, hostile mass of antipathy, tradition gets flushed.

In a moment of pure irony you understand and accept that throwing your life on the line for these people who don't even pay their taxes that are used to pay your salary, becomes a real cynical euphemism called 'Community Service."

Community Service . . . community relations. Within the fire department, the division tasked with making personnel approachable to the neighborhoods and maintaining the public image of the department the people of the city is the Community Services Division. Since the department and the citizens it serves and protects constantly cross paths during a time of tragedy and emergency, the importance of portraying it's members as human beings is a critical issue.

Some communities are friendlier than others, but some thrive on hostility and apathy. In the 15th battalion, any semblance of maintaining positive relations within the immediate neighborhood is akin to attempting to befriend both Ali Baba and the larger portion of his forty thieves or Genghis Khan's Mongo hordes. It is not a matter of hatred, because during daylight hours the vast majority of the folks populating 'the Penny' act and appear normal. Only as the sun drops and darkness falls does that aura of evil and danger begin to mount, despite the wide, sunny smiles and giggles of two dozen children visiting the firehouse for a field trip or the day-long street party replete with hot dogs and burgers and free soda in the middle of Fort Avenue. There are distinct reasons for everything inside the firehouse to be bolted in place and secured with the heaviest, most secure locks industry can provide.

Adding insult to the injury of having everything in the firehouse stolen, more than once, is the constant threat of assault outside the firehouse in the course of just doing the job. Life is not just an inexpensive commodity on these streets, it is exquisitely cheap.

A running joke in the firehouse revolves around the cost of life in the district, a chicken wing. During an otherwise pleasant summer's evening, two men, cousins became embroiled in a heated argument over the ownership of the last piece of chicken at the KFC near the projects. That last piece, a wing, would have been joined by another three dozen had the two cousins been patient enough to wait an additional forty-six seconds. The decisive effort to lay hold of the wing came when one cousin produced a nine millimeter automatic and proceeded to place five rounds, center mass into his familial competitor point, game and match.

Take a run into the Pulaski Homes and you find a body bleeding into the gutter, compliments of two entry wounds in the lower abdomen. You've been called there by the two paramedics from Medic 35, one of the five paramedic units that struggles to answer eight thousand calls each year in this district alone. Within a minute or two the now familiar zip of a passing bullet lets you know your presence is not wanted, a not-so-subtle hint that the body in the gutter didn't get there by accident and is supposed to stay there; untouched by you or anyone else, until firmly and certifiably dead. Of course, there is another popular means of rendering unwanted humanity to a state of vegetation, ramming an ice pick between the second and third cervical vertebra with the sole purpose of permanently paralyzing said humanity for the rest of their life. Both methods, bullet and pick, are the going rate for having the poor taste of strolling along the wrong side of the street holding drugs from a local competitor.

Unless you've lived in a cave on an isolated Micronesian island for the quarter of a century, it has become relatively easy to recognize an ambulance or fire engine in the streets of any given city. Among the generally civilized nations of the world the arrival of such identifiable vehicles at the scene of an emergency is welcomed. Not the case in the eastern district on Fort Avenue.

For the personnel accompanying the emergency vehicle, rule number One is to determine the ebb and flow of the crowd gathered for a victim prostrate in the street. If assessment dictates treatment, a constricting crowd around said victim's body space augers further, imminent injury. If that mass of humanity expands to allow emergency personnel access to the victim, there is an even chance egress will also be granted. Constricting crowds means 'swoop and scoop,' no treatment, put the victim on a stretcher and get yourself out of the neighborhood.

You apply for the job of firefighter and anticipate, with good reason, that if accepted, you will fight fire. After four months at the fire academy and subsequently, being assigned to a busy company, you settle into your logical role of being a firefighter, no glory, some people claim minimum brainwork also. But then the city develops the concept that emergency services, firefighting, should also include healthcare, and since the city runs the fire department, it's easy to slip the ambulances and paramedics under that big umbrella.

You had already put your life on the line putting out fires for a whole lot of people who don't give a damn to begin with and now you are also responsible for helping provide healthcare to the same crack heads, increasing your exposure to their apathy, antipathy and inscrutable logic. For some guys the job of paramedic is the cat's meow, the high-priced cheese instead of the other stuff. Most of the females coming out of the academy want to be paramedics, and that's fine. A parallel is found in Kipling and paraphrase it so that: Ambulances are Ambulances and fire engines are fire engines and never the twain shall meet.

At least part of that is true since some people can't wait until they get a rotation on the ambulance. Almost all of the older guys abhor ambulance duty like Dracula hates garlic and crucifixes. The new guys would rather be smeared with honey and stake over an anthill than work in the ambulance shift. This new generation of academy graduates grew up sitting in front of their televisions watching 'emergency' or 'Squad 51' but not a majority of the men.

To the companies in the Fort Avenue firehouse, the 'Medic Assist' runs are the bane of their existence. Reduced to its basics, a 'medical assist' is essentially, a call for more man power. That means, of course, one of the two companies is turned out, lights flash on, sirens scream, the whole nine yards, to join the ambulance. It can mean removing a victim from a crumpled car using the Hurst tool to open a vehicle like a can of tuna or assist in moving a patient who is so grossly heavy, the task requires half a dozen people.

Sarah Caldwell is one of those awesomely overweight specimens of humanity whose growth to planetary proportions has taken place within the 15th battalion boundaries. Sarah is on the downward slope of middle age.

"I didn't join the fire department for this," Jerry March glowers at Burger, who is acting officer of the shift. The precise title 'Acting Lieutenant' will pay Bill an officer's scale for the duration of his time of 'acting man.'

The shift's first run of the night comes at five-fifteen, a call to assist Medic 10 at 11012 Gloucester Street, Apartment B. Every paramedic unit that has driven through the east side knows the address, Sarah CardWhale lives there, or more accurately, lays there.

Years ago, Sarah's somewhat frail, milquetoast husband, Xavier, converted the couple's living room into a permanent bedroom for his planet sized spouse. In that converted living room, spread and mounted on a reinforced double bed, the enormous woman has done little more than lay, eat, watch television and expand geometrically. Bill Burger can see the woman through the first floor window as he slowly approaches the front door. A paramedic greets bill, shrugging apologetically before any words can be exchanged.

"I know, I know," Bill nods, bare-headed, wearing only his turnout coat. "It's Sarah, we know the address."

"I'm sorry Bill," the paramedic, Sharita, is an attractive street-tough woman who does not countenance bull. Her smile is a dazzling white display of perfect teeth and she uses it effectively, knowing her request for assistance does not sit well with the firemen. "Seems like our girl has developed breathing problems and after I spoke to St. Joe's on the radio they want her transported to the hospital." Sharita looks over Bill's shoulder and sees Terry Buck and Filthy Nick, two of her favorite firefighters. "Hi guys," she greets them with that dazzling smile.

"Transport her in what?" Burger scowls. "You gonna call a tow truck?" The small procession enters the apartment where a second paramedic, Juanda Hurlock, is attempting to begin an intravenous line in the patient's massive arm. "Use a harpoon," Bill rumbles.

Loud, watery wheezing fills the room, the desperate attempts of a very obese woman to work air into her lungs. Sarah Caldwell lies in her bed perspiring profusely. Behind the oxygen mask covering her nose and mouth, the woman's eyes are wide with terror. Burger can hold his breath only so long inside the apartment, the stench is overpowering. Years of infrequent bathing, incontinence, inadequate cleansing after other bodily functions and a dozen other breakdowns in basic hygiene leaves the interior of the dwelling smelling somewhat barn-like.

"Did you mess yourself, Sarah?" Burger asks in a loud voice, seeing the woman nod as Sharita answers "Yes," simultaneously; Bill rolls his eyes.

"You got the I.V.?" Sharita asks her partner.

"I can't find a vein in all this fat," Juanda struggles, slapping and examining wide expanses of pale skin.

"Uh Sharita," Burger nudges the paramedic, "When was the last time this whale was dragged ashore?"

"I dunno," Sharita shrugs, "why?"

"I don't know how we are going to get her out of here," Bill nods at the doorway. "If she was transported before, I'd like to find our how and see if maybe she's grown a little bit." Nick and Bucky are pressed against the far wall of the room. Xavier Caldwell stands steadfast at the head of his wife's bed, furtively stroking her sweaty brow.

"Mr. Caldwell," Sharita speaks loudly, the way people raise their voice in the presence of someone who doesn't understand English. "The firemen want to know when your wife was taken to the hospital the last time. Can you remember?"

"Y . . . y . . . yes," Xavier nods anxiously. "I . . . i . . . it w-was a . . . uh . . . month a-a-ago," his stammer has Burger unconsciously nodding his head, silently coaxing the words from Mr. Caldwell. "T-th . . . the fire department h . . . h . . . had t . . . to c . . . c . . . cut out th—th—the d-d-doorway," he finally pushes out the words to the joy of Burger whose neck is beginning to ache.

"Lovely," Bill rolls his eyes and glances at Sharita, rewarded with another of her smiles. "We shoulda called for the Rescue," he mumbles, pulling his cell phone from a coat pocket. Pushing the button for the automatic dialer, the big man wait's a moment. He is dialing the quarters for Rescue 3, the heavy-duty Rescue Company assigned to the First Division.

"Hey Babe," his tone is friendly when the call is taken by Rescue 3' watch desk. "This is Burger, Engine 50. Who's the officer working tonight?" A pause before, "Ronnie . . . Bill Burger here. Engine 50," Bill nods and smiles into the phone. "Listen Ron," Bill's voice takes on a pitiful tone, "We got a medic assist to Sarah Caldwell . . ." He holds the phone a full three inches from his ear and everyone in the room hears the loud guffaws ringing through the receiver.

"Yeah, okay." Bill finally speaks after fifteen seconds of overly dramatic derision, "I just wanted to call you privately and ask you to call Communications and put yourself out of service to come over here and takedown the doors and walls so we can get this lady to the hospital." The officer at Rescue 3 speaks quickly. Bill turns to Sharita. "The Rescue wants to know if this is a medical emergency." When the paramedic assures Burger that Sarah's life is, indeed in jeopardy, the information is relayed through the phone. Seconds later the handie-talkie on Burger's shoulder comes to life, informing the Division that Rescue 3 is being placed out-of-service to assist Engine 50 and Medic 10.

"We oughtta try to get Sarah as secure and stable as possible," Bill glances at Miller and Buck. At that moment a loud watery explosion rumbles through the soft tissue forming the range of Sarah Caldwell's gut. Within seconds of the thunderous report, the room fills with a smell overwhelmingly and singularly disgusting in its vile pungency. Eyes blink and Sharita searches her pocket for a small surgical mask. Terry Buck and Nick are working their jaws, opening and closing their mouths in an attempt to prevent themselves from gagging.

Once the initial olfactory shock subsides, Burger is able to draw enough breath to remark with appropriate solemnity, "Maybe I shoulda' called for a Haz-Mat response instead.

Each year the fire department sets aside one weekend for 'Open House." It is an opportunity for members of the neighborhoods and communities, whether taxpaying citizens or dependant upon taxpaying citizens, to visit the local firehouse, mingle with the men and become familiar and its hoped friendly with individuals who are charged with protecting their lives and property. In the majority of instances, the occasions are filled with the innocent laughter of children and the general questions from adolescents and adults while strolling through the fire house, maybe sipping a soda or enjoying a snack. In others, the more ominous communities of the 'Open House Weekend' presents a decidedly guarded and suspicious environment. Locks are checked to make sure they are secure, personal possessions are hidden and secured in the nearest resemblance of a vault. In the Fort Avenue firehouse every member of both companies reports to duty and ring the apparatus floor while at least one man keeps watch over the back parking lot. Jerry March has suggested metal detectors be installed at the front door and Mike Greenstreet has offered to help erect barbed wire to keep erstwhile visitors in plain sight and under control. Neither offer is seriously considered although both were seriously given.

Visiting the firehouse though, is not limited or restricted to the designated 'Open House Weekend.' In practice, anyone can stop at the firehouse, introduce themselves and receive a quick tour. Even the more benign of the dopers and befuddled brain heads who manage to lurch their broken, derelict selves through the firehouse door have been handed a dollar or two on the sly out of sheer pity at their plight. One of the 'regular' visitors to the firehouse, the occasions a source of both humor and frustration, is 'Pops' one of the last remaining white residents living on Presstmen Street.

Nobody knows "Pops' real name. He has always been 'Pops,' his wife's name is 'Moms' and has lived on Presstmen Street for nearly six decades. His hair is thick, curly and completely white, the freckles and age spots battle for sole possession of his pale skin. To the men in the firehouse, Pops is the last surviving memory of the time when this neighborhood was not a postcard for urban decay, proof that despite the continual spiraling down of civilized society there is a remnant of a better, genteel time.

The debate whether Pops retains his original teeth is ongoing, his wide smile and gravelly, high-pitched voice recognizable immediately. Dan Kemp, for all his brusqueness and cutting cynicism, leaves standing orders as house captain that Pops is to be accorded every courtesy and favor normally rendered to a 'friend of the firehouse.'

Pops rarely visits during the winter months when the biting, icy cold works hard at his ancient arthritic joints and the walk to the firehouse is too long to endure the discomfort. Other than those painful weeks, however, it is not uncommon for the old man to wander aimlessly through the big front doors, when they are raised, or totter through the smaller pedestrian door with body slightly bent at the waist, head bobbing with each step and a crooked smile on his lined, weathered face as he greets each man crossing his path.

At midday during the first day of the four day trick, Pops comes through the big doorway in front of the engines. The sky is clear and, despite a slight chill, the exit door has been raised. He wears a pair of battered, green corduroy slippers and a thin sweater. His flannel shirt is tucked into a pair of tan trousers and, in place of a belt, a length of clothes line holds his trousers just above his bony hips. Once inside the firehouse the elderly man makes a straight line to the watch desk where Terry Buck has been watching his entrance with a bemused smile.

"Hey Pops," Bucky stands up from his chair and grins at the old man.

"Howdy," Pops nods and waves at the chair, "sit down, sit down."

"Where you been?" Terry asks, sitting as ordered. "You ain't been around for a while. We figured you and Moms probably were down in the Bahamas or something . . . laying on the beach and drinking."

"Horse poop," Pops chuckles quietly, "if I was gonna go to the beach, I wouldn't be takin' the old woman," he grins wickedly. Terry feigns shock.

"Why wouldn't you do that?" he asks. "She's your wife."

Pops glances over both shoulders and leans forward, lowering his voice to a conspiratorial whisper, "She ain't got enough curves, in fact she's flat as a pancake." Terry begins to giggle. "I ain't kiddin," he protests, "if I was gonna go to them Bahamas, the first I'd do was get me a younger woman."

When Buck is able to compose himself, he acts surprised. "You'd take a younger woman?"

"Hell yes," Pops looks at Terry like the younger man suddenly grew a second head, "I ain't takin' no old bag with me when I want to have fun." He pauses thoughtfully and shrugs, "I guess sixty's be young enough, you think?"

"Yeah," Bucky is barely able to say the word without his shoulders heaving.

"I hear they got nude beaches down there," Terry prods the older man.

"Don't matter," there is an emphatic shake of his white-haired head, "when I want to have fun, I do!" The frail old man makes a fist and pumps the air as forcefully as an eighty year-old man can pump air. When the thin bony arm has been lowered, Pops smiles sheepishly, "Where's that big fella today?"

"Which one?" Buck asks.

"That big blond fella," Pops does a tight figure eight in the air as his octogenarian-mind struggles with placing names and faces, "the fella always wears a white shirt."

"The captain?" Terry nods understanding and hit's the transmit button on the box. "Hey Cap," he calls loudly, "you got a visitor demanding to see you."

Several seconds pass before Dan Kemp treads heavily down the spiral stairway at the rear of the apparatus floor. He is scowling until he spies the slightly stooped figure of Pops at the cubicle. "Hey Pops," his greeting is loud and echoes through the firehouse. "How are you?" he puts a big arm around the frail shoulders, gently embracing the elderly visitor

"Howdy," Pops grins and bobs his head. Dan 's booming greeting attracts the attention of some of the other men and Burger, Miller, Holland and Bridges troop from the lounge. The old man watches the single file approach, an open-mouthed smile on his face. Terry looks closely at the thin face and notices that Pops needs a shave. Snow white whiskers form stubble over the other man's chin and jaw.

"I'm glad you came by." Kemp's face becomes serious although his eyes sparkle with mischief. "I got a bone to pick with you."

"Oh yeah," Pops looks at the bigger man without blinking.

"You sold me some apples about a couple months ago," Dan prods the old man's memory. The sale involved a paper grocery bag filled with apples, the bag brought to the firehouse by Pops, and sold to the captain. The old man and his wife struggle to survive on their fixed income in the decadent neighborhood and Dan offered to purchase the entire bag for fifty dollars.

"What of it?" Pops squints at the officer

"They were all bad," Kemp declares, "rotten, spoiled. The whole bunch was bad. I went through every apple in the bag and didn't find one that I could eat." The accusation has no effect on the elderly man, who remains pensive and then purses his lips and places a thin finger at his chin.

"You sure it was me who sold them to you"

Dan's face reddens and he struggles for composure, "Yeah, I'm sure," he says emphatically, suppressing a smile. "How many old goats you think come in here selling apples?"

"How the hell should I know?" Pops shrugs and looks into the faces of the men surrounding him, each man observing the old man with a personal fondness, "That's why I was askin' if you was sure it was me you bought them from?"

The radio horn on the front wall sends a transmission echoing through the high ceilinged room and Terry lowers the volume. "I think you sold the Captain them bad apples," he suggests softly.

"Mebbe," Pops thrusts out his chin, defiant "I ain't sayin' it was me . . . ain't sayin' it wasn't." The firefighters exchange smiles.

"That's against the law," Tim Bridges interjects, "this is a city building and if you sold bad goods here . . . well," he takes a deep breath, "the law says we gotta call the apple police."

"Horse manure," the old man looks at Tim in mock anger, eyes sparkling, 'there ain't no such thing as apple police."

Tim puts a hand flat against his chest and staggers backward a few steps, "There isn't?"

"You think I fell off the turnip truck yesterday, son?" Pops wheezes and his expression becomes somber when he glances at Kemp. "When did you say them apples was bad?"

"I checked 'em an hour after you left," the burly officer claims.

"I shoulda figgered," Pops scowls and nods like a man who has solved a mystery murder. "I shoulda known and so should you."

"Known what?" the captain is teetering on an outburst of laughter.

"Them apples was good, y'see?" Pops launches into an explanation concerning fruit, his intensity and sobriety the envy of an agricultural agent. "When I sold 'em to you, they were good and when you took 'em they were good." Kemp's hands are in his back pockets and he leans forward to listen carefully. "But you didn't use 'em right away," the visitor explains, hands making short rolling movements over each other in front of his chest, like he is shaping a snowball.

"If you had used 'em right then and there," Pops declares, "it woulda been fine." He nods with the confidence of a physician making a correct diagnosis. "But you waited . . . you waited, see? And any dummy with half a brain knows you just can't sit back and wait on fruit . . . especially apples."

"Huh?" Dan's shoulders begin to shake.

"I'm telling' you the truth," Pops raises his right hand, oath-taking style, "you wait mebbe twenny or thirty minutes tops on apples and they go bad on you," his hands slap together, . . . just like that!"

"Like that?" Kemp mimics the hand slapping.

"Yep," Pops shrugs, knowing his explanation has satisfied the captain's complaint, unaware Dan could care less about the apples, regretting only he hadn't doubled the amount of money he paid Pops.

"Pops is looking for a new girlfriend," Terry introduces a new topic to the assembled group.

"You are?" Donald Holland is grinning, his mouth opening wider.

"Damn right," the old man confirms Buck's information.

"Your wife know?" Burger asks, a hand over his mouth to hide a smile.

"Don't need to know," Pops bobs his head and leans against the outside of the cubicle. "But even if she did, I don't care."

The smiles fade and allows Kemp to address a more serious topic. "Y'know, Pops, you need to think about moving out of this miserable neighborhood."

"You say that?"

"Hell yeah," Dan nods, "this is a terrible neighborhood, it's violent."

"Don't bother me none," Pops stands defiant, chin thrust out, shoulders squared. "Ain't none of them people around here bothers me."

"Really?" Terry Buck looks hard at the old man in front of him.

"Anyone ever try to break into your house?" Dan inquires.

"I got a big, heavy, front door," Pops declares with a thrust of his chin. There is a moment's pause before he adds, "Ain't got no lock though," and the laughter erupts all over again.

Dan fishes in his pocket for a handkerchief, wiping his eyes, "You don't have a lock on your door?"

"Uh uh," Pops shrugs, "but that don't matter," he continues, "I got a gun."

Instantly the mood turns serious. "You got a gun? A real gun?" Bridges asks.

"Sure do," the old man surveys Tim's face, remembering the 'apple police,' "I got me a good gun, a hand gun."

"Do you know how to use it?" Donald Holland's eyebrows come together in a frown and he pushed his glasses back up on his nose.

"Of course," Pops looks at the EVD with disdain, his hoarse, high-pitched voice has a sarcastic edge to it. "Why would I have a gun if I didn't know how to use it?"

"I was just asking," Donald is apologetic.

"You ever need to use it?" Dan Kemp wants to know.

Pops shakes his head, "Nope, no . . . never used it," he sighs and shrugs at a goal yet to be attained.

"In this neighborhood?" Dan is skeptical, "never used it?"

"Nope," the old gentleman assures the officer, "I scare the little bastards with it . . . but I ain't never used it to fire." The assurance is settling, the concern for this man is genuine. His well being is not taken for granted. A short pause ensues, perhaps ten seconds, before Pops adds quietly, "Ain't got no bullets for it anyways," and six grown men collapse with laughter.

The ebb and flow of humanity around the firehouse during 'Open House Week' finds it's counterpart in an outreach program not listed in the Lafayette Park directives concerning Community Relations. Home visits, inspections, smoke detector installation and Fire Prevention Week comprise a formal person-to-person aspect of what the department considers 'community relations.' Personal relationships of the memorable kind are forged as the result of 'informal,' spontaneous circumstances occurring everyday on the street, few find a corresponding category in an MOP.

"Place Truck 105 in service in the district for driver training," Paul Gulfee speaks to communications in a clipped voice over the watch desk phone. On the apparatus floor Holland, Hagan, Killen and Bridges are pulling on their turnout coats and climbing on to the truck. The outing is for the benefit of Mark Hagan who is tillering in place of Greenstreet, the side trip to the credit union goes unmentioned by Gulfee.

"We ready?" Paul settles into his seat in the cab, glancing at Holland, Donald hears the buzzer sounding from Mark, the signal he is ready, and winks at the lieutenant.

"Now we are," he grins and releases the brakes. The credit union won't close until four o'clock and there is no rush. Donald turns left and at the corner of Fort and Jefferson reaches over and hit's the air horn. A slender brunette jerks her head around at the noise and her hardened face breaks into something resembling a smile. Her attention is focused on the rear of the truck where Mark leans from the open door of the tiller cab and waves. The prostitute returns the greeting with an enthusiastic wave of her own, blowing a kiss at the husky man steering the back of the truck.

"Jessi," Donald identifies the hooker for the sake of his lieutenant.

"I thought this was Diamond's corner," Paul cocks his head to the side, leaning back in his seat, relaxed.

"Jessi and Diamond are the same person," Donald confides.

"You're kidding me?"

"Nope," Holland hit's the horn again, a quick double tap. "Apache," he nods in the direction of a solidly built blonde.

"Apache?" Gulfee cranes his neck to follow the woman as the truck glides past. He turns back to Donald, confused and unsure. "What is that name?" he grins. "A white hooker named Apache working the streets of an all black neighborhood?"

"It's called diversity, Paul," Holland observes.

In the seats behind Gulfee and Holland, Tim Bridges stares blankly out the side window, "You want to go fishing with me and Burger?" Sam Killen's question breaks Tim's concentration.

"Where you gonna go?"

"South River," Killen answers noncommittally. "We're gonna take his boat out . . . make a day of it." The idea is Burger's.

"Yeah," Tim accepts the invitation, "I'd like that," his eyes narrow as he looks at Sam. "What are we fishing for?"

Killen gives the other man a dour look, "Fish," he replies. The truck slides through an intersection and Sam adds, "You bring the beer . . . and get the good stuff. None of that cheap crap, okay."

"That's why you asked me," Tom frowns, "this isn't anything more'n a glorified beer party." His comment draws a "So what?" expression from the craggy face.

"And your point?" Killen asks without looking at Tim. His gaze is fixed on the herds of people moving along the pavement. "I can't think of anything we do that doesn't center on beer." It is another sociological fact, beer and firefighters. Occasion or location doesn't matter. Union meetings, shift parties, baseball games, football games, funerals, weddings, births . . . the list continues. The common denominator is always beer. Three years ago, when Mike Greenstreet had been hospitalized after falling through the roof of a burning dwelling, the big man spent several hours in surgery. Finally returning to his room where a horrified nurse found Sam, Bill Burger, Jerry and Donald Holland encamped around the hospital bed, an ice cooler of Budweiser atop sheets and the firefighters dividing chili-dogs among themselves wondering when Greenie would be hungry.

East Franklin Street has cars parked along both sides, creating a narrow channel through which Holland carefully steers the truck.

"Whoa what have we here?" Paul Gulfee points out the window.

Three black youths are doing the 'walk' along Franklin. That self-assured, cocky don't mess with me stride that has become the 'march' the semi-official sway, immediately shared by the locals when two or more are headed in the same direction. In this instance, all three homeboys have that arrogant chin-up, arm swinging step that would allow them to cover more ground if they weren't carrying heavy rolls of black conduit on their shoulders. Their guilt is sealed when the trio do a crisp three sixty at the sight of the truck.

"I think we got an 'Act Three' in progress," Holland suggests.

Before any building, invariably vacant, gets burned down, there is a scripted, though informal, process to strip the structure in question of whatever may be of value. The process has been observed and codified by the firefighters in three specific stages . . . 'Acts' . . . and is inviolable as the rising and setting of the sun. Only upon completion of those three 'Acts' can it be expected that the building will be set on fire.

'Act One' involves a wholesale carryout of anything not nailed or bolted down, carpet, tile, tables, chairs, appliances and the like. The second stage, 'Act Two' includes fixtures, faucets, door knobs, lights and even light bulbs. When the Kentucky Fried Chicken store in South City was finally lit off, the premises had been vacant for several months. The first wave of 'shoppers' had been so thorough that even the urinals in the men's room were stolen. The last 'Act' of this sad trilogy was the stripping away of the plumbing and electrical entrails inside the empty building . . . electrical conduits precisely like this kind carried over the shoulders of these three stooges trying to shuffle their way out of sight of the firefighters on the truck. Removal of the last vestiges of civilization, electricity, is the trip wire. Once the interior is denuded of all indications of previous life, the final step is this low-drama restructuring of the city, the gasoline can and match. It is cause and effect.

"You just sit and watch where the homeys and the yo's are carrying out the wiring from some empty building and you just mark the spot 'cause sure as hell there's gonna be a fire in two weeks."

Gulfee and Holland spy three yo's strutting along Franklin with all that stolen conduit and know they've stumbled on a gold mine.

"Hold up bro," Gulfee calls loudly from his open window of the truck's cab. His door opens and the lieutenant is standing in the street facing the trio, pulling back the front of his turnout coat to show the department badge pinned to his white shirt. One benefit of dealing with nitwits is the fact they don't grasp the fact Gulfee doesn't have any law enforcement power, but he has a uniform and badge which makes him 'the Man' until they find out the truth.

"Whattup?" the response is a dull monotone from the tallest of the youths who does a shuffle in his two hundred dollar Nikes and gives Paul a loose limbed waggle of one arm. All three youths are dressed in their Projects finest; hooded sweatshirts drawn loosely around their heads, baggy sweatpants whose crotch hangs below the knees and nylon bandanas, formal wear in the 'hood.'

"Whattup?" Paul smiles and shakes his head at the version of proclaimed innocence. The Projects-version of friendly distraction, an attempt to allay Gulfee's suspicions. *They know we caught 'em,* Paul thinks to himself. "C'mon, man," Paul says, "Don't piss in my ear and tell me it's rainin', okay?" He nods at the coils of black conduit, "We're gonna confiscate that in the name of the city."

"Huh?" the three exchange nervous glances and turn back to Gulfee with confused, concerned frowns. At the same time Killen and bridges join Paul facing the three young men.

"Now I know you just didn't stroll out of Home Depot with that conduit" Gulfee gives them a wry smile, "And I know you aren't taking it home to Momma so you can put a nightlight in her bathroom."

"Aw, c'mon, man," the shortest of the three is tossing his head around like Stevie Wonder, "we ain't done nothing' wrong, okay" We just found this layin' up in the alley and figgered it' be worf something'."

"Oh yeah," Paul agrees, "only problem with that is all the buildings around here belong to the city," he can't be sure they will buy the statement, but he's willing to carry it on as long as he can.

"So?" the tall homey shrugs, still doing his shuffle in those two hundred dollar shoes, like he's dancing' in place.

"So, if this belongs to the city," Gulfee doesn't miss a beat, "then we gotta confiscate it in the name of the city," he shrugs, "we're duly authorized representatives of the city." If the three want to walk away there's nothing Paul can do, but they are still not sure of his authority and linger, nervously, at street side.

"You're foolin' wit us" the tallest one says, eyes narrowing slightly with suspicion.

"Now why would I stand here and mislead you?" Paul asks innocently, considering his next move.

"We aren't allowed to bluff," Killen's deep voice rumbles ominously, "not on city business."

"Man, this is crap," the shortest homey complains, his head still doing figure-eights as though his neck is rubberized.

"Life's a bitch," Gulfee agrees with a shrug. East Franklin Street is empty of traffic, but the parked cars on either side makes it seem choked. Truck 105 sits in the narrow channel formed by bumper-to-bumper cars, motor running and although the flow of pedestrians is steady back on Fort Avenue, nobody ventures along Franklin, allowing this confrontation to remain private.

"The only other way," Paul continues, "is for me to call the police and let them figure it out," he absently fondles the Handie-Talkie hanging from his shoulder. "But then you know how the cops are," he drops the reminder, "they'd probably think you guys stole all this and want to take you down to the Eastern District station . . ."

"We don't need no *poleeces*," the tall boy interrupts.

What a revelation, Gulfee thinks to himself, *these creeps probably have sheets on them, pages long.*

The tall kid can hide his frustration no longer and stops shuffling to stamp a foot on the pavement. He doesn't take his eyes off Gulfee and Paul can see suspicion in them slowly morph into restful hatred. The officer knows all that saves him from bodily harm is the presence of Killen and Bridges. Tall yo boy nudges Shorty, "Give it up Buggy," he speaks softly.

"Yeah Buggy," Gulfee addresses the smaller youth, receiving as baleful a glare as a brown skinned munchkin can give and still be taken seriously.

The exchange is made quickly, and three heavy rolls of electrical conduit are handed to the firefighters who, in turn throw the contraband into the cab of the truck. Gulfee climbs back into his seat, taking care to move slowly and confidently, like he is King of the Hill, showing no signs of nervousness. Once in his seat, door shut, the lieutenant gives the three brain deads a friendly wave. The look he gets in return can only be described as classic hatred.

"You SOB's gonna have a real big fire around' here one day," the tall Einsteinian mumbles, empty hands now thrust deep in sweatshirt pockets.

"Yeah Jerk," Paul murmurs, "and I'll know just who set it."

The truck pulls from the scene of the heist and Gulfee twists in his seat, looking back at Killen; the big man is carefully examining the conduit, running the coils through his hands. "How much?"

Sam is quiet for a moment, estimating weight multiplied by price, considering what businesses would show the best interest. "We got enough here for a real big meal, Loo," he smiles. "A real big meal."

Gulfee slaps his hands together, rubbing them hard. "I knew this would be a good day," he laughs.

Success and satisfaction are hard-earned by-products of careful planning and beginning with a solid foundation. The easiest, and most careless follow-up to what is called 'The Big Copper Caper', would have been to present the electric conduit to one of several scrap metal yards in the city, collect the money for it's copper and divide the spoils among themselves. Such haste, however, has implications. If the stolen-then-confiscated conduit has indeed been reported missing, it's appearance at a scrap metal/salvage yard would involve the firehouse in breaking the law. There's little sense in drawing attention to their prize possession and nobody could guarantee the three homeboys on East Franklin didn't go to the poleeces their own selves and file a report against the firemen. Although the concept of 'Finders-Keepers/Losers-Weepers' and 'Possession is Nine-Tenths of the Law' continue to remain sound principles on the street, there are no guarantees once 'the authorities' become involved.

Instead, and after careful, prolonged counsel with Dan Kemp and Jerry March, the big rolls of conduit remain carefully stored in the back of the firehouse, tucked among the bevy of tools, lockers and equipment that crowds the apparatus floor around the three firehouse vehicles. Like treasure liberated from a Spanish galleon or payroll from an Old West stage coach whose whereabouts are being searched by an enthused posse, the electrical conduit is allowed to 'cool off' before seeing the light of day once more.

When the time arrives, it is not the light of day that greets the modern-day treasure, it is the florescent lights of the firehouse at night.

During the evening of the second night, on a trick three weeks after the East Franklin Street incident, the decision is reached to deal with the 'buried treasure.' There is a protocol to be followed. Haphazard, indifferent habits could bring disaster, at least such paranoia accompanied the stolen conduit as it sat in the firehouse. Nobody in the city cared where the wiring has disappeared, but firefighters, conscious of their own role in the bloodless stick-up will not be comfortable until no further link between themselves and the conduit exists.

Shortly after dinner on a Friday evening, Dan Kemp saunters innocently to the watch desk and lifts the department telephone from it's cradle. "Hey Bunk," Dan speaks to an unidentified communications technician at the other end of the phone. "Cap'n Kemp, Engine 50 . . . put us out of service for the report of a dumpster fire, four hundred block of Concord Street," there is a pause and Dan has a loose grin on his face, . . . "we had a passerby report the fire to us in-quarters." When the call is ended Dan slaps his hands together.

"Terry!" his voice booms across the apparatus floor, "get that conduit and throw it on the wagon." He leans out of the cubicle and spies Burger walking to the front from the lounge, "Hey Bill, grab the five gallon can will you?"

Bill gives a snappy salute and veers to his right, disappearing to the far side of the truck where a red-painted hand pump dispenses gasoline; using the pump to fill the five-gallon container sitting against the wall. Task finished, Burger hoists the can and transports it to the engine, securing it inside the cab where he will be seated.

A faint breeze is stirring as Engine 50 turns into the small parking lot outside Elementary School 459 on Concorde Street directly across from the main entrance to the Pulaski Projects. Huge brick buildings looming ominously in the dark, forbidding and threatening, the perfect backdrop for a 'dumpster fire.'

Terry Buck spreads the conduit in wide loops across the open lot and Burger follows, spouting gasoline from the can, soaking every inch of the black insulation and creating a miniature lake of gasoline centered on the wiring. "Good thing it's night," he observes, shaking the last drops from the container, "no cars in the lot." He laughs, "Can't you picture a lot full of cars lighting off if they were running school at night and this place was packed?"

Dan Kemp checks that Miller is ready with the hose, "We ready?" It requires half a pack of matches before Dan finds one that remains lit. "Shoulda brought a flare," the captain laughs, tossing the lighted match in an arc toward the center of the python-like conduit. In a flash and dull thud, the middle expanse of the parking lot is transformed into a sea of flames, the faces of the firefighters caught in the brilliant illumination.

The heat makes Terry blink and step back, unprepared for the intensity of the flames. "Damn," he glances at Burger, "you think we used too much gasoline?"

All eyes are riveted on he boiling clouds of black smoke rolling skyward. "You think somebody over in the Homes is gonna see the fire and call it in?" Miller speaks loudly to Kemp.

Dan looks over his shoulder at the darkened canyons across the street, "Don't matter," he shakes his head, turning his attention back to the conflagration he has helped engineer on the parking lot. "If it gets called in we're already here," he notes with a shrug, "but those dimwits are already too busy settin' their own fires to worry about this one."

The fire is not as intense as at first but smoke continues to roll upward blotting the light of a nearby street lamp. The once bright flames have consumed the gasoline and are working on the black insulation, a mass of smaller, steadier flickering flames causing the conduit to liquefy and oxidize, revealing a solid mass of shining copper underneath.

Kemp strolls to the perimeter of the smoky, flickering mass and examines it carefully. A full three minutes pass before the officer retraces his steps and waves to Nick. "Hit it," he orders. The stream of water erupts from the pipe as Nick plays the line over the dwindling fire. A massive hiss sweeps through the dark lot and massive clouds of white smoke replaces the inky black clouds.

It only takes a few minutes to extinguish the fire and when Miller shuts down the nozzle, the loose knot of men step closer to see the consequences of their handiwork.

"Damn," Burger is impressed and the word escapes his lips as he looks down on several hundred dollars-worth of gleaming high-grade copper.

"Let's roll this stuff up," Kemp says, "and get it on the wagon. Paul said he'll run it over to Orleans Scrap Metal in the morning." At his command, the firemen converge on their final prize and begin rolling the lengths of copper into more manageable loops.

"One of the great things about this job," March comments to the captain as the engine heads back to it's Fort Avenue Firehouse, "is the way the people in this neighborhood respond to our needs." He laughs aloud, "Just knowing the poor firemen in the firehouse need money for food . . . look what they did."

"Oh I know," Dan leans forward in his seat, "giving of their own possessions just so we don't starve."

"Real community service," Jerry nods, "giving to firefighters what they've stolen from others."

The engine is backing through the open doorway at the firehouse, the back-up warning bell still *bing-bing-bing*ing when the alarm is received, an odor of natural gas in Pulaski Homes; Engine 50 and Truck 105 investigate . . .

Kemp climbs back up into his seat and slaps the cushioned console in front of him. "We were so close we could have walked across the street!"

"I don't want to walk around that place," Jerry shakes his head, turning left from Fort Avenue on to Sinclair, Sirens and air horns crashing and wailing.

Eight large buildings form the cluster of low income, high-rise housing known as 'Pulaski Homes'; pressed into a twenty square acre expanse of cement, asphalt and packed dirt. Grass does not exist anywhere around the homes although the trees planted there when the housing project was erected have grown upward and outward to form a thick canopy obscuring the majority of street lamps that dot the complex. Given the fact that more than three quarters of those street lights have been shot out and remain that way, the heavy expanse of the tree limbs and leaves makes little difference. The grounds around the eight story, grimy brick towers are perpetually cloaked in darkness. In the building known simply as Building A, a telephone call has been made to the fire department reporting a strong odor of gas.

"Fourth Floor," Kemp shouts, slamming the door of the cab. Behind the engine, Holland brings the truck near the building and the men from both companies slowly clamber from their vehicles, glancing warily up at the fourth floor windows.

"Stretch me a line?" Burger pauses at the side of the engine, ready to pull the hose used for interior work. He's hoping the captain will refuse and is delighted when Kemp shakes his head.

"Nah," Dan scowls, "probably need a wrench."

Paul Gulfee and his company, tools in hand, precede the engine company, entering a first floor entrance and lumbering up a narrow, interior stairway. The concrete steps reek of urine and are littered with a collection of assorted trash and rubbish normally escaping trash bags enroute to the big dumpsters near the parking area. Along the third floor is a large mound of black plastic garbage bags bulging with refuse, as if the owners didn't feel like using the stairs and began building this small hill instead.

"Hey, look." Sam Killen uses the tip of his boot to touch a cluster of plastic milk jugs. Six of the opaque containers form a straight line along the edge of the landing. Each at least three quarters full of urine.

"Is it just me," asks Sam rhetorically as the climb continues, "or does it seem like there's a plumbing problem in this neighborhood?"

On the fourth floor, the door to Apartment G is partly open. Stained and dented with a collection of long deep scratches on it's outer surface, the door's lock has it's metal screws loosened to the point the entire assembly hangs askew.

"Good security," Bridges notes.

"Fire Department!" Paul Gulfee shouts their presence, barely halting at the doorway before shoving his way inside and striding down a short hallway, an excursion into a small-scale Third world. Refuse litters every room opening off the hallway, scattered and crumpled newspapers, empty bottles, plates of half eaten food now covered with green-gray fuzz . . . and cockroaches.

"Hey," Sam Killen nudges Bridges, "look," he directs Tim to an empty picture frame on the wall, a cockroach the size of a man's thumb sits motionless in the precise center of the frame, a living snapshot. "Roach Gothic," Sam is disgusted.

"Fire Department," Gulfee is repeating, approaching the doorway of a tiny kitchen at the very rear of the apartment. The officer stops so quickly the men following him bunch around the doorway. "Uh huh," Paul stares, his eyebrows arch. In the corner of the tiny kitchen, a rail-thin man stands in front of a small stove. He is wearing a pair of sunglasses and a black silk tee-shirt, nothing else. A cigarette hangs from one corner of his mouth and the man returns Gulfee's stare with a 'So what are you looking at,' expression of his own. A woman is sitting cross legged by the stove totally nude and with an expression only someone too high on drugs could have.

There is an uneasy silence at first, no one sure what to say or do. "What's the problem?" Gulfee finally asks. The question brings a look of surprise to Mr. Sunglasses who responds as if Paul was standing atop a dead body asking if someone was hurt.

"Problem?" he might be glaring, but the sunglasses hides his eyes. "Can you smell anything, man? You know what gas smells like?" His indignation causes Gulfee and the others to sniff the air where a slight telltale whiff picks up the unmistakable odor of gas.

"Okay, okay," Kemp pushes himself forward. "Just tell us what the problem is," he doesn't have the time or inclination to deal with a half-naked 'yo' with an attitude.

"The gas . . . the gas!" Sunglasses gestures at the stove.

Paul steps to the stove, "Blew out the pilot light," Gulfee lifts the top of the stove and shines a flashlight underneath.

"We're gonna shut the gas off," Paul calls out to Sunglasses, "but you'll have to call the superintendent to get everything turned back on."

Kemp announces to the rest of the men, "I think our work here is done."

"Place Engine50 and Truck 105 in service," Kemp speaks into his radio. The two companies are standing outside Building A in the Projects. Faces appear at windows, staring out and down at the firemen and the two big vehicles,lights still spasming. Eyes peer out from between horizontal slats of window blinds, a hand holding the shades open, an eerie sense of being alone and surrounded in this foreboding place is made worse knowing you are being watched.

"*Standby Engine five-Oh . . .*" the voice from communications crackles from the radio, then:

"*Truck One-Oh-Five . . . assist the Medic Unit . . . Ashburton Avenue and Houser . . .*" the call for the truck company is met with groans.

"Damn those medic assists," Holland grits his teeth.

"*Engine Five-Zero . . . respond to a report of smoke in the oven . . . Lincoln Park near the entrance to Bell Street . . .*"

"What's with these odor calls?" March is behind the wheel complaining, watching Kemp climb into his seat. The siren begins to rise as the engine pulls out in front of the truck. Donald Holland eases the longer vehicle out of the projects and turns right, glancing in his mirror to see the red flashing lights of the engine going in the opposite direction.

The Lincoln Park call takes the engine past their quarters on Fort Avenue. The apparatus floor is brightly lit, Loughlin's red car sits alone under the lights. "At least Loughlin is getting a break," Kemp grumbles.

Turning into Lincoln Park the engine slows and Jerry rolls down his window, the cool night air slips into the cab bearing the faintest trace of something burning. "I'm just gonna ease along the park road," March tells the captain, their faces gently lit by the lights inside the cab. The dash-mounted computer screen glows a soft green, the data entry giving neither man more specific information than the radio transmission. "Keep an eye out your side for something."

Driving slowly, the engine rolls along the narrow street curling through the park north to south, the men inside occasionally bouncing in their seats over a mounded speed bump. Trees line the asphalt road and become denser and taller, helping obscure any illumination from the mercury vapor lamps dotting the landscape. Inside the cab, the five men are swiveling their heads left and right, peering into the darkness on either side.

Burger sees the flames first, on the left, maybe seventy yards down in a small open area. The engine jolts to a stop and on the ground in the distance there appears to be a small tree blazing away, embers flying and the ground lit up for several feet around. Only when the men climb from the cab and draw closer for inspection do they realize it isn't the tree on fire.

"Jesus, Mary and Joseph," Dan Kemp genuflects in that frantic rapid manner of a back-slidden Catholic suddenly in need of divine intervention. Terry Buck runs forward carrying the fire extinguisher from the wagon and cuts loose with an explosive burst of chemical agent, thick white clouds flush the ground and smother the burning body. Bill and Nick are on their knees immediately, straddling the victim, searching for some place to touch, some area where they can move this person and administer aid.

The warbling siren of a blue and white grows louder, followed by the deeper, throatier siren of the paramedic unit, both responding to Kemp's call for assistance.

Blood and fluid bubble from the victims mouth, the entire body hardened into a blackened rictus of immolation. Charred human flesh leaves a distinct odor in the air.

"What was *that* all about?" Kemp jerks a thumb back at the stretcher where paramedics work on the smoking hulk that has just been extinguished. The police officer with Dan is the sector sergeant. The two men have been working along Fort Avenue for more than a decade and have that easy give-and-take relationship.

"It looks like 'Willie the Bean'," the sergeant is matter of fact, "doper, local crackhead," he holds up a yellow can of lighter fluid for Kemp's inspection. "One of my guys found this about fifty feet away." The two men share a grin, "Willie was movin' in on some of the local corners."

"And they lit him off?" Dan asks.

"The rhythm of the street," the sergeant grins again at his successful imagery. "We were hearing that Willie has burned a couple of customers," he makes a half-hearted gesture in the direction of the hulk, "so I guess they burned him back, literally."

"This whole place is getting unreal,' Kemp frowns. He lights a cigarette and offers one to his aquaintance. The sergeant takes the smoke with a nod of thanks. He is the senior sergeant for the Fort Avenue patrol sector and, through his pragmatic reign, parking tickets written for the members of the firehouse have an extraordinary habit of vanishing. In return, the sergeant knows he can stop at the big granite building at any time and be welcome. During the frigid nights of winter it is not uncommon to find this same officer reclining comfortably near the watch desk, gently snoring, while Bucky or Burger or Miller, or any of the other men, listen to his radio for his call letters. When called, the 'Sarge' is awakened and given his information. The quid pro quo is no formality, it is the classic relationship between the city's two most public agencies at its best.

"Y'know, Dan," the sergeant inhales deeply on the cigarette and blows out smoke rings, "it was always getting outta hand. Remember when I made sector sergeant and you had been here . . . what . . . six, eight years? You told me this was a hell hole." The police officer laughs softly, "The only problem is we never figured just how bad and low this place could get." They pause as the stretcher is trundled past.

"You want a cause of death?" the paramedic at the end of the stretch calls back to the sergeant.

"Sure."

"Overcooked," the reply brings a smile to the policeman's face.

"That's a helluva way to go," Kemp shakes his head.

Ten blocks from the Lincoln Park entrance used by Engine 50, a paramedic unit sits at curbside, lights fluttering, rear door wide open. Directly behind the ambulance, Truck 105 dwarfs the other vehicle and the truck's light creates a revolving kaleidoscope of color moving across the landscape as the long apparatus idles, it's crew huddled between the emergency vehicles. At street side a mercury vapor lamp adds it's illumination to the gathering, the same light shining on the piece of debris that has once held promise of becoming a human being.

Sprawled in the gutter and across the curb, the derelict is bundled in a filthy overcoat, stained trousers and a shirt that had come from the factory white, but has survived the experiences leaving it yellowish-brown. The human flotsam in question lies with his eyes open and rolled up in their socket, globs of saliva drool over toothless gums and down his chin.

"I'm sorry I forgot my camera," Donald Holland surveys the scene under the still-breathing carcass.

"This is a literal piece of crap," Sam Killen rumbles under the streetlight and spits disgustedly on the ground, staring balefully down.

"Thanks for coming guys," Darlene Scotus greets the men from the truck. She is in the rear of the ambulance, the box, wearing blue rubber gloves and drawing up a syringe of Narcan. "I don't think this guy will be any trouble, but I wasn't sure." She looks at Paul.

"Better to be safe than sorry," Gulfee shrugs, appreciating her honesty and glancing over her body at the same time. Darlene wears the navy slacks and shirt of the department's paramedics service, stethoscope draped around her neck. Although her skin is a dark brown, Darlene has hazel eyes that initially surprises people. Her features are well-defined and almost 'delecate', hair highlighted with muted gold streaks, is pulled back in a French braid. He wonders if Darlene dresses in bright colors when off-duty and he reflexively glances at her left hand and sees no wedding ring. He jerks his wandering mind back to reality,. . . *you're married . . . you're starting to think like Bridges!* He smiles absently and watches the paramedic clear an air bubble from the syringe.

"Overdose?" Killen asks, glancing from the syringe to the twisted human rubbish on the curb.

"Oh yeah," Darlene nods, brushing back an errant stand of hair that has played over her face. "I'm gonna give him a shot of juice and he'll be fine."

"A waste," Gulfee grunts.

"You got it," Darlene agrees and her glance at the lieutenant lingers a few seconds longer than needed. She likes the way Gulfee doesn't need to remind everyone he is an officer. *He ain't muscle-bound,* Darlene can see, *but he's manly.* She wonders if . . . *Oh, he's married,* she reminds herself as her eyes catch Paul's wedding band. *I wonder if he'd ever had a drink with me.* The question lasts a second at most. *Get professional,* Darlene mentally prods herself.

"You want us holding him down?" Killen asks, stepping toward the human wreck.

"I don't think so," Darlene shakes her head. Her voice rises, "Bobbi, you want these guys holding down the patient?" Kneeling next to the dirty 'yo' Roberta Champus checks again if the patient was still alive.

"Hell no," Roberta calls loudly, "maybe if he takes a swing or something they can kick him."

"My kinda girl," Gulfee confesses.

Darlene Scotus steps down from the back of the ambulance with her syringe of Narcan and approaches the prostrate overdose victim. "God, he stinks," she makes a gagging sound.

Narcan is fast acting. It's affinity for the drug receptor site on the cell wall is stronger than that of the opioids flowing through the veins of this victim's body. Once Darlene has depressed the syringe, it is a few seconds before the man's eyelids flutter and he begins to blink rapidly.

"What the h-h-happened," the words slide easily from a mouthful of rotted teeth, bulging white eyes slowly evolve around the faces peering down at him. "Who' the h-h-hell are y-y-you fools lookin' at me!"

"I think it's working," Darlene observes with a grin.

The filthy collection of human organs dressed in dirty clothes begins to twist and shakily raise up from the ground. He is bent over, trembling and staggering across the grass, away from the assembled department members. "Git da hell a way from me, . . ." he recoils from the people at curbside, hands clutching wildly at the air.

"Hey," Paul Gulfee calls to the doper.

"Go to hell," the human wreck backs away from the ambulance, stumbling.

"It's the gratitude that makes this job so fulfilling," Darlene flashes a smile.

Gratitude is in short supply where it matters most. The neighborhoods where fires burned frequently and without regard for life. Most FOG's can remember a time, growing fainter each year, when the appearance of the fire department doing its job was a cause celebre anywhere in the city. Now, in the heyday of the welfare state, whatever service is provided is viewed with an attitude that a firefighter willingly sacrificing life and limb is a right, you put yourself on the line because it is owed to these people. In this city, if you're a firefighter, you find heartfelt gratitude in the 'hood' measured in angstroms. If you want appreciation you either head out to some little community still waiting for a Norman Rockwell or go downtown where people who don't live, or vote, in the city depend on television for their image of the job. Or you stop at the corner for a beer.

Beer forms the axis around which the fireman's life revolves, whether the occasion is union meeting, a firehouse picnic, a department outing or a softball game, the event is superfluous, beer is the theme. There are no optimal times for the men in the firehouse to get together for a cold one, one moment is as good as the next, although the traditional observance for the shift falls immediately after work on the second day, and in the morning after the last night of the trick. A few beers at eight or nine in the morning isn't seen as an anomaly and the Pub provides the perfect ambience at that hour.

The Pub is on Water Street at the edge of Midtown; tucked between the FedEx office and the H & R Block building. A narrow, two story building with the second floor given over to storage space and the first floor, a real live hole in the wall, taken up by the Pub itself. Other than a large sign over the front door, depicting an over-sized halligan tool with a firefighter's helmet hanging from one end, the bar is non-descript. However, if you are a firefighter, it is a veritable oasis in the middle of an otherwise hostile universe.

Owned and operated by Bobby Domulevicj and his brothers Glenn and Fred, there is never an unwelcome firefighter at the bar or any of the tables scattered across it's interior. It doesn't matter if you're a firefighter from the city, or New York, Philly, Boston, anywhere. You come through the door and show your ID card and you'll think you've suddenly discovered long-lost relatives who've spent a lifetime searching for you. 'Bobby'—'Bobby Dom'—or 'Bobby Domya,' is invariably behind the bar, shouting insults at his brothers or trading stories with some of the firemen from the west side or a guy in the FDNY who is passing through town, always laughing, always sympathetic and always heavy-handed with the beer tap.

By eight-thirty in the morning, Blue shift had a working fire on Happey Street, Hagan dragged an ancient overweight grandmother from the second floor, saving her life. Shortly after lunch both companies had a second working fire in The Heights, one where Engine 50 had made a great stop of a fire that had rolled through a vacant dwelling and threatened to jump to the next exposed site. To complete the day, 50 had caught a dramatic looking fire over on Mount Street, filling in for Engine 7 out of service on yet another rotating closure.

Leaving the fireouse in the competent hands of their relief, nine men rendezvous at the Pub, parking three blocks from the tavern. Making their way through the weaving mass of pedestrians choking the sidewalks along Water Street, people who having finished their work, answering phones, making appointment, writing reports, fighting frustration until time to go home.

Half the men are still in uniform, sky-blue shirts half hanging out of pants, unbuttoned and flapping around them. The other half are in navy-blue tee-shirts with their company designation over the left breast and FIRE DEPARTMENT printed in bold white or red letters across the back. Moving through the swirling throng of civlians, the men are greeted every few feet by well wishers demonstrating an encouragement and support totally alien in it's earnestness and candor.

"God Bless You," a small, gray-haired woman grips Hagan's elbow and smiles up at him. Mark can only blush and return the woman's greeting.

"I pity you guys," a heavy-set, well dressed man, lawyerly-looking, slaps Donald Holland on the shoulder after shaking the EVD's hand, "The mayor is screwing you guys royally." Donald pushes his glasses back up on his nose and thanks the man, feeling awkward at the demomstration and gratitude. Definitely not people from around Fort Avenue, he thinks ruefully.

Another man, elderly but nattily attired in blue blazer, tan slacks and buttoned-down collar shirt, and perfectly knotted tie, addresses

Tim Bridges, "I can't believe what a job you young men have to do," he pumps Tim's hand. "You deserve twice the salary you get from this city." Each blessing is accepted by the firemen who are more sanguine in their view of the anonymous supporters.

"You can bet these people don't live in the city," Holland observes, his voice kept low. He receives another round of handshakes and glances at Bill Burger.

"At least anywhere near us," Bill agrees.

A passer-by waves a folded newspaper, the headlines dealing with the city's deficit in it's education system, "The mayor oughtta thank God he has men like you workin' for him . . . at least you guys give him his money's worth.

"How do I get transferred down here?" Holland looks around at the buildings in Midtown.

"Or try getting these people to move near the firehouse," Burger suggests.

"NO!' Donald protests, "If these people move into the neighborhood we'd never get any runs."

Hagan and Bridges duck through the door of Halligans. "I need this beer," Tim swears, nodding a greeting at Bobby Dom.

"Fluid replacement," Hagan agrees, "purely therapeutic."

"The Heroes arrive!" Bobby Dom greets the men in a loud voice, the interior of the bar is cool and Bobby is wiping down the service bar, raising a free hand to wave enthusiastically.

"The dummies arrive," Hagan corrects the proprietor, yanking a chair from one of the tables. "You got a funnel?"

"For?"

"Just shove the tip in my mouth and put the other end under the tap," Hagan instructs.

"Tough day?"

"Usual day," Burger announces, wearily sliding atop a bar stool.

Bobby waves his bar towel at the front window, at the constant movement of people on the sidewalk. "Lots of people out there talkin' to you . . . supporting you," he observes.

"And not one of 'em votes n the city," Holland laughs.

"You guys want everything?" Bobby asks grinning. "The people who owe you the most are always the ones takin' you for granted. It's always the outsiders who support you," he shakes his head. "It's your basic problem of society, it's why you guys are supposed to have one of them community relations things. Make sure people know what you do."

"Yeah," Burger gulps his beer and wipes his mouth, "standing there watching us put out a nasty fire in their house," he observes, "must not be enough to tell them what we do."

The ebb and flow of life in 'The Penny' continues unfettered by any attempt to establish 'community relations.' Within that depressing, but expected, microcosm of existence in general are small rays of hope, little vignettes that offer a tantalizing notion that justice, regardless of measure and source, eventually manifests itself. For the men in the firehouse, the concept of any type of relations with the occupants of the 'hood' is strictly a one-on-one exchange, we help you, you help our co-existence. In those rare moments when the hopes and desires of the firefighters intersects with some tiny event serving the better interests of the community, the resultant mood of optimism, however, is viewed as a sign from on high that hope is not an abstract thought.

Shortly before an overly large, round sun disappears behind the sea of broken, crooked, antiqued television antennai, projecting upward from the flat roofs on block after block of the row houses stretching back from Fort Avenue, four men, March, Hagan, Burger and Donald Holland, sit on small, low-backed wooden chairs on the concrete apron of the front of the firehouse. Their chairs are tilted back to balance on rear legs and all four occasionally rock back and forth, attention directed at the intermitten but steady traffic in the street.

"We need to talk Shelley into moving her corner closer to the firehouse," Mark observes, glancing down the street where one of the local prostitutes advertises her availability to potential clients.

"What do you care?" Jerry snorts derisively.

"She brightens up the neighborhood."

"Hey," Jerry directs their attention to the right, "Mauritius is makin' his 'rounds."

A large sedan turns on to Fort Avenue, slowly cruising toward the firehouse. "Maybe you can talk to the man direct, Mark . . . put in for a transfer."

"What a waste," Holland remarks staring at the big car.

"Who? Hagan?" Jerry laughs. The big sedan slows at the firehouse, the pimp leans against the window and gives a perfunctory wave to the firemen.

"Yeah, yeah," Burger smiles back and lowers his voice, as if the pimp might overhear, "Go to hell you worthless piece of crap,"

"Hope your car blows up with you in it," Holland murmurs.

The sedan pulls to the curb where the prostitute has been unsuccessful in procuring interested clientele. Mauritius D-for—Divine Smith slides from his seat and speaks with the girl for a few moments.

Exchange of marketing strategies?" Jerry guesses.

"Yeah," Burger laughs, "or a new motivational technique, . . ." the pimp suddenly slaps her, so unexpectedly and viciously all four men wince at the same time.

"Ouch!" Hagan purses his lips.

"So much for marketing strategies," Jerry shrugs. They watch the pimp shove the hooker, sending her staggering away from him. He stands hands on hips, glaring at her.

A small Toyota eases from the right lane into the left, blinker flashing to indicate a turn. Nobody pays attention to the car's gradual diminishing speed or the window being lowered in a jerky motion, cranked quickly, but awkwardly. A short black tube is pushed out over the half-opened window and it seems like an eternity passes before a large puff of smoke is followed by a sharp staccato explosion.

"Damn!" Nobody remembers who screamed the word, but four chairs in front of the firehouse are immediately emptied.

Perhaps it is a credit to his personal fortitude or maybe the placement of the shot was sloppy, but Mauritius Smith isn't killed immediately. In a display of mental acuity and awareness of his surroundngs, the pimp begins a deliberate, desparate crawl toward the firehouse; his upper torso a solid crimson stain marked by five ragged puncture holes.

"H-help m-m-me," the voice gurgles. Smith is on his hands and knees moving slowly but inexorably toward the big front doors of the one building he is sure will extend protection. "H-help m-mpme f-f—firemans,"

"Go to hell!" Donald Holland lies on his stomach under truck 105 and responds generically.

"Get the hell out of our firehouse," Bill Burger is crouched in the watch desk cubicle wondering if the plexiglass and wood around him is sufficient to stop another barrage.

"Help," the watery voice trails off.

"Is somebody callin' the cops?" Holland yells from beneath the truck.

"Does anybody wanna call the cops?" Mark Hagan shouts from the rear of the firehouse where he crouches behind a row of lockers.

"Who's at the desk?" Jerry shouts from behind the engine.

"Nobody," Burger replies trying to squeeze more of his bulk under the desk.

Sirens begin sounding, tires screeching . . .

"Cops are here," Donald announces. Four police cruisers form a semi-circle around the bloodied, prostrate body of the pimp. Only after Holland confirms the presence of the police officers do the others begin to emerge from hiding.

"What happened?" a sergeant, gun in hand, steps quickly to the firehouse.

"He got shot," Holland explains, climbing from under the truck.

"No kidding!" the sergeant shakes his head, holstering his weapon. "Did you see what happened?"

"Is there a reward?" Burger cautiously walks to the doorway.

"C'mon," the sergeant searches the faces of the four men who have come out of hiding. An ambulance siren sounds in the distance. "Did any of you guys see what happened?" the group has collected under one of the apparatus doors.

"The jerk was slapping one of his girls," Jerry begins explaining. "Next thing I know there's a shot and we duck inside."

"He got it with a shotgun," the sergeant motions toward the inert form of Mauritius Smith leaking body fluid all on to Fort Avenue. "Looks like buckshot from the holes," Mark Hagan offers the policeman a cup of coffee. "Nice neighborhood, huh?" The sergeant looks up and down Fort Avenue while paramedics work on the unresponsive body of the pimp as a stunned, bewildered hooker watches the effort.

"Mr Rogers would be jealous," Hagan shrugs.

"Did any of you guys try to help him?" the police sergeant wants to know, half expecting the reply.

"Him?" Mark is ready to laugh, "For what?" The men quickly look over at the body of the pimp, almost hidden behind a pile of medical supplies being used by the paramedics in a half-hearted effort to find some sign of life.

"Damn," the police sergeant shakes his head, "you guys are cold."

"Whoa," Jerry, overhearing the comment, saunters to the officer, "We were helping a vital community function here," he asserts.

"Oh yeah?" There is a hint of a smile in the police officer's eyes.

"Vermin control," Jerry announces, keeping a straight face, "I figure we ought to get a community service award."

"Community service?"

"Yep," March replies as the stretcher with Mauritius D-for Divine Smith is loaded in to the back of the ambulance, "we don't just fight fire," the pump operator declares. "We're real big on Community Realtions . . . we do home inspections, smoke detector," he glances at the ambulance door being slammed shut . . . "pest control."

CHAPTER 10

"Consequences"

Two tricks, five working fires, two second alarms, the weather cools and the 'hood' gets hotter. The fires continue through the first days of the new trick and by the first night, there is a palpable need for rest in the firehouse. A working fire in Pulaski Homes started the day shift. Three families living in an apartment meant for one, made dramatic photos of rescues for the newspapers. Fresh from that fire, Engine 50 caught a second alarm in The Heights and Truck 105 filled in for Truck 9, shut down for yet another rotational closing—now known throughout the city by it's euphemistic 'enhanced training.' Red shift caught a second alarm and another working fire in Pulaski before day shift came back and got called to that crapper on Mount Street, within an hour of coming on duty. By lunchtime, the same day some simpleton in Washngton Square managed to light off his whole apartment and the fire spread to the two arartments overhead. Loughlin held the fire to one alarm but special called enough equipment for a two-and-a-half alarm deal.

"I'm tired of smelling smoke!" Dan Kemp's complaint is loud and echoes around the firehouse. "Gimme a nice quiet night so I can get some sleep and I'll fight the next city-wide fire by my own damned self." He has just scrawled his name on the company roster, beginning this last night of the trick. The burly captain walks the length of the apparatus floor; a cup of coffee in the sanctity of the lounge beckons him.

"Here, here," the agreement comes from Mike Greenstreet, whose backside overflows the chair at the desk. There comes a time, even for the two companies out of Fort Avenue, that enough is enough.

"Tonight's the night!" Jerry March checks off a space on the coonskin, can of icy soda in one hand. "I got a call from Bob Hannah just before coming to work," he declares, "and he says all the signs are there." A slurp from the soda can makes Dan Kemp wince and he fixes the pump operator with a glare.

"Bob Hannah can kiss my butt," he stands at the coffee machine pouring the last dregs of the pot into his cup. "We been working our butts off these last couple of tricks. Any of *that* showing up on his charts and cartoons?"

"No way, Cap," March takes another watery slurp, "all I know is that there's gonna be one helluva fire tonight." Kemp is now rummaging through the refrigerator, pushing through brown paper bags of food, examining Rubbermaid containers and frowning.

"We got food in here with hair growin' on it."

March looks over at Donald Holland who is assiduously studying a book while sprawled on one of the sofas. "You bring your firefightin' jammies tonight, Donald? The blue ones with the feet in 'em? We're gonna sleep on our wagon tonight."

"Forget the wagon," Kemp growls, now rummaging through the snacks on the shelves, the crackling of the snack bags sounds like flames.

"I forgot my special jammies," Holland replies without looking from the magazine "so I'll just sleep nude."

"Dedication," March points out.

"Forget dedication, too," Kemp adds above the crackle of cellophane bags.

Billy Burger enters the lounge, arms stretching wide in open confession of exhaustion. "Anybody hear anymore about that pimp that got shot?" he asks over a massive yawn.

"He's dead," Holland shrugs, as concerned as if the deceased had been an insect squashed underfoot. "He don't need to worry about his girls anymore."

"No kidding, Sherlock," Bill glances at the EVD, "I remember you layin' under the truck watchin' everything." March, settling into an armchair with the newspaper, rattles the paper as he folds and creases it. "Ol' MO—ritius," he informs them, "got on the bad side of some doper named 'Whitey' Jordan . . ."

"The heroin guy on the west side, Kemp recognizes the name.

"Same guy," Jerry nods, "and it seems like our man 'DEEvine wasn't satisfied with pimpin' wholesale, he was getting some of his girls to sell some powder to their friends out west," he arches his eyebrows up and down Groucho style.

"The mills of justice," Burger yawns again, examining the cupboard.

"It don't matter who's doin'what," March tosses the newspaper atop the coffee table and heads for the lounge door, soda in hand. "This whole city is going down the drain, one piece at a time."

Jerry shrugs, standing in the doorway, "Either way," he conceded, "I just wish I was the one with my hand on the plunger."

"Your sensitivity overwhelms me," Donald murmurs, turning the page of his magazine.

March strolls toward the watch desk, soda can in one hand, his other arm swinging briskly. "I got the watch, Greenie," he calls loudly to the front.

Moore's Park Drive runs north and south along the extreme boundary of first-alarm district for both companies in the Fort Avenue firehouse. Dwellings lining both sides of the street are considered 'row homes' although they are massive, three-story structures, testimony to a time prior to white flight to the suburbs when affluent families considered the neighborhood sufficiently removed from the busy 'downtown' business center.

Although the houses are large, the street itself is narrow, made narrower still by the line of cars parked bumper-to-bumper along either curb and limiting passage down the street to one vehicle at a time. This congestion also serves notice that, despite the size of the homes, they are as packed with people as the street is with their cars. Three and sometime four extended families struggling to share space in dwellings meant to provide comfortably for a single family.

Fire Communications Dispatcher, David Goodyear unrolls the top of the large grocery bag containing his sumptuous feast for the evening. The aroma of the food brings a smile to his face, two extra-large Italian coldcuts, extra thick Pastami on Kosher rye, three chocolate cupcakes, two apples and an orange. A quick glance at the vending machine in the hallway outside the Communications theater shows it to be well stocked. Goodyear is confident the twelve-hour shift, seven-to-seven, will be a little slice of heaven. He isn't bothered when the other dispatchers refer to him as "The Goodyear Blimp,' he's not that fat.

At the time of construction, the building codes allowed these rows of impressively large homes to share a common space, a cockloft, above the attic in each dwelling that ran the length of the block. Subsequent codes required builders to construct a firewall, a firebreak along the entire block of houses. Unfortunately, words like 'cockloft, 'firewall' and 'fire extension' have little meaning to the family members who have occupied these homes for the past ten years.

"The problem," Jerry March is pontificating at the watchdesk, chair pushed back, feet propped on the desk's edge, "is that we're too good for our own selves." He shrugs matter-of-factly. "The more the city takes from us, the harder we work to maintain our reputation," his hands come back behind his head. "If we were any other city agency we'd just sit back and say 'the hell with it' and do exactly what the rules say we're supposed to do." He shakes his head, bent arms waving like elephant's ears. "But do we ever learn that? Noooo," he draws out the negative reply. "We just keep on doin' this same stuff day in and day out."

"For the same lousy pay," Tim Bridges adds.

"Yeah, for twenty years," Jerry laughs, "I'm not sure how it makes us old guys look," another derisive laugh. "This has been goin' on ever since I got in the department." There is a moment's tension as the radio speaker on the front wall spews out a string of information, the sound echoing over the apparatus floor.

"A married guy is stuck," Nick Miller observes, "how do you get that across to people?" The thick silver mustache above his lip twitches.

"You don't," Jerry shakes his head again. "You come to work, do the job and go home and enjoy your kids."

Ken Shaw strides past the cubicle, "Red car goin' in the district," he anounces stiffly; his eyes fixed ahead of him, a stern expression on his face.

"Uh oh," Jerry smirked at Nick and Tim, "trouble with the fun couple." Confirming March's assumption, Tom Loughlin materializes on the opposite side of the watch desk, wordlessly moving to the passenger side of the red car.

"Oughtta be an interesting ride through Oz," Miller rolls his eyes as the Jeep Cherokee lurches out the exit door.

"I bet Ken turns on the rap music," Jerry laughs.

"What music?"

"Anytime Shaw is angry with the chief," March tells them, "he turns on the radio in the red car to one of them rap music stations," the pump operator does a pantomime of Shaw's movements. "But he won't turn it on loud. The whole time they drive around that music will be playing and it drives Loughlin crazy. He hates it with a passion." Jerry laughs aloud, "but Loughlin won't say a word to Ken because that'd be a sign Ken won."

"I love it," Bridges chuckles.

The suddenness of the triple *Clang* takes all three men by surprise; the warbling tones come across the system loudly.

"*Smoke in the dwelling, Engine Five-Zero respond . . .*" the teleprinter behind the cubicle begins to zip and whir.

"I got the door," Tim yells. The engine is rolling into the street in less than a minute and as Bridges hears the siren diminish in the distance, he punches the thick red button that automatically lowers the door.

"Pulaski Projects again," Jerry yells at Kemp.

The captain rocks back and forth in his seat, staring out the window at the passing derelict buildings and dirty broken facades that coalesce under the heading 'East Side.' What a way to live, the thought wanders through Dan Kemp's mind for about the billionth time since beginning work in this hellhole. From the corner of his eye, Kemp sees Jerry lean forward and slide a disc into the slot of an electronic system secured under the instrument panel. Seconds later the captain becomes aware of an addition to the siren and air horn; a rapid rise and fall in tempo with definite form and meter. By the third bar of the music Kemp is staring at his pump operator.

"What is that?" the question has no malice, the officer recognizes what he is hearing. Dan Kemp wants conformation. He twists in his seat and spies Burger in his jumpseat, a grin spread across his face.

Engine 50 speeds down Fort Avenue, slowing at each intersection, weaving through halted traffic as the unmistakable strains of 'The William Tell Overature' blast through the sound bar at the top of the cab.

"Hi ho Sil-l-l-l-l-v-e-e-r-r," Jerry is grinning malevolently, not daring to return the incredulous stare of his captain and enjoying the expressions of surprise and recognition on the faces of the homeys and semi-literate yo's stopping along the sidewalk to pump their arms in the air.

"The 'Lone Ranger'?" Kemp places a hand against his forehead and closes his eyes.

"Nah," Jerry shouts above the philharmonic orchestration, "It's 'The William Tell . . .'"

"I know what that is," Kemp has to grin. "When did you come up with . . . that?" he gestures to the disc player.

"Me and Bill been working on it for a while," March confesses, earning Burger an eyebrow-arching glare from the captain.

The engine turns into the projects, the blaring music announcing it's arrival sixty seconds before the apparatus comes into view. In the ominous canyons of Pulaski, the loud, driving rhythm is recognized. The crescendo of music draws children like the bells of an ice-cream truck in summer.

"Incredible," Kemp grumbles, sliding from his seat to the dirty cement outside.

"Can we keep it? Huh? Can we? Can we?" March peppers the officer.

"You need medication," Dan Kemp looks across the seat at Jerry and slams his door.

The quiet of the firehouse reflects the general inactivity of the city itself. Since the engine cleared from the Pulaski Projects, a smell of smoke directly linked to a smoldering pot of macaroni and cheese left too long on an unattended stove. The night becomes the answer to Dan Kemp's plea for a time of rest. Neither company, Engine 50 nor Truck 105, has turnd a wheel. Other than short, echoing, bursts from the radio there have been no sounds other than the men's conversation and laughter and the constant background noise of the television.

In the lounge, Kemp sips from a final cup of coffee, Ken Shaw sits on a sofa reading the newpaper hiding his face. "So Loughlin is gonna transfer?" Dan relates the latest rumor in the form of a question.

"Yep," Shaw replies from behind the paper, his blue shirt is unbuttoned and open down the front, the shirttails are pulled free of his pants. "Worked with the man for ten years and he can't put in a word to get me transferred with him." The reason for the evening's chilly relations between Tom Loughlin and his aide is confirmed. The chief has put in for a transfer to the 9th battalion without so much as a whisper to the man who has been his constant traveling companion for a decade.

"Is that bad?" Dan asks, standing in the middle of the room, swirling the coffee in his cup and paying superficial attention to whatever is on the television, a production intended to prove there are no differences in genders. "I mean," he searches for the right words, "you two didn't always hit it off, y'know?"

"Doesn't mean he couldn't at least make the effort," Shaw replies sounding like a wounded spouse.

"Who's gonna be his replacement?"

"Donovan," the response is curt and clipped. The newspaper lowers and for a moment Howard glances at the captain, "but that's not for public consumption."

"No problem," Kemp shrugs. There could be lots of worse replacements than Gary Donovan, called 'Big Cat' when he was captain of Engine 5.

Shaw sighs deeply and looks at his watch, "I'm gonna turn in, it's past eleven." He gathers himself and rises from the chair, silently walking to the lounge door. Kemp drains his coffee and gives a final glance at the television, convinced that if a woman wants equality it didn't always need to take the form of physical toughness. If the world needs saving it will take a joint effort from both sexes. The captain puts his cup in the kitchen sink and follows Shaw from the lounge.

The chief's aide trudges slowly up the spiral staircase and Kemp decides to stroll to the watch desk. He seems oblivious to the fact he is clad in a navy blue company tee shirt and a pair of white boxer shorts. Just above his right ankle is the tattoo of the firehouse emblem, 'East Side Lightning.'

"Now that is a sight," Killen is grinning broadly at Kemp's appearance. "What?" Kemp grins wearily and looks at his bare spindly legs, "You don't like white meat?" He leans against the entrance to the cubicle.

"It ain't the white meat, Cap," Killen replies laughing, "it's the scarcity of white meat!" He glances at the officers skinny legs one more time, "You need to find the chicken those legs belong to."

Proper planning and husbanding of his resources has allowed David Goodyear to enjoy his feast over an extended period of time. By midnight the dispatcher has consumed one of the biggest Italian coldcut sandwiches and the aroma of it's onions and peppers remains heavy around him. Half the pastami is gone. The remaining half is carefully wrapped in deli paper inside the brown shopping bag. He has sliced an apple and contemplates the sweet tartness, congratulating himself on the uniformity of each piece he's cut.

Goodyear works fire dispatch, a separate division of the room from the emergency medical services. The room itself is large, almost twenty-four hundred square feet, and at this time of night the overhead lights are dimmed. Another six dispatchers work the computer consoles in the big room, the 'Pit' they call it, two dispatchers work the computer consoles.

At the front of the room two large displays cover most of the wall. The first, on the left, shows the location of every firehouse on the east side of the city, the companies in quarters show as blue, those out of service as red. The units considered engaged in 'enhanced traning' are cicled in black. The second display shows every street, intersection, housing project and community in the 1st Division. The computer screen in front of David Goodyear is an exact duplicate of the second wall display. A a keystroke, Goodyear can change his display to match the firehouse map, or, another keystroke enlarges the screen until the dispatcher can identify an exact address. The electronic stylus at Goodyear's console, applied to his screen, opens windows of the successive information that allows the dispatcher to identify and assign companies across the division to any report of any emergency. Atop the computer screen a digital clock keeps twenty-four hour military times. Every fifteen minues the clock triggers an update of all activity within the division. It is one-fourteen when Goodyear shoves the last slice of apple into his mouth and cleans his hands with the towlettes in his bag.

Soft snoring fills the second floor bunkroom, a soft light shines up through the pole holes; its source the watch desk below. Although it is no longer required to keep the desk manned after midnight, Communications automatically triggers the alarms. Tim Bridges is engrossed in a the techno-thriller novel and cannot bring himself to close the ragged, dog-eared paper back and go to bed. Besides, he rationalizes, I got the next four days off. He can spend the next ninety-six hours in bed if he wants.

Chantelle Henley skips up the steps of her house, door key in hand. The television is playing loudly in the living room and Cantelle's first worry is the argument she will have with her father. The lock assembly turns and Chantell pauses, taking that last deep breath befor facing her Grand Inquisitor, and pushes open the front door.

James Henley's last cigarette has smoldered quietly in the sofa cushions. The smoke it produced consuming the padding in the cushions, asphyxiated the slumbering man, without awakening him. There is enough smoke to fill the first floor of the row home, the accompanying fire burning the sofa and surrounding carpeting but, by that time the oxygen needed to sufficiently fuel the slow burning flames had been utilized. 'The Beast' was forced to lower its metabolism and 'hibernate,' slumber, until some event, some natural occurrence, fed precious oxygen-containing air to waiting embers, like the opening of a door.

The force of the explosion propels Chantelle Henley backward from the top step, her clothing burned off, skin seared. In the upstairs bedroom the open window that served to bring cold air into the room, becomes a flue; liquid fire flows upward, searching, rolling over ceilings, reaching for that second source of air. Already a seething furnace, the living room fed fire, sent smoke up stairways, mushrooming over ceilings and forcing it downward to consume whatever combustibles lay in its path. The fire burns in all directions, including the common walls between the houses on either side.

Heston Sharpe parks his car at the opposite end of the block from the Henley house, happy to be home after driving a bus for eight hours. He is a punctual man, used to maintaining schedules and knows the time is precisely one twenty-five in the morning. Having maintained this schedule for the past fifteen years, Sharpe is also innately aware of the smallest details in his neighborhood at that hour. The bright glare at the far end of the street is decidedly out of place and attracts

Heston's immediate attention. His first thought is that he is looking at a miniature solar flare starkly brilliant against the inky black sky. After staring in amazement at the fire blowing flames from the windows of the house almost a block distant, Sharpe's adrenaline kicks in and he rushes to his own front door, fumbling with his keys. By the time he lifts the phone to dial the emergency number, the fire at 305 Moore's Park has ben burning for over ten minutes.

Betty Whittley thought the muffled explosion came from an airplane overhead. For several minutes the tiny woman lay in her bed half asleep, wondering why an airplane would be flying so low. When she noticed the eerie orange flickering movement across the wall in her bedroom, she realized the glow came through the window. There was no need to go to the window and look out, she reached for the bedside phone.

David Goodyear tenses involuntarily at the electronic *beep* sounding in his headset. The muscles tensing that accompanies unexpected stimuli and releases that adrenaline rush increasing blood pressure and causing the mouth to become dry.

"City Fire Department," Goodyear speaks into the headset curled around one ear. "What's the nature of your call?" his computer screen already pinpoints the origin of the call, a small red circle pulses at a street corner and red letters appear next to the indicator:

302 Moore's Park Drive
Whitely, Elizabeth

"There's a fire across the street," the woman's voice is calm, slightly slurred from sleep, Goodyear focuses on the address.

"What's the address of the fire?"

"Three-oh-four . . . no . . . no . . . sorry . . . three-oh-five Moore's Park . . ."

"Is this an occupied dwelling, Ma'am?" Goodyear asks patiently.

"What?" the woman sounds confused.

"Is this a residence or a business?"

Silence initially greets Goodyear's question. Then, "Oh my gawd . . . all those children in there . . ."

David Goodyear suddenly forgets the remnant of his meal, something in the caller's last words form a knot in his stomach. He becomes aware of sounds around him, sounds within the Communications room.

"I got a phone call for a dwelling fire . . ."

Dwelling fire reported on Moore's Park Drive . . ."

David Goodyear applies his electronic stylus to the red circle identifying Betty Whittley's residence; the screen enlarges to show 305 Moore's Park.

The overhead lights flash on, illuminating 'The Pit' in a bright glare.

"Tactical Box," the words come from the dispatch supervisor standing at the head of the room. He is wearing his own headset and has keyed into each console in Communications, "Occupied dwelling, multiple family . . ."

Paint and turpentine neatly arranged against the walls in the Crandall home ignite, the fire seething on the third floor of the Henley row home burns through the common wall. The same fire is working into the Henley's attic and, dangerously, the open cockloft.

"Dispatching a Tactical Box to Three-Oh-Five Moore's Park Drive," Goodyear speaks slowly and concisely into his headset, informing his supervisor of his action, "additional information received of a second dwelling fire in an adjacent dwelling . . . Three-Oh-Three Moore's Park . . ."

The tip of the stylus on his screen gives Goodyear a list of companies available, highlighting those specific companies assigned to the first alarm. Goodyear sweeps the stylus tip down the company listing, marking each to be alerted. To his right an inch-square button glows red, labeled 'House Gong.' David checks the companies that the Prometheus system has identified to be sent on this alarm. Through the miracle of electronics those companies will be hearing the alert tones and bells clanging once the square button is depressed. Heading the top of the Prometheus list are Engine 50 and Truck 105.

Memorable events, good and bad, often cause their preceding circumstances to become as etched in the mind as the events themselves, precursors necessary to the recall and, many times, as vivid as the event itself. Tim Bridges, engrossed in the techno-thriller at the watch desk can recall the chain of images linked together ultimately leading to 'the night.' Months afterward he is able to recount a string of rapid fire mental pictures as though viewing them through a mental camera.

Turning the page of the paperback, bridges sits back in the watch desk chair and stretches. In the moment that passes there is an eerie sensation, a pregnant pause in time that falls over the shadowy apparatus floor, and then passes quickly. The idea of finishing the remaining pages of the novel crosses Tim's mind in the split second he hears the metallic '*click*' of the firehouse gong arming itself.

The reverberating *clang-clang-clang* echoes over the warbling tone, the voices of the dispatcher blurts from the gray radio horn so quickly he sounds inpatient announcing the alarm: *"Occupied dwelling, Tactical Box 5-1-504 Moore's Park Drive and Jilly Street . . . Engine 50 . . . Engine 9 . . . Engine 24 . . . Engine 19 . . . Truck 105 . . . Truck 15 . . . Battalion 11 . . . Rescue 3 . . . Squad 40 . . . respond as RIT . . . Med 15 . . . multiple family dwelling . . ."* the report repeats the assignment, ringing over the high ceiling.

"I'm standing at the watch desk," Tim describes those moments four months later, "pulling the run sheets from the printer and it's like I'm seeing little video clips . . . short ones . . . just popping up around me. Everything just disjointed but connected at the same time.

Donald Holland appears first, sliding down a pole at the rear of the firehouse and charging to the front, his turnout pants drawn up, suspenders over shoulders and blue shirt unbuttoned and flapping behind. One arm is extended for the first glossy print-out from the teletype, the other arm reaching for the door of the truck's cab. Greenstreet jams stubby feet into turnout pants and climbs to the tiller cab. Dan Kemp standing on the painted cement floor, door to the engine open, slides his arms into his turnout coat. Burger and Miller face each other wordlessly as they secure their turnout pants and reach for their helmets. Terry Buck takes a second copy of the teleprinter report from Bridges' hand.

Jerry has the engine's motor rumbling, lights beginning to flash and pulse, melding with the lights atop the truck. Ken Shaw buttons his uniform shirt, walks quickly, but calmly past the cubicle, pauses long enough to get the last copy of the response report. Tim steps down from the raised slab and pushes one foot, then the other into boots of his bunker pants, then yanks suspenders up over his shoulder. Once up in the truck's cab, Tim settles into his seat and takes his helmet from Killen's hand.

Doors slam simultaneously, adding their own sharp echoes to the noise on the floors. The grinding rattle of doors raising, long, loud hissing of brakes releasing and the first small jolt as Truck 105 rolls out the front door.

The truck exits first, turning right, Killen and Bridges are sliding arms through the shoulder harnesses of their breathing apparatus and fitting the protective hoods over their heads. From the semi-darkness of the backseats, Tim watches Paul Gulfee clipping his coat closed and donning his own breathing equipment, bending slightly so his ear is inches from the truck's radio. The lieutenant listens a moment, lifts his head to say something to Holland and then turns to give the two men in the back a thumb's up. Paul speaks to communications briefly and then slips his own head covering up, pulling it snugly around his face.

In the front seat of the engine, Dan Kemp is bare headed, staring at the back of the truck's tiller cab caught in the headlights of Engine 50. Terry Buck tugs at his gloves, flexing his fingers into a fist. The nature of the alarm, it's time and content says this is the real deal. Communications does not arbitrarily dispatch a tactical box at this hour and tack on such specific information.

The engine has a small radio speaker directed at the jump seat area in it's extended cab, its volume distorting sound, but the men rocking back and forth in their seats can understand the broken snippets snapping from the speaker.

"Units . . . five . . . four . . . receiving . . . additional . . . in . . . multiple dwellings . . . Heavy fire condition . . . report of . . . and heavy smoke."

"Watch for 9 Engine," Kemp is shouting to March, "they're gonna pop out along one of these little streets off Washington and scare the hell outta us." March, staring straight ahead, nods. At the left turn on McKean Avenue, the flashing red lights of Rescue 3 can be seen a few blocks down to the right as the big apparatus approaches the intersection. Three blocks further and the little three-vehicle parade crosses Fullerton Avenue, the pulsing red-and-white lights of Squad 40 weaves through a line of halted cars to the left. The Rapid Intervention Team, RIT, is moving fast, its quarters are further from the fire ground than Fort Avenue.

The ride, fraught as it is with the knowledge of the type of fire, seems interminable. On the small computer screen jutting from the instrument panel, green light forms letters and images, addresses and hydrant locations. Kemp studies the screen momentarily before twisting in his seat to shout to the men behind him, "We got a crapper," he yells, "there's a hydrant at Moore's Park and Blount Street, end of block. We'll hit the hydrant and Engine 9 will follow and pump it." Dan peers at Terry Buck, "Terry, make sure when you lead-off you give 9 Engine plenty of room to get down the street."

"Close," March yells. In front of them Holland turns left and then right, the long truck twisting snake-like. For a moment Kemp and March get an unobstructed view of the rooftops ahead. Lights blaze, Holland brakes quickly.

"Oh damn," Kemp yells the words.

Paul Gulfee stares at the fire rolling from the houses at the end of the block, bright, undulating balls of orange and yellow and red, brilliantly stark against the night sky. Thick smoke flows so heavily from the windows it seems to hang in the air, frozen in place. From Gulfee's seat it looks like a huge bonfire at the end of the block. His first reaction is to grasp the Handie-Talkie hanging from his left shoulder. The sheer volume of the fire combined with the size of these row houses and the numbers of people still inside races through Paul's mind, a rush of pure adrenaline.

"Truck One-Oh-Five to communications . . . transmit a second alarm at this location . . . repeat . . . Moore's Park Drive . . . request second alarm."

Thomas Loughlin nervously drums his fingers against his thigh, his habit when responding to what he knows is a very intense fire situation. As the red car approaches the turn at Moore's Park, he hears the request for an additional alarm and, at the same time, sees the flames rolling skyward over the tops of the big houses. Loughlin is considering another factor beyond the fire and exposures, the time factor. He faces a rapidly moving, quickly expanding fire that has already been burning unchecked for at least twenty minutes and the distances to be traveled by additional companies only adds time for this fire to grow. It is already beyond the scope of the first alarm units. In the moments it takes for the thoughts to cross his mind and translate into intelligent facts, Loughlin sees fire push out from the rear windows of the houses at the end of the street.

"Battalion One-Five to communications . . . transmit a fourth alarm at this location . . . extremely heavy fire conditions . . . multiple family dwellings . . . request a fourth alarm be transmitted immediately."

Events unfold slowly, even amidst the rush of synchronized chaos on the fire ground, like freeze-frames in an already slow-motion video. A surreal crystallizing of specific moments in time made more eerie by the yellow-orange hue cast by the fire mixing with the glare of lights from the fire apparatus.

The truck isn't at a full stop before Killen and Bridges are out of the cab, Gulfee, stepping down into the street, watches the two men throw a ladder to an adjacent roughhouse, Bridges is halfway up the ladder. Donald Holland transfers power to the turntable, he's already in the street setting up the stabilizing jacks with Greenie's help. Engine 50 fills the street with it's bulk, coming to a jolting, hissing stop behind 105, hose stretching back up the street to the hydrant where Bucky is making the connections. Burger and Miller, each with a fold of hose over a shoulder, move to the front of the middle house on fire, the house totally involved, every floor a mass of flames. Dan Kemp yanks more hose from the crosslay bed while Burger and Miller flake their sections behind them.

Sirens continue to wail, flashing lights appearing from all directions, it's impossible to tell what companies are coming from which directions. Overhead the big aerial of 105 is lifting, hydraulics humming as each section telescopes outward; men gathering to scale the ladder when it is in place. Another engine stops at the street corner, taking the hydrant where Buck connected the coupling to the hydrant connection at the pump. A third engine jolts to a halt near the corner in front of 105, hose dropping behind it, trailing back to a hydrant somewhere on Jilly Street.

Paul Gulfee is a lieutenant, his knowledge of fire ground operations pales in comparison to Loughlin's or that of the 11th battalion now arriving at the rear of this fire. But Gulfee can do the math involved and the empiric summation is as ugly as it is precise. The fires have been burning out of control for several minutes before the first alarm came in, more time elapsed in the long run to Moore's Park. Now second and fourth alarms have been requested, each alarm bringing companies a greater distance than the initial companies traveled. Nobody knows if even a fourth response will suffice for this firestorm and, during all those minutes, the fire will continue to grow. The whole process takes a moment to crystallize in Gulfee's mind. A nightmare!

Inside 307 Moore's Park, the smoke and heat form a solid wall, rejecting the firefighter's initial entry. Somebody on the roof, maybe Holland, is working away with a chainsaw, struggling to vent the row house. Six inches down . . . angle away and cut again . . . the hole immediately fills with smoke and orange threads of flame. Across the roof an EVD from Truck 15, second best truck in the division, 15 Hook, has cut halfway through. The second truck is at the rear, it's aerial somehow raised, a great job by the EVD. Heat envelops the roof, smoke blows across its surface.

"Donald!" the EVD from 15 is shouting and motioning at the vent hole he has begun. "I got smoke and fire showing here!" Holland stops cutting, more fire shows from his own vent. A short distance between the EVD's, two more men from 15 work fiercely with an axe, their progress slower than the chainsaws; silhouettes appearing and disappearing in the drifting smoke.

"We got fire under us," one man yells and Holland feels his stomach tighten. Fumbling with his portable radio, Donald calls for Loughlin.

"Truck One-Oh-Five portable to Battalion One-Five . . . emergency." Loughlin's response is immediate.

"Battalion to One-Oh-Five, report!"

"Chief, do these row houses have a common cockloft?" The question alerts Loughlin to his worst fear.

"Affirmative, One-Oh-Five. What is your status?" Loughlin's reply confirms Holland's fears.

"The fire is in the cockloft, Chief. I think it's running the block." The cockloft, that long shared, common space running the length of this row of houses, has been breached by the fire. How long it has been burning in that shared space is anybody's guess, but the mere fact that the cockloft is involved changes the dynamics of the fire ground. In addition to burning vertically, this fire is also burning horizontally, with no firewall or fireblock to impede it's expansion.

Heat from the roof of 307 is oppressive, the fiercely burning house at 305 adds to the problem. Like a cancerous tumor metastasized to other parts of a body and feeding the metastasis like a 'mother lode,' the inferno that was once 305 Moore's Park Drive is feeding heat and flames along three floors, an attic and, now the cockloft.

Somewhere in the thickly flowing ink-black of the third floor, Bridges and Killen are, literally, on their bellies, inching over the floor. Outside, on the ladder, Greenstreet yanks what's left of the window frame from the wall, letting it flutter to the ground. Just over the roof's edge, Greenie can hear the whine of chainsaws and thud of axes. He adjusts the thousand watt spotlight on the ladder into the black void in front of him. Orange tinted smoke fills the room so heavily the illumination reflects back onto his face.

Dan Kemp hunches behind Burger and Miller, assuming his familiar position, watching the effects of the water from the pipe disappearing into the furnace of 305. It's the proverbial drop of water in a bucket, and Dan waits to hear Loughlin order the hoses to move to the adjacent exposures, the order confirming the middle house is completely lost. The fire is so intense there is no attempt to gain entry and the best that can be hoped for is to control this nightmare until sufficient resources arrive to really attack it.

A touch at his shoulder causes Dan to turn. Loughlin stands behind him, face lit by the fire, surveying the extent of the flames. "I want you to move your line down to the next house," Tom says pointing to the upper floor of 307. "And get up inside if you can, I want to try and stop this between 307 and 309 if I can," the chief pauses to listen to a report from the 11th battalion in the rear of the burning houses.

"These places have a common cockloft," Loughlin returns his attention to Kemp, "and I know it is extending, just not how far."

Kemp glances quickly over his shoulder at the fire behind him. "What about this middle house?" Loughlin looks past the captain for the briefest of moments.

"It's lost," the chief replies.

While Kemp supervises the repositioning of the hose, Loughlin and Shaw demonstrate a misleading sense of calm, moving about the street marking the position of each company. The chief is listening intently to his radio, calculating the time factor and estimating the arrival of the additional companies. He has three lines of operation at the front and a fourth in the rear, men are on the roof probing for the furthest point of extension. There are men inside 307 conducting whatever search and rescue is possible. The chief's jaw aches from clenching them in frustration and he knows he will be relieved when a higher ranking officer arrives to assume command.

Tim Bridges moves slowly along the floor of the front bedroom, his only guide is his sense of touch. Killen seems a thousand miles away, the occasional crash of furniture, like trees toppling in the wake of a bull elephant, the only evidence that Sam is around. Behind him, Tim knows Greenie is at the window. Every few moments there is a pale, brownish flash of light, the ladder's spotlight attempting to cut through this dark, nasty flame whispering around him. *Somewhere in here, in this fire,* he thinks, *are people still in bed.*

Jerry March uses a piece of chalk to mark a hose coupled to an outlet on Engine 50's pump panel. The line, Engine 32's is thick and rock hard with pressurized water. Jerry examines the maze of dials and gauges on the panel, adjusting the throttle slightly, and steps back to look over the top of the engine at the fire rolling into the sky, "Good Lord," he mumbles and shakes his head.

It looks like a fire apparatus convention has descended on Moore's Park Drive.

The center of the street is a continuous line of the red-and-white vehicles, lights pulsing, motors rumbling, and the blue-white brilliance of halogens making the whole scene assume a dream-like sequence. The deafening noise resulting from the metallic scratch of radios cranked too high, and sirens screaming in the distance, interspersed with blasts from air horns. Eleven minutes after the first alarm, companies arrived at this inferno.

The moment Tom Loughlin confirms the size and scope of the fire, adding that multiple dwellings and occupants are involved, Communications alerts the department's chain of command and dispatches the field communications unit. Once at the fire ground, the division's Field Com assumes command of all radio communications, switching all radios on the fire ground to a separate channel.

"Second alarm, multiple occupied dwellings . . ." the recorded message sounds on every pager and cell phone in the department's system.

Gregory Ryan, 'The Predator,' is already en route, tight lipped and mentally categorizing a dozen scenarios he might be facing. Todd 'The god' Monroe receives the message while in his pajamas, sitting on the edge of his bed. The page will alert his driver, Kevin Diehl, to pick up Monroe at home and get him to the fire ground. It is while waiting for Diehl that Monroe receives the message, *"Fourth alarm requested . . ."* and he knows the chief of Department Thomas Callahan will be at the scene too.

At the moment Todd Monroe is buttoning his crisply starched white shirt and checking to ensure his gold badge is pinned properly in place, Tim Bridges is slithering on his belly along the floor of 307, breast-stroking through charcoal pudding. He is taken by surprise when a gloved hand hits something solid and rubbery.

"I got one," Killen's voice sounds hollow in the blackness. Tim grunts a response, he has also found a victim.

"Oh damn," Tim talks to himself, his mind racing, "not another baby!" the feel and weight in his hands tells Bridges the victim is a small child, but definitely not an infant.

Tom Loughlin's head jerks up. Framed in a smoky window, caught in the halogen lights below, Sam Killen is cradling a small figure, maybe a child. On the other side of the street the omnipresent mass of spectators has gathered like Israelites at the foot of a burning, smoking Sinai, gripped in awe and fear at the glowing, flaring sights before them. Shouts, whistles and screams accompany Killen's appearance, noise that makes Loughlin look at the window.

"Here," Bridges slides along the floor, pushing the elastic body of a young boy. "I think there's more," Tim is gasping.

"How's your air?" Killen asks, eyes wide and white behind his mask.

"About gone," Tim manages to reply.

"You got fire!" Greenie is shouting from the ladder. Behind the two firefighters, from the same direction they'd just come, a dark-orange ball of light pulses out of the brown soup stuffing the room. Heat moves in a wall that staggers the two men at the windows, something has lit off the rest of the interior of the floor. Part of the ceiling collapses and glass shatters from somewhere inside. A muffled roar fills the room and white super-heated steam turns the interior into a rolling sauna. Somewhere, somehow, an engine company has gotten a hose line opened up

"Any closer?" Kemp is shouting above the roar of water. He is crouched so low he is peering over the tops of the helmets worn by Burger and Miller. The face piece of his mask is flecked with water drops and the white, roiling steam engulfs the trio fused into a single huddled mass.

"No way!" Burger is shouting, chin tucked to chest, slowly playing the powerful stream of water through a huge hole that had been a window. He feels as though he's at the edge of a fiery furnace, any closer and he'd end up as black as Killen.

"Second Line?" Kemp shouts.

"Only if you want to put this thing out" Bill yells back.

"Tom?" The Predator identifies Loughlin in the brilliant lights in the street, "What we got?" The division chief makes his way to Loughlin, both men in white helmets and coats, the only distinguishing feature is the heavy soot and dirt layering Loughlin's coat.

Loughlin pauses, listening to David Marriott of the 11th Battalion report from the rear of the houses. "A whole lot of trouble," Loughlin finally tells his boss, "second alarm companies are setting up. I have four hand lines operating along the front, one in the back. But," he frowns, "all three houses are lit off in the rear." The battalion chief nods at the middle house and then at 303, "Some type of accelerant lit them off." There is a moment of silence before Loughlin adds, "An officer from one of the engine companies . . . I didn't get the number . . . reported some neighbors told 'im this closest house was having a lot of painting done. I'm assuming that's what lit it off."

"Extension?"

Loughlin looks up the street at the flashing lights and for a moment, thinks the sight is enough to send an epileptic into seizure. "Common cockloft, Greg," and he sees his boss stiffen. "It runs the length of the houses. I have Truck 15, Rescue 3 and some men from 105 on the roof, they were venting and found the cockloft burning. Right now I pushed them down further to see how far down the fire has gotten, but it's definitely horizontal."

Gregory Ryan nods quietly, biting his bottom lip. Raising his own Handie-Talkie to his mouth he requests a fifth alarm. The third alarm companies haven't even arrived yet.

"Mr. Mayor," the voice of Michael Danning on his telephone makes Myron Sprague sit up in bed. Glancing at his clock, he notes the time.

"Danning?" his voice is thick with interrupted sleep.

"Mr. Mayor," the Special Assistant for City services speaks quickly, "we have a potential nightmare scenario developing on the east side . . . a rather large fire in a series of occupied row homes." A wake-up call from hell.

"Where?" Sprague is fully awake now.

"The east side, sir," Sprague's boy repeats himself, "a very big fire; it just reached five alarms."

"What are our liabilities?" the consummate politician is already dealing in public relations.

"It's in the middle of three closed firehouses . . ."

Sprague experiences a moment of icy cold.

"Do you want your car?" Danning asks.

"Right away," Sprague orders, "has Feldman been notified?"

"I assume so," Danning replies, "he'd be contacted by Fire Communications."

"Okay, okay," Sprague is thinking fast, "this has to be a fire department operation, top to bottom. Make sure we get out a notice that it's the fire department deciding what firehouses are being closed tonight, got it? I'll want a statement on that to be ready by the time I get to the scene." Hizzoner had covered himself.

"Done," his aide promises. "I'll fax it through to your car en route."

"I want to get to the fire," Sprague orders, "I'll be ready in five minutes." When the call ends, Sprague is already out of bed, pulling on a pair of socks, trying to remember where he keeps his L.L. Bean boots and if the blue shirt and khaki slacks will look workman enough. It won't really matter, he thinks, I'll be wearing the fire department windbreaker and ball cap.

The mayor's vehicle is a 'car' in name only. The gray-blue Lincoln Navigator is outfitted with heavy duty tires and suspension, red-and-white lights behind the grill are augmented by an emergency warning system affixed to it's roof and an electronic siren completes the effect. His driver, a city police lieutenant, specially chosen for his driving ability and intimate knowledge of the city's streets, arrives at Sprague's townhouse precisely four minutes and fifty seconds after the mayor hangs up from Danning's call.

"Mr. Mayor," the police lieutenant addresses Sprague, "Mr. Danning is on his way to the scene and says he'll meet you there with your press secretary. He's arranged for a press car to bring a television and radio crew from City Hall, and has made sure the newspapers will be represented."

Myron Sprague settles back into his heavily padded seat and smiles contentedly, the radio in the Lincoln is locked on the fire department fire ground channel. If Danning has the press release ready, he thinks, he's in good shape. Myron Sprague, Mayor, gubernatorial hopeful, understands his position. If the fire department looks good on this, the mayor is at the scene as a concerned executive surveying a catastrophe and supporting the city's heroes, 'the Bravest'. If this whole thing is a massive foul-up, it will be Mayor Sprague on the fire ground investigating what went wrong and demanding heads roll, he is the 'Vigilant Protecting Angel.' Above the wailing siren and flashing lights, Sprague knows he is in a win-win scenario, his only loss will be the votes of any fatalities. "*What the hell,* he reminds himself, *"half those people come from out of state anyway."*

Inside 303 and 305 Moore's Park Drive, the fire burns particularly hot, paint and turpentine acting as super rich fuel for the flames. The field com is set up around the corner, on Jilly Street. The interior of the large walk-in van is brightly lighted, state-of-the art electronics taking over all the fire ground communications and operated by three Communications officers working the controls. A large status board inside the van now marks the exact location of every company on the scene and arriving companies will be directed from the van. The continual screaming of sirens above the fire ground din announces the third alarm companies are nearby and two further alarm groups have yet to arrive.

Loughlin and Ryan stand at the corner of the street, faces lit by the fire, studying the progress of the inferno while looking elsewhere for indications the extension can be checked. Power saws rip through the roofs along the block, sparks and embers blow upward in a vortex of superheated air. Both men greet the arrival of Todd Monroe with tight-lipped nods.

"No progress?" Monroe asks, clipping shut his white turnout coat. Whiter, even, than Ryan's, the coat has bright orange reflective lettering across the back, at shoulder level, with Monroe's name and title instead of the generic 'FIRE DEPARTMENT.' It is assumed the average firefighter with a single digit IQ knows a white coat and helmet signifies a chief officer. Monroe wants to insure he is recognized as a ranking chief officer, as if the pearly white coat and shiny white helmet with it's gold front piece left any question.

"We're lucky to be where we are, Todd," The Predator replies flatly. "The SOB was rolling for a good twenty minutes before we even got the first line on it."

"Looks like a back draft in the middle house," Loughlin points out, "but the fastest extension has been over there," he points to 303. Marriott is in the back and says the way it's burning indicates a great deal of accelerant involved and we've been told the house was being painted extensively. The fire breached the houses and just took off."

"The whole row has a common cockloft, Todd," Gregory Ryan says.

"Well damn," Monroe curses and stares at the ground, "any survivors?" The silence in response to the question makes Monroe wince. Loughlin's radio scratches loudly.

"Engine Five-Oh to Battalion . . ." Dan Kemp sounds exhausted.

"Go ahead, Five-Zero," all three chiefs listen.

"We split the fire at 307, chief," Kemp's voice is faint, almost overwhelmed by background noise. *"Main body of the fire is from 307 back down to the end of the row . . . the extension in the cockloft goes another two houses I think, but it's just up in the cockloft . . ."*

"Affirmed, Five-Zero," Loughlin looks at the other two commanders. "That's a break."

"Let's knock out that extension," Monroe suggests, "and pull back the hand lines to exterior operations." Ryan and Loughlin know what will follow. "Once we know the cockloft is knocked down and the lines are pulled back, we can place master stream operations to drown this bastard."

In a horrific instant Bill Burger disappears. It happens so quickly . . . so quickly all that saves his life is the tight muscle-aching grip he maintains on the nozzle, the same hold Nick has kept on the hose itself since getting inside the house next to 305. Surrounded by impenetrable smoke and battered by heat, the men on the hose move to a better position and suddenly hear a terrible wrenching sound of breaking wood, one second prior to Bill literally disappearing, his helmet clattering to the floor.

The big man's weight nearly dislocates Nick's shoulders, bending the smaller man in half and almost dragging him through the same hole into which Burger has plunged. There is a moment's dramatic pause before a rush of smoke, super-heated gas and wisps of flame push up through the hole. Hanging on to the nozzle, Bill is suspended from the ceiling in the basement, fire and smoke everywhere around him. Burger is screaming in pain, his legs are on fire and the flames are reaching further at him.

Kemp shouts and lunges over Nick's shoulder to place his beefy hands on the hose. Two men holding the rock hard length are all that prevents Bill from falling into the caldron below. Behind the face piece of his mask, Bills' eyes are saucer-plate wide with terror and the pain in his lower torso paralyzes him and prevents him from pulling himself upward. Like a one sided tug-o-war, Kemp and Miller heave back on their section of the hose, an impossible task for Nick alone. When Bill's knees clear the ragged edge of the hole, the big man lurches to one side, steadying his bulk and pushing himself clear.

In front of the trio, the fire, in the absence of water, reaches out, building it's intensity once more. Burger is in a semi-fetal position, slowly rolling back and forth with arms around his own drawn up legs. Kemp is about to yell at Nick to open the nozzle on a fog pattern, reducing the heavy stream of water to a fine misting spray of billions of droplets. Each droplet absorbing many times more it's own weight in heat, but the veteran Miller already knows what to do and in moments all three men are behind a curtain of fog. Back and forth, Nick directs the vaporous pattern from the fire pushing at them to Burger's mass on the floor, one direction to fight the fire and the other to keep Bill cooled down.

Kemp is backing Miller on the line now and searches quickly over the floor for Burger's helmet while, simultaneously yelling into his radio for assistance. The room is filled with black that takes on a dull orange hue, never a positive indication. Above the men and to their front, the dull orange hue looks like it is drawing into itself, the fire gathering strength. Unabated, the dull orange heat ball will transform into a mass of heavy, clearly defined flame.

Thumping, clattering, and crashing sounds signals the entrance of assistance into the smoke laden room. Dan Kemp feels the hose lifted, the immediate back pressure straining his arms is partially relieved and Kemp recognizes Terry Buck leaning into the hose. "Jeezz, I'm glad to see you in here," the officer yells his gratitude.

Buck's eyes narrow in a grin. "Jesus was busy, so He sent me instead," Terry yells back. Beside the men are two guys from RIT, kneeling beside the prone Burger and helping him to his feet. "He okay?" Terry watches the ministrations to Bill while getting a better grip on the line.

"Fell through that hole," Kemp nods at the gaping hole in the floor. "There's fire under us," he explains and Terry watches orange fire push up through the hole as if wanting to prove the captain's words. "As soon as they get Bill outta here, we're going to back up." Kemp has no idea how long there has been fire under the floor where they stand, how long the wooden joists have been exposed to flames weakening them to the point the entire floor gives away. Regardless, he doesn't intend to be standing around to experience that crashing, flaming phenomenon.

The RIT duo moves quickly, the huddled mass disappearing into the smoke between them and the doorway. Their exit is covered by water from the nozzle, Nick Miller making broad sweeps back and forth across the face of the fire crowding back at them. "Okay Nicky," Kemp is yelling again, pushing his face close to Miller's, "just start backing out low . . . we'll guide you back. We gotta get outta here." There's just a nod from Filthy Nick, his eyes locked on the fire and glancing occasionally at the hole just to his left, a hole that is filling fast with flame.

Burger is carried as far as the street where a stretcher has been set up in anticipation of his arrival. He is trundled around the solid line of the fire apparatus filling the street, bumping heavily over hoses strewn everywhere. At the far end of the block, the department's Mobile Hospital Unit has it's rear doors wide open, it's interior brilliantly lit. The MHU is the size of a transit bus and inside is a virtual emergency room, four beds surrounded by IV poles and tubing, trays of instruments waiting to be opened. Responding to the third alarm, the MHU is staffed by the department surgeon and three paramedics. Bill will be immediately treated inside the unit and then transported to University Hospital.

Standing on the rungs of a ground ladder, Tim Bridges helps move a hose toward a fireman above him who directs a stream of water into the third floor window of 307. Tim is between the second and third floors and the blowing smoke flows around him, partially obscuring him from view out in the street. After pulling a victim from one of the bedrooms, the young fireman couldn't get back inside, electing instead to help Engine 9 get their hose up the ladder and remaining amidst the heavy smoke to support their operation.

Somewhere overhead but unseen through the drifting smoke, Tim hears a saw working. Shouts from other firefighters carry through the thick soup moving past him. Peering upward, Bridges can see grayish black smoke bleeding rapidly and thickly from under the eaves along the edge of the roof. Unless attacked, the smoke will give way to fire and Tim is hoping the condition has been recognized.

Over Tim, working on the roof, a man from rescue 3 is operating a saw on the cornice of the big dwelling. He will cut away the cornice so the fire building underneath is exposed and extinguished. It is difficult work, heat and smoke battering him. Vision is limited even on the outside of this burning house. The saw whines and clatters, chewing through the roof material. With a sudden jerk, the saw cuts through and swings clear, releasing that section of roof to fall to the ground beneath.

Unfortunately, Bridges stands almost directly beneath the section of cornice when it breaks free. The falling chunk hits Tim squarely atop his head, thudding on the crown of his helmet with such force it almost separates Bridges from the ladder. His vision blurs, like losing the horizontal control on the television, and Tim sways precariously on the rung where he stands. It feels like he is momentarily outside his body, sounds seem muffled and distant and everything moves in an eerie slow motion, dream-like. He is slightly disoriented, knowing he is on a fire ground, but unaware which one. Tim isn't sure if he is on a ladder or not, and if this is a dream. The thought passes through his mind, he can take a few steps and find out.

The face peering down at him is clean-shaven and unfamiliar. Bright lights cause Tim to wince and he is unable to recognize his surroundings. Panic rips through him and he involuntarily surges upward wanting to clear his head. "Hold on, son," a strange gruff voice sounds nearby. Smells of alcohol and disinfectant fill Bridges' nostrils and he sees hospital beds neatly aligned on his right. "Settle down, Tim" a woman's voice calls to him. "You're at University Hospital . . . do you remember what happened? Do you remember falling off a ladder?" Bridges wants to respond, but suddenly feels dizzy, the brightly illuminated room around him begins to spin faster, left to right. He falls back into the bed, closes his eyes and vaguely remembers hearing a man and woman talking about an MRI on. . . . "that fireman's head." The remark sounds out of place and he wonders what fireman is being discussed.

"Uh oh," Deputy Chief of operations Todd Monroe recognizes the big Navigator carrying 'Chip' Sprague approach the Mobile Command Center. His swearing makes Gregory Ryan and Tom Loughlin raise their heads from the tactical schematic hastily drawn across a Dry-Erase board.

"What is it?" Ryan squints under the Center's bright lights.

"The damned mayor," Monroe grimaces and his lips draw into a straight line.

"Before Tom?" the division chief frowns and shakes his head. "I don't need this headache on top of everything else," he curses softly under his breath. In response to their silent prayers, the radio speakers inside the Command Center erupt into a metallic squawk.

"Chief of Department on the scene . . . hold this fire at fifth alarm . . . " the announcement followed by a formal, somewhat ominous declaration,

"Chief of Department Thomas Callahan on the scene taking command of fire ground operations . . . on orders of Chief of Department, fire at Moore's Park Drive and Jilly is being held at five alarms." The black SUV carrying Callahan glides to a halt at the rear of the Command Center. The lights atop the roof continue fluttering red and white as Callahan exit's the front seat, slamming the door. Approaching the brightly lighted van, Callahan's face is a mask of concern. From over his right shoulder, the head of Myron Sprague bobs up and down as he follows the chief to the center of operations.

"Gimme the update," Callahan's voice is clipped, no trace of humor and not the slightest nod to any of the commanders standing there. In response to the chief's request, Monroe glances at Loughlin, his signal to begin.

"It's all a loss," Loughlin places a finger on the schematic where a large sketch of the block has been made, his fingertip rests on the middle of the group. "This is the seat of the fire, the dwelling is a total loss. The houses on either exposures are both fully involved . . ."

"Did it spread?" Hizzoner the mayor interrupts the briefing, brusquely entering the command van and sliding sideways past Gregory Ryan to stand over the schematic. "Fatalities? How many dead? Did you guys pull anyone out alive?" 'Chip' Sprague proves to be the smallest individual in that small knot of men, made smaller still by the absence of bulky gear. He is, however, their ultimate boss and his tone demands an answer. There is, however, the long standing policy during operations that the President of the United States cannot usurp the authority of the chief in charge. With Sprague's outburst, uneasy glances are exchanged. "Tom?" Sprague's voice is too loud and his eyes lock on Callahan's face.

"I was getting that data, Mr. Mayor," the chief explains softly and looks at Loughlin.

The battalion chief has his lips in a straight line and nods at Callahan. "There's no survivors," Loughlin manages to say before Myron Sprague lets out a cry of disgust, both arms raised in frustration. "It looks like the fire is stopped at 307 . . . Engine 50 made an interior attack and was able to prolong their presence and hold off extension until we put more water on the fire."

"Good . . . good job," Callahan murmurs.

"Any bodies able to be brought out?" another interruption by the mayor

"Mr. Mayor," The Chief of Department focuses a glare at the mayor, "all information will be forthcoming. That's why Chief Loughlin is doing the briefing."

The reprimand causes Sprague to noticeably bristle.

"The fire is still too hot to conduct a body search," Loughlin intercedes for the big chief. "We are just now getting enough water to bring it under control," he attempts to explain the operation to the civilian. "It's going to be another ninety minutes minimum," he says, shaking his head. "This thing had too big a jump on us . . ."

"You're saying not enough companies arrived?" Sprague sniffs the hint of an accusation.

"It wasn't the amount," Todd Monroe tries to explain, "it was the timing. Apparatus had too far to travel . . ." his words are anathema to the politician who begins shaking his head, the visor of his department baseball cap swaying.

"No. No," Sprague's face flushes. "You will not be reporting that information . . . that is an executive finding. No mention of time or distance is allowed." The forcefulness in Sprague's tone surprises the other men. It is purely rubbish to ignore the direct factors of this disaster.

"Nobody said anything about reporting anything," Chief of Department Callahan intercedes, glances at the other chief's with a look that says, "What is he worried about?" and looks down at the much shorter mayor. "Battalion chief Loughlin was simply explaining part of his briefing, something you insisted on," the latter remark stings 'Chippy.' The entire group turns to see the approach of Alan Rocky Feldman.

The commissioner looks even more emaciated than normal. "Quite the fire, huh?" his greeting is more like he's coming in at halftime to the big game and noticed the score.

"Battalion One-Five Alpha to One-Five . . ." Ken Shaw calls to Loughlin. The chief's aide watches the fire from the street, standing between two vehicles. Around him the activity takes on that expectant atmosphere of a large-scale operations preparing for action, the slightest lull in aggressively pursuing the fire as more powerful applications are being made ready. Heavy, wide diameter lines are being pulled from storage compartments and stretched, 'wye' connections, strange-looking manifolds bringing three more lines into one large one are being connected.

"One-Five to One-Five Alpha," Loughlin responds, the Command Center now becomes the 'switchboard' for fire ground communication.

"Preparing large stream operations, Chief," Ken's voice is nonchalant, like he is telling Loughlin the sky is dark.

"Interior people out? Roof men down on the ground?" Callahan's questions are perfunctory, he's sure of affirmative answers but as fire ground commander, he is now responsible for all activity and decisions.

"Large operations?" Alan Feldman looks at the chiefs around him, his civilian attire in stark contrast to white coats and helmets. The phrase is alien to the commissioner and when Todd Monroe answers, he misses the short sigh of condescension preceding it.

"Surround and drown," the Deputy explains. "Monitor pipes and ladder pipes."

These exchanges between the professionals and the intrusive mayor and his naïve commissioner captures the fire department's miseries perfectly. "But before beginning operations we need to make sure none of our men are inside any of the structures," he pauses and looks at the faces around him, making damned sure the little twit in blue windbreaker and baseball cap realizes the chief must touch chin to chest to see him. "The amount of water and pressures are so large, anyone inside would get washed out." Not exactly but almost.

"I ordered any interior lines pulled back," Tom Loughlin manages to respond to his big boss, "and the roof was becoming unstable anyway. Roof operations were stopped awhile ago." The Chief of Department nods.

"Okay, Tom," he pats Loughlin's arm, "you had your butt in a sling the moment they announced the box." To the Mayor, Callahan holds out an arm toward the entrance. "I suggest we move this conference outside where we can supervise operations."

Myron Sprague moves uncomfortably, a small man among men in every way, painfully aware of his diminutive stature as well as his ignorance of the department's methods. He will remain quiet until momentum and environment shifts in his favor. *Besides,* he is thinking to himself, *the media will be collecting around here and both Danning and me will handle things.* And like the chastened schoolboy he has become, 'Chip' Sprague stares between the shoulders of Thomas Callahan, following the towering chief from the Command Center, and controls the overwhelming desire to make disrespectful faces . . . wanting to stick his tongue out at the *big, tall know-it-all,* he derisively hurls the mental insult at Callahan's back.

In the street, the movement and work of the firefighters continues unabated but takes on a different focus. Under the brilliance of dozens of halogen lights, many of the companies engage in the evolution necessary to place master stream devices into operation. It is the indictor this fire is too large to continue using hand lines and, simultaneously, a declaration the dwellings are considered a complete loss.

Donald Holland finishes securing the large monitor pipe to the distal section of the truck's big aerial ladder. He has brought the ladder back to it's bed and hefted the heavy pipe from it's compartment, kneeling among the rungs to fasten it in place. Trailing down the length of the section is the wide diameter supply hose that wide feeds over seven hundred gallons of water per minute to the pipe. Greenie kneels in the street beside the truck, coupling smaller lines to an engine, perhaps two that will supply the water.

Jerry March drags the uncoupled end of a line to an available outlet on the pump panel, locking it in place with quick turns. An additional hose rises from the street to the top of the engine's hose bed where it is attached to the Stang pipe pointed in the direction of the middle dwelling. The device looks like a shortened, curved 'cannon' and will add another seven hundred or so gallons per minute to the drowning of this flaming debacle. There are identical operations taking place at a dozen department vehicles, most sitting in the street fronting the row of houses, others in the rear, including two tower ladders, the telescoping platforms made for this type of attack.

"About ready?" Paul Gulfee calls to Donald who pushes his glasses back from the tip of his nose. The EVD is sweating profusely, his face grimy.

"Two minutes," Holland shouts his reply.

"I gotta check on Tim," Paul turns and tells Killen. All four men around the truck have suppressed their immediate concern at Bridges fall. Sam has had the greatest difficulty, asking every five minutes if further word had been received on Tim's condition.

"All I know is that he was unconscious when they took him in," Paul cannot remember when the huge black man has shown so much anxiety. "I know you're worried."

""Hell no," Killen is not a good liar, his eyes darting about nervously. "But I gotta be worried, it's a state of mind." He kneels beside Greenie to move the 'wye' connection into position where the hose lines will not 'kink' when water begins flowing.

"Yeah," Gulfee nods cynically, watching the placement of the 'wye.'

Similar concerns are reflected among Engine 50 although Bill remains in the Mobile Hospital.

"He's gonna get sent to the Burn Center at Memorial Hospital," Dan Kemp announces loudly, relaying the information he has just received from a paramedic inside the MHU. The captain lumbers along the street looking up at the upper floors of the involved houses. Flames roll dramatically upward from the dwelling, sending a steady flow of embers swirling in it's path. Moments before, the roof of 305 finally gave way, crashing inward with a groaning roar and splintering wood. About a third of the adjacent roof, the one over 303, followed within seconds and the fresh air fueled an even brighter explosion of fire into the darkness. The collapse, however, makes it somewhat easier to direct the big master streams directly into the very seat of the flames.

Terry Buck's face is lit by the brightness of the fire, "What a colossal disaster," his comment draws Jerry's attention.

"Hey," the pump operator shrugs, "no guts, no glory."

"There ain't no glory in that grief," Nick Miller shakes his head and flicks a cigarette into a growing pool of water fed by the spray of a leaking hose coupling. The flick of the cigarette causes Nick to wince; he feels the quick movement all the way up his arm to the shoulder unexpectedly yanked when Bill went through the floor.

"Let's just put this out," Kemp grumbles loudly.

In the air over the fire, short spurts of water fall to the ground from the tower ladder platforms. Water surges up into the big pipes on the platform, furtive at first, but as the pressure builds, the staccato-like spurts lengthen in time and volume until becoming a solid, powerful stream cascading directly into the middle dwelling. Three of the tower ladders are on the fire ground, one at the front and the remaining two stabilized on their jacks in the rear. Caught in the glare of the fire ground lights, three aerial ladders begin telescoping up and over the fires, each carrying a ladder pipe. Spurting intermittently like the towers had done, all three pipes suddenly open up, the Niagara of water against the rolling backdrop of fire creating a dramatic visual.

Jerry cranks rapidly at the controls of the monitor pipe atop the engine. Along Moore's Park Drive, three companies are following March's

271

lead, the resultant heavy streams crashing through smoking, blackened holes that, hours before, had been windows. The powerful application of the big pipes creates a thunderous roar, the air immediately around the apparatus becoming chilled from the water's resultant temperature change.

Just inside the police lines established to control the gathering spectators, two dozen reporters, cameramen and sound technicians have joined in a jostling, straining, irregular line. Work lights are erected on tripods, illuminating faces and cameras anxiously and expectantly waiting for the fire department's Public Relations officer for the usual packaged information . . . "yes we arrived as soon as possible . . . no there was no way to ascertain the immediate cause of the fire . . . No, it is a five alarm fire, not ten alarms."

Several of the media recognize Myron Sprague's Navigator and crane their necks to glimpse the short man. If cameras and microphones were magnetized the mayor can't be drawn faster. No sooner is he free of the confines of the Mobile Command, Sprague strides confidently toward the reporters, making sure he wears the appropriate somber expression, the one saying he 'really cares'. The street is wet from the thousand gallons of water being expended on the fire and the myriad of halogens reflected from a dozen different pools. 'Chip' Sprague blesses himself for remembering the low-cut Pacs he threw on in haste. The most cautious step still plants a foot in an inch of water. He's hoping a camera captures his short thoughtful sojourn to the media line. Sprague feels more confident when Michael Danning looms from the dark, looking quite different without his ever present three piece suit, but like his boss, official looking in a fire department windbreaker. Better still, Danning has a manila folder stuffed with MetroStrat reports and their subsequent conclusions.

"Any survivors?" the first question is the only one audible from the immediate babble rising from the reporters.

"Too early to ascertain," Sprague's face is a mask of pity and concern and he forces a frown. "Fire units got to the scene as quickly as humanly possible, but found these dwellings," he gestures toward the hulking row houses on his right, "so fully involved it was impossible to conduct the type of thorough searches they always perform." *At least I assume* they *did,* the mayor keeps this thought to himself.

"How quickly did the first units get here?" another question from the faceless reporter, the voice though is female.

"You'll have to check with the department," 'Chippy' responds. The words are nearly lost in a sudden crackle of communications echoing in the street but the follow-up question rings clear in the subsequent lull.

"There are three closed firehouses within ten blocks north and west of these two houses," the interrogator is a young, slender male wearing a woolen coat. He kneels in the front row, light brown hair in a short ponytail and tortoise-shell framed glasses low on his nose. "In addition there are two closed firehouses four blocks to the south and several disbanded companies located well within immediate response."

"Firehouse closings are rotational," Sprague interrupts before the entire statement is finished. "Closings are fire department decisions not mine." The Mayor glares at the young journalist.

"City policies require your approval," ponytail asserts, ignoring Sprague's glare. "And the stated rationale behind even the temporary closures was for training . . ."

"Correct," Sprague agrees quickly, glad the explanation of 'enhanced training' was broached.

"The city's fire academy isn't open at night, Mr. Mayor," ponytail replies once Sprague has stepped completely into the ambush. "Why are firehouses closed for training when no training is even possible?" The question creates a moment of silence before two dozen more break out, a virus released in the air having immediate results.

"I will say again," Sprague's voice rises, irritation unveiled, "the decision is a department policy, not city hall's." Spray from the tower ladders drifts over the assembly of reporters, they shudder and murmur uncomfortably.

"Is that prompted by the cutback in the department's budget?" the question is loudest, demanding it's answer. The diminutive mayor shifts his weight back and forth and glances at Danning. The MetroStrat expert thumbs a report.

"Is it true each subsequent alarm had to travel further and further?" the question causes Danning to reverse his thumbing. Somewhere, he knows, are the numbers for distances and responses.

"Maybe we're missing the point. These heroic firefighters have exerted themselves to the maximum to try to save lives," Sprague needs to switch focus, immediately.

"Could closed companies have been here faster and actually saved them?' It's ponytail again, scribbling furiously in a marbled notebook. "Between the closed firehouses and disbanded companies," Ponytail has not waited for an answer, "how much apparatus and how many men would have been on the scene before the first fire trucks arrived?"

"Six companies and thirty men," the answer rises from somewhere in the rear of the group. Heads turn, reporters look quickly for the source of information but the source is not identified.

"Is that true?" Tape recorders are thrust forward.

"You are asking questions best suited for the fire department to answer" Myron Sprague is in over his head. The questions being posed are among the least he has expected. "Perhaps the department Public Relations officer would serve you better at this juncture." he turns abruptly and strides toward the group of white helmeted commanders standing in a loose circle several yards away. Michael Danning falls in step with his boss.

"Where'd *that* come from?" Danning hopes Sprague has a better sense of things.

"*THAT,*" the mayor hisses, tight-lipped, face growing darker, "is what is known as a damned ambush . . . a set-up." He glances quickly at his Metrostrat 'Boy.' "You didn't know the content of the questions?"

Danning spreads both arms in a display of innocence. "Hell, no," his voice is high and tight with indignation.

"Chief Callahan," Sprague almost yells at the Chief of Department, "a moment please?" The mayor and Danning stand ten feet from the assembled white helmets.

"Holy hell," Thomas Callahan allows the frustration to simmer over into the murmured epithet, "a five alarm fire to run and I need to answer this twerp's questions?" He turns in the mayor's direction and waves an indication he's heard the request. "I'll return gentlemen" he informs his subordinates.

"Tom," the mayor begins rapidly, eyes narrowed in barely concealed rage, "I was just made a sham by the media." He jerks his thumb in the direction of the reporters behind him, the group observing the exchange.

"Do you have any idea why I'm being asked for *my* responsibility in closing firehouses and disbanding companies?" He searches Callahan's face for any clue the chief may have known that ponytail was waiting. "I had some longhaired smart ass asking about closures and questioning the 'Enhanced Training' explanation. Can you tell me why?"

Thomas Callahan is able, honestly, to shake his head dolefully. "I cannot," the reply is direct and Callahan looks down directly into Sprague's eyes. "I have never spoken with, met or even know anyone like that." He glances back at the fire. "And nobody on my staff speaks with the media, it is a cardinal rule all information goes through the PR officer. Period." For a moment Sprague studies the chief's face before relaxing with a shrug.

"Anxiety, Tom," Sprague rubs both eyes. "Just concerned about the loss of life and property." He has a good idea Callahan believes him. "I'm sorry to take you away from your duties here . . . my apologies."

When Callahan returns to the chief officers, there are no questions regarding the mayor's continued interference. Callahan is thankful further exposure to Myron Sprague is unnecessary. He had answered truthfully, technically. The pony tailed reporter was Jeffrey Kennedy's cousin. Callahan wasn't aware the slender man was also a reporter for one of the city's two evening newspapers. A faint smile crosses his face. And Kennedy had simply remarked a few weeks earlier that the two men had shared several beers at a local tavern, family talk, gossip, he'd said. And of course, Manny Rojo had been pacing back and forth over there behind the reporters, for reasons only the union president knew. Callahan wonders if his staff 'wunderkind' deserves a steak dinner.

"Tom," the big chief looks at Loughlin, "who was first due with you at this box?" he nods at the fire.

"Engine 50 and 105 Truck," Loughlin identifies the two companies immediately in front of 305 Moore's Park Drive and quickly adds the rest of the assignment.

"Get the names," the chief of Department speaks quietly, "I want them written up for Meritorious Action Medals . . . this had to be the nightmares of all nightmares for them to pull up on."

Exhausted, sweating still in the night air and their attention divided between the smoking, shattered dwellings in front of them, the men from both companies are standing in a crooked line abreast of the row of houses. Dan Kemp, helmet askew, coat open has an empty stare on his face, looking at the smoking shell that had once been 305. The torrent of water falling into the house has reduced the inside to a blackened skeleton. Smoke rises heavily from it's interior, but it is white smoke, the welcome indictor this fire is beaten. He knows there is still work to do, the interior still needs to be torn apart and pockets of fire extinguished by hand lines. But this fire is done for, although it has taken it's toll. Kemp's face is dirty, streaks of pale skin showing where sweat and water have tracked from forehead to chin. He thinks of Burger lying in an ambulance by now on the way to the hospital and his eyebrow arches at the remains of the fire.

Nick Miller and Terry Buck lean against the engine, faces strained and backs aching. The filth and soot somehow looks natural on Nick. The same accumulation on Bucky gives him a rugged appearance although his two little girls wouldn't recognize him. Both men are bare-headed, helmets in hand as they watch the cascading master streams falling into the burnt out shells before them. Atop the engine, Jerry March wears a turnout coat, cigar clamped in his teeth and follows the flow of water from the monitor pipe into a second floor window. "Now I feel like a firefighter!" he shouts to the men in the street.

"For once," Dan Kemp grumbles. "Let's get ready for the inside war,." he speaks loudly. As he fastens his coat Dan watches Terry and Nick wearily place helmets on their heads and hunch aching shoulders one last time. "The city pays us lousy wages to do this," he reminds both men with a cynical smile, "so let's give 'em their money's worth.

Less than two dozen feet away, Paul Gulfee takes a last drag on his cigarette before flicking it into a lake of water near the truck. Beside him Greenstreet and Holland hold ceiling hooks in one hand, they look like medieval pike men standing guard. Paul smiles thinly. Greenie's massive gut pushes out from his open coat and two buttons are missing from a filthy, wet shirt. Donald's glasses are spotted with water and he pushes them back on his nose. "We're gonna be here forever," the EVD observes quietly.

"Lookin' for bodies also," Greenstreet adds in a gruff voice.

"Sam gonna be okay?" Gulfee glances up at the ladder pipe in operation atop 105's extended aerial. On the ladder Killen directs the nozzle, making minute changes in it's direction, occasionally gazing down into the charcoaled interiors that had been furnished homes a few hours before.

"He'll be fine," Donald observes. "Once he finds out Tim's okay he'll be fine."

""Helluva way to make a living," the lieutenant comments, pulling his gloves tighter. Greenstreet shrugs at the words.

"The hell with it," he growls in a raspy voice, "us heroes don't need no pay for this. Just ask the city." The three men laugh briefly. It's true.

"He had a dream in which he saw a stairway resting on the earth, with its top reaching to heaven and the angels of God were ascending and descending on it." Genesis 28:12.

EPILOGUE

When the fire ground at Moore's Park Drive had been secured, more than a dozen black body bags were arranged in single file along the front sidewalk. The newspapers and television reporters did the research and claimed the fire had been the deadliest in the city in four decades. A reporter from one of the evening papers wrote a four part series on the fire, including within the text, the bare facts concerning the closed firehouses and the deadly consequences of blithely reducing fire protection. Governments, all of them, are always reactionary, he had written. City planners and budget 'gurus' always assume the status quo is an eternal state. Furthermore, the adventurous reporter hinted, the fire department may have planned the rotational closures, but most assuredly, it was done in the face of a dwindling budget and under the threat of permanent disbanding of companies.

For two weeks the fatal fire remained the center of attention. Blame and accusations were hurled, radio talk-shows couldn't handle the tidal wave of critics of city hall. And then a drug-related triple murder re-focused attention on the growing crime rate in this city. The fire department and it's problems fell quickly to a hail of nine millimeter bullets that quickly extinguished the lives of a police officer and two addicts caught on the second floor of a crack house. The deaths came as a blessing for Myron Sprague who pointed to the need for greater police presence and who found agreement in a population more concerned with the chances of being shot than burned. After it's brief moment in the public eye, the fire department returned to its role as 'that other branch of guys wearing blue.'

Time brought changes to the big firehouse on Fort Avenue, inside and out. After a quarter century in the department, Dan Kemp retired after placing fifteenth on the promotion list for battalion chief. There were only five openings for the position and Kemp knew there was no chance for him. Two days after the official list was posted, the captain had his papers in at Lafayette Park.

After recovering from his injuries sustained at Moore's Park, Bill Burger became an EVD for the 3rd Battalion, finally retiring after three years. His best friend at Engine 50, Jerry March, took the lieutenant's test and was promoted, assigned as a lieutenant in a company somewhere out in the 'East.' He put in his papers after two years, his heart had developed an arrhythmia deemed too clinically significant to allow Jerry to continue working. He never returned to driving the bread truck either.

"Filthy Nick' Miller stayed at Engine 50 for eighteen months after the Moore's Park fire and then transferred to Truck 13 in the Western Division. He is still working there as of this writing. Terry Buck is now *Captain* Buck of Rescue Company 1, one of the youngest captains in the department. Tom 'Tomcat' Kelly, 'Mr. Howdy Doody,' remained at Engine 50 for two years before being transferred to Engine 51 in the city's wild-west side; currently the busiest in the city. Barry Kramer, Barry-Fred, returned from his injuries, having the existence of his neck affirmed medically and immediately transferred to the maintenance shop where he worked under Elmer Rawley for nineteen months. Barry Fred seemed to do much better maintaining the engines and their pumps than operating them. He retired to Florida.

Paul Gulfee remained a lieutenant at Truck 105 for two more years before transferring to Truck 22 in a quiet, sedate neighborhood where people still brought baked goods to the fire house and a 'crapper' was a once a month occurrence. He still works there as of the writing. Donald Holland, Truck 105's EVD with a near photographic memory concerning anything related to the fire service, experienced a meteoric rise within the department, becoming a lieutenant on Engine 19 and then captain of Truck 15, replacing the legendary 'JC' Somerville. Donald was placed second on the list for battalion chief, a virtual shoo-in for the position.

Michael Greenstreet, Greenie, died shortly after this story was completed, a victim of diabetes and a heart overworked by a perfectly round body. Richard Simms recovered from the injuries sustained from the fall into the backyard of the dwelling fire and returned to Truck 105 for two years before transferring to Truck 13 where he worked with Nick Miller. Sam Killen, the dark giant, retired from the fire department one year after Tim Bridges fell from the ladder at the Moore's Park fire. He worked for the State Fire marshal's Office and was as imposing as ever.

Tim Bridges returned to Truck 105 after two months' sick leave. Eligible to take the promotional examination for lieutenant, Tim was promoted and assigned to Truck 15 where he worked as an officer under Donald Holland. Within six months of that fatal fire, Mark Hagan was involved in an auto accident on his way to the firehouse. Mark sustained head injuries to the extent he was retired with one hundred percent disability. Today he is barely able to recognize the men with whom he once worked.

Thomas Loughlin followed through with his decision to transfer to a different battalion and worked in a quiet upper, middle class neighborhood for twenty-eight months before finally retiring. Not once did he ever pay for a fire house meal. Loughlin's aide for ten years, Ken Shaw, stayed on as EVD and aide to 'Big Cat' Donovan for two additional years before retiring to open a fire department-related tavern in the county. He still serves drinks from behind the bar, a living version of 'Mr. Clean.'

Even the big, granite and brick firehouse went through a dramatic change. The city closed the firehouse on Fort Avenue due to structural concerns. It was purchased by a private firm, renovated and subsequently rented back to the city as a Department of Public Works garage, essentially the same use by a different agency.

The companies themselves, Engine 50 and Truck 105, were relocated along with the battalion's red car to a newly constructed fire house two blocks from city hall. Six months later the division's rescue unit and the Field Communications Unit were added to the single story firehouse. Both engine and truck respond to less than two-thirds the calls they once did. The surrounding buildings and businesses are a far cry from the crumbling, brown 'hood' they'd called home for so many years. In many respects it has been better that most of the men on Blue Shift are elsewhere, the reduction of runs and 'first-in' fire would have surely driven them crazy with boredom.

There are constants in the department, however. Like firefighters everywhere, regardless of the city, neighborhood, or make-up of company, they remain convenient heroes.